Notes from the Lightning God

John W. Schouten

BeWrite Books
www.bewrite.net

Published internationally by BeWrite Books, UK.
32 Bryn Road South, Wigan, Lancashire, WN4 8QR.

A CIP catalogue record for this book is available from the British Library

ISBN: 978-1-906609-12-2

Also available in eBook format.

Produced by BeWrite Books
www.bewrite.net

For Diane Martin

John W. Schouten is a writer and a poet, who has also worked, with varying levels of distinction, as a ski instructor, a machinist, a mental health worker, an optician, a roofer, a Spanish teacher, and, most recently, a marketing professor and consumer researcher. John describes his academic research as an anthropology of the American dream. This is his first novel.

Notes from the Lightning God

For Bonnie
Dec. 2009
cheers!

Part One: Leaving Home

Deep within him he believed that the Andes held the baffling secret of life.

– Ciro Alegría, from *El Mundo es Ancho y Ajeno*

Bigger than life and quiet as ever. That's what I thought as I took my turn at his open casket. All in all, my father was more approachable in death than he had been in life. I could touch him now, and I did. I laid my hand against his cool forehead. It felt like plastic.

Goddamn you, Dad. What am I going to do now?

Mitch came home from Seattle and stayed with Mom for a few days. After the funeral, I couldn't stand to stick around. I drove to a convenience store and bought a pack of cigarettes, Camel filters. I hadn't smoked more than a few social cigarettes in the six years since high school, but suddenly I had the urge. On my way out of town I pulled over to the side of the road where I could sit, in a new suit I would probably never wear again, on a highway crash barrier with a view of the Willamette River. It was October, 1983, and early fall rains had given way to a crisp Indian summer. I tapped one cigarette out of the pack and smoked it with deep French inhales. I considered what my father's reaction would be if he could see me.

"But you can't see me, can you, Doc?" My voice, hanging in the autumn air, surprised me with its brittleness. I listened as if there might be an answer. I smoked a second cigarette. Then a third, a fourth and a fifth. My head was spinning and my mouth tasted like shit. I stood up, a little unsteady, bent my head back and looked at the sky. It wasn't just my father I was talking to then. It was God, or the universe, or whatever. "Fuck you," I said.

For Thanksgiving break, I went home again. Home meaning my parents' – strike that – my mother's house. My apartment in the med-student ghetto had never qualified. It was less than a month since the funeral. I got home mid-morning and found Mom in her bedroom packing Dad's shoes and clothing into boxes.

"What's this?" I asked.

She blew a strand of hair out of her eyes and tipped her head toward the boxes on her left. "Consignment," she said. And, tipping her head in the other direction, "Salvation Army."

I peered into one of the boxes for the consignment store: expensive sweaters, slacks, dress shirts, polos. In the Salvation Army box: teeshirts, jeans, bedroom slippers. It felt a little macabre, like a funeral for Dad's wardrobe.

"Is Mitch coming down?"

"No."

"Where's Dad's car?"

"Sold."

The news hit me like the sudden realization of an empty stomach. Dad's BMW already gone. I loved that car. A black M5. He had never let me drive it. "What about Dad's practice?"

"I've got a buyer."

Who are you? I thought. Where's my mother?

"Listen, Sammy, why don't you walk through the house and pick out any of your father's things that you want to keep?"

"What about Mitch?"

She shook her head, meaning that Mitchell didn't want any of Dad's things. Well, he wouldn't, would he?

In the den, I found the last of Dad's crossword puzzles. He used to work crosswords religiously. Besides aiming me unflaggingly toward medical school, his one clear legacy to me was a love for words. The *New York Times* puzzle was reprinted a week later in our local paper. Dad preferred the more difficult, late-week puzzles. Often, he would pick up those from early in the week and work them in his head, filling in only certain letters to form a pattern of some sort. For example, he would fill in only the perimeter squares or the border-to-border phrases, leaving the rest blank for me to complete, or not, as I was able. They were his table scraps, and I had gobbled them up. At his size-thirteen feet, I'd been an anxious, sad-eyed, mop-headed puppy dog, eager for any semblance of affection or recognition he might unexpectedly dispense.

I would never reach my father's six-four stature, nor have his natural charisma, but at least with respect to crosswords, I had become his equal, or better, before he died. The puzzles I found were some he had begun but failed to finish, probably because of the combination of morphine, scotch and blackouts that defined his final days. I sat in his chair and finished each one, scratching out mistakes and supplying the correct answers. Then I crumpled them, one at a time, and lobbed them into the cold fieldstone fireplace. When I completed the last puzzle, I pushed them all together and dropped in a match. As they flamed, blackened and curled into smoke, it felt, for the first time, like a goodbye.

Mom and I had Thanksgiving dinner at a local restaurant. Our table was one depressing island in an archipelago populated by people with nowhere else to go.

I began to have trouble in medical school. Concepts became slippery and details escaped me altogether. I would open a textbook and the words would swim before my eyes. It was as if they actively resisted me, rebuffing my efforts to grasp them. Some evenings, I sat for what seemed like forever, staring at the same two pages, trying to penetrate a new chapter or make sense of a new diagram. I would snap out of a trance, see from the clock that an hour had gone by, and get a sudden feeling of disapproval from my father.

One morning, I showed up late for my class in cellular physiology, only to find there was an exam in progress. I took a copy of the exam to an empty desk, folded back the cover sheet and stared at the first page. Nothing made sense. What did it mean? Was I in the right place? I looked around me. The faces looked familiar in the way of actors you know you've seen before but can't put names to. The room looked like some place I had dreamt about. I returned my attention to the exam and tried again to focus on the material. The first question had to do with the process of metastasis, the spread of cancerous cells. My mind began to reel out a movie in the style of b-grade horror: *The Disease that Ate Doc Young.* Suddenly, a bell rang and the class period was over. I turned in a blank exam and melted back into an otherwise forgotten day.

On the Friday before finals, I was moving through my afternoon anatomy lab like a zombie. The professor called on me with a question that didn't even register. When I failed to answer, he asked, "Is something wrong, Mr Young?" I shrugged. What could I say? That lately I had the weird sensation of my father looking over my shoulder every time I cracked a textbook or peered into a cadaver? The professor mistook my gesture for indifference. He asked me if I thought I had the right attitude to be in medical school. I shook my head. I had no answer.

I left the lab in mid-session, went straight to my car and pointed it toward the family home. The radio came on to an NPR story about Reagan and the nuclear arms race. I turned it off. A winter rain had set in and the hissing of the tires on the drizzle-damp pavement became my meditation. I wanted nothing more at that moment than to be in my old bedroom, to climb into my old bed and to close my eyes long enough for the world to make sense again.

The next part of my memory always plays back in slow motion. A car I don't recognize, a Celica convertible, blocks the driveway, so I coast to a stop by the curb. The trashcans are there for collection, filled to overflowing with gallon cans emptied of house paint. Next to the sidewalk, buried in the lawn like a stake through its heart, stands a sign: For Sale, Century 21.

It felt like all the air had been sucked out of my car. The car door was heavy as if I were opening it under water. I forced it open. Dragged myself out. Pressed it shut. Click … click. I walked to the house with enormous effort. Opened the front door. Music leaked out: Eurhythmics. "Sweet dreams are made of this …" A pair of tennis racquets lay on the floor with crossed handles. "Everybody's looking for something …" I heard the sound of ice cubes ringing into glass bells. I floated to the kitchen. At the sink stood a woman, her back to me, holding a glass in each hand. I saw flowing hair, a short robe, cream-colored silk, hanging open. Tanned legs. Turning. Breasts. Naked, plush, beautiful, terrifying …

"Sammy."

I could not say "Mother."

I turned aside to see a man, thirtyish, athletic and naked, disappear in the direction of the master bedroom.

"I'm sorry," I said. I bolted for the door.

"Sammy!"

In my panic I recognized my name, but not the voice that called it. It was the voice of a monster. A voice that would seduce me, that would call me back, comfort me, tell me everything was going to be all right, and then break me in pieces.

I woke up shivering from the cold. It was dark. My head hurt. My guts hurt. All around me crackled a sound like endlessly splintering wood. At first, I didn't know where I was. Just as it was dawning on my battered consciousness that I was inside my car, an ocean wave of nausea came over me. I fumbled open the door, leaned out and sprayed a geyser of puke into the blackness.

I fought my way back to a sitting position and leaned my head into my forearms against the steering wheel. With the door ajar and the dome light on, I could now see, glinting from the floor of the passenger side, the slight but impudent remains of a bottle of José Cuervo. I stared it down for the duration of two or three breaths, enough time for the briny smell of seawater to penetrate the reek of stomach acid and tequila.

Oh, right. The beach. I'm at the beach.

The splintering-wood sound was the static from my car radio, tuned between stations. The energy required to raise my head off my arms, reach over and turn it off nearly exceeded my reserves. But the ensuing silence was worth it.

Slowly, I rolled back the rock of my recent memory. I remembered the sun setting over the ocean and the moon appearing mid-sky, out of nowhere, like a ghost. Further back, I remembered the rain on the windshield as I crossed the Coast Range and the blinding flashes of dappled afternoon light streaming through the trees whenever there was a break in the clouds. Suddenly, the rest of the picture became clear, and I was hit with another wave of nausea.

That afternoon, after I had bolted from the madness of my mother's house, I'd driven in aimless circles around town until I came upon a liquor store. After producing my driver's license to counter the under-age impression made by my boyish face, I'd bought a bottle of tequila and headed for the coast highway. When I passed the town limits, I'd already twisted open the tequila and taken a long swig.

Very slowly, very deliberately, with my head throbbing, I closed the car door, started the engine, switched on the headlights, and turned the car away from the lonely viewpoint where I'd lodged it hours before. Highway 101 was empty and I was grateful to have it to myself. By the time I was rolling into Portland, some two hours later, the sky had cleared and the first traces of daylight were beginning to outline Mount Hood with an aura of pink. A fresh layer of snow would have made it a beautiful day to ski. It also would have been a good day to study, with final exams starting in two days. All I could do, though, was swallow a double dose of Advil with as much water as my stomach would hold, pull the blinds in my apartment and crash.

I woke up again sometime after noon, feeling vaguely human. The message light on my answering machine was blinking. The message was from my mother: "Sammy? Samson? Are you there, Honey? Listen, I know you're upset … I understand … I wish you would have called before you came … Please don't be angry with me … Okay … well … call me when you get this message, will you, Sweetheart?"

I didn't call. I couldn't. I couldn't even think about my mother without spinning into another funk of confusion. I erased the message, gathered some books and headed for the library by way of an all-day pancake house.

Her second message came on Tuesday, during finals week: "Hi, Sammy? Are you okay, Honey? Listen, I called to see about your plans for Christmas. Call me, will you? I need to know that you're okay."

Again, I didn't return her call. I couldn't think about Christmas yet, and I wasn't ready to say that I was over the shock of seeing a naked man, probably not much older than me, slipping into her bedroom. Or that I was still struggling to block out images of my mother as a hot piece of ass.

I took the first two of my final exams, but I put no effort into them. I really didn't care about the outcome. The other two I blew off completely. In my mind and heart, if not in the official books, I was through with medical school.

The first real signs of cracking in our family structure had shown up when I was finishing my second year of undergraduate studies in biology. Mitchell had come home late one school night and announced he would not be going to college. He'd decided, instead, to try and make his way as an artist. Dad, in the imperious way he used to achieve by holding his head still and erect and looking you up and down only with his eyes, asked him how he planned to support himself with such nonsense. Mitch said he would figure it out, walked away, and thus threw down the first counter-challenge in a Young family cold war.

Dad was the superpower, but Mitch found strength in resistance. With his high school graduation only a few days away, Mitch told the parents he planned to move to Seattle. Dad said good luck but not to expect any financial help in ruining his life. Mitch suggested he could sell his car for money to live on. Dad reminded him it wasn't his to sell. Mitch dropped his keys on the kitchen counter, went to his room and emerged a about fifteen minutes later with a duffel bag, just as a brand new, pearl-colored BMW coupe appeared at the curb in front of the house. The driver, a tall, dark-skinned, sharply-dressed older man, got out of the car and opened the trunk for Mitch's bag. Mitch never came home that night or the next and he refused to attend his high school graduation ceremony.

Within a month, Mitch had moved to Seattle, rooming with and receiving support from Sameer, the friend with the BMW. Mitch didn't come right out and say that Sameer was his lover, but whereas Mitch exhibited a soft masculinity, Sameer was flagrantly effeminate.

My father, the respectable internist, Gregory S. Young, MD, had kept up a stony façade, which was not unusual. I can easily count the number of times I'd seen him smile. Fewer were the times I'd seen him laugh. Despite his apparent stoicism, I suspected that inwardly he became a cauldron of guilt, anger and self-doubt. He had cut Mitch off completely. He refused to give him any kind of financial support or even to hear Mitch's name uttered in his presence.

For another month after Mitch moved out, we heard nothing from him. Not a phone number. Not a forwarding address. Eventually, he called Mom at a time he knew Dad would be at his practice. I got his number from Mom and gave him a call. He was doing fine, he said, sketching and trying to paint.

"Are you working?" I asked.

"Yeah. I bus tables and stock the bar at a club downtown. The waiters tip me out pretty well."

"What club?"

"You wouldn't know it," he said. "What about you? What are you up to?"

"The usual. Summer classes. I'll try to squeeze in a couple of climbs before the ice gets too soft."

"Mount Hood?"

"Yeah. And maybe Rainier."

"Be careful up there," he said.

"Yeah. You too. Be careful, I mean."

Other than birthdays, we hardly talked after that. There didn't seem to be anything to say that was worth the effort of getting past the awkwardness of the one topic that came between us: the fact of his homosexuality, my inability to fully understand it, his fear about my judgments of it, and my fear about the judgments I might form if I got too close to his new life and lifestyle. Silence was easier.

I'm sure my mother kept in touch with Mitch, and she probably sent him some money on the sly. But, ultimately, she wasn't doing so well herself. Unable to reconcile the divisive forces at work in the family, she had become depressed. Watching her with my father had been painful – Mom moving with robotic emptiness and Dad acting like everything was perfectly normal.

With Mitch gone from the picture, at least as far as my father was concerned, all the weight of my father's expectations seemed suddenly to fall on me. Any question about my following his footsteps into medical school was erased. In our few terse conversations on my visits home, he would ask after my grades and then furl his substantial brow and disappear into his den and whatever book, newspaper or crossword puzzle that currently occupied his attention. The things he didn't say echoed in my brain like drumbeats.

For my college graduation Dad gave me a new car, a black Volkswagen Jetta with a personalized license plate: MD2B.

The next major blow to our family occurred when my father died. I was finishing my first year of medical school when he was diagnosed with cancer. Ironically, he hadn't had a thorough medical exam since he was in med school himself. The good doctor must have been ignoring signs of his own illness for months. The cancer had started high in his colon and migrated to his stomach, his liver and his brain. Little missionaries of cellular chaos. Six months later, I was helping carry his casket. He was fifty-two. Mom had rallied from her depression during Dad's illness and nursed him with a focus and intensity I had never before seen in her. Suddenly he was gone and, with him, the very lexicon by which, for better or for worse, we had defined our lives.

My next phone message, a couple of days later, was from Mitchell: "Hey, Sam. What's up? Mom called me. She's a little worried about you. Why don't you give her a call? Oh, and uh … if I don't hear from you in the next day or two, then Merry Christmas. I'm going down to Cabo with my friend Daniel for the Holidays."

So it was Daniel now. Would I be expected to remember this one? And for how long?

I was actually at home the next time my mom called. I let it go to the answering machine anyway. "Hello, Samson. Since I haven't heard from you, I went ahead and made some holiday plans …"

Just the sound of her voice kicked up an emotional shitstorm in me. I felt need, embarrassment, anger and guilt all at once. I needed her to be my mother. I was embarrassed to have crashed in on the middle of her romantic interlude, angry at her for being with another man so soon after my father's death, and guilt-ridden about my anger and my embarrassment.

"I'm going out to Nebraska to spend some time with my mother. If you decide you're ready to talk to me …"

I picked up the phone. "I'm here."

"Hi, Sammy."

"How's Grandma?" I asked, to keep the subject matter safe. Grandma Zabriski was my only remaining grandparent. She still lived in the same Nebraska farmhouse where my mother, then Sally Zabriski, had grown up. Sally had been an eighteen-year-old college freshman when she'd met the young intern, Gregory Young, at the Chicago Medical School Hospital. He had treated her for a broken ankle, she surrendered her phone number, and they were married within the year. She never finished college.

"She's all right. I invited her to come here but she says the travel is getting to be too much for her."

"So you're going out there? For how long?" I struggled to keep the emotion out of my voice, to sound indifferent.

"A couple of weeks – just through the New Year."

"Give her my love."

"I will. Sammy?"

"Hm?"

"About last week …"

"It's okay," I lied. "Forget about it."

"No, Sam. Neither one of us is ever going to forget about it."

Silence moved in between us as I absorbed the truth of her words.

"I'm sorry, but your father is gone, and he isn't coming back." I heard the stress in her voice. I felt my throat constricting and fought back tears. "I didn't have a contingency plan for this …"

Suddenly I realized that, in my own grief and confusion, I'd never really considered what my mother might have been going through since Dad died.

"I may have half a lifetime ahead of me, Sam. I have to start figuring it out somehow."

"What about the house?" I asked.

"I can't stay there. Not by myself."

"So …"

"So, I'm selling. When I get back from Nebraska I'll be moving into a condo by the racquet club."

"That's great. Listen, I gotta go." I couldn't say more or I would cry. My sense of shame and loss were overwhelming. Dad was gone, and now it seemed I was going to lose my mother as well.

The day before Christmas, I took my back-country skis up into the Cascades, parked my car at a trailhead and skied into the woods. I caught a Forest Service road that was closed for the winter. Breaking trail the whole way, I climbed steadily for about four hours, stopping only for swigs of water and concentrating on the only sounds I could hear: my breathing, the rhythmic swishing of my skis through the unbroken snow, and the occasional call of a bird. Finally, by mid-afternoon, I made it to a ridgeline with spectacular views of Mt Hood to the north and Mt Jefferson to the south, two near-perfect cones of intense white, streaked by giant buttresses of igneous rock. I felt glad to have such a wide, empty place entirely to myself, to absorb the sights and sounds without distraction.

I wolfed down a couple of cheese sandwiches from my pack and watched as Hood became wrapped in a huge lenticular cloud. Other clouds, advancing toward me from the south, engulfed Jefferson and took away any possibility of a moonlit night. In a fairly flat spot between two trees, I tromped a platform in the snow with the bases of my skis, pitched my orange nylon dome tent and piled the bulk of my gear inside. I spent the remaining hour or so of daylight carving tracks in a clear cut, climbing back up each time in the same set of zigzags and descending each time through a new string of esses in virgin snow. S for Sam. S for solitude. Sss for the sound of skis on snow.

That night the darkness was complete – emblematic of my future. When I used to fast-forward my life story I saw something like my father's life ahead of me. No longer. Now there was nothing but a void. Mom, apparently, was embarking on a new life as a tennis-club widow, beating back her grief with a racquet and … I didn't want to know what else. Mitch was making ends meet as a waiter and working on his art. As baffling as they were to me, it seemed that both Mitch and Mom were forging new identities that would at least carry them forward, if not bring them some form of happiness. But who the hell was I? With that question nagging me, I cycled in and out of sleep in my down mummy bag. Wind picked at the corners of my tent flaps. Blasts of snow strafed the windward side.

The only voice I heard on Christmas morning was my own. "Ho, ho, ho," I said as I pissed a yellow chimney into the snow, a prelude to packing up and skiing down the mountain into the blank white pages of an unwritten future.

During much of the Christmas break, I killed time in the university library, wandering the stacks with no particular aim in mind, operating with a kind of mental divining rod. A book would catch my eye. I'd peruse it, looking for any kind of connection to me. Sometimes, I'd reshelf the book right away. Other times, I'd read for an hour or two. I found philosophy incomprehensible. Sociology intrigued me, but it also tended to depress me. I really enjoyed literature, but scholarship about literature was like what Mark Twain called the Book of Mormon: "chloroform in print."

Just as the new semester was beginning in January, I discovered cultural anthropology through a flyer posted in the Student Union building. It announced a public lecture titled 'Life with Cannibals: Adventures in Papua New Guinea' by Professor Jack Bentley of the Department of Anthropology. I went. I listened. I saw possibilities. Where better, I reasoned, to find the meaning of life than among people whose lives were still unmediated by the complexities of modern technology? How better to crack open the nut of self than by hurling it against the anvil of another culture? What better cure for suburban nausea than exotic faces in exotic places?

Those impulses led me to the office door of Jack Bentley. We hit it off immediately. I think he was intrigued by the prospect of mentoring a medical-school dropout. He took me under his wing, registered me for independent study credits and loaded me up with books. I dove into the new discipline with the zeal of a convert. By the next fall, I had completed the equivalent of a master's degree in anthropology and was accepted into the doctoral program as Bentley's assistant.

Field notes, March 12, 1986

The research site: *La Clínica San Vicente para la Salud del Obrero.*

Housed in a cinder-block building with two examining rooms, a waiting room and a bathroom, the migrant workers' clinic serves the Latino population of Oregon's Willamette Valley. Kept alive by private donations and a small government grant, it provides basic health care for those who are in the country illegally or are simply too poor to go to a hospital.

The patients arrive in ebbs and flows with conditions ranging from severed fingers to severe fevers to problem pregnancies. My job as a volunteer is admitting them and trying to help them find some comfort in a strange and probably menacing place. I take their names, often from immigration documents that are obviously faked, I record their complaints and, when I can, I elicit their personal histories.

As a one-time medical student, I also assist Doc Spock occasionally, when the nurse, Giselle, is unavailable. The most common reason for Giselle's indisposition, ironically, is that she spends probably twenty percent of the average workday standing outside the back door smoking cigarettes. Parliaments. Two packs a day.

Today was a slow day at the clinic. Doc Spock saw three patients, all before 10:00am – two pregnancies and a case of chicken pox. I asked her if she was any relation to the other Doctor Spock. She said no, but that she still had a crush on Mister Spock of the trim physique, grim logic and pointy ears. I confided that my biggest media crush had been the Bionic Woman, but that I had given it up when I finally realized I could never measure up to Colonel Steve Austin and his six-million-dollar angst.

Spock is maybe four or five years older than I am (she won't say), petite and Semitic. Her dark, wiry hair grows from close around her face, threatening to encroach on it by way of silky sideburns, always pulled back with an elastic tie to create a solid, backward-expanding cone like the feathers of a shuttlecock. She moves efficiently and purposefully in her standard-issue lab coat, giving the impression of someone who knows exactly why she's here and exactly what she wants. My father used to emanate the same kind of sureness – must be part of the same arrogance that makes them think they should be doctors in the first place. I think about how that could be me – the lab-coat part anyway – if I hadn't dropped out of medical school.

Well, no regrets. Medical school was my dad's deal, not mine. I didn't come here to practice

> medicine. I came to practice anthropology. I'm here to improve my Spanish and to learn the venerable art of field work. I am here to observe the 'enactment of culture' and get the hang of recording everything I see, hear, smell and think in field notes.

"Sam, these aren't field notes," said Jack Bentley, looking over my first few entries.

"No?"

"No."

"What are they then?"

Normally, we had a pretty good relationship – something Bentley didn't foster with most doctoral students – but I suppose my question was a little too cheeky.

"What they are," he snapped, "is narcissistic crap."

I gulped, adjusted my posture to convey humility, kept my mouth shut and fidgeted. Bentley glared at me.

"You need to get out of your own head. If you're going to be an anthropologist you need to tell your informants' stories first, not your own. Give them richness. Thickness. Detail. When I read your field notes, I need to feel like I'm right there with you. I need to feel like I inhabit the world you're writing about. You need to convince me that you've found a way to belong in your research site and, more importantly, that you've learned to understand it from your informants' points of view as well as your own."

He looked to see if I understood him. I nodded.

"Don't be hasty with analysis and interpretation. Describe, describe, describe. It takes a long time, a lot of observation and a lot of description just to figure out what it is you're seeing."

"What about my own thoughts and impressions?" I asked.

"Your reflexive entries are important, too. But keep them separate. Put them in a journal or give them a separate designation. They will function to frame the story, to tell the reader where you were coming from. Eventually, they help us to understand and, we hope, to trust your conclusions."

I pondered what he was saying for a few seconds and then I began to think about how I would describe activities at the clinic. Bentley reeled me in again. "You'll find that your field research actually has two sites. There's the outer site, the physical and social landscape you're working in, and there's the inner site, your own mental landscape. You won't understand either of them accurately at first. It takes time and attention. Your work isn't done until they both come into focus."

From Field notes, March 22, 1986

> At about two in the afternoon a man came in with an injured arm in a makeshift sling. I packed it in ice to control the swelling and gave him pain killers. While the medicine started to work, I obtained some basic information from him. He was from Michoacán. Thirty-one years old. Spoke good Spanish and a smattering of English. Worked for a local tree nursery. He had been making a repair to a greenhouse roof when his ladder shifted and bucked him off. He had landed on a stack of pallets, with his arm twisted beneath him …

"What have you got?" asked Spock.

"Broken arm," I said.

The man winced with pain as Spock palpated his forearm. "It looks to me like a clean break of the radius and a spiral fracture of the ulna," she said. "I'm going to need …"

Just then, the clinic door flew open to the sounds of screaming and cries for help. Two men carried a pregnant woman between them. Her legs were streaked with blood and dirt and her face was blanched gray.

"Sam, set this arm and splint it. Give him Demerol for the pain. Giselle!"

I hesitated. I was nervous about my lack of credentials. "Is that legal?"

Spock set me straight with a ferocious look. "Ask him if he gives a rip about your diploma."

Giselle had just come in from a smoke break, overheard Spock's reprimand and released a hoarse cackle that degraded into a smoky coughing fit as she followed Spock and the trio of migrants into the other examining room.

I set out a splint and bandaging as I explained to the man that the bones had to be returned to their proper positions to heal well. I had never set a bone before. I knew it would produce extreme pain, even with the Demerol, and I knew it was best done quickly. I was nervous as hell. It must have been obvious, because the man with the broken arm looked at me as if I might sprout horns.

"*Lo siento, señor, pero esto le va a doler.*" As the scream was forming in his belly, I thought maybe I shouldn't have warned him about the pain.

Last night, I dreamed for the first time in Spanish. I dreamed I was sitting with a group of men in a bean field. We had been harvesting and it was time for a break. They were laughing and telling jokes. I didn't remember any of the jokes, but I remembered having understood them. I understood them, and I laughed myself awake.

At first, at the clinic, it was difficult for me to understand most of the patients' complaints and personal information. Some spoke neither English nor Spanish, but indigenous languages, such as Mixtec. Oregon sits right between California and Washington State on the migrant trail, a route that attracts workers from all over Mexico and Central America. Those who speak Spanish do so with various accents and idioms and their speech sounds very little like the deliberately slow, articulate phrases from my Spanish classes. Nevertheless, through a combination of patience, practice, repetition, pantomime and inference from context, I was finally becoming conversant in the language of the Latin American countryside.

Until today, I spent hours every night hunkered over my dictionaries translating field notes from English to Spanish. From now on, I resolved to record them all in Spanish.

At noon, Spock and I were sharing plates of food from Jimmy's Taco Paradise, the Metro-van-slash-mobile-kitchen that parked across the street every day. Local Anglos called it Jimmy's Roach Coach, but we more discriminating eaters knew that Jimmy made *tacos al pastor* to die for.

"Do you ever dream about this place?" I asked Spock.

"No. I mean the tacos are pretty good, but …"

"Funny. I'm talking about the clinic. Like last night, I dreamed I was out here on the sidewalk. A car drives by – a red Dodge, actually – and two guys shoot at me from the car windows."

"God, Sam." She captured a stray bit of shredded cabbage from her lips with her tongue. "You do know I'm not a psychiatrist …"

"And that's not even the interesting part. They've shot me, right? And I'm full of holes and staggering toward the clinic door, except I'm not *me* any more. Suddenly I'm somehow watching it all from off to the side, and the guy with the bullet holes is Moisés Blas."

"Moisés? The big Peruvian?" She wiped her mouth with a handful of paper napkins and dropped them into a pocket of her lab coat. "I wonder whatever happened to him."

I had wondered too. About a thousand times.

Most of our patients were from Mexico – highland villages in the states of Oaxaca, Chiapas, Guerrero, and Michoacán – places where it was no longer possible for them to eke out livings on tiny farms with degraded soil. A few others came from Guatemala or El Salvador, some having fled their homes in the middle of the night with death squads still pounding at their doors. Most were small, stringy men and women, barely over five feet tall. Moisés was different. At a heavily muscled six-foot-one and dark as a chestnut, Moisés was easily the largest indigenous person I had yet encountered. He was also the farthest from home, and one of the sickest.

I'd arrived that morning weeks ago at a little after eight o'clock to find him standing on the sidewalk in front of the clinic just looking at the building. It had already rained twice that morning and his wet clothes were sticking to his body. "*Buenos días,*" I said as I walked by. I noticed that his left earlobe had been split at some time, giving it a shape that reminded me of a ginkgo leaf. The only sign that he even heard my greeting was a slight deepening of the frown lines around his eyes and brow. It was a busy morning for the clinic. Several people were already in the lobby waiting to be seen. By eleven-thirty or so, we'd finally dealt with all of the morning's patients and I was thinking about lunch. Spock had some kind of Tupperware-clad concoction from home, so I headed alone toward Jimmy's. When I pushed my way out of the clinic door, I discovered the big *campesino* still rooted in the same spot. As far as I could tell, he hadn't moved a muscle all morning.

"*¿Puedo ayudarle, señor?*" I offered.

At first he gave no sign of accepting my help. He merely hung his head and balled his fists at his sides. When his voice came out, it was like a low rumble. "*¿Usted es médico?*"

No, I told him. I wasn't a doctor, but I could take him to one. He neither moved nor spoke again, but perspiration began to bead on his forehead and the lines in his face deepened.

"Why don't you come with me into the clinic? I'm sure the doctor can help you." I gestured toward the entrance and took hold of his upper arm to encourage him forward. Through his thin cotton shirtsleeve, his arm felt more like wood than flesh. He raised his head, tipped it back to look at the sky for several seconds and finally took his first reluctant step. While Spock finished her lunch, I took care of the big man's paperwork and took his vital signs. He had no identification of any kind and would give no address or surname. When I asked him for his name, he simply said, "*Me llamo Moisés*." He said he was forty-five, but with his jet-black hair and taut skin, he could have passed for thirty. The most important information I got was from the thermometer. He had a fever of a hundred and five.

I helped Spock with the examination, translating when her need to communicate exceeded her scarce Spanish skills. When Moisés removed his shirt for the stethoscope, I nearly gasped. His upper body was a mass of scars. Spock showed no sign of surprise and I admired her equanimity. Moisés' lungs were clear. His heartbeat was regular. More than strong. It was like the banging of a bass drum. When Spock asked about pain he indicated his gut. He couldn't eat. Yes, there had been blood in his stool. My first thought was colon cancer, and suddenly it was my father sitting on the table rather than this stoic stranger. Fortunately for Moisés, my hasty diagnosis was wrong.

"You are very ill," said Spock, and I translated. "Have you been drinking water from any streams or irrigation pipes?" Moisés' eyes narrowed and he nodded. "For how long?"

"*Pa' siempre, pues.*"

"Long time," I said.

She rolled her eyes. Her best guess, borne out later by blood tests, was advanced giardiasis. In a test of my translation skills, I described to Moisés that microbial parasites from water contaminated by livestock had probably infected his gastrointestinal tract, that is, his stomach and bowels, and from there the rest of his body. "The parasites appear to have grown very strong," I explained. "If we don't stop them, they can kill you." He just nodded. "The way we stop them is with medicine that attacks them. Do you understand that?" A nod. "The best way is to deliver it directly into your blood."

Moisés sat rigid and attentive while Spock set up an intravenous drip. I normally would have tried to keep up a reassuring chatter, but Moisés' demeanor defied small talk. A few times, I thought I saw him mask a wave of pain or nausea, but I couldn't be sure. At my coaxing he reclined but did not relax, on the examining table while Spock inserted the needle and began the drip. I had never seen such bold and pronounced veins as the ones that mapped Moisés' arms.

When the IV was completed, I translated additional admonitions and instructions. "That wasn't so bad, was it?" Moisés shook his head no. "You need to come back every morning for a few days. The microbes are crafty," I said. "If we don't kill them all, they may act like they are gone, while really they are just gathering reinforcements to attack you again. If that happens, they will be stronger than ever. Do you understand?" Another nod. "Will you come back tomorrow?"

"*Sí. Puedo regresar.*"

"Good … and Moisés?" He met my eyes directly for the first time. "It was good to meet you." He nodded with pursed lips, turned and walked out through the once-again crowded lobby.

Before I waded, lunchless, back into my regular duties, I asked Spock the question that had been needling me since Moisés had first unbuttoned his shirt. "What did you make of those scars?"

"Knife wounds, mostly. And at least one looked like a bullet hole."

"Jesus."

"It's funny ..."

"What?"

"As sick as he is, his heart should be racing like a speedboat. His pulse is slower than mine. And his lungs are cavernous."

Moisés returned as promised. Each day for almost a week, he received a follow-up injection and a quick check-up. At my request, Spock let me administer the injections. It gave me a chance to talk to Moisés who, frankly, fascinated me. Maybe it was because of his scars – like the lines of a text between which great stories reside. Maybe it was his looks. Moisés' features appeared to have been chiseled in solid walnut and varnished to a brilliant sheen. He reminded me, more than anything, of one the heroic proletariat figures from the murals of Diego Rivera. He should be holding a massive sledgehammer against a backdrop of steel-wheeled industry. As an amateur mountaineer and back-country skier, I was in pretty good shape, but Moisés made me feel like a soft, bookish schoolboy.

On his second return visit, I had learned that Moisés was from Peru and that he had reached the USA two years earlier by stowing away in the hold of a cargo ship out of the Port of Callao – days without food or water in a cramped, steel-walled cell. "That must have been terrible!" I said stupidly. He shrugged.

The next day I asked him why he left Peru. "*Porque quisieron matarme.*"

"Who wanted to kill you?"

"*Todo el mundo,*" he replied. He didn't say *why* everybody wanted to kill him, but new patients had arrived, and I didn't have time to ask him.

On his next visit, I learned that Moisés had grown up in the Department of Ayacucho and had worked as a miner farther to the north in the Central Highlands of the Peruvian Andes. Hence his unusual cardio-pulmonary capacity. The following day, I got up the courage to ask about his scars.

He had been pulling extra duty as a night watchman when the mining camp was attacked by rebel guerrillas in search of explosives. His bullet holes had been courtesy of the guerrillas, who'd left him for dead with wounds that looked more serious than they really were. Of all the guards that night, only Moisés survived. When the army finally arrived the next day, they found him self-bandaged, having dug a bullet out of his own thigh with a spoon handle. Another round had passed cleanly through his left shoulder and a third had torn through his ear, the blood from that giving the impression of a fatal head wound. His gingko-leaf ear probably saved his life.

The army, not contented with Moisés' story, arrested him on suspicion of terrorism and began to ply him for information about the guerrillas. The knife wounds were courtesy of a sadistic officer who preferred that particular instrument of persuasion. Moisés escaped the army stockade, having killed two guards with his bare hands, and made his way to the coast, traveling mostly on foot and only by night.

On Moisés' last visit to the clinic, Spock declared him well on the road to recovery and gave him a bottle of pills to finish his treatment. I asked him to stop by again sometime. I said I would buy him lunch. He said he might. Just as he reached the door, he turned and said, "Blas."

"Blas?" I repeated.

"*Es mi apellido.* Moisés Blas Iturbide." So now I knew his full name. Then he walked out. In my mind, Moisés' stories lingered vividly, and Peru had begun to loom large, distant and exciting. I watched for Moisés every time I drove near a migrant camp, a working field, or a group of men who appeared to possess a drop of indigenous blood. I never saw him again.

Spring semester ended, and with it my doctoral coursework was finished. I also wrapped up my field work at the clinic. I reduced my volunteer time to one day a week and spent the rest of my days in June poring over my field notes and writing up my conclusions. With Jack Bentley as a co-author, which, by the way, was a more adversarial than collaborative working relationship, I managed to get a paper accepted to a mid-level Anthropology conference.

My phone rang late one afternoon.

"Hello?"

"Hi, Sammy."

"Mom. I'm twenty-five years old. Don't call me Sammy."

Silence.

"Sorry. Samson … Sam, I … uh… just called to see how you're

doing."

What could I say? That after two years I'd replaced anger with indifference? That she and Mitch had become like complete strangers to me? That as long as I kept my head in my studies, as long as I immersed myself in this other world I had discovered and didn't allow myself to think about my vanished home and family, then things were mostly fine?

"I'm all right."

"Studies are going well?"

"Mm-hmm. Yeah. Fine."

Silence.

"You know, there's a guest room in the condo if you ever want to visit."

"Okay."

"Mitch has been asking about you. He says you boys don't talk much."

"Yeah, Mom. I, uh, I've just been really busy."

More silence.

"You know your brother really loves you ..."

My chest and gut began to tighten as if my whole body were trying to squeeze moisture to my tear ducts. I swallowed, closed my eyes and fought it all back. Mitchell, I thought. Two years younger than me, two inches taller, my best friend all through childhood, and now ... what? A stranger? The old family photo albums are filled with pictures of us, always together, two sandy-headed imps with perpetually uninhibited smiles. At least that's how it was when we were children. Once Mitch hit adolescence, his smiles had become rarer and more considered.

"Sam?"

"Yeah?"

"Do you need anything, Honey? Is there anything I can do for you?"

"No. I don't know ... Maybe. I'll let you know, okay?"

Day of Heroism! read the flyer pinned to the cork board on my kitchen wall. I was crossing campus on this summer evening, heading home from the library, when a small, scruffy demonstration caught my eye. Normally I ignored political rallies and other such noise, but this one was different. Four students – I assumed they were students, although most had left for the summer – were chanting, "Workers of the world unite!" These were workers? A skinny kid with a face full of acne held a hand-painted sign that read 'Free Peru!'

I sidled closer, keeping my posture casual and non-committal. The girl, a homely punk-type with cornrows dyed crimson except at the blonde roots, and with a safety pin through her earlobe, held a sheaf of flyers printed on red stock. She turned in my direction. I made eye contact and she zeroed in on me like a yellowjacket to a picnicker.

"Workers of the world unite!" she insisted, thrusting a flyer in my face.

"Okay," I said and snatched the flyer. She blocked me before I could take a step, squared up like a boxer. "Okay, okay. I'll read it. I promise."

"Okay." She seemed suspicious, as if unprepared for acquiescence. It was very awkward.

I got back to my apartment and decided to heat some soup for dinner. I opened a can of something with beef and barley and poured it into a small saucepan with a hollow metal handle that I had acquired from my mother's stock when she downsized to her condo. As I stood watching the sludge slump into the pan, I started to think maybe it was time to try out another relationship. Trouble was, I didn't even know what I wanted from a relationship, other than sex and some undetermined level of companionship. And women seemed to sense it. As a result, I'd had a few dates and an occasional night of lovemaking, but nothing that survived the awkward dance of morning conversation. Turning on the stove tonight was just another tiny surrender in an apparently unwinnable battle.

My stove was a small, four-burner electric range. One burner was dead, two were dying and the fourth burned with a malevolent intensity that was frightening. As it was the only burner with the power to heat the soup before sometime the next morning, that was where I put the pan. I dropped two slices of bread into the toaster, with which I was surely taxing the limits of the apartment's electrical circuits. Then I picked up the flyer from where I had set it on the table and began to read.

> *Last week the Peruvian government brutally murdered three hundred prisoners of war in Lurigancho. Setting an example for the oppressed everywhere, our comrades took over the prison and continued to fight the people's war from the very dungeons of the enemy ...*

When was this? Three hundred? Had there been anything in the news?

> *The government agreed to negotiate with the prisoners about conditions in the prison, then sent in soldiers armed with machine guns, grenades and antitank weapons. Prisoners fought back using slings, homemade crossbows and a small number of captured guns. Inmates defied the commandos for a full day. The majority of the deceased were executed after the prison was recaptured ...*

I flashed for a moment to an image of Moisés and his knife wounds, courtesy of a Peruvian army officer. I tacked the flyer to the kitchen wall with a push pin and stood reading the final paragraph.

> *The Peruvian Communist Party has issued the following statement: "The deaths of these martyrs stand as a glorious banner to Justice, and before that banner we sons and daughters of the people pledge our unwavering commitment to follow their illustrious Crimson Road to freedom, to advance the people's war and to serve the world revolution until the inextinguishable light of Communism dwells upon the earth! Glory to the fallen heroes! Long live the revolution!*

That last word, *revolution,* was lingering in my mind when suddenly, from the stove behind me, came a cacophony of hissing, spitting and shaking that sounded like a standoff between a tomcat and a rattlesnake. My soup was bubbling and frothing at the lip of the saucepan and splashes were starting to reach the burner where they immediately burst into little dancing flames. I grabbed for the pan just as the toast conspired to pop up, I and hit the handle at a bad angle, causing hot soup to splash onto the back of my hand, down to the burner and into a full-on stove-top conflagration. The brand new smoke alarm, which the landlord had installed just the week before, started shrieking with the intensity of a heart attack. I couldn't put the pan back down because of the fire, and I didn't dare drop it. Meanwhile, the soup continued to scald my hand.

I managed to jettison the soup into the sink, smother the flames on the stove with baking soda and stick my hand under a stream of cold water. The screaming smoke detector was not so easy to deal with. After several unsuccessful button pushes and at the very edge of sanity, I finally simply ripped out the battery, wires and all, and tossed the whole apparatus into the sink. I tossed the toast in afterwards for good measure.

The fridge was empty except for the standing assortment of condiments, a half gallon of milk and two tallboy cans of Rainier beer. I contemplated having a bowl of cereal for dinner and decided on the beer instead. I carried both cans to the living room, settled into the recliner (a Mom castoff), opened one of the cans and held the other one against the back of my scalded hand like an ice pack.

I managed to finish the second beer just before that critical juncture where it turns to piss without the intervention of a digestive tract. When I went back to the kitchen to turn out the light, having decided the mess could wait, the red paper flyer shouted at me from its place against the drab kitchen wall. It floated there as if it had will of its own. A will and an abiding sense of rage.

I met Jack Bentley today at Beau Jest. I'd asked for the meeting. He'd picked the place. Usually just called BJ or the Bo, Beau Jest is Dog Town's best coffee shop by day. By night, they push the tables back to make way for competitive improvisational theater. It was an ordinary afternoon in Dog Town, the strip of coffee shops, head shops, barbershops, pubs and bookstores that flank the east edge of campus. Ordinary in every way but one; I was more excited than I had been in years. I'd finally figured out where I wanted to conduct my dissertation research to complete my PhD in anthropology. I was sure Bentley would approve if I proposed it properly. I'd rehearsed my pitch all morning.

Nice thing about the Bo, when every other café in town had caved into paper and Styrofoam, the Bo still washed dishes and served coffee in stoneware mugs with real metal spoons. We took a windowed booth and huddled over the black elixir of social interaction. We were like bookends to the Baby-Boom generation. Bentley had helped usher in the Sixties. I had just missed them, coming of age in the Seventies, and felt pangs of loss for the era of political idealism, mescaline and free love. Now, in the era of Ronald Reagan, I was pretty sure the loss was becoming permanent. Sharpening my nostalgia was the fact that, through most of my youth, I had suppressed my hunger for adventure in order to make the grades that would get me into medical school. Well, I was about to change all that.

"What really intrigues me," I said, warming up to my announcement, "is the clash between modern and traditional cultures. I see some of that among the migrants here, but in their case it's a situation they've chosen. I want to know what happens to a traditional culture when it's overrun with modern political and economic forces. Can they maintain their cultural identity? Do they want to?"

Bentley sucked in his cheeks and looked thoughtful. "You know there are cases of tribal cultures embracing Western consumer goods in all kinds of interesting ways ..."

"Right, right ... But I'm looking for something with more intensity, more stress on the culture." I swirled the coffee in my cup. "I've been thinking about Peru."

"No way, Sam."

I opened my mouth to protest, and he cut me off.

"Forget it. Have you forgotten what's going on down there?"

I hadn't forgotten. There was Lurigancho Prison with its three hundred dead. A more recent news item had reported the murder of an American biologist who had gone to the Peruvian Andes to study vicuña, the wild cousin of the llama and the alpaca. There had been several other attacks on Americans and Europeans over the last couple of years, many of them fatal, and most of them attributed to Communist guerrillas that called themselves the Crimson Road. No, I hadn't forgotten. On the contrary, Peru had become an obsession for me. I'd been reading everything I could get my hands on; Peruvian history, Peruvian literature, contemporary Peruvian fiction. I'd been buying tapes of Peruvian folk music. I even began stocking a flower vase in my apartment with alstremaria for the simple fact that they were commonly called Peruvian lilies.

Once again, I opened my mouth to speak and Bentley cut me off with a shake of his head. "It's way too dangerous, Sam. A dead doctoral student does nothing to advance the field." He dropped a dollar on the table and stood up to leave. "Call me when you have a more reasonable proposal."

In 1776, two American movements advanced the cause of freedom. In North America, Thomas Jefferson wrote the Declaration of Independence, and in South America, Inca Tupac Amaru II petitioned the Spanish High Court in Cuzco to end the slavery of indigenous Peruvians. Jefferson and the colonists eventually prevailed and won their freedom. Tupac Amaru II did not. In 1780, he raised a revolutionary flag and began turning miners into soldiers. Beginning in the mining region of Tina, the new Inca's forces captured and executed an abusive Spanish official. The revolution gathered grass-roots support and won battles, but as it did, the middle-class, mixed-blood *mestizos,* or *mistis*, became alarmed. Frightened by the messianic character of Tupac Amaru II, the *mestizos* turned against the revolutionaries. When Tupac Amaru II attacked Cuzco in January of 1781, he was repelled. In April he was captured, and in May, along with his entire family, he was executed.

The Spaniards had beheaded the original Inca Tupac Amaru, last of the ruling Incas, two hundred years earlier in order to subdue his people. For his revolutionary namesake, they had even less mercy. After a long period of torture, which included ripping out his tongue with iron pincers, The Spanish court had him drawn and quartered in the central plaza of Cuzco by four horses pulling toward the compass points.

Today was the fourth of July. Independence Day. Last night I dreamt of Tupac Amaru. He had the face of Moisés Blas.

I cornered Jack Bentley in his office. It had been three weeks since our meeting at the Bo, and I'd made an interesting discovery. I stopped by unannounced and knocked on his closed door. No answer. I waited. Knocked again.

"Come in."

A faint odor of marijuana lingered in the air.

"You've been holding out on me," I said.

"What do you mean?" He betrayed a hint of nervousness.

"Alfredo Ramirez. Professor of Anthropology at *Universidad Nacional*. You never told me you had a former doctoral student in Peru."

I saw relief pass over his face as he realized that I wasn't referring to the ganja. "Ah, yes. Fredo. You never asked."

"I'll bet he could help me get established for my field work."

"Sam, I told you ..."

"C'mon, Jack. The place is perfect. Some of those Andean villages are still as deeply indigenous as you can find anywhere. And it's a cultural crucible. Between the army, the *Camino Rojo* and the coca trade, they're facing fascism, communism and rogue capitalism all at the same time."

"And you want to see what emerges from the mix? It's crazy."

From what we could tell from international news, Peru was mired in civil war. The *Camino Rojo* – the Crimson Road was the popular name for the revolutionary Peruvian Communist Party – had brought the national government to the brink of disaster with a campaign of terror and sabotage. Started and led by an ex-university professor named Miguel Fortuna, the *Camino Rojo* had become increasingly violent, at least in part, as an answer to violent abuses by the government's own army and national police forces.

I once again recalled the scars of Moisés Blas. It was an image I couldn't seem to shake from my mind. I pressed on. "I'd be careful."

Bentley shook his head.

"You agree it would make a good study, right?" I persisted.

"Yes, but ..."

"I think it's worth the risk. There must be dozens of Americans working in Peru. Probably hundreds. It's not exactly a death sentence. I could start out in Lima. Take my time. Get a feel for the political situation. Learn the ropes from Professor Ramirez. I could work my way into the Andes gradually, if at all, through more stable zones …" By the time I ended my argument, I had both hands planted on the top of Bentley's desk and he was leaning back as far as his creaky office chair would allow.

"Look, Sam. It's not just the danger. There's not a single granting institution that would fund anthropological research down there right now."

I'd thought about that too. "It doesn't matter. I can fund it myself." As I said it, I hoped I was right. It would mean asking my mother for an advance on my inheritance.

Bentley raised his eyebrows, took a deep breath, and then let it out with a sigh. "Maybe so," he relented. I relaxed into a less emphatic position. He remained thoughtful. "Why don't you give me a day or two to think about it and check it out with Fredo? In the meantime, if you're really serious about this, write me a formal prospectus."

It was September first, coming into my favorite season in Oregon. As my plane waited on the tarmac, I considered that I was heading toward springtime in the southern hemisphere. And eventually to the Andes. Only a short flight and a change of planes at LAX stood between me and the adventure of a lifetime. Jack Bentley had taken me to the airport in his beat up old Saab. He walked me to the gate and, just as I was getting ready to board, he handed me a nine-by-twelve manila envelope. "I'd like you to take this to Fredo for me. It's a little archival research he asked me for."

In the hour and a half it took to get to Los Angeles, I pondered what I was leaving behind. It didn't seem like much. I had no love life. Of the women I'd dated in graduate school, none had any desire for a lasting relationship. At least not with me. It was probably my own fault. It seems I either ignored them or suffocated them. Or both. Debbie A, a social work masters student and the one woman I actually lived with for a while, had put it like this while she was boxing up her things: "Jesus, Sam, it's like living with a goddamn split personality. You're either closed up like a clam or you're climbing all over me! I need …" she bracketed the word 'need' with both hands like she was holding an invisible beach ball to her face, "... a little consistency."

And no home life either. A few years ago, I was comfortably situated as the older of two sons in a stable, all-American nuclear family. We weren't particularly communicative, but it seemed like everybody had a part to play, knew that part well enough, and played it without creating a lot of grief for anyone else.

But that was a lifetime ago. Now, I was on my way to Peru, leaving behind a barren personal life and a disintegrated family.

At LAX, I made the trek to the international terminal carrying only a flight bag over my shoulder. In order to blend in as well as possible in Peru, I had cultivated a look that was deliberately generic, a task made easier by bland genetics. My build was athletic, but not ostentatiously so. My brown hair was not too long, not too short, and cut a little too neatly for my preference. On advice from Alfredo Ramirez, I carried no tape recorder, no photographic equipment other than a simple point-and-shoot camera, and no clothing with obvious US branding – nothing, in fact, that would identify me easily as an American. To the Peruvian Army, all Americans were suspected supporters of the *Camino Rojo*. To the *Rojistas* the *yanquis* were despised as imperialist pigs. Under the circumstances, I hoped to keep a low profile.

What I did carry included a couple pairs of good wool socks, cotton boxers, a plain canvas jacket, an extra blue work shirt, some basic toiletries that I would jettison in Lima in favor of locally branded ones, and a single, bound notebook. I'd decided that even my notebooks should be of common Peruvian manufacture. I carried only about two hundred US dollars in cash, another thousand in traveler's checks and a Visa card for emergencies. Runaway inflation guaranteed that any dollars converted to *soles*, the Peruvian currency, would begin to evaporate almost immediately. For that reason, my money would be apportioned in small amounts sent monthly from my bank in the US to an account at the main branch of *Banco Europa* in Lima. I could then access it from one of the smaller branches scattered about the country.

With the help of Alfredo Ramirez, I had obtained credentials from the National Institute of Peruvian Culture attesting to my scholarly purpose. The credentials should help me avoid certain kinds of trouble, at least with police and other government officials. What they might mean to *Rojistas* remained to be seen, or not, if I was lucky.

Night was falling by the time the plane leveled out into its southerly trajectory. I wanted to arrive in Lima with my wits about me, so I had made preparations to sleep on the flight. I swallowed an over-the-counter allergy pill with a Seven and Seven and fell asleep almost immediately.

About four hours later, I woke from a dream. I'd been climbing in the lead position with a group on a glaciated mountain – it had seemed like Mt Hood, only an unfamiliar ascent – when a patch of rotten ice gave way beneath my feet. I slid out of control down the steep slope, trying without success to plant my ice axe. As I careened past the second climber, to whom I was roped, I saw his face set in judgment against me. It was my father. I was headed for a blue crevasse and had just reached the end of the rope when I snapped awake.

Shaking off the chilling effect of the dream, I leafed through the in-flight magazine and completed its too-easy crossword puzzle. Once I'd completely exhausted the magazine's entertainment value, I decided to try the booze and antihistamine trick again. I rang for the flight attendant and groped in my flight bag for my allergy pills. There in my bag, tempting me with its blank exterior, sat the envelope Jack had given me for Alfredo.

My curiosity battled with my sense of propriety. On the one hand I wanted to know what kind of research Jack had done for his former student. On the other hand I felt as if opening the envelope might be a violation of confidence. I pulled the envelope from my bag and hefted it. It was quite thin. A few sheets of paper at the most. I turned it over. It was held shut with a metal clasp, but not sealed. Surely, I reasoned, that meant the contents weren't particularly sensitive or private. Curiosity won out.

I loosened the clasp and extracted the contents. Only three sheets: two photocopied documents and a hand-scrawled cover letter. The documents were in German and bore swastikas. I was more interested in the letter.

> *Greetings Fredo,*
>
> *I believe the enclosed documents will provide the evidence you were looking for. It's too bad the truth so often comes out only after these guys are already dead. I managed to find these records through a Swiss colleague with special access to the archives. Do you know Susanna Schoen, out of NYU, currently at Leipzig? She said it was*

tough digging. Seems we both owe her a favor.

By now you've met Sam. He's a bright kid, if a little headstrong. As you know, I advised him against working in Ayacucho. If he didn't have his own funding, he never could have gotten as far as he has. Anyway, I hope you can help steer him out of harm's way.

Best wishes,
Jack

I hope so too, Jack. I read the letter a second time, feeling slightly jealous of its collegial tone. Jack and Fredo and Susanna Schoen all belonged to an elite professional club that excluded me. But not for long. I would soon earn my own entry.

With the documents and letter back in their envelope, and with an alcohol and Benadryl cocktail working its magic on my central nervous system, I eventually fell back to sleep.

At one point in the predawn hours, a bit of turbulence woke me again. Through the window, somewhere over the Pacific Ocean, I watched as lightning spread across the sky in great, lacy curtains. My next recollection was of the cabin lights coming up, the air temperature plummeting, and the first stirrings of breakfast service making its way down the aisle. Soon a voice advised me, first in English, then in Spanish, to prepare for our descent into Lima.

The image I will always carry with me of Lima International Airport is one of men with guns. At both Customs and Immigration, soldiers stood guard with grim expressions on their faces and automatic weapons slung over their shoulders. A customs official, wearing a look that combined boredom with meanness, emptied out my flight bag and searched it thoroughly. He shook out my folded clothes and let each garment fall into a heap. He leafed through my notebook and dumped the toiletries out of my kit. When he was done, he held the flight bag upside down, gave it a shake, dropped it on top of everything else and then simply pushed the whole pile off to one side and stamped my customs form. Welcome to Lima, I thought.

Outside the terminal, I hailed a taxi and haggled a price for transportation to National University. Thanks to advice from Alfredo Ramirez, I already knew the going rate, which was about half what the cabby first quoted me. On the way there, a single theme stood out: Men with machine guns. They stood at the entrance to every bank and every government office or installation. At certain street corners, they stood by armored vehicles. I leaned back low in the seat, keeping one arm draped over my travel bag, and tried to take everything in as the cabby bullied, honked and gestured his way through the heavy, anarchic traffic.

"*¿Usted es Mexicano?*" inquired the cab driver at a point where a traffic cop dammed the metallic river with a white glove to allow movement along a cross street. The question caught me off guard.

"*¿Cómo sabía?*" I let him believe I was Mexican.

"*Su acento.*"

Smugly, I filed away the information that to at least one Lima cabby I sounded like a native Spanish speaker with a Mexican accent.

As we approached the university, the cab swung wide around the burned-out remains of an old Dodge panel truck. On its side, I could make out most of a hand-painted hammer and sickle.

"How long has that been there?" I asked the driver.

"Who knows? A couple of days? A month?" Not his neighborhood.

At the university, I made my way to the Anthropology Department where I located a Fifties-era office and a bespectacled, mid-thirtyish professor with curly dark hair, almond-shaped brown eyes and a skin tone that resembled a deep tan over slightly jaundiced skin. He wore dark gray slacks, a white, poorly ironed shirt with the sleeves rolled above the elbows, black wingtips and a narrow blue tie.

"Doctor Ramirez?" I based my guess on the nameplate by the office door.

"*Sí,*" he answered without looking up.

"*Me llamo* Samson Young."

"Ah! Of Course. Welcome." Alfredo Ramirez suddenly radiated enthusiasm. "I've been looking forward to meeting you. Jack speaks highly of you."

I smiled. Modestly, I think. Inside I was throwing myself a congratulations party. Bentley had never spoken highly of me to me, and I appreciated this vote of confidence.

"I studied under Jack when he was still at A and M. I did my field work in the US, a study of informal economies along the Texas-Mexico border."

"I've read it. It's required reading in Bentley's methodology class. I've cited it in some of my own research with migrant workers."

Ramirez's mouth twisted to suggest something like a wry private thought. "Ironic, no?" he said. "My going there. Your coming here. Maybe it would have made more sense for us both to stay put."

"Don't you think anthropology is best served when we work outside our familiar cultural frameworks?"

"Spare the lecture. I've given it a thousand times." Oops. I suddenly felt like a pretentious ass. "Still, given our current political situation, you might be better off working someplace more peaceful."

"I'd be bored."

"Better bored than dead."

It was hard to argue with that. I remembered the manila envelope. "By the way," I said, "Jack sends this with his regards."

Ramirez took the envelope and, without looking at it, flipped it onto the top of an overstuffed in-basket. He picked up his phone, dialed an internal extension and announced my arrival. "*El Señor Young ha llegado*." Then to me he said, "You must be tired from your trip." I wasn't especially tired, but I didn't contradict him. It turned out his statement was more of a transition than a diagnosis. "I've made you a reservation at a hotel nearby where you can rest up. Tomorrow we can talk about your research site."

"Have you found a suitable site already?" Faster than I expected, I thought. My metabolism stepped up a notch with excitement.

"Maybe," said Ramirez. "I have to confirm a couple of things still, but …"

His train of thought seemed to be derailed by the approaching staccato of heels in the tiled hallway. The sound stopped at the door and a young woman entered. Ramirez introduced us. Her name was Marivela Santiana. She was a Peruvian graduate student and, apparently, she was to be in charge of me. Maybe five-foot four in red heels, she seemed very fit, or at least solid with a kind of compact voluptuousness. She had dark eyes and a broad mouth framed in a parenthesis of dimples when she smiled. Her long, thick, black hair was curled and loose and had a few reddish highlights. Her black skirt and white blouse both fit like they were a half-size too small. Her bust tugged at the buttons revealing glimpses of a full-coverage brassiere and a flat stomach. Over the blouse, she wore an unzipped short red jacket. The only jewelry I noticed were her earrings, simple gold hoops, and a ring with a tiny red stone set in gold on her right pinky.

"*¿Tuyo?*" She asked as she scooped up my flight bag from the tiled floor and slung it over her shoulder, over the top of a small red handbag. She sang more than spoke the word, enunciating the syllables with an inflection that rose in perfect time with the arching of her eyebrows. I nodded. She cocked her head toward the door. "*Vámonos pues.*"

Off we went. I glanced back at Ramirez. His wry look had returned. "You're in good hands. I'll see you tomorrow for lunch."

"What time? Where?"

"Marivela will fill you in."

My hotel was only about four blocks away from campus in the direction of downtown. On the way there, I struggled to keep up with the pace of Marivela's legs and conversation. Where had I lived in the States? Had I been to New York? She dreamed of going to New York. And how was it to work with Doctor Bentley? Wasn't he brilliant? Didn't it seem like an enormous privilege? Those buildings over there were student housing where, of course, she lived with only one roommate because she was a graduate student. And did I have a girlfriend? No? Brothers and sisters? Only one? And this coffee shop was absolutely "*precioso*," a must for breakfast. Seriously, no girlfriend? And then, "*Aquí estamos.*" There we were in front of a Spanish colonial building with multiple entrances. A pair of worn stone steps led to a wide wooden door with a bronze plaque that read 'Hotel El Moro'.

While I checked into the hotel, Marivela, with her hands clasped behind her back, did a slow circumnavigation of the small, high-ceilinged lobby, craning her neck to inspect every picture, vase and bit of carved stone or woodwork with extraordinary intensity. She didn't seem inclined to leave. The matronly desk clerk plunked down a heavy skeleton key, indicated the carpeted wooden staircase and disappeared behind a curtain where a black and white television broadcasted the snowy images of a daytime talk show: *Habla Peru con Cassandra.*

"Hungry?" asked Marivela, now standing close behind me and once again holding my flight bag.

"Yes. But I'd like to get cleaned up before I eat."

"*Per-fec-to*," she sing-songed as she snatched the room key from the counter and practically skipped toward the stairs. Mentally, I was a little off kilter as I hurried to catch up. Watching her red pumps twist into the dark carpet of the stairs, taking in each orbiting movement beneath the fabric of her skirt, I felt as if I had stepped through a movie screen into a bygone era. I may not have been in love with her the by the time I hit the middle of the stairway, but I was strongly interested. I had the empty-chested feeling I associate with a strong – and usually unrequited – desire for a woman. When the feeling becomes persistent enough, I have been known to make a fool of myself.

As she reached the top of the stairway, Marivela stopped and abruptly turned toward me. My momentum carried my face right into her bosom. I recoiled and had to grab the heavy railing for balance or risk careening back down the stairs. She grinned, cocked her head toward the hallway on the left and pointed with her lips. "This way, I think," she said in English.

Marivela turned the key in the lock, pushed the door open, deposited my bag onto the room's only chair and then perched on the edge of the standard double bed. "I'll wait," she said.

I hung my jacket over the chair back, took the toiletry kit out of my flight bag, went into the bathroom, closed the door and stood there with my back against it. Marivela had me totally off balance. She was sexy and forward and unpredictable. Was this a cultural thing, I wondered, or simply her individual personality? Whatever it was, I found it intriguing and energizing, as well as discomfiting.

I took stock of the bathroom. There was no shower, only a sink and mirror, an old-fashioned toilet with its tank high on the wall, and a claw-foot bathtub. I peed, trying to be quiet by keeping the stream on the porcelain rather than splashing into the water. I washed my hands and face, took one deep breath, exhaled heavily and eased myself back into the bedroom.

Marivela stood next to the chair, holding my open flight bag by one of its two handles. "Is this all you brought?" she asked. I nodded.

"You need to do some shopping."

"You speak excellent English."

She cocked her head to one side and smiled. "I require Fredo to practice with me. I would like you to please do the same." I nodded. "All right then, let's go downtown."

I locked up my room and we walked a few blocks to a busy corner where we could catch a microbus to the city center. For every step I took, Marivela seemed to take two, and still she stayed just ahead of me all the way. All the micros were packed with riders. Each one stopped, squeezed out a few people, swallowed up a few more and it went on its way. Within a couple of minutes, along came a bus for the route we wanted. Marivela hailed it. It lurched to a stop at the curb and Marivela bounded up the two steps. I had only managed to get halfway inside the door when the driver hit the gas. I grabbed the steel handrail and hauled myself in as the bus plunged back into the stream of traffic. Marivela dropped a few coins of fare into the driver's palm. All the seats were filled and those of us standing in the aisle were stuffed in like Vienna sausages. Passengers with upcoming stops were already pushing forward, forcing us farther back.

"Watch your wallet," cautioned Marivela. I slipped it into my front pocket and kept a hand on it. A strange hand reached out from somewhere and gave Marivela's breast a squeeze. Before I could even process a coherent thought, she threw a jab, and a man in the nearest seat buckled over, holding his throat and gasping for air. No words were uttered, but chuckling laughter rippled through the surrounding passengers. Marivela's face remained serene. I tipped my head to her with raised eyebrows to acknowledge how impressed I was. She rolled her eyes as if to imply, "What did the *chingado* expect?"

The tango of boarding and exiting passengers continued and, eventually, it was our turn to begin the surge forward. We landed with several others at the *Plaza de Armas* and Marivela steered me onto *Jirón de la Unión*. Both sides of the broad pedestrian boulevard were lined with boutiques, restaurants and hotels.

Our first stop was a bank to change dollars to *soles*. Then I bought us a late lunch at a corner restaurant. We shared a *pollo a la braza*, so tender that the meat sloughed off the bones, with French fries and a scorching yellow chili sauce. This was *so* not Colonel Sanders or my mother's Shake-n-Bake. We also ordered a large bottle of the local lager, *Cerveza Cristal*, and two glasses.

"Were you born in Lima?" I asked between bites.

"In Trujillo. In the north. On the coast."

"Do you have family there still?"

"No. No family. I was an orphan at the age of thirteen. I went to live with an uncle in the sierra. He is a teacher and he took charge of my education. I owe him everything." She said it matter-of-factly with no show of emotion. "What about you? Tell me about your family."

"There's not much to say. My father was a physician. He died a few years ago. My mother lives near Portland, Oregon. I have one brother. I told you that. He's younger. An artist in Seattle … so they say. I've actually never seen any of his work."

"No? How so?"

"Opportunity, I guess. I've been pretty busy with my studies and field work."

"Is Seattle very far away for you?" She was looking right at me with an intense gaze that almost made me squirm.

"No. I guess not. Not so very far."

Later, as we strolled along the heavily touristed boulevard, I resisted buying clothing, even though Marivela periodically tugged me toward a shop window and insisted that I would look handsome in this or that disco-styled get-up. I wasn't absolutely sure whether she was serious or just having a little fun at my expense, but I felt flattered by the attention. Clearly, everything in the shop windows was too urban for my needs. Eventually, I bought socks and underwear, several bound notebooks, a new ballpoint, some postcards and a few toiletries, including a cologne that Marivela playfully picked out for me.

By evening, my energy was starting to flag. It had been a full and incredible day. I'd never really gotten my bearings, and so the hotel kind of sneaked up on me. Suddenly, Marivela and I were standing on the street in front of it.

"That was great," I said. "Will I see you tomorrow?" It was more of a plea than a simple question.

"Would you like that?" she asked.

"Very much."

Her face brightened. "Good! Then we'll do something after your lunch with Fredo."

Fredo? Not Alfredo? Or Professor Ramirez? For some reason, I had expected a more formal relationship between student and teacher in Peru. Maybe I didn't really know as much about Peruvian culture as I thought I did. Or maybe Marivela was just a singularly interesting and progressive exception to rules I thought I'd learned. So full of surprises.

"I'll come by for you in the morning. I'll look for you in the café." Then she put a hand on my shoulder, stood on her tiptoes and kissed me tenderly on the cheek. "Welcome to Lima. *Duerme con los ángeles.*"

Her wish that I should 'sleep with angels' used the familiar, more intimate 'tu' form of speech. I watched her stroll toward the university without a look back. Her walk was music that made me want to dance.

I had a light dinner of pasta and wine at an unremarkable Italian restaurant a couple of blocks from the hotel. Then I returned to my room, ran through the day's events in my mind and jotted a few lines in my journal. I confined my entry to the whos, whats and wheres of the day. There was no way I could get enough of a handle on my feelings to commit them to paper. It had been an emotional whirlwind, ending with the playful, flirtatious and altogether captivating Marivela Santiana.

I went to bed, but I tossed and turned, unable to quiet my mind. To make matters worse, the hotel mattress sagged like a hammock. Over and over again, I'd try to empty my head of thoughts, and every time, it would fill back up with images of Marivela. Finally, I gave in. I concentrated on my mental pictures of her; the smooth, brown legs ending in red daggers of footwear … her beaming smile alternating with a playful pout … her flashing, dark eyes … the vigor with which she pulled me this way and that, leading me by the arm, while my heart and brain struggled constantly to catch up … the femininity that seemed overlaid on an almost animal energy … the nonchalant punch to the groper on the bus …

Then, I was spinning out sexual fantasies. Slipping the buttons on Marivela's blouse. Unleashing her breasts from her brassiere. Her skirt unzipped and sliding to the floor. Soon, the physical discomfort of sleeplessness was amplified by the presence of an insistent erection …

The next day, I bathed, had breakfast at the *precioso* coffee shop and spent the morning fleshing out my journal entry from the night before. The café turned out to be some kind of bohemian intellectual hangout. The clientele seemed younger than me by a few years and markedly stuffy. They gathered in groups of four or more, struck poses of intentional sloth and talked about who knows what. I thought I overheard one young man with sandy hair and the very soft beginnings of a beard propounding evidence of nihilistic philosophy in Shakespeare's King Lear. Occasionally, I would look up from my writing to find one of them looking at me surreptitiously and then, before I could make eye contact, make a point of ignoring my existence.

At about a quarter to twelve, Marivela's musical "*¡Hola!*" rang out from the café door. She looked like a character from a Sixties Italian movie in a white, scoop-necked top, tight black jeans, black pumps and, for dramatic flair, her red handbag and a red scarf around her neck. She strode around behind me, bent down and kissed me on the cheek. I was so grateful I could have kissed the table top. Mister sandy-hair-and-beard squinted a look at me that could have been disgust or jealousy or even outright loathing. I snapped my notebook shut, giving the impression, I hoped, of having captured in it some damning observation.

Marivela stayed in the lobby while I dropped off my notes in my hotel room. Then we walked straight to campus. Marivela's pace was slower and more subdued than that of the day before.

"I had a nice time yesterday," she said.

"I did too. Really nice."

As few as our words were, I felt as if the air between us was heavy with emotional energy.

"I thought maybe this afternoon I could show you some more of the capital."

"Great. I'd like that."

With practically nothing else said, we arrived at Ramirez's office.

His door was open and he stood rifling through folders in the second drawer of a four-drawer filing cabinet. His desk was cluttered with maps, handwritten notes and what looked like stacks of articles and student papers. Off to one side, I saw the envelope I'd delivered the day before and, on top of it, the two German documents.

"Ah, Sam. Ready for lunch?"

"Sure."

"Marivela," he said, "would you like to join us?"

"No, no. You boys go ahead. I have some things to do here. I'll see you when you get back."

Alfredo closed his file cabinet, glanced over at the papers on his desk and nodded to Marivela as he joined us in the hall. She slid past him into his office, gave us a little wave and closed the door.

"Professor Ramirez ..." I said, as we exited the building.

"Just Fredo, please."

"Fredo. I was curious, what kind of research was Jack helping you with?"

"Oh, nothing much. Just some genealogy."

He didn't elaborate, so I let it drop. We lunched in the street. Our first stop was a corner just off campus where an old woman sold spinach tarts from a covered straw basket. Each tart was about six inches across, with a flat bottom crust and a domed top crust crimped at the edges. It was filled with a mixture of spinach, white cheese and garlic, topped with an egg that lay perfectly centered, its yolk intact, just under the crust. The next stop was for *anticuchos*, skewered squares of heart braised over live coals on a hibachi.

"Beef?" I asked. It was delicious.

"Probably," answered Fredo. "But it could also be llama. You always want to eat it well cooked. It can carry parasites."

We finished off at a plaza where a man sold fresh sweet-potato chips from a pushcart. We each ordered a bag, then watched as he sliced wafers of pink tuber, tossed them into a pot of sizzling oil, pulled them out golden brown, hit them with salt and dumped them into brown paper bags that immediately darkened with grease. They were so tasty, all I could say was, "Wow."

On the way back to campus, thinking about Fredo's comment on genealogy, I asked him about his personal history. He took so long to respond that I began to wonder if he hadn't heard me or, worse, if I had offended him.

"I grew up with my parents and three sisters," he began at length. "My father is half Chinese. A fierce advocate of education. My mother – I suppose you would have described her as an Afro-Chinese mulatto – was a gentle woman, very dignified. I think some people found her aloof. She had a regal bearing."

"Had?" I asked.

"She died while I was studying in the States."

"I'm sorry."

He gave me that very North American gesture of shrugged shoulders and raised eyebrows that signifies water under the bridge.

"I was in the field," he said, "making good progress on my dissertation. I didn't go home for the funeral. My father never forgave me for that."

"Is he here in Lima?"

He clasped his hands behind his back as we sauntered and turned his eyes to the ground in front of us. "Arequipa," he said. "He's a druggist. The whole family is there; my sisters, their children. I don't see them much any more."

Fredo's candor plunged me into silent contemplation of my own family. Ghosts and strangers. It seemed Fredo and I had that in common.

As we neared his office again, he broke the silence.

"So, what do you think of Marivela?"

The question caught me off guard. What should I think? What should I admit to thinking?

"She's very … energetic. Helpful. Smart."

We took two or three more steps in silence.

"Do you like her?"

That question also made me a little uncomfortable. I wasn't sure how to interpret it.

"What's not to like?" I asked.

When we got back to the office, Marivela was gone. I noticed that the documents I had delivered were no longer on the desktop.

Fredo stood across the desk from me and spread out one of the maps that were lying there. "This is the Department of Ayacucho," he said. "And here is where I think you should conduct your field work." His finger rested on a little dot near the border with Apurimac. The name of the village was Santa Rosita.

By field work, he meant the combination of observation and

interviews that ultimately would form the data for my dissertation. My first task would be to find a way to fit into the community, to develop the trust of the townspeople. It probably wouldn't be as easy as volunteering at the clinic had been, but I was pretty sure I could manage it in a fairly short time.

Fredo then indicated a wide circle on the map with a sweep of his hand. "Most of this area has been declared an Emergency Zone at one time or another."

"Emergency Zone?"

"A place of heightened rebel activity, theoretically under martial law. I've done some calling around and things have been relatively peaceful lately. More than that, it turns out that with everything else that has happened in the wider region, Santa Rosita has managed to stay out of the fray."

"How so?"

"I'm not sure. Perhaps she has a powerful patron saint."

I waited for him to explain further, but he didn't offer and I didn't press the issue.

"How close is ... the fray?" For different reasons, I hoped for different answers. I wanted to be close enough to conflict to be able to study its impact on the culture, but I also wanted to feel reasonably safe from harm.

"It depends. The priest there says he has heard of *Rojistas* as near as Uchurimac, which is just a few kilometers away." He indicated another small dot. "On the other hand, the fact that there *is* a priest in Santa Rosita is pretty remarkable. Priests in the *pueblos* tend to rank pretty high on the rebels' shit lists, especially if they get political. A number of them have been executed."

I tried to banish images of slaughtered priests from my brain. "So," I said, "Santa Rosita."

"Does that seem all right to you?"

"It sounds terrific. How do I get there?"

"Well, unfortunately, getting there isn't easy."

"No?"

Fredo shook his head. "There are no public flights in and out of Ayacucho. The airport has been occupied by the Army but it is constantly under siege by *Rojistas*. There are buses, but they take forever, and they frequently get held up."

"By *Rojistas*...?"

"Or bandits. Your best bet is probably to drive."

"Drive?"

He nodded. "It's no more dangerous than any other mode of transportation. At least you have control of the vehicle, and when you get there you'll need a way to get around. If you want it, I know a guy who will sell you a Jeep for five hundred dollars."

"That sounds great."

His lips twisted into a wry smile. "You haven't seen the Jeep yet."

Fredo had just jotted down the name and address of the owner of the Jeep when Marivela reappeared in the doorway.

"Ready to see some sights?" she asked.

I looked to Fredo to see if he had anything else for me.

"Away you go, then," he said. I thought I detected a hint of irritation in his voice and I wondered briefly if I had done something to aggravate him.

At the same subdued pace as earlier in the day, Marivela guided us to the cathedral where we saw the remains of Francisco Pizarro, Peru's first Spanish conquistador, in a glass-sided sarcophagus. I was struck by what a small man he had been. A tiny man, I thought, to have brought ruin to such a grand civilization as the Incas. Such was the power of gunpowder and steel. We browsed the cathedral's many shrines and the sacristy with its museum of religious art. The amount of gold on display was impressive, and only a miniscule portion of what had been plundered from the Incas. I noticed that Marivela didn't genuflect like most of the visitors.

"Would you like to get a cup coffee?" I asked.

"Sure. That would be nice." She smiled and took hold of my arm with a gentle squeeze.

I was liking this day a more and more.

At a small café, I ordered coffee with cream and Marivela asked for a Coke. We sat facing each other on either side of a small, round table. As she lifted her glass, the napkin beneath it rose up and floated to the floor. She leaned over to pick it up, affording me a generous view into her scooped neckline. I tried not to look. No, that's not true. I tried to look as if I were trying not to look. She crumpled the retrieved napkin and set it aside, took a sip of her Coke and gave a couple of soft taps on the end of her straw. For the first time, I noticed she had artificial fingernails. Painted the same red as her scarf and handbag, they softened what I also noticed to be very strong and surprisingly rough-looking hands.

"You're not Catholic," I suggested, recalling her failure to genuflect.

"Ay, no. I have worked hard to – how do you say? – conquer my own ignorance. I try to live with my eyes open, not blinded by superstition."

"How is that working for you?"

"So far, so good, I think."

I hovered over my coffee, breathing in the steam and aroma. It was good coffee.

"Marivela?"

"Yes, *Cariño*?"

Cariño. My dear. How should I interpret that?

"What can you tell me about the *Camino Rojo*?"

"I don't know. What do you want to know?"

"I'm not sure ... Who are they, really? Where do they come from?"

"Well, above all, they are ordinary people. Many are *campesinos* and many are poor people from the cities. Some have good educations and others have practically none."

"Their leader is an academic, right? A university professor?"

"*El Colibrí*? Yes. He is far from being 'ordinary people'."

"Why do they call him 'The Hummingbird'?"

"I don't know. Maybe," she said with a coquettish smile, "because he flits from flower to flower? Or maybe because he is ... agile and elusive? If you meet him, you must be sure to ask."

"They say hardly anyone ever sees him. That he's like a ghost."

"That is what they say."

From the café, we walked toward the Museum of Anthropology and Archeology. I was beginning to recognize a few landmarks and get a sense of direction, at least in this limited sector of the city. It was a good thing, for without landmarks I would have no means of navigation. There were no visible mountains and the sky was so heavily overcast that it was impossible to get a bearing from the sun. The light itself was bright enough but so diffuse that it cast no shadows.

Once in the museum, I felt sudden, bizarre moments of familiarity. I recognized many of the artifacts and exhibits from pictures in my archaeology textbooks. I marveled at the examples of trepanning, human skulls with surgically removed windows of bone that attested, according to some literature, to successful pre-Columbian brain surgeries. I saw famous artifacts of solid gold from Cuzco and thousand-year-old textiles from Paracas with still-vibrant colors. It was incredible to be seeing it all in three, real dimensions.

"It's funny," said Marivela, "but I've never really spent much time in here before."

"Sometimes it's good to play tourist in your own town."

We spent almost three hours soaking up ancient culture. By then, evening was upon us. "Can I buy you some dinner?" I asked. Marivela nodded. As we left the museum, she reached over and took my arm.

We made our way back to *Jirón de la Unión* and the *Plaza San Martín*. There, facing the square, stood the stately *Gran Hotel Bolívar*. Built during the first years of the Peruvian Republic with no expense spared, the palatial fifty-plus-year-old structure looked like a rich but tired old lady.

"Have you ever been in there?" I asked.

Marivela looked wide-eyed at the imposing white stone façade. "No."

In a reversal of our pattern of the last two afternoons, I took her arm and steered her in that direction. "C'mon. Let's check it out. They're bound to have a restaurant."

For the first time Marivela was very nearly speechless. We pushed our way through the heavy front doors and into a world of sweeping staircases, massive chandeliers, heavy, ornate draperies, gilded lamps, tired velvet furnishings and Persian rugs on mirror-like marble floors. At the front desk, I asked for the restaurant, and a crisply uniformed young woman led the way.

"A table for two?" asked the maître d', who showed us to a richly draped table by a window overlooking the gardens of the plaza. The few other guests in the restaurant, all dressed in suits and evening wear, paid us no attention beyond first glances.

"What is a Pisco sour?" I asked Marivela, looking at the drinks menu.

"It's what you might call the Peruvian national cocktail. It's quite delicious."

I ordered two. The frothy concoction, made in highball glasses with the local Pisco brandy, citrus, whipped egg whites and I didn't know what else, was delightful. Marivela's left a delicate mustache on her upper lip, which she erased with a deft flick of her tongue.

The dinner menu was printed in ornate script on one side of a parchment-colored card stock. It looked good to me – limited, but upscale. Marivela seemed rather awed by it. I got the distinct impression that she had never encountered such menu items before.

"I'm not sure what you like," I said, "but I'm leaning toward the filet mignon." It was served with a claret reduction, bleu cheese crumbles and braised yucca spears garnished with yucca flowers. I never ate this kind of meal back home, but here it seemed absurdly affordable.

"That sounds good to me."

So the waiter replaced our empty cocktails with a bottle of Chilean cabernet and we embarked on one of the most memorable meals of my life. Our only words were in praise of the food and wine. My thoughts were divided between appreciation for the food and the growing feelings I had for Marivela. It was as if an aching vacuum were tugging away inside of me at the same time as the realization that Marivela just might be able to fill it. I wondered about the possibilities. As we lingered over the last sips of wine, I searched her eyes, and she searched mine.

Coming out of the restaurant, she walked closer beside me than she had going in, her shoulder brushing against my upper arm. It seemed easy, in that moment, to reach my arm around her, and so I did, and drew her even closer. In the opulent lobby, we lingered as a tall, thin, silver-haired man played a soft medley of Burt Bacharach songs on a grand piano.

"Sam," said Marivela, turning to face me and placing her hand gently on my chest, "let's look at one of the rooms."

The same young woman who had shown us to the restaurant now led the way with a room key. At the third floor, she held the elevator doors open for us, then after knocking gently, unlocked the oversized door to number 307. Marivela walked in almost reverently and I stood behind her. A crystal chandelier hung above a massive, carved wooden bed, flanked by ornate wood and marble end tables. Floor-to-ceiling windows gave way to a balcony with a wrought iron railing and then to a view of the *Plaza San Martín* and the surrounding colonial buildings. More marble surfaces were visible through the bathroom door.

Still and speechless, Marivela stood and took it all in. After perhaps a minute, I placed a hand on her shoulder. She turned toward and into me, held my gaze for a moment and slowly nodded her head.

"We'll take it," I said impulsively.

Marivela stayed behind while I went back to the lobby and registered for the room. As I produced my passport and Visa card and completed the form, I could scarcely believe it was happening.

Back at the room, I opened the door slowly, suddenly unsure of myself. Marivela wasn't there, but her clothes lay folded neatly on the foot of the bed. The bed was flat and firm. I heard a splash of water from the bathroom and smiled. The door was ajar. I gave a little knock.

"Mmmm ... *pasa adentro*."

I accepted the invitation and stepped in. She lay fully extended in the big marble tub. Patches of bubbles drifted on the surface of the water like puffy clouds in an otherwise clear sky. Beneath it, her body created the hills and valleys of a dream landscape. She seemed weightless, eyes closed, face perfectly relaxed. Opening her eyes slowly, her long lashes transporting flecks of foam, she smiled. "Join me?"

In the morning, I woke up gradually to a feeling of warmth and well-being that far exceeded anything I could conjure up for comparison in my sleep-addled brain. Nope. This was unique. I felt great. My gently rising consciousness took in folds of soft linens, low morning light, a warm, seashore smell combining soap, fruit, flowers, body salt, sex and a lingering scent of cinnamon from Marivela's perfume. Then my memory kicked in. An overwhelming montage of Marivela. I breathed deeply, stretched and rolled from my side onto my back and then burrowed toward the side of the bed where Marivela ... wasn't.

"Mari?"

I rolled out of bed and stood, naked, looking at the tangle of sheets and blanket. The reality of the empty bed taunted my memory of the night of before. A night of tenderness and passion and laughter and, oh my God, Marivela. Beautiful, brown, fierce, soft, hard, transcendent, electric Marivela.

"Marivela?"

No answer. I padded into the bathroom. My clothes were still strewn on the floor where I'd left them. But no Marivela.

Back to the bedroom. Her clothes, her shoes, her handbag: all gone.

Breakfast, I thought. She's gone for breakfast.

I took my time washing and dressing, all the time expecting Marivela to come through the door with ... what? ... coffee? ... croissants? ... fresh-squeezed orange juice? It wouldn't matter. Anything I ate with Marivela this morning would be perfect.

But she didn't show up. Finally, I picked up the room key from the nightstand, pocketed it, had a last look around and went downstairs.

At the registration desk, the same clerk from the evening before was working again. I set the room key on the counter.

"*Buenos días*," I said.

The clerk took a quick look at the key. "*Buenos días, Señor* Young. How was your stay?"

"Fine. Great. Say, have you seen my ... umm...?" I didn't know how to fill in the blank.

"*Sí, Señor*. She left about two hours ago." I glanced at the clock on the wall: seven-fifteen. "She said to give you this."

He slid a letter-sized envelope across the counter. It was the hotel's stationery. I thanked him, left the key, and settled into a chair across the lobby.

My Dear Sam. Thank you for a wonderful night! I am sorry to leave you this way. I couldn't bear to wake you. Don't be angry. I have to go away for a while, and I may not be able to see you before you leave for the sierra. No! Go away? Where? Why? Why now? And why couldn't she have told me last night? *Please write to me when you can.* She signed it, *Con Mucho Cariño, Marivela.* With much what? Warmth? Caring? Affection? Shit. *Cariño* may be the most ambiguous word in the whole Spanish language.

The Jeep wouldn't be ready for two more days. For most of the first, I kicked around downtown and then I killed some time at the university library. By evening, I was bored and restless. I kept thinking about Marivela. I carried her letter around with me, had read it so many times I had it memorized. I wanted to see her, to know more about her. I had no phone number or proper home address for her, just a vague wave toward the big student housing blocks on the day we met, and I didn't feel comfortable asking Fredo. At the library circulation desk, I found a campus directory, complete with student names, room numbers and a campus map.

Her dorm was an ugly, four-story cement block surrounded by a flowerbed that had turned to something like cement itself and appeared to be planted mostly with cigarette butts. The entry was glass double doors. The door on the right was spider-webbed with cracks and stabilized with a criss-crossed pattern of duct tape. I sat on a bench a few yards away and watched for a while. Males and females went in and out in about equal numbers. It was obviously a co-ed dorm. Nobody seemed to require a key or a security code.

I looked again at the address to be sure of the room number: 3K. Did I dare to knock? What would I say to Marivela if she was there? "Hi, I was just in the neighborhood?" Jesus. How about, "I was just wondering if you might still be around, despite what you said in your letter, and that maybe you might want to, oh, I don't know, get a drink or something, fuck my brains out, and disappear on me again?" Or maybe I could say, "Hello, I'm conducting a study of the resiliency of the human heart." Shit. I should just go away and trust that Marivela had good reasons for leaving like she did. The problem was, I was a bumbling mass of desire and insecurity and confusion, and I couldn't let go of it.

So in I went.

Inside was a foyer of chipped, grey-and-green streaked tiles with a steel and concrete stairway going up and hallways running to the left and right. Room numbers such as 1F and 1H painted on green steel doors indicated that I wanted the third floor. The halls and stairwell were empty of people and furniture. At the third floor, I turned right and found 3K at the end of the hall. I stood for a while and listened. I heard music from 3L behind me, but 3K seemed quiet. There was no doorbell, so I summoned my courage and knocked.

I was groping for something to say when the door opened to the length of a security chain. The face in the gap was not Marivela's. This girl was taller, heavier, plainer and lighter complexioned.

"Hi. I was looking for Marivela."

"She's not here."

"Oh. Umm… Do you know where she is?"

"Who is asking?"

"Sam. I'm a friend from the United States."

She gave me a look of pure incredulity. "She went away." The door closed, and I heard the deadbolt click into place.

Early the next morning, I followed Fredo's directions to a mechanic's garage carrying five hundred dollars in traveler's checks. The Jeep he had arranged for me was an ancient, loose-jointed Willys with a tiny, four-cylinder engine that had been transplanted from something Japanese. It had only one seat, the driver's. None of the four tires matched any of the others. The pale yellow paint looked like it had been applied with a broom. All that was left of the tailgate was a pair of rusting hinges, and in its place hung a doubled length of sisal rope. None of the gears had functioning synchros, which made shifting a matter of double or triple clutching while searching almost mystically for the exact engine speed that would allow the gears to mesh. It was not what I was used to, but, all things considered, I thought it was perfect. Back home, it was the kind of beater car you could leave parked anywhere – a trailhead or a city street – without fear of theft or vandalism.

I left the Jeep at the hotel and started to walk back toward the University to check in with Fredo. It was just after ten o'clock and I was daydreaming about bumping into Marivela again. With no warning and no prior experience to help me interpret the sound, I heard the *whump* of an explosion. Turning in the direction of the concussion, toward downtown, I saw a halo of white smoke hovering in the air. Less than a minute later, there was another *whump* and another cloud of smoke above the skyline. People on the street stood and stared. Then sirens began to blare and people started to disappear indoors. I went straight to Ramirez's office walking as fast as I could without breaking into a run.

"Fredo!" I said as I reached his open door, "did you …?"

He held up one hand to silence me as he worked the tuner of a radio with the other. "… Crackle, crackle … two buildings downtown … *TelePerú* … crackle … almost certainly … crackle … *Camino Rojo* …"

Alfredo listened intently for a minute or two then turned the volume down. "If you still want to go to Ayacucho, this would be a good time for you to travel," he said. I nodded. Of course I still wanted to go. "Go to Santa Rosita as quickly as you can and contact the priest there. He'll be expecting you."

"Now?"

"Yes, now. If this bombing was an attack by *Rojistas*, then they'll be lying low for a few days. There will be more *Guardia* on the roads, but your chances are better with them."

"My chances?"

"Of getting there alive. Here's a clean map. Don't mark your route. If you get stopped by police along the way, don't say you're going to Ayacucho. Say Cuzco."

"What if I get stopped by *Camino Rojo*?"

"Don't."

Then he handed me his card and added, "And call me when you get there, will you?

"I will. By the way …"

"Hmm?"

"Have you seen Marivela?"

Fredo pursed his lips, as if trying to remember, and shook his head. "Not for a day or two. Why?"

"No reason."

His eyes narrowed, and he studied me as though he were probing for a secret. For a moment I felt I'd sensed some kind of veiled hostility coming from him. But I shook it off.

My planned route to Ayacucho led from Lima through Puerta del Sol, eastward over the Andean continental divide at Ticlio, through the Mantaro Valley and the city of Huancayo and into the Department of Huancavelica. Lima seemed to stretch on forever, becoming poorer and dirtier the farther I got from the city center. Visible signs of poverty downtown were mostly limited to street vendors and the homeless. Children, as young as five or six and dressed in rags, sold Chiclets, shoe shines or cut flowers on every block. Most were shoeless and dirty. Some were spectrally thin with big, brown, pleading eyes, while others looked stringy, tough and shrewd. I tried to speculate about the world they lived in, about reality as they perceived it, and I was thwarted by the horror of the mental pictures I conjured. Along the highway, I did a double-take at a man squatting alongside the road, pants accordioned around his knees, defecating. Farther along, whole settlements rose improbably from the sand. Constructed of found materials, they looked less like neighborhoods than animated landfills exerting structure on their surfaces in a grotesque parody of suburbia.

From Lima to Puerta del Sol, the road was flat and busy and the Jeep's engine ticked along. At one point, the urban squalor gave way suddenly to a rural landscape with no transition through middle-class suburbs. The predominant view consisted of open spaces planted with dusty orchards or the remains of crops. Somewhere in each expanse of field or orchard sat one or two small buildings, mostly constructed of adobe blocks and corrugated steel, that could have been animal sheds or very minimal human dwellings.

Everything was covered with a layer of dust. Dry ditches ran alongside the two-lane highway. Alongside the ditches ran narrow walking paths, dusty tracks worn through dust-covered grass or tamped and smoothed into rougher patches of dirt the same dusty color. Even the sky looked like dust.

The open spaces were interrupted here and there by walled properties with impressive gates. On those walls grew the only exceptions to a monochromatic universe. Virtually every wall was clad in bougainvillea. In some cases, the flowering vines grew along the tops of the walls like brilliant, ropy ice cream toppings. In other places, heavy tendrils reached over the walls as if groping for some invisible prize on the other side. Elsewhere, entire walls were hidden by cascades of color. Vivid reds clashed with hot magentas and flirted with muted yellows. A few walls shunned the flamboyant bougainvillea for the more modestly dressed and Catholic vines of passion fruit with their bizarre flowers evoking the crosses on Calvary.

At Puerta del Sol, the gateway to the Andes, I encountered a *Guardia Civil* roadblock – more men with machine guns. I queued up behind a small cargo truck and a microbus burgeoning with passengers. A soldier commanded the truck driver to pull over to the side of the road and get out of his cab while uniformed officers made a show of studying his documents. It looked like he was going to be there a while. Another officer approached the driver's window of the micro, papers were passed and the bus was cleared to go on.

My turn. I pulled forward to where the officer stood waiting.

"*Buenos días*," I ventured.

"*Documentos, por favor*," was the gruff response. I produced my international driver's license, my passport and the letter of credentials from the Cultural Institute. He gave them all a once over then, without returning them, said, "*Los documentos del vehículo.*"

I started getting nervous. I produced all the papers that I had received when purchasing the Jeep, including the bill of sale.

"*Estos no están en orden.*" Not in order? What did that mean? "You are going to have to come with me to the station."

"The station?" I was starting to feel panicky.

"*Sí, la estación.* The fine for incomplete paperwork is one thousand *soles*. Of course I will also have to impound the vehicle until the papers are in order. The price of the impound is one thousand soles. You can probably have the vehicle back in, oh … I'd say … three or four days."

Shit. Shitshitshitshitshit. Goddamngoddamngoddamn. My brain short-circuited in a string of helpless obscenities. I was a fish with a hook set firmly in the roof of my mouth.

"Of course," continued the humorless officer, "if your time is valuable, it might be possible to clear things up here."

The fisherman was feeding me line.

"How much would that cost?"

I ran with the line and jumped from the water.

"Five thousand soles." Zip! He reset the hook and reeled me in.

Of course I paid. The amount came to less than fifty bucks US – a gringo tax. The soldiers waved me on, and I ground my gears getting started. Driving away from the roadblock, I experienced a weird combination of relief, optimism and nausea.

From there on, the road climbed relentlessly and became more and more degraded. The rapidly increasing altitude started taking its toll on the Jeep's power. By the time I got to the town of Matucana, I was struggling along in second and resisting the need to drop down into the granny gear. In a way, it was just as well that I had to drive so slowly. I was so constantly astonished by the world around me that at higher speeds I probably would have driven off the road or shaken the poor Jeep to pieces. Just as I approached Matucana, I hit the brakes and sat staring in amazement and delight. Crossing the road was an old man with deeply furrowed brown skin and posture like a question mark leading a string of llamas. It was a scene I would soon come to regard as commonplace, but there and then it felt like an exotic discovery, a once-in-a-lifetime moment.

Since I had already stopped, I decided to tinker with the carburetor. Pretty soon, by trial and error, I had the engine running smoothly again. Feeling pretty hungry, I pulled up to a café called the *Restaurante Vicuña.* It was a small, whitewashed cinder block building with a door and window to the front and the name of the establishment lettered in blue on the side wall. In keeping with the theme of adventure, I ordered frogs' legs and fried potatoes. It felt great to be there. I opened my notebook and jotted some impressions:

> These mountains are as dramatic as I expected, but in a different way. They lack the cragginess of the Rockies and look, instead, like enormous piles of loose stone. The exception is where sufficient water allows for cultivation. Even steep slopes are planted. According to the server in the café, the main crops are potatoes, barley and *habas*, a broad white bean. In a few places the steep mountainsides are terraced with stone walls to create flatter ground for planting and water retention. This terracing dates back to the time of the Inca.

From Matucana I continued, drunk on the scenery, and occasionally grinding a gear, to Ticlio and the summit of the pass into the Central Andes. Less than five hours out of Lima, this was the spine of the continent. All the water I'd seen so far had been on its way to the Pacific Ocean. Any drop hitting the ground in front of me now would eventually join the flow of the Amazon on its way to the Atlantic. According to the sign there, Ticlio was the highest point on the planet with a working railroad station. The station was no more than a worn wooden platform. At around fifteen thousand feet of elevation, it was also the highest I had ever been, outside of an airplane. Even in my mountaineering in the Cascades and the Rockies, I had reached summits of only twelve to fourteen thousand feet. At that elevation those peaks had been permanently snow-capped and glaciated. Here at Ticlio, because of proximity to the equator and because all the precipitation falls during the summer months, the ground was bare except for scattered patches of thin, crusty snow. Flanking Ticlio on the north and the south rose peaks that must have reached seventeen or eighteen thousand feet. There the snow was permanent.

Curious about the effects of the altitude, I parked the Jeep at the side of the road, got out, and began to jog. After about a hundred yards on a slight downgrade I still felt pretty energetic despite what I knew had to be a profound lack of oxygen. I turned around and began to jog back toward the Jeep. The very slight upgrade took its toll after only a few steps. By the time I reached the Jeep, I was gasping for air and remembering jealously the mighty lungs and heart of Moisés Blas.

A minute or two later, my breathing almost back to normal, I bent slowly at the waist to stretch my hamstrings, straightened back up, and took one last long drink of scenery. The top of the world, I thought. Here it was more than just a cliché. Then, with my shadow stretching out in front of me, I determined it was time to go. I reached for the key in the ignition, but a sedan coming from the other direction pulled off the road and stopped in front of me. Two uniformed members of the *Guardia Civil* emerged from the car.

Shit. Not again. I'm about to get hit for another bribe.

"*Buenas tardes*," I greeted them warily as I stepped down from the Jeep.

"*¡No te muevas!*" Don't move, came the response from the man on the left. He was a slight man with gray hair and epaulets on his shirt. The man on the right, the driver of the car, was short and fat and held a lower rank. He had a glistening divot of straight black hair and a reddish mole the size of a raspberry clinging to his upper lip. Both men wore pistols on their hips, and Fatso had drawn his.

I held my hands out to my sides, palms up, in a questioning gesture. For a microsecond, I'd been tempted to raise my hands above my head, but had caught myself and avoided acting out the embarrassing American television stereotype.

"What are you doing here?" asked gray-hair-and-epaulets. Fatso had moved around to stand at my side and just slightly behind me.

"I'm just enjoying the scenery."

Fatso gestured with his gun as he spoke. It seemed like a natural extension of his hand. "What the lieutenant means is: what is the nature of your business?"

"I'm an anthropologist," I said, then added, "working with the National Institute of Peruvian Culture."

"Your papers," demanded the lieutenant.

I pulled the letter of credential from my shirt pocket. The lieutenant snatched it away and began to scan it.

"Not this," he said. "Your identification papers."

I nodded my understanding. "They're in my bag."

I reached for my flight bag and, at that instant, Fatso drove a fist into my side, just below the rib cage, doubling me over. For the second time in the last few minutes, I was gasping for breath.

"You need to get down," he said, resting his pistol with surprising weight on my shoulder, its barrel cold against the side of my neck. I got to my hands and knees, but that didn't satisfy Fatso. He put one booted foot against my back and sent me sprawling face first into the dirt and gravel.

Still sucking wind from the lack of oxygen and the belly punch, I coughed and wheezed. My lungs burned with inhaled dust. I tasted gravel. I blinked in an unsuccessful effort to clear the grit from my eyes. I didn't dare try to move my arms. Instinctively, I had landed with my left arm stretched forward to cushion my impact and my right arm crooked beneath my face for the same reason. With my chin planted on my right forearm, moving only my eyes in their sockets, I could see my left arm from the elbow forward, a dun landscape stretching from just under my nose in monotonous detail to a very near horizon of pavement, two sharp-creased pant legs from about the thighs down, a dusty pair of black oxfords with one frayed shoelace, and the lower third of the Jeep.

The lieutenant emptied my bag onto the ground next to the Jeep and scattered the contents with the toe of his shoe. He picked up the leather wallet that doubled as my passport holder.

"Gringo," he said, practically spitting the word. My passport hit the dirt at his feet. "Let's see what else we have: International driver's license, traveler's checks ... Hmm..." I could hear the sliding, rustling movement of paper money. My wallet landed about a foot from my passport.

I tried to lie perfectly still. I did, except for the irregular heaving of my diaphragm. I struggled to calm my heart and regulate my breathing. Meanwhile, the lieutenant proceeded to examine every inch of the Jeep. He searched under the hood, beneath the dash, under the single seat and inside the fender wells. Anything that wasn't fastened down he tossed to the roadside.

"*Aquí no hay nada.*" The lieutenant sounded disappointed to have found nothing of value. "Go figure. A gringo driving such a total piece of shit."

"*¿Le mato?*" Fatso asked if he should kill me in the same tone of voice he might have used to ask, "Care for a drink?" I couldn't believe what I was hearing or how powerless I was to do anything about it. My heart raced like an engine about to throw a rod.

"*Espérate,*" said the lieutenant. Yes! Wait! I thought.

At that moment, the clattering sound of a diesel motor announced the imminent arrival of a truck along the highway.

"Don't move a muscle," commanded Fatso, his voice coming from a point ominously close behind me. I strained my eyes to see as much as I could in the direction of the highway. Moving from the top to the bottom of my weirdly orthogonal field of vision, a farm truck rolled past to the labored sound of gears shifting. A row of solemn brown faces peered out between the wooden slats of the bed. Witnesses, I thought.

Fatso's knee came down on my rib cage, grinding with the force of his weight. "I think you should stay here for a while," he said. Suddenly, lightning flashed in my head and everything went black.

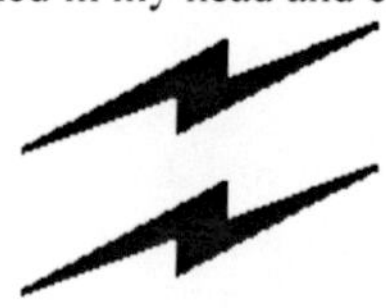

Part Two: Fat-Sucking Vampires

I know the wild and treacherous rivers. I know how they run, how they swell, what power they hold within. I know where their blood flows.

– Jose María Arguedas, from *Los Ríos Profundos*

Alejandro Ganz de la Vega stood on the bank of the stream that ran through the property of his ancestral home. The calm surface reflected a blue sky with only a few shreds of cloud to mar, or perhaps underscore, its perfection. This stretch of stream bank was where Alex Ganz felt most at peace. Here a shallow pool gathered behind a dam of stones reaching from one bank to the other – stones Alex had set in place as a child some twenty-five years before. In those days, he had sometimes floated tiny boats he fashioned from the wood and leaves of a eucalyptus, the only trees that grew abundantly at this elevation in the Peruvian Andes.

If the creek ever had a name, it had been forgotten for generations. Ganz had never called it anything but *mi arroyito*. He admired its cool clarity, a trait he believed he had developed in himself over the years. Often he had pondered its fate as a tributary of the tumbling Rio Apurimac and eventually of the muddy, mighty Amazon. Who could say? Maybe one of his tiny craft had actually sailed down out of these mountains, over tumbling rapids, past the city of Iquitos with its floating houses and on to the Atlantic Ocean at the far eastern edge of the continent. *Mi arroyito*, he thought. I know where you're headed. But what about the rest of this country? Where is it going? He recalled his recent experience flying over the village of Cocharcas. Rows of fresh-mounded graves. Everything that would burn had been torched. What had been homes were smoldering adobe shells exuding the bitter smoke of eradicated lives.

Although he maintained his official residence at the family home in San Isidro, Lima's prestigious Embassy Row neighborhood, Alex Ganz, at thirty-two and still single, preferred life on the old de la Vega *hacienda*. The ranch house, built in Spanish Colonial style around two open-air courtyards, lay high in the mountains of Ayacucho, nestled in the center of a small valley known as el Valle del Cóndor. No walls surrounded the house but its security was subtly thorough. El Valle del Cóndor was a sixty-square-kilometer crescent of flat, stony ground cut by ages of erosion from a breach in the soaring *cordillera*. Only one road entered the valley from below. It approached through a steep, narrow canyon where it was gated. Inside the iron gate and set against the sunnier southern wall of the valley stood a heavily shuttered stone house that, to the casual observer, might have appeared to belong to a prosperous local farmer. A sharper eye would have seen it as the guardhouse of a fortress.

Ganz looked around him and considered the tranquility of his valley. Along with the nearby town of Santa Rosita, it had remained unscathed by the violence that raged in the countryside surrounding it. The townspeople below, aware of their miraculous state of grace, showed their gratitude at the chapel of the *Santísima Virgen de Dolores*, to the benefit and satisfaction of the local priest. Ganz, however, knew it was not the Most Holy Virgin of Sorrows that protected these people and his own holdings from the ravages of the *Camino Rojo*. The peace existed as an agreement between him and one man, a man rumored by some to be dead, who lived as an outlaw and yet had become one of the country's most powerful figures.

Across the stream, where the sun now fell with its full morning force, Ganz's hobby herd of llamas grazed in the pasture of short, fine grass that blanketed the valley. To Alex, these were not beasts of burden but living works of indigenous art. Their statuesque profiles and slow, deliberate movements drew a link to the prosperous era of the Inca. They also evoked for him the essence of femininity, the long, graceful legs and necks, the proud postures, and the eyes. Above all the eyes.

Framed in luxurious lashes, the llama's eyes combined mahogany and sapphire polished to brilliance. Their depth and luster were mesmerizing. When Alex needed more than anything to just unwind, he would sometimes send Indio, the old caretaker, out to the pasture to lead in one of his favorites. He would spend a few minutes running his fingers through the soft wool of its neck, feeling as much as listening to its nasal hum, and gazing into its eyes as if into an oracle. No creature on earth possessed eyes of such intense liquidity as those of a llama. The eyes of his sister Cassandra came close, he thought, although without the innocence.

Such was the state of Ganz's mind when a flash of light on a windshield ended his reverie. The estate's black Land Rover made its way slowly across the pasture and rolled to a stop. The driver's door opened and out stepped Manolo Ruíz. Where other people had to clamber in and out of the Rover with its high profile and ground clearance, Manolito simply turned his massive frame and unfolded it, keeping his head low to avoid the upper doorjamb. His brow overhung brooding eyes like the eaves on a house. From there his forehead sloped back and up, laddered with faint scars from the times he had neglected to duck. Although his title was Estate Manager of el Valle del Cóndor, a more accurate description of his duties would have been head of security for Mr Ganz.

Manolo straightened himself respectfully and announced, "Sanchez *está aquí.*"

"*Bueno.* Take him to the parlor and pour him a glass of Chivas, neat. And Manolito, make sure he doesn't wander."

Outside the gate, Porfirio Sanchez leaned against the fender of his own car, a tan, late model Plymouth sedan, and smoked a cigarette. For years, he had been lead investigator of the PIP, the investigative arm of the Peruvian national police force, here in the province of Ayacucho. As a younger man, he had compensated for polio-stricken legs by working out his upper body, but in his later years, he had let much of the muscle recede to thick slabs of fat. With his heavy upper half and his thin, bowed legs he reminded Ganz of a hut on stilts. Unlike most officers of the PIP in the provinces, Sanchez had no burning desire to be transferred to Lima. Granted, a position in the capital was more prestigious – there was no possibility of further promotion without it – but it could hardly prove more profitable than the situation in Ayacucho, which allowed him to feather his nest deeply and regularly with American dollars.

Sanchez' two primary targets of investigation, by mandate from Lima, were the *Camino Rojo* and coca cultivation. The *Rojistas* were too well entrenched, too vengeful and too deadly for Sanchez to take on. Instead, he captured his quota of 'subversives' by falsely accusing and extracting 'information' from men that he knew beyond a doubt *not* to be affiliated with the guerillas. To deal with coca cultivation, he went straight to the source.

Ganz shunned a ride to the ranch house, preferring the calming walk that would keep Sanchez waiting long enough to drain his first glass of scotch and initiate a second. When Ganz finally entered the parlor, he found the inspector well and predictably buried in an overstuffed cordovan leather chair, glass in hand.

"*Buenos días*, Inspector," Ganz announced himself and invited Sanchez to remain comfortably seated. "*No se levante, por favor.*" He poured himself a glass of ice water from a carafe on the same heavy, alder wood sideboard that held the liquor, and remained standing there, leaning with ankles crossed. "How goes the war?"

"One survives. You know how it is. I bring in the occasional *terrorista*, I uproot a few acres of coca, and Lima leaves me alone."

"Mmm. Which guerrillas have you taken lately?"

"Oh, a big prize. The notorious Camilo Vargas."

"The old cattle rustler? I thought he was already in jail."

"To be sure, to be sure. The old *cholo* was wily. Very tight-lipped. But we learned a thing or two before he expired." With this smug statement hanging in the air, Sanchez savored the last swallow of his second glass of Chivas. Ganz refilled it.

It was Sanchez's standard ploy and Ganz understood it perfectly. The inspector, whenever his career required another *Rojista* arrest, simply chose someone from among the region's current inmates or at-large petty criminals and pointed an accusatory finger. If he needed two arrests he would press his first scapegoat to inform on yet another, usually one of Sanchez's choosing. In Sanchez's way of thinking, it was an efficient way to preserve his record and protect the law-abiding populace from scoundrels without running afoul of the *Camino Rojo.*

"And how can I help the esteemed servant of the people?" Ganz asked, even though he knew the answer. It was a dance they did, a protocol of feigned respect.

"Ah, *Señor*, you know how much the government appreciates your ongoing support." Sanchez tacitly acknowledged the monthly 'retirement contributions' he came to collect. "It makes all the difference in my ability to keep the peace. Unfortunately, it is time for the Government once again to eradicate the horrible coca menace."

"I feel much safer," said Ganz with a touch of scorn, "knowing you are here to protect us from such dark dealings."

The nine-by-twelve inch, unmarked envelope Ganz lifted from the end of the sideboard and handed to Sanchez contained two items. The first was a thick stack of American twenty-dollar bills, Sanchez's 'retirement benefit'. The second consisted of a map and an accompanying set of directions. In the center of the map, outlined in red, was an isolated tract of *selva*, the high Andean fringes of the Amazonian jungle. The marked tract of land had been planted for almost a decade with a single crop of coca. The plants had grown tall but had begun to suffer from blight and now yielded less than in previous years.

In a couple of weeks Sanchez, with much fanfare, would direct a small unit of *Guardia Civil* down the precipitous and rutted road that led to the coca field. There they would pull the plants, pile them high and burn them as part of the international campaign to eliminate illegal coca production. The unit of *Guardia* would return to its barracks with sore backs and hands, Sanchez would reinforce his exemplary record with the PIP and the government would turn its bureaucratic gaze away from the Ayacucho region for a time.

A few days later a small group of local workers would enter the field, spread the ashes with a few sacks of fertilizer and replant healthy young coca plants, which would grow and produce for yet another decade.

Sanchez took the envelope and nodded his approval without glancing at its contents. “Always a pleasure, *Señor*.”

“The pleasure is mine, Inspector,” replied Ganz. “Now if you will excuse me, Manolito will see you back to the gate.”

As he watched the dusty Plymouth pull away, Alex considered the legacy of coca he had inherited as a part of Ganz Enterprises. His father, Oswald Ganz, had migrated to Peru in 1945 with a German passport and a small fortune in gold and jewels. The latter he turned into a larger fortune through international trade in commodities. Within twenty years he had acquired a controlling interest in Banco Europa, a bank with strong connections to Frankfurt and the Caribbean.

At the age of forty-one, and already one of the most powerful men in Lima, Oswald Ganz converted to Catholicism. At forty-three, he married Pilar de la Vega, the twenty-year-old only daughter of an aged, wealthy landowner with holdings throughout the central Andes. The marriage cemented Ganz’s standing in Peruvian society and, at the same time, broadened his base in the Peruvian economy. The de la Vega *haciendas* had once employed thousands of peasants in the raising of cattle and the cultivation of various crops, including potatoes, corn and other grains … and coca. The union of Ganz’s business, with its banking, shipping and distribution networks around the world, to the de la Vega agricultural empire, and particularly its coca production capacity, had proven extremely lucrative.

Oswald and Pilar made their home, like most wealthy Peruvians, in Lima. They lived in a grand San Isidro house and kept a horse ranch in the Andean foothills near Puerta del Sol. Two years after the wedding, Alejandro was born, and three years after that, a daughter, Cassandra. Alex, and later his sister, attended a private American preparatory school in Lima, to and from which they were driven each day in an armored BMW. He was a quiet and reflective boy. In addition to scholastics, at which he excelled, he also became an accurate marksman. He played soccer competently enough to defend for his school team, but he was neither impassioned nor brilliant on the field. He paid little attention to girls, although the reverse was not true. Combining many of the best features of Oswald and Pilar, he made a striking impression. He bore his mother's olive skin and dark hair but ended up with his father's height, broad shoulders and silvery-gray eyes.

On completion of prep school, Alex was sent to the United States, where he earned a degree in economics from Harvard. From there he returned to Peru to begin his transition to the helm of Ganz enterprises. The transition ultimately had to be accelerated when Oswald suffered a series of strokes. In the nine months between his father's first stroke and the one that killed him, Alejandro Ganz de la Vega grew from a talented heir apparent into a focused, studious and cautious captain of industry. The years since then had made him tougher, wiser and richer, though not necessarily happier.

Within an hour of Sanchez's departure, Ganz heard the approach of a small plane. He had been expecting it and he was prepared for the meeting. Always before, he had met this man on neutral ground, usually at some remote landing strip. For some reason the man had insisted that this meeting occur at el Valle del Cóndor. It was unsettling for Ganz to have Miguel Fortuna, or *El Colibrí*, as he was popularly called, coming to his own home. Fortuna was the elusive head of the *Camino Rojo* and Peru's most wanted man – the Hummingbird. Ganz inhaled slowly, straightened his back and shoulders and walked out to face the man who was, according to one's politics, either an inspired revolutionary or a murdering terrorist.

A pair of armed guards deplaned first, followed by the bearded and slightly-built Fortuna. "You should choose your friends more carefully, *Señor* Ganz. *Ese polizonte*, Sanchez, *es un chancho y un bufón.*"

He knows about my meeting with Sanchez, Ganz considered, and he wants me to know that he knows. "A pig, perhaps," Ganz agreed, "but not a fool, and certainly not my friend. I throw him little bones in order to keep him in line."

"He picks the bones, but they do not make him strong. He is a mere placeholder. I allow him to live only because his weakness is useful. He cannot turn aside the revolution, and if your loyalties should turn, he could not pluck you from the path of destiny."

Ganz felt a twitch of revulsion at Fortuna's arrogant sureness. "I trust, *Señor*," he replied, with countering self-assurance, "that my cooperation with your cause is not in question."

"It is not my cause. It is the cause of the people. And I don't believe for a moment that it is your concern. Still, as they say, politics makes for strange bedfellows. Shall we work out the details of our continuing arrangement?"

Fortuna had no real idea of the true profitability of Ganz's coca production operation, let alone of the rest of the pieces of Ganz Enterprises. If he had, he most certainly would have increased his demands. As it was, Ganz had always paid. He acted like it hurt, but he always paid. All he asked in return was that the *Camino Rojo* stay away from his property in el Valle del Cóndor, from the town of Santa Rosita and from his coca fields in the jungled foothills of the *Cordillera*. He had made a Faustian deal, but it was a deal that made good business sense and allowed him to protect a fair swath of his beloved Ayacucho from terrorism.

Apparently satisfied with the new terms for the 'protection' he offered, Fortuna extended his hand to Ganz. He had never done this before. Ganz shook the hand with only the briefest hesitation, and Fortuna turned to go. He took a couple of steps then looked back over his shoulder and said, as if it were an afterthought, "Oh, there is one other small matter – your sister."

"Cassandra? What about her?" Ganz was alarmed at the turn of conversation. His family had never been an issue in his dealings with *El Colibrí*.

"The bourgeois swill she feeds the people concerns me deeply. A *chica* who is so well loved should have a mind for the consequences of her influence, don't you think?"

"Cassandra's not political. Her television show is nothing but sweet custard."

"Yes, but such a diet soon leads the people into complacency. And many a poison is delivered in the guise of sweetness. You should take care for your sister, *Señor* Ganz. A little brotherly counsel may be in order."

Two Jeeps merged into one fuzzy Jeep, which finally cleared up and solidified. I got to my hands and knees and resisted an urge to vomit. Hot cables of pain crackled forward and upward from the base of my skull, where I found a prodigious knot garnished with a fresh scab. Everything I owned was lying in the dirt. I did a slow inventory and found that my cash was missing. Shit, I thought bitterly, and winced from another surge of pain. Gringo tax.

With my belongings stuffed back into my flight bag, I climbed behind the wheel of the Jeep and put my hand to the ignition, which to my immense relief still held the key. Rather than fooling with the clutch and balky gears, I simply started the Jeep in first gear, causing it to lurch back onto the roadway. Driving was difficult because I could barely control the muscles in my legs. My head still throbbed as I began the long descent into the Mantaro Valley.

The Mantaro River was a braid of silver ribbons turning to black on an undulating surface of gold and green velvet. Spring temperatures had already begun to waken the fields of grain and potatoes. A network of mortarless stone walls and occasional dwellings of raw adobe and red tile roofs further humanized the landscape. In contrast to the agrarian idyll, a line of enormous electrical towers stretched from horizon to horizon like a zipper. The Mantaro Valley was Peru's powerhouse, a fact that made it a favorite target of Crimson Road attacks. A key part of the guerrillas' strategy was the regular disruption of electrical services. A well-placed bomb in a remote stretch of the Mantaro Valley could bring much of Lima to its knees in darkness.

The vulnerability of the region's electrical facilities made the provincial capital, Huancayo, one of the country's most heavily garrisoned cities. The presence of the military didn't escape my attention as I pulled into town, hungry, sore and fatigued. I avoided stopping at the *Hotel de Turistas*. Swarming with military personnel, it looked more like a barracks than Huancayo's finest inn. Instead, I worked my way along side streets until I found a neighborhood café that catered to a civilian clientele.

I parked the Jeep and carried my bag into the café. A short Indian-looking woman met me just inside the door.

"*Buenas tardes, Señora,*" I said. "May I please speak with the owner of the restaurant?"

The woman frowned then nodded in the direction of a roundish man just visible through the door to the kitchen. As I approached him, my movements drew every eye in the house.

"*Señor,*" I said, "I wonder if you might help me." There was no response beyond a silent willingness to listen. I lowered my voice. "I have been robbed of all my cash. I need food and a place to stay. I have money, but only a traveler's check in American dollars."

The man straightened from his aproned slouch and stepped forward so that his chin practically touched my chest.

"Follow me," he said quietly. He led me to a doorway that opened on a back storage room. I entered and turned to find the proprietor brandishing a shotgun. The ancient, double-barreled firearm had been resting in the corner just beside the door.

"Who are you?"

"My name is Samson Young. I'm an anthropologist."

"Show me some identification."

I produced my passport and my credentials from the Cultural Institute.

The man relaxed but held his grip on the shotgun. "My name is Mauricio. I can accept your dollars … as a favor to you. And you may eat here. I have no rooms, but my cousin operates a small hotel not far away. Let me see your traveler's check."

I pulled out a single twenty-dollar check. Mauricio looked it over carefully and compared the signature with the one on my passport. Convinced it was genuine, he began to quote an exchange rate and prices for a meal and a room that, coincidentally, totaled the US equivalent of twenty dollars.

After a meal of *chifa,* Chinese-style fried rice with bits of ham and green onion, and a liter bottle of beer, I followed Mauricio around the corner and down the street to a building announced by a small brass sign as the *Posada San Martín.* Mauricio gave a sharp knock and a moment later a bright blue door opened within a much larger door of the same color. A man somewhat taller than Mauricio and with less hair on top led us in, past an old Ford Cortina and into a patio upon which opened a dozen rooms on two levels. After the two men conferred quietly for a moment, Mauricio introduced me to my host, who, in turn, showed me to a vacant room furnished with a single bed and a wash basin atop a wooden table.

I tossed my bag onto the bed, a canvas ticking filled with lumpy cotton on a wooden platform, pulled out my notebook, sat down with my back against the cold plaster wall and spent the next hour or so writing about the day's experiences. Most of the rest of the night, I tossed and turned, trying unsuccessfully to ignore skittering noises from the bare wood floor. At one point, I walked out of the room and into the open courtyard. With no electric lights to wash them out, the stars shone so brightly and so close that the whole courtyard was suffused with a pale natural light. A mordant combination of awe, doubt and loneliness hit me at that instant. It was as if each star stood tethered to my chest by a bitter-cold filament of glass.

Eventually, I fell asleep. I dreamed I was caught up in a crowd of people shouting and shoving in the middle of a street. I was searching for something without knowing what. Suddenly, I caught a glimpse of my father through a café window. I tried to call out but my throat was too dry. I pushed through the crowd and into the café, but when I reached the booth where I had seen him, all that remained was a half-empty coffee cup and a sprinkling of coins. I looked up and, passing by the window and disappearing into the crowd, was Marivela. I cried out and startled myself awake. The darkness I woke to was thick and disorienting and the knot on the back of my head was throbbing. Eventually, I remembered where I was, and sometime after that I managed to go back to sleep.

In the morning I woke again, but to daylight. I used the toilet in the small inn's shared bathroom, washed my hands and splashed my face with cold water from the only tap. A *pancito,* or small bread roll, with fresh, white cheese and a cup of coffee awaited me on a side table in the lobby.

"Compliments of the house," said the balding innkeeper.

"*Muchas gracias, Señor*." The crust was tough and chewy but, inside, the bread was warm and tender.

Also on the table, the morning newspaper showed a picture of a building with windows missing and ran the headline *PENTHOUSE AND TV STATION BOMBED*. I read some of the news article:

> … bombs ripped almost simultaneously through two buildings in downtown Lima. One exploded on the roof of the *TelePerú* studio stopping all transmission for several hours. The other destroyed the penthouse apartment of Cassandra Ganz, star of the popular show *Habla Perú con Cassandra*. No casualties have been reported. Police suspect members of the *Camino Rojo*, although no one has yet claimed responsibility …

The paper also ran a picture of Cassandra Ganz. Even from the grainy news photo, I could tell she was beautiful.

"*¡Qué cosa, ¿no?!*" said the innkeeper.

"Yes," I agreed. "Really something."

With directions from the innkeeper, I found my way first to the local branch of *Banco Europa* to cash another traveler's check, then to a PetroPerú station to fill the tank of the old Willys. Everywhere I went I had the feeling of being watched with suspicion. It was as if all activity stopped when I came close and then resumed cautiously after I passed by. In Lima I hadn't drawn much attention, but here in the sierra, being taller and paler than virtually everyone, I stood out like the stranger I was.

As I pulled out of Huancayo on my way toward Huancavelica and then to Ayacucho, it was with the feeling that I needed three sets of eyes: one to watch the road ahead, a second to watch for dangers from behind, and a third with which to absorb the beauty of the Andean landscape. The views alternated between snow-capped peaks, broken canyons, lush river banks, terraced gardens and broad expanses of prickly pear cactus. Everywhere there was water, there were crops. Everywhere else grazed assortments of farm animals including skinny cattle, goats, sheep, ducks, chickens and pigs in various combinations. For more than eight hours, I navigated the bucking and rattling Jeep along a road that, with its constant ruts, potholes and washes, was often only marginally smoother than the surrounding terrain.

Cassandra Ganz de la Vega had grown up pretty and precocious. Almost the photographic negative of her brother, she had her father's blond hair and fair complexion, and in startling contrast, she inherited the large, deep brown-black eyes of her mother. After earning a degree in broadcast journalism from UC-Berkeley, she had returned to Lima to work in television. She currently anchored *Habla Perú con Cassandra*, a popular daytime program gliding superficially over news and social issues and delving more deeply into stories of human interest, shopping and 'domestic production'. At least twice in every episode, the camera zoomed in for a sustained close-up of Cassandra with her unblinking brown eyes and trademark blonde tresses. Two years ago, when *Habla Perú* first went on the air, she exuded enthusiasm, facing the television camera with freshness and fire. More recently, however, she wondered if her posture and smile might not reveal a trace of the irony she felt.

Living between a downtown penthouse and the family horse ranch at Puerta del Sol, she remained one of Peru's most sought-after single women. She had taken her share of lovers, always with discretion. Some had been Peruvians. Others were foreigners. All of them eventually bored her with their self-importance. That was her problem, she thought. Her life bored her. Yet it was more than that. Life pretty regularly pissed her off. At first, she thought *Habla Perú* was the solution. At school in the US, she had allowed herself to fantasize about a life in journalism, about tracking down important stories, stories that would make a difference to the people of her country.

And what am I doing now? she thought from the back seat of her chauffeured Mercedes-Benz, the *Today Show* 'lite,' a happy little daytime TV show-and-tell for middle-class Peruvians. The network refused to let her her handle anything even approaching serious or controversial material. "Cassandra is not about negativity, darling," the producer had said. "Cassandra is about beauty! Optimism!" The policy had been effective in one way at least. Cassandra had become the darling of Peruvian viewers, the one dependable icon of middle-class tranquility, the one sign people could always cling to that, somewhere inside the boundaries of their suffering nation, people could live modern, bountiful lives. In her mind, Cassandra imitated the effeminate voice of her producer while supplying words of her own: "Cassandra is not about life, darling. Cassandra is about smiling while your whole being wants to puke."

There was a time, remembered Cassandra, when such a charade would not have seemed so distasteful, when it might have posed an interesting challenge for an aspiring young actress. As a young girl, she had loved the old Hollywood movies that her father encouraged her to watch to perfect her English. Her favorite had been *The African Queen*, which in pre-VCR years her father had purchased on film, along with a projector that remained set up in the large playroom at the rear of the house. Cassandra could recite every one of Katherine Hepburn's lines, and if she couldn't quite produce the gravelly tone of voice, at least she had mastered the accent.

Hollywood's countless scenes of tenderness, passion and betrayal had offered not only entertainment and language practice but also an emotional content that was largely absent from Cassandra's home life. Her mother had seemed to live in an emotional sarcophagus, especially when Oswald was alive. For public occasions she came out, put on her finery, dressed up her face with a smile that never quite touched her eyes, and acted the part of a society wife. Privately she was withdrawn, mustering only enough energy for disapproval when Cassandra's ebullience led her to unladylike behavior. And her father? He had doted on his baby girl, but Oswald Ganz was dead. Of course, she had always adored her older brother, but Alex was three years older, an eternity in the timeline of school-aged children. For all his kindness, Alex focused forward on life, a focus that had kept a little sister always in his peripheral vision. And now … now he was just plain infuriating.

With less than an hour until airtime, having just arrived at the front of the *TelePerú* building, Cassandra was still fuming over the paternalistic attitude of her older brother. What nerve, she thought as she climbed from the rear curbside door of the Benz, to suggest that she should cancel her season. He had intimated that she might be in danger. "That's preposterous," she had told him.

At that moment, an explosion tore across the rooftop of *TelePerú*, bruising the air and raining rubble from the sky. Cassandra dived, ass-upward, back into the car, covered her head and cringed as bits of glass and concrete peppered the car. When the moment of crisis had passed, she sat up quickly, grateful that no tabloid photographers stood nearby to immortalize her indignity. The dust hung in the air like an unanswered question as the reverberation of the blast faded to a ringing in her ears. People in the street began the hasty retrieval of the packages they had dropped. Cassandra emerged once again from her car as a second explosion ripped the Lima skyline.

Although a couple blocks away and no immediate threat to her safety, it was this second explosion that cracked the foundation of Cassandra's composure. The smoke that still billowed into the sky appeared to emanate from the blown-out windows of her own penthouse apartment. A crowd stood watching the spectacle with their backs toward her. All except one. A woman in a floppy hat and sunglasses stepped forward and raised her hand to point at Cassandra's face with a pantomimed pistol. *Bang, bang*, she mouthed silently and slipped back into the crowd.

It was dusk when I rolled the Jeep to a stop in front of the adobe chapel across from the *plaza de armas*, or town square, of Santa Rosita. The chapel, although smaller and plainer than many of the churches I'd seen on my way here, was the only building facing the plaza on this particular block. The rest of the block surrounding it was devoted to what looked like a walled garden. There were no other cars on the street.

The chapel door was a heavy, unadorned wooden affair with black iron hardware. Above it was a small round window of plain glass. I gave the door handle a cautious push and noted with admiration the smooth, quiet movement of its hinges. The low interior light revealed an empty chapel with virtually no adornment. Wooden shutters stood closed over the few narrow, unglazed window openings. Three columns of a dozen short pews separated the vestibule at the back from the altar at the front. The altar was flanked on the right by a pulpit-lectern and on the left by a curtained doorway. The Virgin herself, for whom the chapel was named, looked like a case study of clinical depression in wood and oxidized paint.

The curtain moved and a gangly, black-frocked priest appeared. I guessed him to be five to ten years my senior.

"*Buenas tardes, Padre.*"

"*Buenas tardes*."

"Would you be …?"

"Father Pedro Buenaventura. How may I serve you?"

"My name is Samson Young."

"The American! I was expecting you. Welcome to the *Santísima Virgen de Dolores.* How do you do? How was your trip? Won't you come in?" He closed the distance between us with a few long strides, shook my hand and led me into the chapel with an arm around my shoulder, easy since Pedro Buenaventura was at least five inches taller.

Not knowing which of his questions to answer first, I just said, "Thank you," with a feeling of relief at the open hospitality.

"So, tell me about your trip. Oh, I'm sorry. Please, sit down. May I take your bag? Would you like some tea?"

"*Gracias, Padre*. Some tea would be nice."

"*Bien. Muy bien.* I'll start the water." The priest moved to the curtained door, held the curtain aside and beckoned, "Come, come. Now, how was your trip?"

"From Lima?" He nodded noncommittally, as if it didn't matter which trip I described, and indicated one of two chairs next to a small wooden table. I set my bag on the chair and stayed standing. A second full day in the broken-down seat of the Jeep had cured me of wanting to sit for a while. "Well, it was like two different trips, really. Yesterday I thought I was a dead man, and today I thought I had gone to heaven."

"A dead man?" He filled a kettle from a tap over a deep sink and placed it on one of two burners of a propane range.

"I was robbed at gunpoint yesterday and knocked unconscious. At Ticlio. By *policía.* I honestly thought they were going to kill me. But today … today was different. Driving across Huancavelica into Ayacucho was a waking dream. There were greening fields, red-cheeked children playing along the roadside, herds of llama and alpaca. It was magnificent."

He nodded with a smile that seemed to combine understanding and a bit of sadness. "I'm glad you made it here safe and sound."

There followed a moment of silence between us and I chose not to fill it.

“Tell me,” Buenaventura resumed. “What is it you hope to learn here in Santa Rosita?” He poured steaming water over a scoop of herbs in a porcelain teapot.

“I’m not exactly sure, *Padre*. Generally, I want to understand the cultural dynamics of the people here. I want to know how they live their lives and how they view the universe. But, more than that; these people face difficulties that most people of my country never see and perhaps can never really appreciate. I suppose I would like to understand those difficulties. And I would like to understand how the people learn to cope with them.”

“I would like to think that God helps them cope. But I fear that isn’t the answer you’re looking for. Frankly,” he added, “I’m not even sure it’s true.”

I chewed on those words while he filled two stoneware cups with swirls of golden liquid. I took one and breathed in the aroma. It smelled like chamomile.

“Not sure it’s true?” I left the phrase hanging.

“Not sure of a lot of things.” He said it with a note of finality that told me the topic was closed.

I wondered if he was experiencing doubts about his own beliefs. Or did he mean that he was skeptical of my purpose here? Would he prove antagonistic? I didn’t get that feeling. I reminded myself not to speculate too much. I also mustn’t give in to the temptation to talk too much or to volunteer my own opinions too readily. My job was to observe and to listen. I mustn’t say or do anything that might significantly alter the paths of behavior or the fortunes in this town. Having grown up with *Star Trek,* I thought of this injunction as the anthropological Prime Directive.

Father Pedro, with his scarecrow frame and black cassock, seemed to me like an anachronism. Only the relative modernity of industrial-age fixtures and appliances kept the scene from being downright medieval. As I pondered the setting, I think we must have exchanged looks of bewilderment. Finally, it was the priest who broke the silence.

“As I promised your colleague, Professor Ramirez, I’ve arranged for you to have a room and take breakfasts with someone in town, Doña Rosario Flores. She will welcome the income, and her godson, Enrique, will enjoy the company.”

"Enrique?"

"Yes. An orphan, eight years old, sharp and inquisitive. They're not expecting you until tomorrow. You can sleep here if you don't mind a hard bed, and I'll introduce you in the morning."

"I like a hard bed," I said. It was a little after 7:00pm. I wondered what the typical bedtime was and what people did to occupy their evening hours.

"If you don't mind me asking," continued the priest, "how do you plan to get acquainted with the people of Santa Rosita? They are likely to be guarded around you unless they get to know you well. Do you have any skills?"

"Skills?" The question caught me off guard.

"Skills. You know, some way to help them out, to gain their trust."

I suddenly felt stupid for not thinking of it myself. "Well," I said, "as a matter of fact, I have some experience in a medical clinic."

"Excellent," said the priest. "Then there is someone else you should meet. In the meantime, I was about to cook some supper. Would you join me?"

Father Pedro reheated a pot of soup that he must have made the night before. It was a simple chowder made from potatoes and corn and flavored with a bit of bacon. To make it stretch to feed a visitor, he added water and a white flaky substance.

"What are you adding?" I asked.

"*Chuño.*" I shook my head to indicate I was unfamiliar with the word. "It's a kind of naturally freeze-dried potato. A staple food, really, of the poor people here. The farmers prepare it in the open air during the winter."

As simple as it was, I was impressed with the soup's heartiness, especially as he served it with *pan semita,* a dense, fiber-filled brown bread.

I volunteered for after-dinner clean-up, which consisted of hand washing in cold water two bowls, two cups, two spoons and an aluminum pot, and placing them in a rack to dry. Above the sink hung a bare light bulb with a simple switch at its base. Its exposed wiring ran along the ceiling and was fixed in place by staples. It also fed one electrical outlet on the outside wall. I had noticed no electric lights in the chapel at all.

As I washed the dishes, Pedro Buenaventura retrieved a pair of heavy wool blankets from a wooden storage bin, shook them out and refolded them on the end of the first pew. Hard bed, I thought. No kidding. He also provided an alcohol lamp and matches and then showed me the tiny bathroom with its commode, its basin and its curtainless shower with only a cold-water pipe, and a dangerous looking water-heating showerhead plugged directly into an electrical outlet. Showering here would require courage.

"You have chosen to live among humble people," said the priest without apology. "Please make yourself at home. I will be retiring to my room for the evening."

"*Gracias, Padre*. I appreciate the hospitality."

"Until tomorrow then, *que Dios te bendiga*."

"From your mouth to God's ears, *Padre*. May He bless you too."

He looked at me for a prolonged moment as if he was actually considering the likelihood of such a thing.

I folded one of the blankets twice lengthwise for padding and doubled the other one over it. It was not yet nine o'clock. I still needed to write in my journal and jot a few field notes, but first, I wanted another look at the town. With my flight bag tucked out of sight beneath the pew, I slipped quietly out the chapel door.

Up and down the street, all was quiet and growing darker. At random intervals light leaked out of gaps in curtains or worn wooden shutters, throwing feelers across the cobblestones. I crossed the street to the *plaza de armas*. Dimly lit by four of the town's few streetlights, the plaza was crossed from corner to corner and from side to side with gravel footpaths. A few rosebushes in bare dirt beds had begun to show the first leaves of the season. Where the paths met in the center of the plaza, they circled a statue of Simón Bolívar, the hero of Peru's war of independence from Spain. I was examining the statue when a sudden crashing sound engaged my fight-or-flight reflexes. I spun around and caught a view of a skinny dog departing the plaza with its tail between its legs. A metal trash can lay on its side next to a park bench. My heart and lungs were scrambling to catch up with my adrenaline response.

Once I managed to relax again, I resumed my survey of the town. Across the street, facing the plaza opposite the church, stood the municipal buildings, which I assumed would house all the government functions of the town with the probable exception of the jail. Facing the plaza to my right was the town's most modern building. It was two stories tall, white, and made of concrete. On top, I could see a white plastic or fiberglass water reservoir. On the ground floor, at the corner farthest from the church, was the entrance to the local branch of Banco Europa, its doors and windows protected by roll-type steel shutters. That would be one of my first stops tomorrow. At mid-block, another door appeared to lead to either offices or residences. Whether that part of the building pertained to the bank or something else, I couldn't tell. The rest of the bank block held a pharmacy and a little *bodega*, a typical mom-and-pop style grocery. I circled the plaza and took inventory of the remaining buildings. The last block facing the plaza contained a shoe repair shop, a second *bodega*, a small *papelería* or stationery store and a restaurant called *Los Tres Chanchitos*.

When I came back around to it, I noticed that my Jeep had received a visitor. On the curbside rear tire, a dark spot indicated where a dog had recently pissed.

Just as I was about to head back into the chapel, I heard the soft crunch of a footstep in gravel. In the center of the plaza, at the base of the statue of Bolívar, stood the silhouette of a man. A very large man, I thought, as big as my dad. Six-four and two-forty. Maybe bigger. Watching me, unless the darkness and my eyes were playing tricks. Against the man's dark shape, I detected the orange pinpoint of a lit cigarette. When he takes a drag on the cigarette, I thought, it will light up his face. But the man dropped the smoke, ground it out on the gravel path, slipped away to the far side of the statue and disappeared. I caught one more glimpse of him in the penumbra of a streetlight as he rounded the corner beyond the plaza. A few seconds later, I heard the sound of a car door. It closed with a distinctive, out-of-place, expensively European clunk.

Inside, the chapel was quiet and the only light was that which fell in through the window above the door. I lit the alcohol lamp and set it on the altar rail. I took my time writing field notes, describing my day's journey, my meeting with Pedro Buenaventura, and what I had seen so far of Santa Rosita. I carried the lamp to the bathroom, where I noted with chagrin how every sound I made was amplified by the still night.

The only way to get even somewhat comfortable on the wooden pew was to lie flat on my back. Doing that, I slept reasonably well until, I would guess, about two in the morning when something, possibly my own snoring, or more probably aching joints from the hard surface, woke me. I opened my eyes into darkness so complete that I could scarcely tell I had opened them. I turned to my right side, pulled the wool blankets more tightly around me and eventually fell asleep again for maybe another hour, at which time I repeated the process on my left side. I slept a while longer, turned on my back and slept again. Each time I woke, it was with a fresh set of aches and the sense of vivid dreams slipping away.

Shards of light appeared at the edges of the curtained doorway while it was still pitch dark outside. My watch said five o'clock. I shut my eyes and tried to ignore the priest's quiet predawn activities. By six o'clock, he already had devoted an hour to reading the scriptures. Now he was refreshing candles at the altar of the Most Holy Virgin. I kept trying to sleep until the bang of a car door shattered the last illusion of slumber. A peasant woman carrying a small bundle of something burst through the chapel door. She looked like she was about to shout greetings to the *padre* when she spied me rising from my heap of blankets on the pew. She held her tongue and walked quickly around the side of the chapel to join the priest by the door leading to his private quarters.

As the woman and the *padre* spoke in quiet tones, I rubbed my eyes and tried to roll some of the stiffness out of my shoulders. I couldn't hear what they were saying, but based on the glances from the woman – a pretty woman, I noticed – I concluded they were talking about me. They walked through the door to the kitchen and Father Pedro began making coffee. I dressed, and then, wearing one wool blanket like a robe against the chilly morning, I joined the priest in the kitchen.

"How did you sleep?" asked the priest.

"Not too badly," I lied.

"I see you chose *el banco de las viudas*."

"Widows' bench?"

"The second pew. As long as I've been here, that's been the Sunday-morning territory of a little group of widows. My most reliable parishioners."

A clamor of pipes and the sound of water running onto concrete came from the bathroom.

"You have a housekeeper?" I asked with a nod toward the bathroom.

"Oh, my, no. Well, yes, actually, but that isn't her. That's our doctor."

I struggled to reconcile the priest's words with the image of the young peasant woman I'd just seen. "Doctor?"

"*Sí. Médico*. Her name is Mercedes Marquez. She really is quite talented and she has excellent rapport with the *campesinos*. Coffee?"

The heavy mug felt good in my hands. I was grateful for the warmth creeping into my fingers. I was preparing to take my first careful sip, peering through the steam rising off the surface of the coffee, when the bathroom door swung open with its own burst of steam. My expectations were jolted once again. Instead of the peasant clothing I had seen before, the woman emerging from the steam wore blue jeans, a baggy alpaca sweater and unlaced army boots. She unwound a towel from around a cascade of black hair, gave her head a toss and turned to face me with a look that seemed, for some reason I couldn't guess, defiant. My heart raced. I felt, in that moment, like I had never seen such an exotic and intriguing woman. If I had thought at all about Marivela in that moment, it would have been only to reflect on how long a time had seemed to pass since I had awakened to her imprint in an empty bed.

"Allow me to introduce Mercedes Marquez Acevedo," said the priest.

"*Encantado,*" I said. Enchanted, in Spanish, is a common greeting with no real meaning beyond cordiality, but I meant it literally and thoroughly.

Mercedes nodded cautiously. "You are an American, *¿no?* So what brings a gringo to Santa Rosita?"

"The last person who called me a gringo nearly had me shot."

"A US passport won't win you many friends around here."

"Then I'll have to earn my friendships some other way."

"You haven't answered my question. Why Santa Rosita?"

Damn, I thought, she doesn't waste time with pleasantries. "I guess the short answer is that I'm an anthropologist. I'm interested in traditional cultures. I want to understand the life of a Peruvian *campesino*."

"I can sum that up for you in a single word. *Sufrimiento*." She practically spat it.

"And you work to ease that suffering."

"I do what I can."

"Maybe I could help you."

"Oh, that would solve *all* my problems." Mercedes returned to the bathroom and gathered her things. On her way back through the kitchen, she thanked the *padre* for the use of the shower. She refused to make eye contact with me as she blew by me and out of the chapel.

After a light breakfast with Father Pedro, I followed his directions across the plaza and up a side street to the local telephone company, the only place in town with a public phone. The tiny space, sandwiched between two other shops, held only a short counter, a long wooden bench along one wall and two enclosed wooden phone booths. Behind the counter sat a young woman reading a paperback. The two booths took up the entire end wall. Both booths were occupied, and four other people sat on the bench, presumably waiting their turns ahead of me. A minute or so later, a middle-aged man in a worn brown suit emerged from booth number one on the left. A second man, older, in a patched gray gabardine suit and a stained gray fedora, took his place as the first one paid for his call.

In the booth on the right, number two, through the window-paned door, I could see the figure of a woman hunched over the handset. She rocked gently back and forth. A few minutes later, the man in gray finished and paid and an old woman in a heavily embroidered skirt and vest stepped into the booth on the left. Her call apparently couldn't be completed, so she gave way to a young man in chino work pants, white shirt and blue sweater vest. The woman in the right-hand booth still sat, rocking forward and back, clutching the phone to her ear with both hands. In the meantime, two more customers had come in behind me.

The young man finished his call and the clerk motioned to me that it was my turn. One old man, looking like a large-sized skin draped and folded onto a small-sized frame, still waited on the bench and should have been ahead of me. Wringing the shape out of an old felt hat, he appeared to be waiting worriedly for the woman in booth number two. I wondered what life drama held her so tightly to the phone.

The phone had no dial and no instructions, and when I picked up the handset, no dial tone. As I was debating whether to ask the girl at the counter for help, I heard a click and a voice, "*El número, por favor.*" Wow, I thought. It's like Mayberry RFD in Spanish. I read Alfredo Ramirez's number from his card. Expecting a ringing sound, I was mildly disconcerted by the loud *clack-clack-clack* sound that came from the earpiece.

"*Hallo.*"

"Fredo? Hi, it's Sam Young."

"Oh, Hello, Sam. Are you in Santa Rosita?"

"I am. But I have to say, getting here was no picnic."

"No, I don't suppose it was."

I gave him an abbreviated version of my trials and tribulations, to which he offered the observation that I wasn't in Kansas anymore. It seemed like his way of emphasizing that he knew a lot more about my culture than I knew about his. On that count I was fully ready to concede his superiority. In fairness to myself, I supposed that my culture had been considerably safer to investigate.

"Listen, Sam," said Fredo, about the time I was thinking the conversation was over, "I'm pretty busy, but I would be willing to help you interpret your data. Why don't you send me a weekly outline of your field notes? Maybe I can serve as a sounding board, help you get your head around your project a little faster."

Good idea, I thought, with some relief. I agreed to keep him updated, thanked him and walked back out into a room full of waiting customers. As I opened the phone booth door, I had the sense of several conversations instantly falling quiet. The sudden somberness persisted while I paid for my call and it trailed behind me like vapor as I walked back into the street.

After the bombing, Cassandra Ganz dropped out of the spotlight. *Habla Perú* was given over, temporarily at first, to a fresh-faced young journalist who probably regarded Cassandra's sudden retirement as his big chance at stardom. Cassandra never went back to the show or to the ruined penthouse apartment, preferring instead a life of apparent solitude on the ranch at Puerta del Sol.

The bombing had been big news for a couple of days. The tabloids were especially lurid in their headlines but short on real news. *Peru's Media Darling Target of Crimson Road Bombs! Cassandra Lucky To Be Alive! Industrialist Brother Flies to Lima to Console Cassandra!*

Cassandra Ganz gave no interviews. When Alex arrived late in the morning following the explosions, he found his sister surprisingly calm.

"Why don't you let Manolito bring some men down to guard the ranch?" Alex asked.

"No, *hermanito.* I'm in no danger. If the *Camino Rojo* wanted to kill me, I would be dead already."

"I hope you're right," he said after a thoughtful pause. "Is there anything I can do?"

"No, *nada*. I'm going to follow your advice and take a break from work for a while. I just want some peace and quiet and some time with the horses. I certainly don't want Manolo or any goons skulking around."

Alex pursed his lips and nodded. "All right, Cass. But give me a call if you need anything."

"There is one thing. Talk to *Mamá*. Make sure she knows I'm all right. She'll believe it if it comes from you." There had been little direct communication between Cassandra and her mother – mostly just the obligatory holiday-dinner conversations – since the funeral of Oswald Ganz. Pilar de la Vega was old-school Catholic, despite the lack of religious observance by her late husband and her children. When Cassandra had rejected her mother's wishes for marriage and family, Pilar had felt as if she had nothing left to say to her daughter, nothing left to offer. They had become veritable strangers to each other.

The previous night, after the dust from the explosions had settled, after the press photographers had drifted away and after the police had finished an investigation that consisted of ninety percent ogling and ten percent stupid, pointed or pointless questions, Cassandra's driver took her to Puerta del Sol. He dropped her at the door of the house then parked the Mercedes in the livery where he also had a small apartment. Nothing seemed amiss. A small light glowed inside the house, but that was not unusual. The young housekeeper, Luisa, always kept one burning. Cassandra turned her key in the lock, swung the door open, flicked on a light and gasped to see the woman from the street standing and facing her from her own living room. The sunglasses were gone and she held the floppy hat in both hands. She was young, maybe twenty-four, short and strong-looking. The sun, or something, had given her hair some faint highlights.

The woman smiled. Seated in a chair by her side was the man with the bearded face that adorned more Crimson Road banners and more wanted posters than any other image. Cassandra's heart leaped and she couldn't have said whether it was from fear or excitement. No journalists had interviewed this man since the Seventies.

"*Señor* Fortuna," Cassandra acknowledged him. "Or do you prefer *Colibrí*?" He just smiled and shrugged his non-answer. "They said you were dead."

"They might have said the same about you after tonight, my dear," he replied.

"And you are here … why? To finish the job?"

"No, no. There has been enough noise for one night, don't you think? Those fireworks were merely to get your attention."

"Well, you have it." Cassandra placed her handbag on a tall sofa table just inside the door. Her stomach churned with nerves. "Would you mind telling me how you got in?"

"Our Comrade Luisa is a soldier in the people's army." For the first time Cassandra noticed Luisa standing at attention at the entry to the hallway on her left. Apparently there was more to the girl than met the eye. Considerably more. Treacherous little bitch.

The Hummingbird continued, "Now why don't you close the door and make yourself comfortable?"

Cassandra did as she was asked and settled at one end of a large suede-covered sofa. *El Colibrí* gestured for the standing woman to take a seat at the opposite end.

"Allow me to introduce *Comandante* Rita," spoke *El Colibrí*. "Had we really wanted you dead, she would have delivered the fatal shot."

Bang, bang. Cassandra remembered it only too well. Then she remembered the phone call she had received from Alex advising her to abandon her show. The realization hit her hard.

Alex knew, she thought. And then to *El Colibrí* she repeated the question, "Why are you here?"

"I have come," he said with a confidently gentle tone, "to discuss the new, more meaningful life of Cassandra Ganz de la Vega."

Cassandra had been ripe for some kind of meaningful change in her life. Without ever expressing it openly to anyone, she had begun to feel the hollowness of her current media existence. She had grown weary of the parties, weary of the stuck-up, self-important, chauvinistic men that buzzed about her, and weary of the sugarcoated stories she was obliged to tell, week after week, to voracious cameras and cynical producers. She was more than ready for some kind of change, but she had been at a loss to define it. She hadn't sensed the direction a change should take and she didn't know how to overcome the inertia of her thriving career.

El Colibrí, in one night, had brought explosive clarity to both questions. Sitting larger than life in her own living room, he struck a deal with Cassandra. She would abandon her show for ninety days and retire to the ranch with only *Comandante* Rita and Comrade Luisa for company. During that time, she would have complete access to Rita's knowledge of the revolution, a journalist's dream. Nothing would be held back, short of specific plans of action or the whereabouts of *El Colibrí* and other key personnel. Her safety was guaranteed, as long as she made no attempt to betray *El Colibrí* or the *Camino Rojo* before the three months had passed. At the end of that time, she would be free to choose her own path, whether it took her back to her job, with the journalistic story of a lifetime, or in some other direction.

Within days, Cassandra had released all her staff, except Luisa, with generous severance checks. With Rita always at her side, she undertook the tasks of running the ranch. Comrade Sandra, as Rita insisted on calling her, reveled in the physical labor and the mundane pursuits, feeling closer to the earth and more authentically alive than ever before. Rita proved to be an interesting companion, narrow and dogmatic to be sure, but also intelligent and engaging. Of course, Cassandra's main interest, she kept reminding herself, was her exclusive journalistic access to a high-ranking member of the *Camino Rojo*.

Sitting in his office in the modern Banco Europa building in Miraflores, the stylish coastal neighborhood adjacent to San Isidro, Alex Ganz scanned the financial pages of the newspaper. The front section, with its dwindling coverage of the *TelePerú* bombings, lay to one side. A double ring from the phone on his desk indicated a call on his personal line, a line not routed through the company switchboard. He picked up the phone and swiveled his chair to face the gray ocean view. It was Manolo Ruíz.

"News, Manolito?"

"*Sí, Señor*. An American has arrived in Santa Rosita. I kept an eye on him. He spent the night at the church. In the morning he and the priest had a visit from the lady doctor. She spent about half an hour inside."

"What do we know about this American?"

"He came into the bank branch today and chatted up the teller. He claims to be a student, *un antropólogo*. He has taken a room with one of the old biddies in town, *la Señora* Rosario Flores. He came driving a piece-of-junk Jeep and carrying only one bag. Also, it seems he already has established an account with *Banco Europa*." Manolo read off data that included Sam's name, passport number and bank account details.

Ganz placed Manolo on hold and requested the account balance on a separate line. He found it to be reassuringly small. Perhaps this Samson Young really was the student he claimed to be.

"*Bien*, Manolito. Continue to keep an eye on him for a few days. Is that everything?"

"No, *Señor*. About the lady *medico* ... She has been asking for credit at the local pharmacies."

"I see. Thank you, my brother."

Alex broke the connection and dialed the local number of a contact with ties to the US intelligence community. He would soon have the complete story on the American newcomer to Santa Rosita. Then he turned his thoughts to the situation of Mercedes Marquez.

Enrique Morales walked along the tall curb that turned the cobblestone street into a virtual river during summer thundershowers. Along this section of street connecting the house of Doña Rosario Flores with the *plaza de armas* and the chapel of the *Santísima Virgen de Dolores*, there was no sidewalk, only a narrow strip of concrete that separated the curb from the high concrete and adobe walls enclosing the homes and businesses of Santa Rosita. The sun was already warm, and the boy was thinking about the good fortune that brought a foreigner to live with him in the house of Doña Rosario. He tapped a rhythm on the walls with a stick as he walked.

A pile of rags in a deep-set doorway marked it as a temporary shelter from the night before. Enrique stepped just wide of the bundle on his way by, and as he did, a hand snaked out from beneath it and locked a strong grip on his ankle.

"I've got you now!" came a voice from a filthy face emerging from of the rags.

"Let go of me, you old *loco*!" yelped Enrique as he brought the stick down hard on the man's wrist and wrenched his ankle free.

"Come back here, you little bastard. I am the spirit of Tupac Amaru. Come back here. I'll teach you a thing or two." The last statement sank with its mutterer back into the stinking rag pile.

"Crazy drunk," Enrique muttered with disgust as he continued toward the chapel. He visited with Father Pedro at least two or three times a week. They were more than priest and parishioner, and more than friends.

Enrique Morales had been born on the day of his mother's death. Eusebia Morales lay alongside the Ayacucho road and writhed from pain that felt like a condor's claws ripping her back and sides. She gave an agonizing push, birthed a male child and began to hemorrhage. She passed out from blood loss. A few minutes later, she died with her thighs wrapped around the child, who was still attached to the umbilicus and nested in the blood-soaked mass that had been Eusebia's only source of warmth, a ragged woolen shawl that had once belonged to her mother.

The identity of Enrique's father was never known, but Pedro Buenaventura privately believed him to have been Eusebia's former employer. Eusebia had been a delicate girl, orphaned in stages. Her father, Gregorio, had died in prison after being convicted of stealing a goods-laden mule to which he had been entrusted by a white *misti*.

Gregorio claimed to have been waylaid by bandits on his way to market. If he actually stole and sold the mule, as its owner claimed, then one thing was certain, his wife and four-year-old daughter never had the benefit of the proceeds. Gregorio Morales left them as poor as a newly sprouted potato field after a hailstorm.

Eusebia's mother, María, died three years later of a fever, probably related to tuberculosis. Seven-year-old Eusebia wandered off from the adobe hut where her mother lay still, cold and colorless, and walked toward Ayacucho. There, she was met on the road by the same landed *misti* who had jailed her father. He offered her work, first in his fields of potato and *quinoa,* and later as a housekeeper. She worked hard for little food and less clothing for seven years. When, at fourteen, she began to grow visibly pregnant, her employer turned her out, forcing her to live on what she could earn or beg from day to day. She weakened from hunger and slept in sheepcotes and fields until the day she traded lives with her infant son.

Fortunately for the boy, Pedro Buenaventura happened along the road in time to save him from death by exposure or wild animals. A condor or a puma would have made an easy meal of the newborn. Buenaventura cut the umbilicus, carried the baby home with him, baptized him, and christened him Enrique after his own grandfather. For a godmother to the boy, the priest turned to one of the more affluent women of the parish. It was to this same godmother, the widow Rosario Flores, that Sam Young had been recommended to lodge as a *pensionista.*

"*Padre*," called Enrique as he pushed open the chapel door. "We have a lodger. He's white. Even whiter than you or I! And his eyes are blue like the sky."

"Good morning, *hijito*. I know about your lodger. He is from North America, an anthropologist."

"What does that mean?"

"His people live very differently from you and me. He wishes to learn more about the way of life here in the sierra, especially among the *campesinos*."

"Doña Rosario says the *campesinos* are ignorant savages."

"I suppose she might think that, but it's not true. They simply have a different culture." Seeing Enrique's confusion he continued, "They understand the world differently. They've learned to think about things in different ways."

"They chew coca."

"Yes, they do."

"And that's bad."

"It would be bad for *you,* but to the *campesinos* it's an important part of life. They use it for many purposes. It helps them endure hunger and pain. It is also part of how they worship and celebrate."

Enrique looked thoughtful. "His name is Sam. He doesn't speak Quechua. He wanted to know if I could help him learn. And he would teach me to speak English."

"That sounds like a good bargain, Enrique. Perhaps you could take him to the *feria.* I bet he's never seen the open market. Maybe you could go with him and show him what's what."

"Good idea, *Padre*. I bet he's rich. Maybe he'll buy me something good."

"Maybe he will." Buenaventura smiled as he followed Enrique out the door.

By that time, the drunkard from the doorway had made his way down to the *plaza de armas* where he stood unsteadily, shouting to no one in particular, "Death to the *Yanquis*! Death to the dogs of empire!" His hair was matted like felt and his skin blackened with grime. Enrique wrinkled his nose. Father Pedro shook his head in sad recognition of Bonifacio Vargas.

The market day transformation of the streets of Santa Rosita began early. It was about 6:00am when I was wakened by the sound of iron wheels clattering over cobblestones. The wheels belonged to a heavy cart pushed by a man recalling a caricature of a Chinese coolie. He was short and plump with almond-shaped eyes and a long, thin moustache. During the week, I later learned, this man called Mongo sold remedies from a small storefront at the edge of town. Once a week, on market day, he went mobile. The top of his cart held an array of bottled liquids, including extractions of coca, alfalfa, malted barley and different herbs. Next to the herbal extractions were a rack of glasses and a bottle of *Ron Rico* rum. Below, heated to near boiling by cans of Sterno, was a tank of water with which he mixed hot drinks to order.

I pulled on clothes and wandered out of my room to find breakfast laid out for me: a basket of *pancitos*, several slices of something I interpreted as bologna, a cup, an immersion heater and a jar of instant coffee.

"*Buenos días, Señor* Samson," said Doña Rosario as she took up the handles of two large woven shopping bags and moved toward the door. She stood maybe chest high to me with her gray hair pulled back tightly into a bun. Her figure was soft and plump, but her hands, feet and eyes gave the impression of hardness. She reminded me of the fruit of a prickly pear cactus with its soft, seedy insides protected by a layer of tough spines. "The milk is in the icebox. Make sure to lock up." Before I could answer, she was gone, and the eight-year-old Enrique stood near the door bouncing on the balls of his feet.

"Have you already eaten, Enrique?" I asked.

"*Claro que sí.*" As if it had been a stupid question. The boy looked anxious. "*Señor* Sam?"

"*¿Sí?*"

"In your country, do all the people have white skin?"

"No, there are people of all colors, brown, black, yellow, red …"

"Red?! Like the devil?"

"No, no. More of a reddish brown, like the *campesinos* here in the sierra."

"Doña Rosario says white is best."

"Some people believe that, but I don't. I think we are all equal, just different."

"*Pishtacos* are white."

"*Pishtacos?*"

"*Vampiros* who suck the fat out of you."

"I don't know anything about *pishtacos,* Enrique. You don't think I'm a vampire, do you?"

"No. Father Pedro told me you are an *antropólogo.*"

After hurrying through breakfast, I walked through the weekly *feria* market with Enrique. The boy was so energetic and ingenuous that I couldn't help being drawn into his euphoria. Doña Rosario had given Enrique the day off from school with the very stern admonition that it was to be the only time, and Enrique was making the most of it. He played the tour guide with relish, tugging me this way and that to make sure I missed nothing.

It reminded me of my first trip with Mitch and my mother to Disneyland. This time, I had the parental role. Enrique, in knee-patched, navy wool trousers and an elbow-patched, red wool V-necked sweater over a green teeshirt, played the dual role of eight-year-old Sam and six-year-old Mitchell. He vacillated between childlike enthusiasm, all vertical and rotational movement, and a curious intensity when I stopped to look closely at anything. In contrast to my sandy mop and watery blue eyes, Enrique's short black hair and black eyes shone in the Andean sun like spun obsidian. Otherwise, we could have been taken for brothers or for a father and son.

Since dawn, a colorful stream of people had been flowing into Santa Rosita from little towns in the surrounding mountains. They had come with hand-drawn carts or leading burros laden with potatoes, grains, chickens, cheese, heads of goats and sheep, breads, blankets, shoes, felt hats, fingerless gloves, sweaters of llama wool and alpaca, and great steaming pots of rice and stews. "*Comida de combate,*" remarked one old merchant.

Kiosks went up with the sound of wood on wood. Fragrant steam rose from impromptu cafés. Vendors spread their wares on makeshift tables or on blankets on the ground. Observing all of this, I frequently asked Enrique to provide a name for some fruit or vegetable. In turn he would ask for the English equivalent. It became a language game that we would play off and on throughout my stay in Santa Rosita.

"What's that?"

"*Tuna. ¿En Inglés?*"

"Prickly pear."

"Prick-o-ly pear," he would repeat.

"That?" I would point.

"*Banano. ¿En Inglés?*"

"Banana. That?"

"*Plátano de isla. ¿En Inglés?*"

"Plantain. Those?"

"*Manzanitas. ¿En Inglés?*"

"I'm not sure. Little tiny bananas …"

"Leet-tle ti-ny bananas? No!"

I shrugged. "What's that?"

"*Chirimoya. ¿En Inglés?*"

"*No tengo la menor idea.* I've never seen anything like it."

For myself, I purchased a wide-brimmed felt hat, an alpaca wool sweater and a tightly woven wool poncho. I reasoned the outfit would be suitable for the coming rainy season and would make me somewhat less conspicuous as I took to walking in the countryside. Truth be told, I bought the clothes because I liked them. I imagined myself wearing them in a dashing, heroic, Clint Eastwood sort of way. The picture I held in my head of myself as an anthropologist was as laughable as it was vain. I was certain that I would fit right in with the local population, and that they would open their hearts and their secrets to me. That's how stupid I was.

I also found and bought a Spanish-Quechua dictionary and phrasebook. It was pretty thin. Quechua has no words or concepts for many of the phenomena we take for granted. I got Enrique a hand-carved and painted wooden toy, a cup on the end of a stick with an attached ball and string. The boy mastered the game of skill within minutes and, for the rest of the morning, walked around clacking the ball into the cup with remarkable precision.

In the street in front of the church, a small group of women in red skirts and black felt hats sat on their heels, nestling themselves like poppies among mounds of produce. I approached the women and stood over them admiring the voluptuous abundance in the neat stacks of vegetables. Strangely, I thought, none of them looked at me. They sat perfectly still with eyes downcast. It seemed to me that they actually trembled, as if the poppies were exposed to a sudden breeze. Then from beneath the skirt of the nearest woman ran a rivulet of amber urine that slowly made its way among the cobblestones and into the gutter. Her facial expression never changed. As I moved away, the other women tracked my departure with darting looks.

Around the corner, Mercedes Marquez sat on a low stool behind the open rear doors of an old Red Cross van. I stood back and marveled. Her slender hands reminded me of butterflies as she worked with the *campesinos* that came to be cured of their fevers and their wounds. Her intense black eyes seemed to contain wisdom, innocence and ferocity all at once. She had tied her hair back with a multi-colored scarf which, when added to the array of layered, colorful skirts, embroidered vest, black derby and unlaced army boots, gave her a look I found hypnotic. She was a gypsy princess, a human kaleidoscope, a flock of tropical birds.

Curtains concealed all but the back quarter of the van's interior. This apparently functioned as Mercedes' mobile examining room. A pair of white plywood footlockers contained her supplies of bandages, medications and examining equipment. I later learned that she had no equipment more sophisticated than a blood-pressure gauge and a reflecting microscope. All but the simplest blood or urine tests she had to send to a lab in Huancayo, and she did this infrequently because of the need to pay cash for the results. To the side of the van sat a wide reed basket into which each of her patients deposited some form of payment for her services. I could make out a few coins, several potatoes, some fresh fruit, a pair of *cuyes* (guinea pigs, skinned and cleaned) and green leaves that I recognized as coca. I resisted the urge to speak to her. Partly I was afraid of how my presence might affect her interaction with her patients. Mostly, I resisted because, in the few minutes I had been standing there, she acknowledged my presence only once, and that with a decidedly hostile look.

From the intersection behind me there suddenly came a pure, clear contralto voice. I turned and moved toward it with Enrique in tow. Inside a ring of onlookers stood a boy, perhaps twelve years old, dressed in ragged clothing and holding a battered wool hat. He sang a cappella about a young girl from the sierra, who fell in love with a soldier and ran away with him. She became known as the girl of the stockade, a lover of soldiers. Her family cried for her return. Sung in a jarring minor key, it was the most haunting song I had ever heard. When the boy finished singing he held out his hat to capture the few coins that came his way. I dug all the coins from my own pocket and sent Enrique to deliver them.

Noon was long gone by the time we turned toward home. Many of the vendors had already packed up and left with their own acquisitions. Across the plaza, partially concealed by the corner of the *Banco Europa*, I thought I saw a large man watching us. I recalled the silhouette of the man in the plaza on my first night in town. "Who is that man, Enrique?" I asked.

"What man?"

The man was gone and a cigarette butt rolled smoldering to the gutter. Enrique swung the red wooden ball into its wooden cup with a clack.

One morning, about a week into Cassandra's deal with *El Colbrí*, she and *Comandante* Rita took turns digging a trench for a water pipe in the ground next to the horse barn. After about an hour, Cassandra asked Rita where she had grown up.

"I was born in Trujillo," said Rita. She sat on an overturned metal bucket as Cassandra worked the shovel point around the edges of a stone lodged in the soil. "My old man was a fisherman. I was thirteen and the oldest of four children when my mother died. The old man never even took a day off work. He just let the public health people take her away. He came back from fishing that afternoon and threw a net at my feet. It needed mending. That had been one of my mother's jobs. Now, suddenly, I was to be the mother."

Cassandra had stopped digging and rested with both hands cupped over the end of the shovel handle. "In what way the mother?"

Rita shot her a challenging look and said, "In every way. No more school. No more friends. I cooked. I cleaned. I mended. The old man would beat me for any reason, or for no reason at all. After a while, he dragged me to his bed. I ran away after less than a year. The rest of my siblings were boys, so they were safe enough. I was on the street for days. Finally, a pimp named Gordo Pacheco picked me up."

"So, you were forced to be a prostitute?"

"Forced? I suppose. Most of Gordo's customers were soldiers. My old man had been a pig. Most of the soldiers were no worse, and if they didn't complain, Gordo didn't beat us."

Cassandra was now on her knees wrestling the heavy stone out of the hole.

"One night, one of the girls came back bleeding from the vagina. Her name was Rufina. Some *capitán* had gotten angry, worked her over with a bottle and dumped her at Gordo's door. Gordo was drunk. He beat her up, and then he passed out. The girl died. I took off that night and stowed away on a farm truck headed for the *sierra*, but not before I'd left Gordo cut open like a pig with his own knife."

She stood up and took the shovel from where Cassandra had leaned it against the barn. "It was there in the mountains, in Cajabamba, that I found myself in an education camp of the *Camino*

Rojo. I went there for the food, but I stayed for the solidarity, the songs and the hope for a better future. In the camp, I had dignity. In the camp, no one tried to fuck me." She put both booted feet atop the spine of the shovel and used all her force to drive it into the ground, widening the hole.

"The greatest day of my life," Rita continued, "was the day *El Colibrí* came to our camp. It was a hot afternoon when the truck arrived. We all gathered around. He gave us water to drink, and before he even took a drink for himself, he spoke to us from the back of the truck. His voice lifted my soul like a powerful wind. For over an hour, he described the world that would rise from our efforts. When he finished his address, he climbed down and walked straight to me. 'What's your name, little soldier?' he asked. 'Margarita,' I said. My throat was so dry I could barely speak. 'From now on you will be Comrade Rita. One day you will do great things for our people.'"

Cassandra leaned with her back against the barn wall and focused her gaze on the bucket where Rita had been sitting. Cassandra was, by training, a good listener. She had absorbed Rita's story with a combination of empathy and guilt. The empathy had more to do with the intimacy of the telling than with any personal experience of hardship. The guilt was a natural by-product of privilege and conscience. Unlike most members of the Peruvian aristocracy, she had never been able to view the poverty and squalor all around her as something right and natural.

"What about you, Comrade Sandra?" asked Comrade Rita as the shovel rang against another large stone. "What is it like being a big television star?"

"I suppose," said Cassandra, "it's a bit like prostitution … but with better clothes." They both let those words hang in the air for a few freighted seconds, and then Cassandra began a tale while Rita continued to dig. "For a long time, I wanted to be an actress. I went to the United States to study theater and film when I was seventeen. To UCLA, a school in California." Whether Rita understood the geographic reference or not she gave no indication. She just listened.

"During my freshman year, I got a part in a campus production directed by my acting professor. He was handsome and he seemed especially interested in working with me. One evening, he offered to help me work on a scene that he seemed to think I was having trouble with. I was eager to do better. I met him in his office and we worked through the lines together."

Cassandra paused to brush a strand of hair out of her face, leaving a smudge of dirt across her tanned cheekbone. "When we finished, he told me that I was beautiful. I had been wonderful. I had moved him almost to tears. He looked into my eyes and I could see he was filled with emotion. I was so relieved. He reached out and caressed my face and I fell into his arms. I wanted so badly to please him. I guess I made it easy for him.

"I thought we were in love, that my life and my career were taking off. We rehearsed for a month and the play ran for two weeks. I was so caught up in it that I didn't even notice I had missed my period. When it finally dawned on me that I was pregnant, I was terrified and confused, but I felt sure that my professor, my lover, would know what to do. I went to his office in the evening. I had seen lamplight through his outside window, so I knew he was there. When I got to the door I heard voices. I knocked on the door, and the voices hushed. I walked on down the hall, rounded the corner and stood with my back to the wall. I heard a door open and close quietly, but without footsteps, as if someone had looked out. A few minutes later, I crept back and eased myself down to the floor next to the door. The voices began again, and then the unmistakable sounds of fucking. I just sat there feeling numb until the door opened again."

"What did you do?"

"I walked away. I got an abortion, quit my classes and applied for a transfer to Berkeley, another university, where I declared my major in broadcast journalism."

"Why journalism?" asked Rita.

"I decided my future no longer belonged to acting out other people's fantasies. Journalism seemed more real – more like a quest for truth. It turns out," added Cassandra after a moment of silence, "people don't want the truth. Least of all from a woman."

"*La verdad es muy dura*," said Rita.

"Yeah," agreed Cassandra. "Hardest substance known to man."

Soon Rita's stories became more politicized. She spoke not only of her plight as a child but also of the plight of her people. And not only of her people presently but also historically. She could talk for hours about the glory and the social equity of the Incas. She spoke bitterly of the conquest, the Spanish inquisition and the abuses by the European invaders.

One day, after a fiery diatribe about European and American imperialism, Rita said out of the blue, "Your father was a Nazi, *¿verdad?*" Cassandra was speechless. She had wondered about Oswald Ganz's past, had considered the chronology, but no one, not Oswald nor anyone else, had ever spoken of it. She could have found out. She was sure of it. She had been, after all, a journalist. She had the investigative skills. But she had never tried to learn the truth. Rita's words caused her to burn with shame. *La verdad es muy dura.*

Other times, Rita went on at length about the *latifundia*, Peru's former feudal system, and the brutal expropriation of peasant lands by wealthy gentry. She knew the names of the abusive dynasties. She knew statistics of wealth and statistics of poverty. With a passion and an immediacy that Cassandra found intoxicating, Rita recounted the merciless exploitation of the *campesinos* by the landowners. One evening, just when she had Cassandra's anger fully primed, she hit her with another belt of guilt and shame. "Your family, *los* de la Vega, were *hacendados, ¿verdad?* How many *campesinos* did they own, do you suppose?" Cassandra hardly slept that night. Hard truth makes a very poor pillow.

I spent the day at my second weekly *feria* without Enrique. That night, as I closed the door to my room, I looked around as if seeing it for the first time. The single, metal-framed bed. The small wooden table and the straight-backed chair. The yellow-painted walls, bare except for a crucifix and a framed picture of the Sacred Heart of Jesus wrapped in thorns and bleeding. In a way, it all seemed unreal to me, a still life composed to make an artistic statement about a quaint way of living and thinking. In another way, it seemed hyper-real. At the moment, these furnishings were the only hard edges I had.

My former life in Oregon already seemed dreamlike. I knew objectively that I had been gone only a couple of weeks, but they were weeks that held lifetimes and infinite distances. When I tried, I could conjure up vague mental images of my mother and my brother, but they were no more real to me than the ones I could construct of my dead father. From my perspective, there was no distinction between the living and the dead.

From the top drawer of my dresser, I took my current notebook and a pen and began to write my field notes for the day. I described what I had seen at that day's *feria.* I catalogued the wares being sold and the nature and locations of the exchanges I had observed. I described people, the clothes they wore, the things they carried and the ways in which they carried them. I noted what I had learned about the different places people came from. As much as I could, where people had spoken Quechua, I attempted to record my descriptions in that language based on phrases I cobbled together or found intact in the dictionary I had bought at last week's market. The rest I wrote in Spanish.

Mercedes had been at the market again this week. I wrote her name at the top of a page, and then nothing more would come. I stared at the remaining whiteness. Where to begin? I felt I could write pages. I could write about the curve of her mouth when she frowned, the flash of white when she smiled at a child and the radiance that surrounded her like some special kind of light. I could describe the way she looked with her hair tied back in gypsy scarves and the way the layers of colored skirts moved when she walked. Or the college-girl look of the jeans and sweater that would place her right at home on any campus in America.

But could I write these things without also recording how they made me feel? How could I capture the strange mix of hurt and desire I experienced in response to the tension that pulsed between us? Should I allow myself to record the tenderness I felt as I watched her at work in the *feria*? As she felt delicately for swollen glands in the neck of a little peasant girl? Or conversed in subdued tones with a man who looked to be a hundred years old? What about the reluctance of my feet to move after my brain had said it was time to go on? Or the abrupt decrease in air pressure when she had walked out of the chapel my first morning in town? And then there was the inevitable question of why she seemed to despise me even though we had barely even met. No, it was impossible for me to write anything sensible about Mercedes Marquez. She was an enigma.

And then there was the other enigma, Marivela Santiana. Two weeks had gone by since our night of passion in the Grand Hotel Bolívar. I had been ready to give her my heart, and she had disappeared without an explanation. I had tried to keep vivid my mental pictures of her – Marivela smiling, laughing, bathing, floating down the street like a dancer, Marivela the aggressor, Marivela naked and vulnerable – but those images, like the images of my family before them, were already starting to blur around the edges.

I took Marivela's letter from its place inside the back cover of my latest notebook and read it for what must have been the thousandth time: *Thank you for a wonderful night! ... Don't be angry ... Please write to me when you can ...*

So I took a sheet of paper and I wrote. *Dear Marivela, I'm not angry, but I am confused. And a little hurt. What happened to you? Where did you go?* No, I thought, too direct. Too needy. I wadded it up and started with a fresh sheet of paper and a little self-restraint:

Dear Marivela,

I write to you from my pensión *in Santa Rosita. I'm settled in nicely now, but getting here was not so easy. I was attacked and robbed near Ticlio by members of the Guardia Civil. It was probably only luck that kept me from getting killed. I will tell you the whole story another time.*

How are you? I must say, I was surprised by your sudden departure from the hotel. I hope you are well. Please write. I would like to know what is going on in your life. I look forward to seeing you again.

Yours, Sam

I enclosed Doña Rosario's mailing address, sealed, stamped and addressed the envelope, and then wrote short postcards to Mom, Mitch and Jack Bentley. Every card served to underscore how lonely I felt. To Fredo I sent an account of my week's activities.

The familiar door-slam of the old Red Cross ambulance drew Father Pedro Buenaventura out of his half-prayer, half-daydream at the altar rail of the chapel of the *Santísima Virgen*. The ache in his knees and lower back indicated he had been kneeling much longer than he thought. It was already after nine, time to face the day. He pushed himself to his feet and walked stiffly across the adobe chapel toward its heavy wooden door. By the time he got there, it was already swinging open from the outside. A narrow shaft of sunlight pierced the dark interior of the church and then spread like a fan. Framed in the light of a clear Andean morning, the petite silhouette of Mercedes Marquez Acevedo was like a holy vision. She had the dark complexion of an *India* – the glossy black hair, coppery skin, and obsidian eyes – but not the wide face and heavy bones. From her *mestizo* parents, she had inherited the finer bone structure of European lineage. At twenty-five, she was some ten years younger than the priest.

"*Buenos días, Padre*, How are the souls of Santa Rosita?"

"Humble as usual."

Mercedes walked into the chapel with a bulging canvas bag slung over one shoulder. As the door closed behind her, both she and the priest blinked to adapt to the dim light.

"What news from out and about?" Father Pedro folded himself into the rearmost of the bare wooden pews.

"Crazy things. Old Asunción Ortíz has a nephew in Tingo María who just bought a new four-wheel-drive pick-up with a sack full of American dollars. He has painted it with the hammer and sickle to show solidarity with the *comunistas*. I don't think he appreciates the irony of his position."

"Coca dollars." He shook his head. "I worry about the influence of such prosperity."

"God knows it's not widespread. I could use a dose of it myself, and so could a good many of the people hereabouts. I still work almost entirely for *papas* and *choclos*."

"Potatoes and corn are gifts from God, *hijita*."

"Well, consider *these* gifts returned to sender." She let the canvas bag fall to the pew with a thump. "For my part, I need cash or I don't know how my mobile clinic will survive. I can't afford the most basic supplies. Pain killers. Antibiotics. I used to be able to count on friends at the hospital in Huancayo to 'procure' a few things for me, but it appears there has been a crackdown. And with so many *Rojistas* on the roads, I hardly dare to make the drive any more. I swear … it makes me so angry."

"Oh, *hijita*, I am sorry. You know that even with the lack of medications you can still make a difference. May I take you into my confidence?"

"Of course, *Padre*."

"I am concerned about Antonia Quispe. Do you know her?"

"*Sí, la conozco*. The daughter of Benito and Gabriela, *¿Verdad?*"

"The same." He cleared his throat as if preparing to give a sermon. "As you know, I cannot reveal that which I have learned in confession …" He left the words hanging while he examined Mercedes' face for her reaction. "Antonia has not been feeling well lately. She is experiencing nausea and vomiting."

"That was a matter of confession?"

"No, *hija*, but when you visit her, whatever you prescribe, I think it would be to her advantage if the treatment were also appropriate for prenatal care."

"I see. *Dios mío*, she's what, fourteen?" Father Buenaventura nodded gravely. Almost as an afterthought Mercedes asked, "Do we know who the father is?"

"She wouldn't say, and we must not speculate. According to her mother the girl has never had a boyfriend." They both knew that incest and abuse were no strangers to the peasant population, but that those were not the only possibilities behind a teen pregnancy. And Benito Quispe seemed like a decent sort.

"Fancy that," said Mercedes with visible disdain. "Virgin birth."

Mercedes started the ambulance and circled the plaza to get headed out of town. On her way past the bank, she happened to see the *gringo antropólogo* standing inside at the teller window. She gave a snort of disapproval, upshifted and hit the gas.

As the whine and clunk of shifting gears faded away, Pedro Buenaventura felt engulfed in a darkness that was deeper than could be explained merely by the dim light inside the chapel. He laid the potatoes and corn from Mercedes neatly in a bin in the small kitchen of his apartment and then returned to the altar rail. He stood rather than knelt as he directed a subvocal plea toward the beamed ceiling.

"*Dios mío*," he began, and then paused as if waiting for his words to ascend. "Please, forgive my jealous heart. Mercedes Marquez is like a savior to these people. What do I offer them? Hope for rewards in the hereafter? I can't even lead them past the basest of sins. And what of the hereafter? Do such rewards really exist? How can I know? Oh God, pardon my lack of faith. Help me know what to do. You must show me. No. Forgive me. You will do what you will do. But I beg you, please show me a way. *Dios mío*, can you hear me?"

As the priest groped for a connection with the Divine, he felt his hope eroding to doubt and, finally, his doubt slipping into despair. None of his prayers even seemed to be acknowledged by the Almighty, let alone answered. What a difference from his first days at the seminary when he had felt, or thought he felt, the constant flow of divine love, when his life was full of meaning and promise. Now the heavens seemed made of iron. He felt abandoned and alone.

As he wondered whether he might be crushed under the darkness of his own heart, a new sliver of light ran across the floor toward him from the opening door. Slipping through the bright opening, then easing the door shut, was a figure that left Father Pedro momentarily disoriented. The man was too tall and too European to belong in this place. Recognition slowly dawned, followed by suspicion, as the priest's eyes once again adjusted from sunlight to darkness.

"*Señor* Ganz. What brings you to this humble house of the Lord?"

"May not a wealthy sinner also be welcomed in this place?" inquired Alejandro Ganz de la Vega.

"Of course. I beg your pardon. How may I help you?"

"By allowing me to help the community, *Padre*."

"I'm listening."

"The woman who just left here …"

"*La Señorita* Marquez."

"*Sí, la señorita*." He repeated the title, which indicated an unmarried woman. "She is a doctor."

"She treats the poor."

"I see," said Ganz. "And she is well funded in this enterprise?"

"*Señor*, her patients are field mice, not lions of industry."

"As I thought. I wish to create a fund to support the young woman's work." He reached into the breast pocket of his woolen sport coat and handed Pedro Buenaventura a slip of paper. "This is the number of an account in your name at *Banco Europa*. I insist that the source of the money be kept anonymous and I would like you to administer it. For that service, I would expect you to retain a certain amount, say ten percent, for the operation of the church in Santa Rosita. Do you agree?"

In a matter of only a few seconds, Pedro Buenaventura's mind entertained both sides of a lively ethical debate. On the one hand, Mercedes and her patients desperately needed medicines and supplies that could only be had for cash. On the other hand, this particular cash almost certainly came from illicit means. Except that Mr Ganz did have visible, legitimate interests from which the money could also have been derived. And since when was it Pedro's prerogative to judge either the motivations or the sources of charity? Should people be allowed to die because Pedro suffered from self-righteous prejudices? On behalf of himself and the church, he could make such judgments, but on behalf of Mercedes and the sick and afflicted people of the region?

"Your offer is most welcome and most timely, *Señor*. I will of course agree to administer funds for the benefit of Miss Marquez's clinic. I cannot, however, accept any additional gratuity for myself or the chapel. May I ask, what is the reason for this generosity?"

"What was your reason for becoming a priest, *Padre*?" Ganz asked the question as he was turning to leave, making it clear that he did not expect an answer.

What indeed? thought the priest. What indeed?

The Quispe family lived in a tiny adobe house at the end of a footpath that wound about a kilometer from the road that connected Santa Rosita with the high mountain *selva*. Mercedes parked on the grassy roadside and changed into the clothing she wore when working among the *campesinos*. Although she spoke enough Quechua to communicate with them about matters of health, she knew the *campesinos* would be slow to trust her if she appeared to them in the clothes of a *misti*. As it was, they were fully aware that this woman they called *la brujita,* or the young witch, was not like them.

She made her way down the path carrying her medical kit and a supply of multiple vitamins, one of the few medicines she had left. If she could convince Antonia Quispe to swallow one each day for the next few weeks it would greatly increase her chances of bearing a healthy child. The house was deserted except for an old ram tethered to a post and a small black and white pig grazing about the front door. In a potato field behind the house several women worked, bent at the waist in the wide wool skirts, loose blouses and felt hats that were typical of adult women of the region. This would be the reciprocal work of an *ayllu,* a community group that traded labor for labor, providing each participating household with a pool of workers for key tasks such as planting or harvesting a crop or building a house. The *ayllu* tradition, handed down from the Incas, had endured through the conquest, through the feudal *latifundia* and, more recently, through the socialist agrarian reforms that had attempted to return the great *haciendas* to the control of peasant cooperatives. The *ayllu* provided for subsistence living. For the ability to participate in the cash economy the men from these households likely were off working at wage-earning jobs. Many, like Benito Quispe, would be in the *selva* working the coca fields.

The women looked to Mercedes like a colorful necklace against rich brown corduroy. They worked their way along the furrows planting seed potatoes and leaving small piles of weeds as they went. Tomorrow the same women would gather in another field, and so on until each household had its potato crop in the ground. Mercedes stood respectfully at the edge of the field until one woman, Gabriela Quispe, stood and moved in her direction. Walking carefully between the rows, Mercedes met her halfway.

"*Señora* Quispe," said Mercedes in her practiced Quechua, "good day."

"*Doña* Mercedes," replied the woman in Spanish. Few peasant women spoke anything but Quechua. Gabriela was demonstrating her sophistication as well as her deference. The title with which she addressed the young witch was that of an aristocrat. "How may I serve you?"

"From the priest, I understand that your daughter Antonia has been ill. I thought you might allow me to help her." The word she chose for 'priest' was intentionally ambiguous and also indicated 'God'. There was no harm in the *campesinos* believing that the young witch communed with spirits. Not if it influenced them to follow sound medical advice.

"Daughter! Come over here!" yelled the woman back in the direction of the other workers.

Antonia Quispe stepped forward from among the line of working women. Like all the children of these highlands she had the liver-colored cheeks called *chaposas*, the permanent chapping caused by sun, wind and altitude. Her bare feet were heavily callused, cut with deep cracks along the sides and soles. What differentiated Antonia from other children was the complete lack of gaiety in her face. At fourteen, she looked almost as beaten and old as her mother who, at thirty, looked in many ways twice that. How sad it must be, thought Mercedes, to be so young and yet to know one's future so completely.

Gabriela saw no reason her daughter should leave the field, so Mercedes examined her right there between rows. While checking Antonia's heart and lungs, Mercedes noticed with a pang of sorrow the girl's still-forming adolescent breasts. When the cursory examination was complete, Mercedes showed Antonia a small paper envelope of smooth red pills.

"These will help you to stay well. You must swallow one every day. More than one or less than one will not hurt you, but one each day gives the most favor. Also, do not chew them. It is good in your tummy, but it tastes nasty in your mouth. One other thing. These little pills are not good for anyone but you. Do you understand me, Antonia?"

"*Sí, Señorita.*"

Antonia tucked the envelope inside the waistband of her ragged wool skirt and without another word returned to the work group. Mercedes took a moment to absorb the scene: a dozen women bent double, just as they would have been four centuries ago, among row upon laboriously tended row, and behind them the partially terraced flanks of mountains rising to stony gray summits and a pale blue sky. Whether for its expansive beauty or its understated sadness, it was breathtaking.

For the first couple of weeks in Santa Rosita, I'd actually felt like an anthropologist. Things were going well, I had thought. All the new sights and sounds fit my eager expectations like collectibles in a lighted curio cabinet. I reveled in the newness, I recorded my observations feverishly, and I sent summaries to Alfredo Ramirez. In my exuberance, I had failed to notice how many people deliberately avoided my presence.

When it finally dawned on me, I felt stupid. With the passage of a couple more weeks, I began to feel frustrated, even fraudulent. I wondered if I would have to write about Santa Rosita from the exclusive perspectives of an eight-year-old child and a priest. Almost none of the townspeople would even talk to me beyond what was absolutely necessary for the purposes of commerce. Mercedes Marquez, the one person I most desired to talk to, wouldn't give me the time of day. Every week she came to the *feria*, but when I tried to engage her at her mobile clinic, she gave me a look that seemed to say, "Don't even think about coming over here."

Enrique remained an eager companion, but he was only available after school and on the weekend. One of the advantages of hanging with Enrique was that he would unabashedly introduce me to people I didn't know. After the introductions, though, things usually got weird. People would act pleased to make my acquaintance and then do everything they could to make it as short an acquaintance as possible. They would smile, but the smiles seemed to be masking something else. Were people harboring some joke that I wasn't in on? Was it nervous politeness or appeasement? Whatever the reason, I had a terrible time cultivating research relationships. Without the ability to interview people in depth and take part in their lives I would never be able to learn about the inner workings of the culture. And if I couldn't even be successful relating to townspeople, I despaired of my prospects with the *campesinos.*

I hesitated to report my misgivings to Alfredo. It would feel too much like admitting defeat. It would be embarrassing. As time passed, I became despondent. It didn't help that I hadn't received a response to my letter to Marivela. The brightest light I had encountered in Peru so far appeared to be dimming. I began to suspect that maybe she had a boyfriend in Lima and that my crazy night with her in the Hotel Bolívar had been just that. One night. And crazy.

Father Pedro tried to help me and most days he was available and willing to talk. He even agreed once, reluctantly, to take me along on one of his periodic visits to the sick and the afflicted. We walked together to the edge of town where homes were considerably poorer than the ones near the center.

"Our first stop," he explained, "is the house of *la Señora* Reynaldo. She has gout and spends most of her days in bed. Her granddaughter Justicia takes care of her."

He knocked gingerly on a door made of a single layer of tin on a flimsy wooden frame. It opened a crack. Father Pedro bowed his head slightly and it opened the rest of the way. We stepped in onto a dirt floor textured with broom strokes. Justicia seemed surprised to be admitting two people instead of one.

"Justicia," said the priest, "this is my friend Sam from the United States." The girl – or woman, I couldn't determine her age – held her head bowed so deeply that her chin pressed against her chest. She never raised it from that position. A worn curtain on a wire draped off one corner of the single-room dwelling. Behind the drape I could see the near end of a bed and, protruding from a woolen blanket, a pair of feet that could have been carved from knotted mahogany.

A voice like bad brakes screeched from behind the curtain and startled me with its volume. "*Padre*, is that you? Justicia? Justicia! Make the *padre* some tea. Stupid girl." The last words were merely cackled, not screeched. I assumed that *la Señora* Reynaldo was also mostly deaf.

Justicia shuffled two or three steps to the other side of the house, which was furnished with a low, unfinished wood bench and a single-burner propane stove. In the corner was a pile of blankets. Unless she slept with the old woman, that had to be Justicia's sleeping place. Father Pedro walked around the end of the curtain to the side of the bed. I moved respectfully to its foot. *La señora* was looking at the priest with beatifically upturned eyes when I came around the end of the curtain. She looked at me, clasped the blanket with twisted fingers, gave a little shriek and fainted dead away. It was the last invitation I got from Pedro Buenaventura to accompany him on his rounds.

It was early morning and the priest was finishing his first prayers when he heard the ambulance's unambiguous arrival. The sun was not yet up but a rosy crown had appeared on the peaks of the mountains to the east. Daylight would be soon to follow. Father Pedro met Mercedes at the door and invited her in for coffee. They sipped their coffee at Buenaventura's kitchen table with a minimum of talking. Pedro asked after Antonia Quispe. She was fine. Mercedes asked about the gringo. He had settled in fine with Doña Rosario and Enrique, but he didn't seem to be happy with the way his work was going. When they finished and had only empty cups between them,

Mercedes rose to wash the mugs and scrub her hands at the same time. Pedro stepped into his private quarters and returned with an envelope he had retrieved from *Banco Europa* the day before. "Before you leave," he said, "there is something I need to give you." He handed her a sheaf of bills. "This should help you obtain the supplies you need."

"*Dios mío, Padre!* Where did you get all this?"

"I'm afraid it is not for me to tell. The money was given to me in confidence."

"This is wonderful!" Suddenly, a connection clicked in her mind. Money from nowhere. An American anthropologist new in town. Oh my God, she thought, this is terrible. She sat back down and leafed through the bills, contemplating more than counting them as she did. "Tell me, *Padre*, what does the gringo … the … American want from me?"

"Sam?" Father Pedro was caught off-guard for a second by the apparent non sequitur. "He has some medical experience. I think, *hijita*, that he would just like to help you here in Santa Rosita and at the same time get to know some of the people. I don't think he means any harm."

"No," she scowled. "Neither did Pandora."

I had spent the day wandering the town of Santa Rosita, making inconsequential purchases: a postcard from the *papelería*, an *empanada* from the *panadería*, a pair of bootlaces from the *zapatería*, an Inca Kola from a *bodega* here and a chocolate bar from a *bodega* there. What I was really trying to do was to scare up any conversation at all that might lead to a research relationship. Frankly, I would have settled for a conversation that merely eased my loneliness and frustration for a few minutes.

Eventually, I gave up on socializing and walked up the hill past Doña Rosario's house to the edge of town, past the green painted jail, which only occasionally held prisoners, and then primarily to sober them up, and past a few scattered houses with heavily eroded walls and ragged-looking gardens to where the street ended against the foothills above the town. The hillside ahead of me lay covered with a crazy quilt of cultivated ground. Each irregular plot had its own hue and texture. Some were covered with stubble. Others were burned black. Some were dimpled with clods of golden turf. Others were waled with chestnut-colored corduroy. A few stands of eucalyptus and the occasional stunted pine marked the ridgelines. Here and there a cluster of scotch broom erupted like a fountain of green and yellow. One solitary brown bird flitted from perch to perch, unmolested by even the possibility of a predator.

I took a seat atop a large stone, which despite the full afternoon sun felt quite cold. From there, I was able to get a better sense of the town in its entirety. The first thing I noticed was the sea of red tile and corrugated steel roofs. Next was its orientation around the central *plaza de armas*. From that nucleus outward, the buildings were, on balance, progressively smaller, less colorful and farther apart. No surprise there, except perhaps about the colors. It costs money to buy stucco and paint. I guess I was a little surprised and saddened to see clear markings of class even in this humble Andean community. What was worse, I actually caught myself feeling a little bit proud of the position of Doña Rosario's nicely painted house in the center of town.

A small orphan cloud passed briefly in front of the sun and sent a chill through me. I trembled violently, as if some fault line deep within me had suddenly slipped. From that same slippage arose, under extreme pressure, the beginnings of tears. They swelled like ice floes behind the corners of my eyes. They closed in on my throat. I clasped my hands for warmth and squeezed them between my thighs. How had I ended up so completely alone?

My shoulders shook again from an icy aftershock. I had decided it was time to leave when the sun burst forth with a warm, calming hand and softened my melancholia. I stayed long enough to appraise the sunset before walking back into town. It wasn't much of a sunset, really. The sun took cover behind the western mountains and faded away with no fanfare, no drama and no party clothes. Taking advantage of the remaining twilight, I walked back to the plaza and to *Los Tres Chanchitos*. It was Santa Rosita's only real restaurant. The sign over the door bore a representation of three little pigs in chef's hats and aprons. One carried a cleaver, one a ladle and the other a frying pan. I sat at a window facing the door. Before I could even order, Mercedes Marquez walked in and took the chair across the table from me.

"I'm sorry I ignored you earlier at the fair," she said. She was once again wearing jeans and a sweater and her hair was loose.

"Did you?"

"You know I did. Anyway, I'm glad I bumped into you. I wanted to apologize. I've been rude to you."

I shrugged it off and ordered a beer. She asked for coke.

"Father Pedro tells me you have medical experience," she said.

"Some. I quit medical school after three semesters to study anthropology. My father was a physician. Medical school was pretty much his idea. Or maybe it was mine. At any rate, it wasn't for me. I also worked summers in a clinic for migrant farm workers. What about you? What's your training?"

"I finished medical school, the class work at least, at the University of Ayacucho. It was my big dream. My father was so proud of me. His baby daughter was going to be a *médico.*"

"*Was* proud?"

"My father died before I could do my internship. A jack stand slipped and he was crushed by a car." She paused in thought for a long moment. "My brothers took over running the garage – the family business. *Papá* was a mechanic. *Papá* had supported me in medical school, but my brothers refused to help. Without the money I couldn't afford to finish."

"So you never got your medical license."

"Correct. Not that it matters to the *campesinos*. But I could never open a legitimate practice."

"I'm sorry. I guess I was wondering if maybe I could work with you sometimes. I'm pretty good at taking vital signs. I've assisted in childbirth and minor surgery."

Mercedes shook her head slowly. "It's difficult. Not because of your skill. It's your color. Among the *mistis*, it would be less of a problem, but in the villages and the country the people are deathly afraid of *pishtacos*, pale foreigners who …"

"… Suck out the fat of innocent victims. I've heard." I remembered the women from the *feria*, the downcast eyes, the trickle of urine. My God, they must have been terrified of me. "To do my work among these people, I have to gain their confidence. You know them. What can I do?"

Mercedes brought her elbows to the table, made a hammock of her interwoven fingers, rested her chin in it and looked me straight in the eyes. I felt like I was having my worth weighed in a very fine, if temperamental, balance. Finally she answered, "Time. And association. I've seen you with Enrique Morales. Hang around with him. People know him. He's a good boy. Pretty soon they'll become accustomed to you."

"Enrique is good company. I live with him and *la Señora* Flores."

"Yes, I know." She continued to look at me as if she were trying to force open a door and see inside. After a few seconds, it became uncomfortable.

"What?" I said.

"Sorry. Nothing." She dropped her eyes and focused on her glass. It was my turn to study her. Without her own gaze to parry mine, I'm sure I stared shamelessly at every minute detail of her face. I laid my hand on the table near the center, wishing she would cover it with her own. I wanted to touch her. I wanted to run my fingertips along the fine line of her jaw. My desire felt like a delicate glass ball. If I squeezed it too hard it would shatter in my hand and make me bleed.

"I've got to go," she said. "Thanks for the Coke." The harsh sound of her wooden chair scraping back across the concrete floor echoed in my guts as I watched her walk away.

"Will the *señor* be staying for supper?" asked Felipe, the Pigs' only waiter, as he cleared away the empty Coke glass. I glanced at the battered one-page menu tucked under his arm. I had been in town for less than a month, and already I knew it by heart.

Father Pedro had conducted a mass, as he did every week after the *feria*, as a service to those *campesinos* who only came to town once a week for market day. It had been a meager turnout, and he was both puzzled and disappointed. As he readied himself for bed, he contemplated the simple demographics of the church in Santa Rosita. When he had first come here eight years ago, the chapel would nearly fill with worshipers from both the town and the surrounding areas. The *Camino Rojo* was no more than a rumor or a bogeyman then, but it was a bogeyman that put fear into good Christians' hearts. A little fear, it seemed, was good for church attendance. As the *Camino Rojo* gained ground in the countryside many of those good Christians stopped venturing out and the congregation began to shrink. A certain amount of fear motivated the people, but an overdose paralyzed them. The only part of the congregation that had grown steadily was the widows' bench. Its occupancy had doubled. Now, inexplicably, he was starting to see a few more people from the surrounding region again. Maybe Santa Rosita's reputation for peacefulness was beginning to spread. At the same time, however, attendance among the townspeople had fallen sharply. Why? One thing is sure, he thought as he climbed into bed, nothing I have done has made any difference.

Jesus Christ hung from a cross on the wall over Pedro Buenaventura's bed. The Savior's face, twisted with pain and sorrow, turned Pedro's thoughts in a different direction. "Unrequited love," spoke the priest, whether aloud or in his thoughts he could not have said. "Your passion for us has never been returned, has it, Lord? You give us your infinite love. You gave us your life on the cross. And what do we give in return? Scorn, sin and indifference." He put out the lamp, lay back, closed his eyes tightly and held onto the vision of Christ crucified.

But the vision began to break up. Suddenly it was not Christ upon the cross but another man. A younger man. Then it was not a cross but a bed, and it was not suffering on his face but ecstasy. Pedro Buenaventura clenched his fists and dug his nails into his palms. He struggled unsuccessfully to re-invoke the body of Christ. His growing erection was a quill reaching for his heart, a splinter lodged in the raw tissues of his soul. He arched his back and neck and pressed his forehead hard against the rough wooden headboard until he could feel the imprint of its grain replicated deep in his skin. At the same time his hips moved of their own accord, churning, driving his unwanted erection in and out of folds in his bedclothes. What his mind resisted, his body knew with certainty; ejaculation would be his only relief. The face of the young man-Christ grimaced in ecstasy-agony and Pedro Buenaventura experienced the inevitable pulsing shame of release. Blackness overtook his spirit and a sob wracked his chest.

Alex Ganz used to think of el Valle del Cóndor as his sanctuary, his retreat from the stresses of an executive life in Lima. Lately, it seemed the situation had reversed itself. Business in Lima and around the world ran smoothly, whereas el Valle del Cóndor and Santa Rosita had become a nexus of preoccupation. Even so, he was glad to be back. His plane was refueled and stored for the night in its hangar next to the airstrip. It was a precaution he insisted on, even during periods of inclement weather. He had bartered a kind of peace with the *Camino Rojo* and also with the local law, but he never took his personal safety for granted. There must always be at least two ways out of any situation. Here, that meant his armored Land Rover and a fully fueled and functioning airplane.

As he came through the door, his manservant, Juan Pablo, took his coat, his briefcase and an order for a late dinner. He communicated the dinner order to Consuelo who, in addition to being the housekeeper and cook, was also Juan Pablo's wife. The two of them had never had children and had worked for the Ganz family since before Alex was born. In all important ways they considered Alex their son. Besides Juan Pablo, Consuelo, and old Indio the caretaker, the only other regular resident of the house was the young woman, Luz Castro.

Luz came from Ica in the coastal desert south of Lima. She was a bright twenty-year-old with wavy brown hair and eyes the color of milk chocolate. From a family that was too large and too poor to support her, she had ventured to Lima with the dream of becoming a schoolteacher and the intention of finding work near the university. Soon she learned that work was scarce and that available work paid barely enough to provide a room, let alone decent food, let alone books. One afternoon, as she stood on a street corner at the edge of the National University campus, waiting for a bus in a worn-out dress that was the best of the three she owned, and wondering what in the world she could do to rise above her dismal state, Luz noticed a well-dressed woman standing to one side and looking her over. The woman approached with a smile.

"Are you a student?" she asked.

"*Ojalá*," Luz told her with an if-only look.

"What is stopping you?"

"What is stopping anybody? Money."

"Are you looking for work?" asked the elegant stranger.

"I have a job."

"I can see that." She nodded toward Luz's hands, which were raw from immersion in hot, soapy water. "I mean, are you interested in making good money?"

"Doing what?"

"Dressing nicely. Acting like a lady. Being a good companion for a wealthy gentleman. Most of the time, you would be free to do as you pleased."

Suddenly, Luz Castro stood at a crossroad. She looked down one road, the one she had been traveling for months, every day with less and less hope, and she knew what lay down it. She knew because she had seen it before. She had grown up with it. It was her mother's life, a life without choices, tired, painful and wasted. The other road looked fraught with danger, but it offered something that her current path denied her. It offered her a chance. It offered her a choice.

The woman, Zenobia, was one of Lima's most discrete businesswomen. She took Luz to a Spanish colonial mansion in the heart of the city where she received her first-ever complete medical examination. After the medical exam, Zenobia called her newest client on his private line. This particular, very special, client had seen the portfolios of all Zenobia's women and had rejected them all. In the end, she'd had to resort to special recruitment. The client's specifications were unusual. In addition to youth and beauty, they included freshness, intelligence and a sense of innocence.

"I have a new girl that you may like." She described the encounter by the university. The client was intrigued. "I'll send over pictures. By the way," added Zenobia, "this one comes with a special bonus. It turns out she's actually a virgin. You can have the choice of well-trained or unspoiled."

Luz received lessons in make-up, clothing and manners. There were also lessons in the theory of sexual pleasure, but for Luz, there was no practicum. Client's choice.

Zenobia's girls came and went at all hours. Sometimes they left for a few hours, sometimes for several days, and always accompanied by one of Zenobia's drivers in one of Zenobia's cars. The girls were allowed to accept gifts from the men they met, but the real money was paid to Zenobia's account by wire transfer.

The girls never spoke the names of their *patrones*. They talked about them privately but referred to them by aliases: "Mr Froggy was a bad boy tonight. I had to spank him." "Sofia looked angry when she came in. She must have had a tough time with the Admiral." "Ginger is worried. It seems the Little Jew couldn't get it up again last night." Luz listened shyly to their banter. Privately, she worried about the kind of man Zenobia would assign her to. It seemed that most of the clients were old, albeit rich, and often unpleasant.

"Your situation is different, my little dove," said Zenobia. "You won't be living here at the house. You have what we call a foreign assignment." The driver delivered her to the municipal airport and a waiting plane where the largest man she had ever seen helped her in. She wondered if this giant, rough-looking man was to be her *patrón*. It was best not to think about it, she decided.

Manolo Ruíz had carried all kinds of cargo and passengers for *el Señor* Ganz over the years. Never once had he taken more than a passing business interest in any of them. Looking at Luz Castro, he wished this time could be different. This girl somehow, inadvertently, through the simple act of walking across the tarmac, looking twice, tentatively, over her shoulder at the car that brought her and accepting Manolo's help climbing into the plane, had lodged a marker near his heart.

When the plane began to roar and lurch forward, Luz forgot her other worries. When it lifted off the ground, she gasped. As it lumbered upward over the mountains and rocketed through narrow canyons, she alternated between awe and terror. At the point where nothing could be seen in any direction except mountains, and ahead of them angry upheavals looked like the sharp teeth of a hungry planet, she knew she had left real life behind her. When they finally landed in the green-jeweled el Valle del Cóndor, she was convinced she was dreaming. And when Manolo led her into the house and introduced her to *Don* Alejandro Ganz de la Vega, she made a silent wish that she would never wake up again. That had been over a year ago.

Luz's problem was not that her *patrón* was too old, too ugly or too mean. *Don* Alejandro was none of those. Luz suffered from being in love and being lonely. She was in love with her *patrón*, something Zenobia's girls had said was impossible, so what did it matter that she spent most of her time alone with her books, strolling around el Valle del Cóndor or keeping company with Consuelo? What did it matter that *Don* Alejandro spent half of his time in Lima, living a side of his life that she knew nothing about? What did it matter that she was invisible to him until the evening hours? How different was that from the way most women lived? And just look at all he had done for her. It was true that in the beginning she had spent many nights with the *señor,* learning how to please him and, in some ways, how to please herself. Sadly, it was also true that the more she learned, the less she seemed able to excite his passion. It was enough, wasn't it, to lie in his arms until he fell asleep? More and more, though, he ignored her completely. Those were the nights she dreaded the most.

On this particular night he came looking for her. The door to her room was open, so he didn't knock. He found her curled in a big chair with a college textbook titled *European History.* As soon as she saw him, she closed the book in her lap and sat up.

"How are the studies going?" Alex asked. He had arranged for Luz to pursue her bachelor's degree by correspondence with a private university in Lima that had benefited from Ganz corporate largesse.

"Well enough, I think." It was true. Luz had completed two years of coursework in one year, and with above-average marks.

Alex extended a hand and she rose to take it. "Would you join me for a drink before bed?"

Normally, she would pour. Tonight he did it, two glasses of cognac. Hers, he sweetened with a touch of Benedictine liqueur. They both sipped wordlessly. She thought she detected signs of tension in his face, a deeper knit to his brow, a weary look to his eyes. She stood behind his chair and placed her hands on his shoulders. The muscles were tight. She kneaded them until they started to loosen. He reached up and took her hands, pressing his thumbs into her palms, then stood and led her into is bedroom. She helped him undress, taking care to hang his clothing neatly on the valet. Then she slipped out of her own brocaded robe and silk nightgown. As she slid into bed, he pulled her close until their bodies twined and she felt his breath warming her scalp. She ran her hand down the small of his back and across his buttock, pleased to feel his response against her body, happy to be pleasing him. He held her tight. She felt elated, hopeful.

How could she know that with his eyes closed, Alex saw the face of Mercedes Marquez Acevedo?

From Santa Rosita, Mercedes drove up the road paralleling the creek that descended from el Valle del Cóndor. She knew that at the end of the road was an iron gate and that behind the gate lay the remnant of a great *hacienda*. More than that, she had no desire to know. The Peruvian upper class had no business with her or she with it. As far as she was concerned, her role was to undo in some small measure the harm they had done through centuries of arrogant exploitation of the indigenous people.

The attraction of this particular road was not the *hacienda* at its terminus but a secluded turnout just below it. Less than a kilometer before the gate a double-track road cut through the grass and weeds and disappeared in the direction of the creek. It faded out in a stony hollow formed by millennia of falling water. Growing in the center of the hollow was a large stand of eucalyptus, and it was here that Mercedes parked her van on the nights she spent in Santa Rosita.

She set the emergency brake and stepped through to the rear of the van, which constituted her only real address. Officially she lived with her mother in Huancayo, but since her father's death she had fixed up the old Red Cross ambulance with a propane stove, a cot, a small closet and, of course, a chest of tools with which to keep it all working. It was her home as well as her clinic. From her supplies she took a pail, and this she carried to the stream and filled with clear water.

Mercedes emptied the water into the heavy aluminum autoclave she had scavenged from friends working in Huancayo's regional hospital. It was designed to sterilize medical instruments but tonight it would serve its more frequent purpose as a stewpot. After cranking open a roof vent, she lit the stove and started heating the water. At this altitude it would boil rapidly, but the autoclave's pressure would raise the temperature and assure fast and thorough cooking. Into the pot went *cuyes*, corn and potatoes she had received in payment at the *feria*. She added salt and dried peppers and screwed down the lid.

With dinner cooking, enough to last two or three days, she wrapped herself in a blanket for warmth and once again stepped outside the van and into the evening air. The sky was clear. It would be a cold night, but the stars would be glorious. Mercedes did not believe in *apus*, the Inca gods of the mountains, but if she did it would be easy to believe that the god of this mountain held her cradled in the cup of its hands. She spread another blanket beneath the eucalyptus and lay down with a book. It was a worn copy of the novel by Ciro Alegría that she considered an anthem to life in the Andes. *El Mundo Es Ancho y Ajeno* was her father Eduardo's favorite book, and this had been his copy. The pages were soft as cotton but nowhere dog-eared or stained. After his daughter, the thing Eduardo Marquez had loved most was to read in the moments of rest between jobs in his garage. He had always cleaned his hands well before picking up a book.

The sun set on the mountains beyond Santa Rosita, laying down a blanket of purple and gray. A few lights flickered in the valley below, but they were no match for the lights that appeared in the heavens. The Incas believed the stars were a great river in the sky that flowed east, joined the great river of the earth, the *Amazonas*, and flowed with it into the sea. Tonight it was as if the atmosphere drew freshness and life from their watery presence.

With dinner cleaned away and her bed made ready, Mercedes had nothing more to do than reflect. She thought about the many burned and abandoned villages that dotted these magnificent highlands. How is it possible, she thought, for cruelty to dominate in the midst of such beauty? It seemed that everywhere, everywhere except Santa Rosita at least, public officials, priests, scholars, even tourists (although few came here anymore), had been slaughtered by the *Rojistas* following their so-called public trials. Any *campesinos* suspected of abetting the *Camino Rojo* were taken away by *sinchis*, the National Guard's red-capped commandos, or more often they were executed in their own homes, but not until any young women in the household had been raped and savaged. The people feared the police as much as they did the terrorists. Whereas the *Rojistas* were motivated by ideology, the army and the national police would rape, steal and kill among the *campesinos* with no provocation beyond boredom or feelings of entitlement. For the *campesinos*, there was no protection *by* the law or *from* it.

As the sky grew darker, the stars grew closer, brighter and bigger. They seemed to emanate needles of icy light that penetrated Mercedes' bones. At such times, she found herself envying the women with men to warm their beds. Of course, she realized many of them paid a high price for that warmth. Some accepted beatings or worse. At the very least they were second-class citizens. Well, she thought, not Mercedes Marquez Acevedo. No man was worth that. Still, as she curled into her cot she was undeniably lonely. Her mind turned painfully to the one man whose bed had also been her own. He had disappeared the same week as her father died. She wondered where he was, as she had so many times before. But on this night the pain was somehow less sharp, more distant. For perhaps the first time, she had begun to accept that he was really gone, that she was really alone in the world.

What did these feelings have to do with the *gringo* anthropologist? What was it about him that upset her equilibrium? There were things that didn't add up – first of all, the money. If he really wanted to work with her, as he had offered, then why disguise the source of the donation to her clinic? Why not use the money for leverage? Even more disturbing than the question of the money was the thread of tenderness that ran through the disdain she felt toward the American. Maybe she could explain it away as the result of her need to be a caretaker. He did, after all, seem particularly naive and vulnerable.

I became a walker. The apparent tranquility of the vicinity around Santa Rosita lured me into longer walks farther from town. They were brooding walks. I would have felt homesick if I'd had a home to feel sick for. Instead I suffered from a kind of generalized homesickness, longing for a home to long for. I felt utterly lost and mostly alone. My work had never really started. I had no direction and no momentum, and I didn't know what to do about it. I thought about writing to Jack Bentley, but it was way too early for that, especially after my insistence on coming here despite his objections.

So I walked. Sometimes, I hiked into the mountains, following sheep trails and stepping over the low stone walls that divided one man's crops from another's. If I chanced upon *campesinos* in their fields, they inevitably grabbed their children and prepared for fight or flight. At those times, I felt a poignant kinship with Dr Frankenstein's melancholic and misunderstood monster.

One day, I rambled my way into a hilltop ruin. It was an ancient settlement, probably of the Huanca or the Huari people, contemporaries of the Incas. The ruin was dominated by cylindrical stone houses with trapezoidal doorways. In the middle was a rectangular plaza, or the foundation of some great house. I pondered the choice of the hilltop for building a city. Was it for the protection offered by the steep slopes below? Or did they build on the hill to conserve the fertile valley soil for cultivation? What would life have been like here? Much different from life today in an adobe hut with nothing but firewood to cook by? Would the fear of marauding Chankas or conquering Incas have exceeded the fear today of raiding *Rojistas* or brutal *sinchi* commandos? A site like this would be an archeologist's dream. But what would that dream yield? The message that nothing really ever changes?

Other times, I just picked a road and wandered. At first I stayed hyper-vigilant, looking always and everywhere for signs of hostile activity. I watched for movement, for flashes of light, for the remains of recent campsites. I imagined what I would do if I came around a bend and found a patrol of *Rojistas* coming my way. Most of the scenarios involved a quick turn-around and then an all-out run in whatever direction offered the most potential cover. Lately, I had stopped being so vigilant.

The sky was blue and the temperature was perfect for walking the day I met PIP Detective Porfirio Sanchez. I was walking along the road toward the village of Huaynatambo when I spotted a beige sedan coming my way at a leisurely pace. Being an American car, in good condition, with no official markings, and driven by a lone individual, it piqued my curiosity more than my fear. The driver was smiling as he slowed to a stop in the middle of the road. He looked sort of lumpy and friendly. Harmless. Like somebody's uncle that you'd meet at a barbecue. The conversation began with reassuring predictability:

"*Hola*," he said.

"*Hola*."

"Nice day."

"Beautiful," I agreed.

"Where are you headed?"

"Nowhere in particular."

"Hop in. I'll give you a lift."

"That's all right," I said. "I could use the exercise."

Still smiling, he produced a shiny silver badge. "No, *amigo*. I think you will accept the ride."

After her first month with *Comandante* Rita, Cassandra was primed for another visit from *El Colibrí*. She had worked side by side with Rita and Luisa in hard physical labor. She had begun to empathize, not only with the hardships and struggles that Rita, and by extrapolation, the entire Peruvian peasantry had suffered, but also with the dogmas of liberation that Rita espoused with a razor-sharp elegance of conviction. In addition, she had again and again felt a deep, twisting blade of guilt for the abuses that her class had heaped upon the *campesinos* since the times of conquest. Closer to home, she felt a need to atone in some fashion for the actions of a father who almost certainly had derived seed money from the blood of holocaust.

This visit began like the first, as an unexpected apparition. Cassandra had gone alone, as was her habit, to the stables to care for the horses. Rita was quietly helping Luisa with dinner. When Cassandra slid open the stable door, she knew immediately that something was amiss. The horses were calmer than usual at feeding time. There was the subtle shearing sound of teeth on oats. The smell of oats, hay and manure was fresh and pungent. As the door opened wider, the air silvered with the glow of late afternoon sunlight refracting through motes of dust. Surrounded by this silver aura, Miguel Fortuna stood in a soldier's fatigues, holding a pitchfork next to a pile of freshly gathered manure.

He was neither tall nor handsome, nor even particularly fit. Cassandra surprised herself with her assessment of his soft physique and graying, well-trimmed beard. It was an image she had once thought repulsive, even fearsome. She now found him attractive in a strange sort of non-physical way. His presence seemed charged and substantial.

"*Señor,*" she said. "You honor me."

"I have shoveled a little shit, that's all. A suitable job for any servant of the people. *Comandante* Rita informs me that the changes in your life seem to suit you."

"She is a big help and a pleasant companion."

"She is a soldier," corrected *El Colibrí*, "who has dedicated her life to the revolution. He leaned the pitchfork against a stable wall. "Come here, Comrade Sandra."

She stood before him at arm's length, as tall as him in her Italian riding boots. He looked her up and down and then locked his eyes on hers.

"Remove your clothing." It was a command, but not a harsh one.

She hesitated, wondering for a moment what it meant. *El Colibrí*'s face, his entire body in fact, was unreadable. She did as she was told. Balancing on her left foot, she reached down and slipped the soft leather boot from the right. She let it fall to one side on the dirt and straw of the stable floor. She did the same for the other boot. Then she unfastened the button and zipper of her designer jeans and slid them down across her legs, removing her socks with them, and let them slump on top of the boots.

By the time she had reached this stage of undress, any of the men in Cassandra's previous experience would be grasping at their own buttons or, at the very least, showing clear signs of diminished composure. *El Colibrí* remained impassive. She slowly slipped each of the buttons of her chamois blouse, beginning with the cuffs and ending with a button at the precise level of the slight bulge in her cotton panties. She let it slip off her shoulders, off one wrist, then the other, and guided it carefully onto the pile that had started with her boots. As she turned her head back to face *El Colibrí*, she felt the comforting weight of her hair moving against her shoulders and back. *El Colibrí*'s demeanor never changed.

Cassandra felt a tremor of confusion. Here she was, in a position that had always put her in charge of a situation, and she felt not powerful but vulnerable, not adored nor even desired, but, rather, on the verge of being crushed. *El Colibrí* waited. The clasp of her lacy brassiere rested between her breasts. She unhooked it with fingers that were no longer certain of their purpose, and her breasts rose to an occasion she could no longer define. What was it he wanted? She forced herself to return her arms to her sides, even though she had a sudden urge to cover herself. Goosebumps appeared on her thighs and upper arms. Her nipples hardened and brightened. *El Colibrí* still showed no sign of emotion beyond the slightest cocking of his head, which seemed to indicate he was waiting for her to finish. With her thumbs in the elastic waistband Cassandra pulled her panties down to the point where they slid unaided to her ankles. Her unsupported breasts suddenly felt silly to her, not like the weapons of seduction she had successfully deployed in the past.

El Colibrí gave a short nod of approval. It was not a judgment of the nearly perfect feminine form in front of him. It was an acknowledgement of Cassandra's obedience. "*A rodillas,*" he said. On your knees.

Cassandra's confusion became tinged with fear, but she continued to obey. She settled first her left knee into the dirt, carefully to minimize her discomfort, and then her right. She held her back straight, her arms close at her sides, and her thighs together. *El Colibrí* slowly crossed in front of her. For the first time, she noticed the fraying at the hems and seams of his fatigues. Raising her eyes to level, she took stock of the sheathed knife and holstered pistol that hung from his belt. The pistol's checkered grip was discolored and worn with use.

He circled around her left side, past the pile of her clothing, and stopped behind her. She kept her eyes forward, focused on the wood grain of the stable wall, and concentrated on taking smooth, even breaths. In. Out. In. Out. *El Colibrí* completed his circle, moving in close by her right shoulder. Still she kept her eyes forward. He reached out to the nape of her neck and gathered her long hair like a rope into his left hand. He held it gently at first, maybe even admiringly, then he tightened his grip. As she heard the knife slide out of its sheath, Cassandra felt an involuntary upward flexing of the muscles in her thighs, buttocks, abdomen and shoulders. *El Colibrí* pulled the rope of hair downward and back, exposing her throat.

This is where it all ends, she thought. The blade of the knife glinted in Cassandra's peripheral vision and her fear whipped into panic like a flock of sparrows beating the air when a cat's hypnotic movements spring into teeth and claws.

The knife glided not to her throat, but to the back of her neck, and she felt its motion sawing and pulling at her hair. The panic eased into a different mix of fear and confusion. In a few seconds, the tugging was gone and Cassandra let her head fall forward until her chin rested against her breastbone. Curiously, the back of her neck felt even more naked than the rest of her body. Then, once again, she felt the knife. The cold flat of the blade at the nape of her neck pressured her to bend forward until her hands hit the dirt and she rested on all fours. She had the feeling that *El Colibrí* wasn't so much threatening her with the knife as *talking* to her with it.

Cassandra examined the shape of her hands against the stable floor – tanned, slender, strong … and helpless. She felt the urge to cry, but she fought it back. *El Colibrí* dropped to one knee beside and behind her. Then, again, she felt the knife. So smooth as to be almost intangible and yet, at the same time utterly present, the blade slipped in between her thighs just above the knees. She yielded to its sideways pressure, taking weight on her arms and sliding her left knee across the dirt floor until her legs were parted and she could feel the cool evaporation of perspiration between them. *El Colibrí* knelt between her calves. He placed his left hand against the small of her back, let her bear some of his weight, reached over and around her and laid the knife gently in the dirt next to Cassandra's right hand.

As she listened to the unbuckling of *El Colibrí*'s belt, she considered the knife. It was hers for the taking; a gift, a temptation, a test. She considered her changing options as *El Colibrí*'s fatigues, complete with belt and holstered pistol, hit the stable floor around his knees. The revolutionary leader stroked his erection and docked it in the shallow groove between her labia. Cassandra felt dry inside, arid.

"Take the knife," said *El Colibrí*. She clutched it in her fist. "The knife," he said, "is your lover."

Then *El Colibrí*, with his hands on her hips, pulled himself into her. She clenched her fists hard as he drove forward, paused to overcome the friction of her dry vagina, then drove again more deeply. Cassandra squeezed the hilt of the knife. Every muscle in her body was tensed. She was a sprinter in the blocks, a cat dug in and ready to spring. In that moment of power she had a choice; take control or yield it. *El Colibrí* held himself deep inside her. Seconds passed as Cassandra struggled with a storm of confusion. Then, in resolution of the current moment, she relaxed her arms and let her upper body roll forward until her breasts brushed against the dirt and her cheek rested against her left biceps. Her body released a sudden flow of lubrication, and only then did *El Colibrí* begin the motion that mounted eventually to an explosive ejaculation.

She remained on the floor with her face down and eyes closed until she heard his footsteps leave the stable. When she opened her eyes, the light had flattened into dusk and the stable floor was empty.

Her clothes were gone. The long hank of her hair was gone. The knife remained in her fist. She stood up, dusted herself off and walked naked back to the house. Neither Rita nor Luisa looked directly at Cassandra as she walked through the kitchen. She ran a hot shower and stood under it until the water started to cool.

Folded on her bed as she emerged from the bathroom was a set of combat fatigues, and nested atop the fatigues, like a jewel in a case, lay a compact semi-automatic pistol. Next to it all, with one corner caught under the stack of fatigues, lay a large envelope. Cassandra picked it up and shook the contents into her hand. There were photocopies of two documents written in German and a single black and white photograph. The photo was somewhat grainy, but two images were unmistakable. One was *El Colibrí*. The other person, shaking his hand in front of a familiar mountain backdrop, was her brother. The scene was difficult to assimilate at first. What did it mean?

She set the photo aside and considered the two documents. Their meaning was clear enough. One was the death certificate of a young German soldier named Oswald Ganz, killed in battle at Alsace-Lorraine. The other was a missing-person report on an equally young clerk in the Nazi SS. His name, Wilhelm Schmidt, was unfamiliar, but his face was not. It was true, she thought. Her Daddy. A history drenched in blood, privilege rooted in evil. Shame surrounded and crushed her like a mountain of rock, compressing the grief in her heart until it crystallized into a seed of rage.

Again she picked up the photo. Did her brother really know *El Colibrí*? Could he be a secret sympathizer with the revolution? Suddenly she remembered his call to her just before the bombing at *TelePerú*. He knows, she thought. Alex knows. Alex understands.

Sanchez leaned back against the car door and the seat, with one foot on the center hump, admiring one side, then the other, of his stainless steel revolver. I sat slumped in the passenger seat and looked as furtively as I could from the gun to the door of Doña Rosario's house and back to the gun again. From the house, I had produced my passport and my letter from the National Institute of Peruvian Culture, but I had given up hoping for any good to come of either. Sanchez gave them a disdainful look and tossed them on the dashboard.

Doña Rosario opened the door a crack, peered out, and then quickly closed it again.

"You know, *Señor* Young, I have worked in the sierra for a long time, in one fucking backwater after another. And do you know who pisses me off more than anybody? It's not the *terrucos*. Oh, the *comunistas* scare me all right, but I don't despise them. It's not the criminals either. You want to know who it is?"

I didn't.

"It's the *chingados antropólogos*. They come here with their notebooks and their cameras as if they were studying animals in a zoo. They cozy up to whichever peasants spew the biggest doses of horse shit and they slurp it up like hungry dogs. Eventually the *idiotas* are dressing in peasant clothes, wearing rubber-tire sandals and chewing coca as if it was their path to enlightenment. Ah, well," he sighed. "There's no law against being a fucking *pendejo*."

He deliberately rolled the chamber of his revolver, one click at a time.

"There are other laws, however," he continued. "Why did you not register at the precinct in Ayacucho?"

"Register?" The rules of my existence here were about to change.

"Every foreign resident is required to register with the *policía*. Surely you knew that."

"I'm sorry, I ..."

"You are in violation of the law. Officially I'm required to take you in." I felt the beginning pangs of nausea as I listened. "However, we may be able to avoid such unpleasantness."

"That would be my preference," I said. "How do we do it?"

"Being the paragon of Christian mercy that I am, I might be willing to take your information and register for you. It would save you a dangerous trip. Frankly, for a *gringo* to be on the road in the sierra these days is foolhardy. Of course there is a fee involved."

Gringo tax. "How much?" Sanchez replied with a figure that was the equivalent of about a hundred American dollars. I let my breath out in a controlled stream. "That seems pretty steep."

"You would prefer to become acquainted with the jail in Ayacucho?"

"For that amount, I'll need to go to the bank."

Sanchez pulled the car to the curb next to Banco Europa and killed the engine. "Cash," he sneered.

I approached the bank's one and only teller window. The teller, a small, dark-complexioned girl in a plain cotton dress, was the same one who had taken my deposit just after my arrival. I withdrew the cash for Sanchez. In a small office at the back of the bank I caught a glimpse of a very large man just as the door was being closed. The silhouette was unmistakable. As I signed for the money I asked the teller, "Who is the big man in the office?"

"Who? *Señor* Ruíz? He works for *Señor* Ganz."

"Who is *Señor* Ganz?" I asked. For some reason I couldn't pinpoint, the name rang a bell.

"You don't know of him? This is his bank."

"You mean he manages the branch?"

"No," she giggled. "The whole bank. *Es el presidente*. He lives in el Valle del Cóndor."

The teller put the cash in an envelope but I took it back out and returned the envelope with my thanks. I wanted this transaction to be visible. With the cash open in my hand, I walked to the passenger window of Sanchez's car. There was no way I was going to climb back in if I could avoid it. Now that I knew he was interested more in money than in my imminent demise, I felt emboldened. With some obvious effort, the detective moved to the center of the bench seat, leaned over and rolled down the window. I handed him the cash.

"Thanks for the help, Detective. Do I get a receipt?"

"Don't be funny, *gringo*. By the way, there is one other thing. I seriously doubt that *Señora* Flores is licensed to run a boarding house. My guess is that you would prefer not to see her fined or yourself placed out in the street. Luckily for you, I am willing to collect the license fees. It will be fifty American dollars a month. No need to deliver it. I know where to find you. Don't be making trouble for these people, *gringo.*" A thin smile flickered across his face as he drove away.

A few days later, I had a more pleasant encounter. I'd just finished my standard breakfast of *pan*, *queso fresco* (a salty, white semi-soft farmer cheese that I convinced the *Señora* to add to the menu), bologna and instant coffee, and Doña Rosario was pushing Enrique toward the door. I'd recently developed the habit of walking Enrique to school. The school year was near to an end for the summer months and I wanted to help motivate him to stay with it. For the last week or so, he had become morose about school. He dragged his feet in the morning, picked at his breakfast and generally resisted getting ready. I assumed that having the *gringo antropólogo* in the house had been a distraction for the inquisitive eight-year-old, one that competed seriously with grammar school.

"What will you be studying in school today?" I asked Enrique as we walked.

"*¿Quién sabe?*" Who knows? "Usually it's a little math, a little reading. Whatever the teacher decides. But today we have our visiting teacher."

"Oh?"

"*La Señorita* Castro. She comes from el Valle del Cóndor. She teaches us about history." We rounded the corner in front of the school at the same moment as a black Land Rover pulled to the curb. "Look. There she is now." He brightened.

Morning sun glared off the windshield, making the occupants invisible. Obviously, Enrique had previous experience linking this upscale vehicle with his visiting teacher. I watched as the passenger door opened. I took special note of the shapely legs that emerged and then of the lithe figure that completed the picture of Miss Castro.

"*¡Hola, señorita!*" cried Enrique.

"*Buenos días*, Enrique." Then, after a brief pause and a glance in my direction, she asked, "Who is your friend?"

"This is Mister Sam Young." Enrique took care to get the correct English pronunciation of my name with its non-Spanish vowel sounds. "He's an anthropologist from the United States. He lives with me and Doña Rosario."

Everything about her seemed to sparkle. Her smile was perhaps the only genuinely friendly gesture I had received from anyone, apart from Pedro and Enrique, since coming to Santa Rosita. "I'm Luz Castro," she said. "I'm pleased to meet you."

"The pleasure is all mine," I replied.

She held her smile for longer than seemed necessary for the sake of politeness then turned her attention to the interior of the Land Rover. "Thanks, Manolito. See you this afternoon." She closed the door with a clunk that I recognized immediately. As the Rover rolled forward and away, I glanced at the driver. It was the same big man from the bank and, so it seemed, from the street fair and the *plaza de armas* as well. Luz turned back to Enrique and extended a hand. "Shall we go in, young man?"

I watched them enter the cement schoolhouse hand in hand, and suddenly, out of nowhere, I felt hit by a jolt of deep joy mixed with sadness. I don't remember ever feeling these kinds of emotional spikes before coming to Peru. Anyway, I took my time walking back to the *pensión*, wondering about the relationship between Luz Castro and the big man, Manolito, who seemed to have a spooky interest in me. And why was that? Did it have something to do with the bank? It made no sense.

When I returned to the house, Doña Rosario was waiting for me in the kitchen. She held a dishtowel, twisting and wringing it with her gnarled hands, even though the dishes had already been dried and put away. Her face looked pained, but behind the pain there was stony resolution.

"*¿Señora ...?*"

"*Siéntese, por favor.*" I sat. "*Ay, Señor* Sam. How do I tell you this? Yesterday afternoon I had a visit from Enrique's teacher."

"Okay …"

"She says that Enrique's friends are avoiding him. They turn their backs as if he is not there."

"What? Did she say why?" I was shocked.

"*Ay, Dios mío*, she says it is because of you." Her narrowed eyes were unwavering. Her hands, with their bloodless knots of knuckles squeezing the dishrag, oscillated like tuning forks. "First you bring the *policía*, and now this."

"I'm sorry, *Señora*."

"He's sorry," she said in the direction of heaven. Then, relaxing her posture, she reached into her apron pocket and pulled out an envelope. "This is for you," she said. "It came this morning."

There was no return address, but I thought I recognized the handwriting on the envelope. I carried it into my room and sat down on my bed to read it.

Dear Sam, it began. *I'm sorry it has taken me so long to answer your letter. I have been away from campus for a while. I don't want to go into the details right now, but it has to do with my own field work, which, I am afraid, has become very demanding.* Field work? You never mentioned field work. What are you studying? *I suppose these days I am not exactly the fun loving girl you remember.* Why? Are you really okay? *You must know, however, that my feelings for you are warm and strong. Don't give up on me. Maybe, if fate is kind, we will be able to get back to that happy place we shared.* She had signed it, *Besitos.*

I read it again. I imagined a care-worn Marivela struggling with problems in her work, whatever it may be, and it made me sad. But it also helped me to see my own difficulties with a little more perspective. Mostly, though, her letter underscored how little I really knew about her and how fragile was our basis for a relationship, regardless of how passionately we had bonded in two wonderful days.

Still bothered by what Doña Rosario had said about Enrique, I dropped in on Father Pedro at the chapel. I found him replacing candles at the altar of the Virgin. "*Hola, Padre.*"

"*¿Qué tal,* Sam?"

"You mean other than being a magnet for dirty cops and an all-round failure as an anthropologist? Not so bad."

The priest mostly suppressed a smile. "And Enrique?"

"I don't know. He's fine when he's with me ... maybe a little less energetic than usual. Doña Rosario says that his classmates are ostracizing him at school." Pedro looked at me with raised eyebrows and waited for me to continue. "She seems to think it has something to do with me."

He nodded thoughtfully and turned away from the altar.

"What do you think?" I asked.

"I'm not sure. The townspeople, schoolchildren included, are a superstitious lot, not very modern in their thinking. You are an unknown quantity and, therefore, an object of suspicion. It could be jealousy. It could be fear. I wouldn't worry too much about it unless it gets much worse."

I nodded. I had thought, or hoped, that Enrique would be my ticket to acceptance in the community. Now it appeared I was having the opposite effect on him. No wonder Mercedes Marquez gave me such a wide berth. Shit, I thought. Things are just getting worse. I decided to change the subject.

"I met someone today, a schoolteacher. Perhaps you know her, Luz Castro? From … where did Enrique say? El Valle del Cóndor?" The priest gave a show of recognition and disapproval.

"What is it? What's wrong?"

"El Valle del Cóndor," he said, "is the domain of Alejandro Ganz de la Vega."

"Who is this Ganz? What can you tell me about him?"

He raised his eyes and appeared to be looking off into space somewhere above and behind me. The solemn, angular priest stood that way, reflecting, for just long enough to make me wonder if he was going to answer me or not.

"Mostly what everybody else already knows. For starters, that he is very rich and very powerful. Educated in the United States. When his father died, he took over the family business; interests in banking, imports and exports, and God knows what else."

"What's his connection to Santa Rosita?"

"Historically, his family owned it. There is still an *hacienda* up in el Valle del Cóndor. We don't see too much of him. I think he mostly flies in and out. He seems to like his privacy. I believe he employs many people from this area."

"Doing what?"

"Working the coca fields."

I knew that, officially, coca was illegal to grow and distribute, but it was deeply rooted in the Andes, both literally and figuratively. It was central to the life and rituals of the *campesinos*, and, of course, it held tremendous potential for profit in the international cocaine trade.

"And Ganz is involved in the cocaine business?"

Pedro took a deep breath and exhaled through billowed cheeks before answering.

"With growing the leaf, yes," he said. "With the production of the paste, probably. With the finished product and exportation, who can say? It's definitely something we're better off not knowing. Or talking about, for that matter. Mr Ganz strikes me as a dangerous man, and yet …" His voice trailed off.

"And yet?"

"Oh, nothing. Ganz and his kind live in one world, Sam, and I live in another. They are like parallel universes that do not often touch. When they do, it can be good or it can be disastrous. But it is never likely to be predictable."

"Hmm. The big man, Manolo, do you know him?"

"I've seen him in town. He takes care of Mr Ganz's business here in the sierra. He's the most obvious reason to stay out of Mr Ganz's business, if you ask me."

"And the teacher, Luz Castro?"

"Mr Ganz's business."

In the back left side of the chauffeured Mercedes-Benz rode a gray-templed man in fatigues. Next to him sat Cassandra, also in fatigues but with the added peculiarity of a small handbag hanging from a slender strap over her right shoulder. She leaned slightly into the older man, rested her left hand gently on his right thigh and gave him an adoring look. As he returned her gaze, she slipped her right hand into the purse.

Ahead of the Benz, from between two parked cars, a baby carriage lurched onto the roadway. The driver braked hard, pulling the two passengers forward in the seat. Cassandra gave a gasp, as if she were startled, leaned farther into her male companion and brought her right hand up to his chest. With a pistol barrel pressed firmly into his solar plexus, she pulled the trigger. Then she brought the gun swiftly to the driver's head and squeezed again.

Before the car had stopped completely, she had rolled out the door into a somersault. At the same time, four men appeared out of nowhere with machine guns and began to spray the car deafeningly. Cassandra sprang to her feet and sprinted a few yards before she turned around and calmly joined the gunmen, the driver, the other passenger and *Comandante* Rita in a semi-circle. The carriage, three cars and several traffic pylons laid out a street scene in the middle of the riding arena at Cassandra's Puerta del Sol property.

"Well done," said Rita. "We will continue to practice this and the other variations until every movement is second nature. Comrade Amador," she spoke to the gray-templed man and the driver. "You and Pablo put the cars back in the livery. Comrade Sandra, come with me. The rest of you take two laps of the bridle path and clean your weapons."

Cassandra brushed the dust from her fatigues and smiled inwardly at the feel of her own firm musculature beneath. Never had she felt so fit, so purposeful, so *good.* The ninety days of her bargain with *El Colibrí* had not yet expired, but she had made her choice. She would be a soldier in the struggle for a new Peru, a free and just Peru for all its people. As Cassandra saw it, the revolution was essentially a militant and overdue feminism. The worlds of Peruvian business and government were all-male clubs, at least at any level where she would choose to participate. But here in the *Camino Rojo*, the women carried guns right alongside the men. Women who were fit for it had positions of command and strategy.

Moreover, Cassandra believed she had found a special calling in the *Camino.* With her access to resources and her personal connections, she could offer things to the struggle that the more rag-tag rank-and-file soldiers could not. One of the things she could offer was the horse ranch as a training arena and sometime barracks that was both close to Lima and safe from detection. Her mother, Pilar, had not been near the ranch since Cassandra took up residence there, and Alex was too busy and too respectful of her privacy to show up unbidden or unannounced.

Importantly, she also believed her choice would have Alex's full support – she had seen photographic evidence – and yet *Comandante* Rita had forbidden her to talk to him about it. "The survival of the revolution depends on the separation of its cells," she explained. "The personnel and activities of one cell must be kept secret from all the others. Anything else creates a house of cards. To violate that principle is to betray the revolution. And to betray the revolution is death." Cassandra understood the logic. One cell might be captured, even destroyed, but it would have no links to other cells. There could be no informing, even under the pressure of torture, where there was no knowledge.

"What should I tell my brother when he calls to check up on me?" Cassandra had asked.

Rita had shrugged. "Make something up."

Cassandra's story, which she later told not only to Alex but also to her about-to-be-ex boss at *TelePerú*, was that she was going to spend her time writing a novel. It would be a good way to stay productive and keep her mind occupied, she explained.

"What's it about?" Alex had asked her.

"I'm sort of thinking," she had replied a little coquettishly, "of a romantic thriller set in the entertainment industry."

Once the men had dispersed from the training session, the two women walked side by side to the ranch house. "You are coming along nicely, Comrade Sandra. You take to the training well."

"Thank you, *Comandante*."

"My question is whether you would be able to do the same with bullets and a real target." Cassandra thought she could. She found it easy, in her private musings, to imagine herself and her brother as secret heroes and *patrones* of the revolution.

I have love, or something like it, on the brain. If I had to categorize it, I guess I'd have to call it some kind of erotic homesickness. With a combination of paper shims and candle wax, I have managed to fix my wooden bed frame so it doesn't squawk like a henhouse when I masturbate. Which I do with near-desperate frequency lately, to my mental images of Marivela Santiana and my imaginings about Mercedes Marquez and more recently, Luz Castro.

Ever since I got to Peru, I've found the women very attractive. Let's not put too fine a point on it … I'm dying for some female companionship here. I find myself falling in lust practically every day. Not only with knockout beauties like Mercedes, who by the way makes my heart flop around like a fresh-caught trout in the bottom of a rowboat, but also with *chicas campesinas*. The younger ones, and even many of the older ones, have lithe, strong bodies from lives of physical activity. Their faces, with their high, wide cheekbones, deep brown eyes and straight, strong noses, project this incredible dignity, even in poverty, that I find very appealing. More than just dignity. Bellicosity. They look like warriors. Mercedes has that look, although softened by some European stock. Marivela has it in spades. It's easy to imagine Marivela wielding a war club or an automatic rifle. Luz Castro is different. She appears to have some African genes as well as European, Inca and maybe even Asian. In her, I see a sweet sensuality that fits her schoolteacher persona beautifully. I assume she must be some kind of ward of *Señor* Ganz.

Of all the women in my album of possibilities, Marivela has been the most approachable. Last night, I decided to write her another letter.

Dear Marivela,

Hello again from Santa Rosita. I hope you are well. I think about you often. I too have found serious challenges in my field work. To be truthful, it has been much harder than I thought it would be. The people from the countryside are often frightened of me. I can't seem to find any common ground from which to communicate with them. Many of the townspeople are friendly on the surface. Certainly, they are curious to know more about me and about the United States. However, except for the town priest, none of them are willing to talk about their private lives or even to share their opinions. I have yet to be invited into anyone's home. The only home I have been in (other than the one where I live) belonged to an old woman I visited with the priest. I think I scared her half to death. Apparently the pishtaco myth is still pretty strong here.

I have a good living situation. I room with an elderly widow and her adopted 'grandson' Enrique. Enrique and I get along great, but sometimes I think the señora has her doubts about having a gringo in the household.

What have you been doing lately? Where are you exactly in your studies? We never really talked about your work. I'd like to know more. Please write again when you get a chance.

Affectionately, Sam

In her last letter, Marivela had signed with kisses. For my closing, I deliberated between 'Sincerely' (too cold), and 'With Love' (maybe a little too hot), and finally decided on 'Affectionately'. It was Goldilocks' Baby Bear solution.

The next day I got a letter from Alfredo Ramirez. It was, by far, his strongest expression of interest in my work to date.

Dear Sam,

Your last report was very interesting. I have heard of Alejandro Ganz. Have you met him? Seen him? He is, indeed, a mysterious character. The effects a man of his wealth and importance have on a place like Santa Rosita must be significant. I think it is imperative that you learn as much as you can about him and his relationship to the town. It may be impossible to grasp the underlying cultural forces at work in the town otherwise. Keep me informed.

Best Regards, Fredo

"Come in, Manolito." Alex Ganz sat at the desk in his study in el Valle del Cóndor. He had just returned from several days in Lima and Manolo was there to brief him on the state of affairs in the sierra. "What's new?"

"There has been some sabotage," reported Manolo. "An equipment shed in the upper section of the *San Mateo* fields. We lost a lot of our processing chemicals. It was dynamite." The upper reaches of jungle across the mountains from el Valle del Cóndor contained some of the most profitable coca fields in the world. "No one knows for sure who did it, but the foreman's dog was found hanged in a tree. Trademark *Camino Rojo*. If it wasn't the *terrucos*, then someone wants us to think it was."

This was a message, thought Ganz. They are upping the stakes.

"Were any of our people hurt?" asked Ganz.

"One man, a campesino called Benito Quispe, was killed."

"The body?"

"Recognizable."

Ganz nodded. "Good. See that *Señor* Quispe is returned to his family. Once that is done, have Indio deliver our condolences, along with twenty thousand *soles* and two kilos of coca leaves." The gift would replace Benito Quispe's normal wages for more than a year.

"What else?" asked Ganz.

"Some kind of meeting between the American and the cop, Sanchez. They showed up at the bank in Sanchez's car. The American withdrew cash, handed it over to the cop. The cop drove away."

"Hmm. All right. What of the lady doctor?"

"Nothing new. At night, she's been staying in her usual place."

"Good. Anything else?"

"Nothing really, except ..."

"Yes?" prompted Ganz.

"Well, the *campesinos* are talking drought." Ganz nodded, a signal that Manolo should elaborate. Without constant prodding, it was difficult to get more than one sentence at a time out of the big man. "There has been some moisture this spring, enough for normal planting, but the summer rains are late. The farmers fear for the potato crops."

"And the coca?"

"Stressed," said Manolo. "Not as much new growth as usual."

"I see. Thank you."

When Ganz was alone again, he closed the study door. Rolling back the Persian rug, he revealed a trapdoor in the hardwood floor. Beneath it, set into reinforced concrete, was a safe. He dialed the combination that only he knew and withdrew a set of handwritten ledgers that recorded the costs, revenues and projections for his coca plantations across the mountains at the upper edge of the jungle. He studied them, made some calculations in his mind, then locked them back away and replaced the rug.

With determined strides, he walked from the study to the front parlor. From a drawer in the sideboard where he kept the selection of liquor for guests, he took out a flat, leather-covered case. Inside lay a .357 magnum revolver with an eight-inch barrel. The custom-made pistol was heavy, but beautifully balanced, and fit his hand perfectly. He emptied a handful of shells from another box into his jacket pocket and left the house.

A dry afternoon breeze licked at blades of grass with their browning points and edges. The sun cut broad swathes through high clouds that carried no rain. Ganz held the pistol in a loose grip as he cut across the field to a spot not far from the guardhouse where the stony mountainside gave way to a soft dirt bank. Rising from the ground in front of the dirt bank was a grayed wooden post with cracks running up its sides and across the top. Digging into his pants pocket, he took out an assortment of coins. Spacing them well apart, he wedged the coins into the narrower cracks in the post so that most of each coin was still visible. As he walked away from the post, he flicked off the safety.

At a distance of about twenty meters, he turned, raised the pistol, took a bead on a bright, silver-colored coin and squeezed the trigger. The coin simply ceased to be there. He squeezed again and another coin disappeared. Again, and another. Again and again, coins disappeared from the post as the sharp crack from the pistol echoed across the valley. Each time he emptied the cylinder, he ejected the shells and reloaded. He fired with very few misses until all the coins were gone, then he carried a handful of spent brass cartridges to the post and lined them up across the top. Backing away from the post he cleaned it of shells as neatly as a child plucking petals from a daisy.

When the shooting stopped, Juan Pablo made his way to the entrance of the house and stood inside the door. A few moments later, Ganz came through the door and placed the pistol in Juan Pablo's hands. The manservant would clean and oil the gun, reload it and return it to its case. All this would happen without any need for instruction. It was a ritual they had enacted many times over the years.

Back in his study, Alex placed a call to a number that he had been required to memorize. The man who answered the phone was the first point of contact in a chain of communication that led, at length, to Miguel Fortuna. The familiar voice answered after one ring. "*Diga*," it said. Go ahead.

Alex spoke the words that meant he desired a meeting with *El Colibrí*. The voice answered only, "I understand," and the line went dead. Now Ganz would have to wait. How long he couldn't know, maybe two days, maybe a week, maybe longer. Eventually a note would arrive in his Santa Rosita post office box and it would contain either a refusal or the particulars of a time and a place.

Things just aren't getting any better, I thought. People should be used to me by now. It's like I'm a leper. A goddamn pariah. I have a pretty good sense of life in Santa Rosita from the sheer amount of my observation and from my accumulated conversations with Pedro, Enrique and, to a lesser extent, *Doña* Rosario and Mercedes. But most of the townspeople still keep me at arm's length and regard me with suspicion. And the *campesinos* at the *feria*? Forget it. I might as well be a ghost.

Up until yesterday, I was feeling almost ready to give up on this project, admit defeat to Jack Bentley and start my dissertation research again, or not, on a totally new topic somewhere else. Today, however, a letter from Marivela lifted my spirits.

My Dearest Sam,

Thank you for your letter. I also think of you often. Do not worry so much, Cariño. You are much too handsome to be a pishtaco. I'll bet those serrana *women are all over you, and you are just afraid to tell me so. Just thinking about it makes me feel jealous! As to the difficulties you are having, I think you must just be a little patient. Things will get easier. I am sure of it.*

You ask about my work. I am involved in what you might call 'applied anthropology'. I am working in the shantytowns with poor people from the sierra to help them develop skills to cope with the difficulties of urban life. Some of it is political organizing and dealing with bureaucracy for things like access to water or public transportation. Such a struggle it is!

By the way, Fredo is very interested in your findings. Write again soon, and don't you dare come to Lima without seeing me!

Kisses, Marivela

Okay. I think she likes me. I had my doubts, but I've read the letter several times and … she definitely likes me. Be a little patient, she said. She's right. In the meantime, I just have to lower my expectations for what I can learn from the *campesinos* directly and rely more heavily on what I can observe and learn from more approachable sources.

Thank God for Pedro Buenaventura. I don't know whether he treats me so well because his religion requires it or because he feels a genuine affinity with me. Pedro is my sole confidant. You might say he has become my father confessor, except that I offer no penance and he offers no absolution. My agnosticism keeps religion out of the relationship.

The days are getting warm enough to sit outside comfortably in the evening, as I did this evening, sipping *pisco* with the *padre*. We sat in the walled garden adjacent to the chapel. Along the walls, I noticed flowers blooming that weren't there a week ago.

"It's starting to feel like summer," I remarked. "When does the rainy season start around here?"

"Usually, it has started by now. The farmers are getting a little restless."

"Does this delay their planting?"

"They've already planted. No, all they can do now is wait and hope. And pray. Attendance here at the chapel has gone up in the last couple of weeks."

As usual, I used Pedro as a dumpster for my frustrations about my work. He listened patiently. I think I hoped he would come up with some kind of magical solution to my problems. Or even a hard-won practical solution. It's not as if I was completely stymied. Some of the people in town now would at least give me the time of day. Mothers didn't latch on protectively to their children when I passed in the street. Once in a while, I could even coax a smile out of someone. A few people, primarily *mistis*, even expressed interest in who I was, where I had come from and why I was here. But to get two words out of anyone about the *terroristas* or the *sinchis* proved to be next to impossible.

I asked Pedro about that, too.

"It's fear, Sam. Pure and simple. Even though we've experienced no incursions by the *Rojistas* here in Santa Rosita, everyone here knows someone – a father, an uncle, a sister-in-law – who has been killed by one side or the other. The problem is that you never know who's a *Rojista* or who might be an informer for the *sinchis*. It could be your neighbor. It could be your own brother. It could be the man sitting half-drunk in the corner of the bar.

"When a patrol of the *Camino Rojo* comes into a village to provision, they force people to make a show of support for the revolution. Sometimes, they ask for denunciations of government sympathizers. In every village, there are people who hold old grudges or who like to gossip. Those who are denounced receive what the *Rojistas* like to call the Justice of the people." Pedro drew a long, bony index finger across his throat.

"Jesus."

"It is no different with the *sinchis*. The *policía* also have their informers. Anyone accused of helping the *Rojistas*, even if they did it at gunpoint, receives a death sentence, probably for his whole family."

"No wonder people are so tight-lipped."

The word 'revolution' seemed less romantic to me the more I came to understand its implications among the people of Ayacucho.

With my work going practically nowhere, I had begun to dwell more on the events that had brought me to Peru in the first place. In particular, I had been thinking a lot about my family, especially Mitch.

"*Padre*," I asked, "what is your take on homosexuality?"

"As a priest? Or as a person?"

"Is there a difference?"

After some thought, during which I began to repent of the question, Pedro answered, "The priesthood is a good place to sublimate questions of sexuality. I think some of our finest priests arrive at their faith by making love to God as a means to resist their natural urges toward their fellow men."

"Do you believe it's a sin?"

"The disposition? Certainly not. The practice? I'm not sure. Against the church it is a sin, but before God? Who can say? I prefer to believe that God loves all people just as he created them." Pedro set his glass of *pisco* on the table and leaned forward slightly. "Why do you ask?"

Suddenly, the pregnant silence of that moment was interrupted by a squeal of brakes, a slam and a rattle that both of us recognized. The thread of our conversation hung dangling, and I felt relieved. Mercedes found her way into the garden having already become the center of attention.

"Oh," she said. "Am I interrupting something?"

"No!" We exclaimed in unison, and Pedro offered her a shot of *pisco*.

"Thanks, I'd love some. As the *padre* fetched a third glass, an awkward silence prevailed between Mercedes and me. Pedro returned and poured her a sturdy shot. She took a sip, set the glass down and spoke again with a solemn tone.

"I'm afraid I have some bad news. I've come from visiting Antonia Quispe. There has been a death. It was Benito."

"Benito? How?" asked the *padre*.

"An accident. Or something. Involving dynamite."

"Dynamite?"

"It happened in the *selva*. They are saying it looks like *Camino Rojo*."

"I don't understand," I said, hoping to be brought into the conversation.

Both Pedro and Mercedes looked at me with a kind of tolerant consideration that underscored my status as an outsider. Mercedes seemed reluctant to elaborate, but Father Pedro filled me in.

"Benito worked in the coca fields, probably for *Señor* Ganz. Many of the local men do. It gives them a cash income they probably couldn't earn otherwise." He hesitated as if looking for the right words to continue. "There are certain … um … non-agricultural dangers that come with the work, especially since the so-called international war on drugs has made its way here."

"Non-agricultural dangers?" I echoed.

"Yes. Well, the *narcotraficantes* have land, crops, factories, workers and a lot of money. The *terroristas* have men and guns."

"I get it."

"Anyway," said Mercedes, "there is a funeral tomorrow at the Huaynatambo cemetery."

"I'd like to go," I blurted. "I mean, if I could."

Mercedes cast a glance from me to the priest. It looked as if she was about to say something but decided to bite her tongue.

Father Pedro nodded to her then turned to me. "I don't see that it would do any harm for you to come and pay your respects."

The mood was dark and I began to feel uncomfortable, as though maybe I had transgressed my bounds. No one seemed inclined to say anything, least of all me. Finally, it was Mercedes who broke the silence. "Sam, if you are going to a *campesino* funeral, there are some things you'll have to know first." I must have lit up like a lamp when she said that. She took a long, perturbed breath. Obviously, she was less enthusiastic than I was about the prospect of an elementary lesson in peasant funerals

She retrieved a small cloth bag from her van and rejoined me and the priest in the garden. "You don't need to," she said, "but if you want them to accept you, then you might consider bringing a gift of coca leaves and chewing with them." Pedro excused himself and Mercedes instructed me in the basic manner of coca sharing. I had read about the ritual in journal articles, but seeing a demonstration was entirely different. It felt like a major breakthrough in my field work. Mercedes could be an extremely valuable informant for my research, and this was the first sign I'd had of her willingness to discuss local customs with me.

Thrilled at the prospect of being included in an important Quechua rite of passage, I had slept poorly that night. Through much of it I tossed and turned, trying to imagine what the funeral would be like. In addition, I wondered what to expect from chewing coca leaves. I knew not to expect the intense rush produced by cocaine. I knew that coca chewing was common among the *campesinos*. I had even seen men, typically men carrying obscenely heavy loads strapped to their backs, like Quechuan moving vans, with lips stained green from the leaf. I also knew that *mistis*, or even *campesinos* with aspirations of acceptance into the ways and economy of town life, looked down on the practice as vulgar and uneducated. My personal bias as an anthropologist leaned toward … hell, why lay the jargon on it? I was jazzed. I was pumped. This was Major Major with no apologies to Joseph Heller.

In the morning, Mercedes, Pedro Buenaventura and I took the ambulance seven kilometers over one of the roughest roads I have ever seen to the village of Huaynatambo. Although I had walked part of the way in my ramblings, I had never entered the village. I offered to pay for gas and Mercedes declined, saying without a trace of sarcasm that I had done enough already. I offered Pedro the passenger seat and sat on a cot in the back. The cot had a thin mattress and was attached to the steel side of the van with welded-on hinges. I guessed that this was where Mercedes slept, at least occasionally. Probably it folded up against the wall to make space for an examining room during inclement weather.

From Huaynatambo, we hiked three kilometers to the tiny

cemetery where Benito Quispe was being buried. The narrow path ascended to the top of a bald, isolated peak. It was the warmest day I had yet experienced in the Andes. By the time we reached the summit, I was hot and sticky with perspiration and carrying my jacket. The cemetery lay in the center of the hilltop, inside a low wall constructed without mortar from uncut native stone. The graves were untended. Adobe headstones were cracked and worn and the older graves were being swallowed by the earth's natural processes. A small group of people huddled around a fresh mound.

As instructed, I waited at the gate while Mercedes and the priest approached the funeral party, which consisted of Gabriela and Antonia Quispe and several others I assumed were also from Huaynatambo. These would be extended family of the deceased. As they conferred in quiet tones, I watched and ran my fingers absentmindedly around the edges of the folded cloth pouch I was carrying. The pouch contained whole coca leaves that Mercedes had given me.

I watched as the group relaxed from the bent-forward positions they had adopted for the serious business of discussing me, the outsider at the gate. Pedro Buenaventura looked over his shoulder and gave me a nod that indicated the invitation to join them. In contrast to funerals I had attended in the Catholic and Protestant traditions, this gathering seemed, on the surface, unstructured and without obvious ritual. There was quiet conversation among some of the adults. Antonia stood silently and bobbed her head in a slow rhythm as if she were hearing a private dirge.

One gnarled old man – I figured him for at least seventy – wove wildflowers into a circle, creating a sort of soft wreath. A younger man had bound two sticks together to form a cross, which he planted at the head of the grave. The old man completed his ring of flowers and handed it to Gabriela with a solemn gesture. She draped it over the cross so that it hung in arcs both front and back. The doubled crescents gave me the impression of a boat or a vessel capable of sailing toward heaven, or perhaps of catching and holding blessings from above.

The priest crossed himself and uttered a short prayer commending the soul of Benito Quispe to the Father, the Son and the Holy Ghost. The younger man took out a bottle of *trago*, cheap cane liquor, and passed it to the woman on his right. She drank and passed it on. When it reached the priest, he crossed himself again and took a swig. Then, I drank. The mouthful of liquid burned my throat and then my belly. I passed it to Mercedes, she to Gabriela, and so on until it completed the circle.

While the younger man drank and then corked the bottle, Mercedes reached into her cloth pouch and drew out three unbroken leaves of coca. She arranged them into what looked to me like a slightly splayed stack and presented them to Gabriela Quispe.

"*Señora*," she said, "may this *k'intu* help to ease your pain." Gabriela thanked her, blew across the leaves to share their blessing with Mother Earth, folded them into her mouth and began to chew, slowly and deliberately. Mercedes proceeded around the circle offering a triad of leaves, or *k'intu*, to each person, finishing with me. Only the priest was passed over. To me, she also offered what looked like a tiny briquette of compressed ash. As I had seen the others do, I received the gift of coca with cupped hands. Mercedes returned to her place in the circle.

I understood from my reading that the coca leaf released its stimulating alkaloids only when chewed with a bit of this ashy substance. I blew across the leaves ritually and then chewed them until they were soft and amorphous. Then I added the ash and chewed them together. I could detect no immediate psychotropic effect, but the bitter flavor of the leaves began to sweeten some.

The *trago* made its rounds again, and then Gabriela doled out *k'intus* from her own ample pouch of coca. This process continued until several of the adults, I included, had offered coca to the group and two bottles of *trago* had been exhausted. The children, Antonia and a boy of about twelve, also partook of the coca, but they did not reciprocate with *k'intus* for the group.

The circle of mourners had broken up into groups of threes and fours. Gabriela wept. Antonia stood by her side with eyes downcast and Pedro Buenaventura spoke to them in muted tones. Mercedes sat atop an old grave and spoke with the younger man and a woman I supposed to be his wife. I remained acutely aware of my outsider status as I moved from one small group to another. People acknowledged me with politeness but also with nervous confusion about why I was there and how I fitted into the scheme of things. Feeling uncomfortable, I backed away from the little islands of conversation and found a seat instead on a high point of the cemetery wall.

As the effects of the liquor and the coca progressed, I began to feel dreamy. I continued to chew the wad of coca as my gaze meandered, almost as if it belonged to someone else, down my own lengthening shadow, across the hilltop, over the valley below and on to the rugged mountains in the distance. The afternoon sun warmed my back and I drifted into a state of being that transcended cognition. The world seemed utterly foreign and, at the same time, intimately familiar and painfully beautiful. Some invisible yet almost palpable thread ran through my body and connected me with everything and everyone around me. I felt for the first time like I was part of this universe. I soaked up the blueness of the sky and inhaled the moist music of the breeze. In that moment of unusual clarity, it occurred to me that, of everything here, I knew myself least of all. I was the single darkest spot in my own understanding.

At some point in my reverie, I felt a chill at my back. The mourners had begun to move about with a nervous energy. There was Mercedes. Was she waving to me? I struggled to regain the crystalline understanding that had just visited me. There was Father Pedro, what did he want? There was the grave. And the mourners, crowding together. So far away. Were they signaling something to me? Was it time to go? What was the matter? I looked over my shoulder. Where the sky had been blue it was a wall of boiling black. It crackled with energy. I began to stand up when suddenly a flash of pure white light surrounded me, then blackness, and then nothing at all.

Part Three: The Son of Lightning

Culture is the sum of the stories we tell to make sense of our lives and our universe. An anthropologist is essentially a collector of stories. A bad anthropologist lets himself become part of the stories he collects. I was a very bad anthropologist.

– Samson Young

I am a child. It's a summer day, and I'm flying high above the earth, holding onto a box kite of balsa wood and paper in primary colors. Far below me, I see the gaiety of a rare weekend barbecue on the grassy commons of a hospital. I breathe in the smell of charred meat over mown grass. The smell draws me downward.

My dad sits in a lawn chair wearing plaid Madras swim trunks and an unbuttoned, short-sleeve shirt. He holds a can of beer and talks quietly to a neighbor. Across his belly runs a scar that looks like a raggedy railroad track. "Daddy," I say. I reach to touch the scar. He winces and turns away.

Across the lawn glides my mother wearing a white apron with tiny pink roses, a white blouse and pink pedal-pusher pants. "Mommy," I ask, "what happened to Daddy?" She turns to face me with a deep frown. She takes my wrist and it hurts. She sets me in a chair in the middle of a floor. Distant walls suddenly are closing in on us. She leans into me. Her breath is hot and her eyes intense. "I'm going to tell you a secret," she says. Her lips are moving, but I can no longer hear her voice …

And then I am older. I walk down a hallway of concrete and brick, ducking to avoid bare wires that hang from the ceiling. In the distance, I see Mitch. He stands in the hallway facing me. The look on his face is one of pain and imploring. It stops me in my tracks. Mitch turns away and begins to run, and I run after him, dodging sparking wires. A bend in the hall, and I lose sight of Mitch. I round the bend at a sprint. Suddenly the floor ends and I am fighting for balance at the edge of a deep, wide cement pit. At the bottom of the pit lie my brother and my father, spooned like lovers. Their bodies are splashed with brightly colored paints. I feel weak. Dizzy. I turn to run away, but I slip and fall …

And look up to see my mother kneeling over me in a brightly colored shawl. Her face is drawn and tired. Her teeth and lips are green. In her hand she holds a cross, but now it is not her hand …

It is my father's hand, and it holds a scalpel. He wears a white lab coat and caresses my face. He rests his hand on my chest. Then he raises the scalpel and hammers it toward my heart.

Still shaken by my dreams, I woke to a blurred vision of the face of Mercedes Marquez and to a body shot through with pain. She backed away into focus and I could see that her lips were moving. A sound like a tiny, shrill voice came from far away.

"Sam. Are you all right? Are you okay? Talk to me."

"Oohh," I groaned. "My head … my chest …"

"*Dios mío*, Sam, you were hit by lightning."

As Mercedes' words began to sink in, I became aware of the other members of the funeral party standing in a circle around me. Everyone, myself included, was soaking wet, and a rainbow stretched across the sky. My head pounded with the worst headache I'd ever had.

As I struggled to sit up, everyone in the party except Mercedes and Father Pedro gasped and stepped back. Mercedes knelt next to me and cradled my head and shoulders for support. Whatever had happened to me, that gesture made it seem worthwhile. My left hand, which I reached back to lean upon, had closed over a crude wooden cross. Gradually, I realized I was lying on top of an old grave in the process of surrender to the weeds and the weather. I yielded to the weight of my throbbing head and let my forehead rest against Mercedes' shoulder.

"Can you stand up?" she asked. Now the priest had joined her at my side. The two of them helped me to my feet.

Inside the close huddle of the family of Benito Quispe, there ran a hot current of conversation that, to me, was unintelligible. Finally, they all stopped talking and stood with heads bowed. The old man approached me. The ancient *campesino* extended his right hand with a *k'intu* of eight coca leaves. Instinctively, I cupped my hands to receive them, and the old man said in Quechua, "Bless us, *Kari Wakli-piqta*." Without understanding all the words, I bowed my head and thanked him. It seemed he was giving me some kind of blessing, or asking for one. As soon as the man had returned to the family group, the next oldest man among them approached me with the same offering and the same strange words. He was followed by each of the women, and then the children in descending order of age, until the entire funeral party had presented me with a gift of coca. Once again, they huddled together with heads deeply bowed.

I struggled to make sense of this unexpected ritual, but my aching brain thwarted me. I got no help from Mercedes or Father Pedro. The priest looked as bewildered as I felt, and Mercedes bore a look of acceptance tinged with worry and disapproval. I looked at her inquiringly over cupped hands full of coca. She took the folded coca pouch that was still tucked into my belt, unfolded it to receive the leaves, carefully wrapped them and placed them in my jacket pocket.

"Come on," she said. "We need to get you down from here. Can you walk?"

"I think so." With a hand on her shoulder for balance, I took a few careful steps. My feet were numb and I had to be careful not to stumble. Everything else seemed to work except for my head, which still throbbed mercilessly. And so with the young witch leading the way, I followed with the priest's support. We filed past the fresh grave of Benito Quispe, on to the gate and down the mountain trail to Huaynatambo. The funeral party followed behind at a respectful, or cautious, distance with the exception of the twelve-year-old boy who ran ahead of us down the trail at a pace that made me dizzy. It was a solemn parade. It took all my concentration just to maintain my footing and to keep my head from exploding.

In the village below, we found another twenty or so people standing around the ambulance – silent watchers, people who had been invisible our first time through Huaynatambo, people who wanted a glimpse of us. I heard whispers: *Kari Wakli-piqta, Kari Wakli-piqta.* I still didn't understand the phrase, but I took it to mean something about me.

On the trip back to Santa Rosita, the ambulance rode like a percussion section on a straight-axle trailer. Pedro sat on the cot in the back leaving me the passenger seat. I sat with my eyes closed, my head cradled in my hands and my elbows planted between my knees. We had to stop once for me to lean out the door and empty my stomach onto the roadside. Mostly, I phased back and forth between the clanging machinery in my head and periods of momentary relief where I actually seemed to be outside my own experience looking in. Finally with one last banshee shriek of brakes, we stopped next to the chapel.

"If you would like to come into the church," said Pedro, "I'll make us some tea."

"Tea would help," said Mercedes.

I settled into a chair in the kitchen. Father Pedro filled a teapot with a blend of chamomile and coca leaves and put water on to boil. Mercedes left the chapel and returned wearing her normal western attire and carrying a bundle of something. She handed me a towel and a blanket.

"Give me your clothes," she said. My clothes had begun to dry on my body, but they were still damp and I realized I was shivering. I stripped down to my boxers and socks, dried and wrapped the blanket around me.

"You should probably have a hot shower to warm you up," said Mercedes.

The thought of Pedro's 220-volt shower head made me shiver anew. I shook my head. "I can't take any more water and electricity tonight."

Father Pedro poured the tea around and followed it with a bowl of brown sugar crystals. The sweet tea warmed me and took the edge off my headache. I spoke first.

"What happened out there?"

Buenaventura looked to Mercedes, who remained taciturn. He shook his head as though he wasn't sure of the answer himself. "A thunderstorm came up. Quickly. We decided to get down off the mountain because of the risk of lightning. We tried to get your attention, and just as you stood up from the wall, lightning struck. I'm not sure if it hit you directly or hit the wall behind you, but … well, it was pretty spectacular. It bathed you in light and tossed you like a puppet. You seemed to be dead. No breathing. No pulse. Mercedes saved your life by pounding on your chest to kick start your heart."

"Thanks, Doc." Mercedes forced a slight smile that was at odds with the worried look in her eyes. "There's more, isn't there?"

Mercedes nodded and explained, "*Wakli,* or lightning, is a powerful god to the Quechua. It is a directed flow of the Sun God's power. You encountered *Wakli* directly and survived. That alone makes you special. But you also died and came back to life. From a grave, no less."

"Thanks to you."

"Yes. Well, the *campesinos* don't understand cardiopulmonary resuscitation. To them you are now *Kari Wakli-piqta*, the Son of Lightning. That could be a problem for them, because *Wakli* is not always a benevolent god. He is known to rampage through the fields, killing livestock and stealing potatoes. But you also happened to meet him at the precise moment of the first big summer storm. That is a very good omen."

"So the coca ..."

"*K'intus* of eight leaves," she continued. "An offering to a god."

"Goddamn!"

"Exactly," said Mercedes. "Welcome to the pantheon, Lightning God."

The sun had set while we were inside the church. Mercedes insisted that I let her check me over more thoroughly for complications from the lightning strike. She led me to her van, carrying my damp clothing, unlocked the side door and let me in. She lit a lamp that allowed us to have light without draining the van's battery and then she pulled the door shut.

"Have a seat," she said, indicating the edge of the cot. She hung my clothes over the seat backs. Then, from their place in one of two wooden footlockers, she removed her stethoscope, thermometer and blood pressure cuff. Across the other footlocker, I could see her indigenous clothing spread out to dry. I couldn't help noticing how beautiful she looked in the glow of the lamplight.

Mercedes sat next to me on the cot, shook down the mercury in the thermometer and held it to my mouth. I closed on the thermometer and rolled the bulb back and forth gently beneath my tongue. It was funny, I thought, how this simple sensation, the smooth, hard bulb, the bitter taste of alcohol, transported me back to my childhood. I would be seated on my single bed, and it would be my mother with the thermometer, not my father, even though he had been the doctor. If it was a school day, I would be willing the mercury upward. On a weekend or a holiday I would part my lips and draw air in between my teeth, hoping to cool the bulb that controlled my immediate fate.

I suffered a violent shiver as she took the thermometer away. She read it then placed her palm against my forehead. Her palm felt hot, so my forehead must have felt icy to her. She sat next to me, warmed the stethoscope between her hands and pressed it to my chest. I studied the shadows in the contours of her face and the pinpoint reflections of the lamplight in her eyes. As I felt the warm bridge of pressure from her fingertips to the heel of her palm, there was a pang in my chest that had nothing to do with CPR or lightning.

Next she knelt, lifted one of my feet gently off the floor, removed the sock and then repeated it for the other foot. "How do your feet feel?" she asked.

"Numb."

"You've got nasty burns on both. They're going to hurt when you get your feeling back. Until then, you're going to want to walk very gingerly."

I leaned over to look. My feet looked as if they had been boiled from the tops of my boot lines down to the soles. She bandaged them with clean gauze and put my socks back on to hold the dressings in place. Then she stood and began to loosen the bedding from around the pillow at the head of her cot.

"Sam, I want you to get under the covers." I slipped out of the blanket I had been wearing as a robe and in between sheets that smelled like warm earth with a hint of talc. Mercedes sat on the edge of the cot, removed her boots and outer clothing and slid in next to me.

"This is medicine," she said. "Face that way." I turned on my side, my nose and knees just barely a blanket's width from the steel sidewall of the van. Her arm closed over my ribs and chest and I felt the warmth of her body flow against mine, cupping … pressing … healing. As long as I remained awake, my thoughts buzzed around in my head like bees in a jar. With no sense of up or down, they were cordoned off from the outside world by a prison they could neither see nor comprehend. Soon, my consciousness grew dark and the bees stopped buzzing.

At the kitchen table in the rear of a safe house in Miraflores, the fugitive, ex-university professor of political science, who called himself *El Colibrí*, struck a match and lit a Marlboro cigarette. He recognized only too well the irony of his preference for an American product, given that he regarded American capitalism as the hothouse and fertilizer that nourished the abusive forces at work in Peruvian government. But it was an irony he allowed himself.

Comandante Rita let the smell of his cigarette carry her back in time several months to another safe house in the city of Ayacucho. The promise of an Andean summer had practically dripped from the heavy clusters of red bougainvillea that poured through the back-yard trellis. Young Margarita Novara still thrummed lightly inside from her recent sexual workout. Robed and relaxing in the shade with a Coca-Cola, she had studied the face of the man who had picked her up out of the dirt and set her on the path of revolution.

Miguel Fortuna was not a big man, nor exactly handsome, but his image and reputation were gigantic, not only in Peru, but also throughout the world. Fidel Castro had praised him publicly as 'the most important freedom fighter since Che Guevara'. Ronald Reagan had called him 'the greatest threat to democracy in the Western Hemisphere'. In his homeland he was both folk hero and fugitive, the government's most wanted criminal.

Comrade Rita and Miguel Fortuna had been sexual partners for about six months. Rita knew there had been many others, and that there would be others still. Sex was not love and even love was not exclusive. Miguel had taught her that. Rita had learned long ago that sex was valuable, above all, as a tool for manipulation and control, and that it worked best with men who foolishly equated it with love. Miguel Fortuna was not so foolish.

Miguel had pulled on a pair of cotton drawstring pants. His only other article of clothing was the faded red kerchief he always wore knotted around his neck, even during sex. The triangular patch of red against his tanned throat had reminded her that afternoon, just at the moment of his climax, of a hummingbird.

There in the partial shade of the trellis, he had let his head roll back and blown a last stream of smoke upward into the profusion of flowers.

"What are you thinking, *¿mi colibrí?*" asked Margarita.

"*¿Colibrí?*" he replied with a smile. She had called him her hummingbird. "I like that. It's unpretentious."

With his thumb and index finger, he had stroked his short beard pensively. It was black with the first few signs of gray infiltrating at the chin and cheeks.

"I was thinking, my flower, that I would like you to continue your education."

"¿Sí?"

"*Sí*. We are recruiting a professor at National University. He may prove to be a major asset in intelligence gathering. I think you should enroll at the university. You could be my liaison with him." He could tell by the look on her face that she was surprised, and that she was pleased by the surprise. He added, "You are my brightest young soldier by far, Comrade Rita. How do you feel about anthropology?"

"I can learn it," she assured him. "Just point me to the books."

He had no doubt that she could learn it. Margarita Novara had shown incredible aptitude for learning from her first experience in a *Camino Rojo* education camp. For that reason, Fortuna had decided to accelerate her education. During summers she had trained in revolutionary tactics and strategies, and during the rest of the year she had gobbled up secondary school curricula as rapidly as anyone could feed them to her. Ultimately, she had cruised through a bachelor's degree at the University of Ayacucho in about two and a half years. She had studied Psychology and English. Miguel Fortuna had personally monitored her progress.

"Eventually," he had continued, "we will need to develop a stronger military presence in Lima." His facial expression had turned steadily from one of post-coital satisfaction back to that of a military strategist.

And now, thought Rita, snapping into the present in Miraflores, that coastal military presence had developed as planned, and almost entirely under her own leadership.

"How are things progressing with Comrade Sandra?" asked *El Colibrí*.

"She does what she's told. I think she feels like she's having a great adventure. The revolution feeds the guilt that eats at her. She wants to believe in herself as an idealist."

"The ninety days of our bargain are drawing to a close." He took a deep drag on his cigarette, held it a moment and blew a thin stream of smoke down across the table top. "Do you trust her?"

"No. It all still feels like a game to her."

"It's time to raise the stakes for our pretty comrade." He ground his cigarette into a ceramic ashtray bearing a representation of the Inca Sun God. "I want you to provide her with a full initiation soon. Before she feels like she has a choice to make."

"*Maestro*," she asked, as if it were an afterthought, "would you really let her return to her previous life when the time is up?"

"Of course not, my dear." His indulgent smile and the slightest shake of his head told her the question had been silly and unnecessary.

She nodded. It was her turn to become pensive.

"I was wondering …" she said.

"Yes?"

"Well … I know that family is a bourgeois construct … but you've never spoken of your life before the revolution. All I know is the rumors."

"Hm…" he grunted. He picked up the box of Marlboros and tapped it several times, slowly, on the top of the kitchen table. After some apparent internal debate, he shook another cigarette from the box, lit it and took a deep drag. Finally, he exhaled and began to talk in slow, measured words. It seemed to Rita that he talked more to his cigarette than to her.

"My maternal grandfather was a lawyer. Quite a well-to-do lawyer, actually. I was his only grandchild. My father was a civil servant and a drunkard, weak and resentful. He envied my grandfather for his success, and he bullied my mother because of it. My grandfather encouraged my mother to leave him." Fortuna's expression and a moment of silence told Rita that he was scrolling past memories he chose not to share. "She wouldn't. Before he died, Grandfather cut her out of his will and set up a trust fund for my education. My great aunt, Grandfather's younger sister, was the trustee. The money stopped when I finished my education, but by that time I had a job at the University of Ayacucho and I neither needed nor wanted my grandfather's money."

He snuffed out the cigarette and the conversation simultaneously.

When I woke, it was night. Mercedes was dressed again and had started the van to let the engine warm up. It must have been the sound and jolt of the starter motor cranking that woke me. Mercedes smiled at me from the driver's seat.

"Well, Sam, I'd say you've received enough notoriety for one day. You don't want to add scandal on top of it. Let me drop you off at Doña Rosario's before it gets any later."

I nodded. My head still throbbed. My clothing was dry and I began putting it back on slowly and with some reluctance. Just the pressure of pant legs passing over my bandaged feet made me wince. I decided to carry my boots.

I crawled forward to the passenger seat on my hands and knees to avoid putting weight on my feet. She pulled the old van out into the street. It was only a few blocks to the *casa* Flores, but I was in no condition to walk that far. As she drove, the headlights pushed the darkness forward and drew us along in their wake. Only forward motion kept us from being swallowed by the blackness.

The brakes issued their standard complaint as she stopped the van inside the cone of light from the lamp over Doña Rosario's door. "Good night, Sam," she said. "Try and stay off your feet as much as you can for a few days."

I looked at her through a haze of emotions as I pulled on the handle and swung the door open. Inside, my feelings shifted like sand on a beach being pounded and scrubbed by one wave after another. I wanted to be in love with her. I wanted her to be in love with me. I knew, in that moment, that neither was possible. She was out of my league in so many ways. Mercedes Marquez Acevedo knew exactly where she had come from and who she was. To me, and my experience, she was a woman of unimaginable clarity and strength. She had a profound connection to this land and this people. Against that backdrop, who was I? I had no clarity about who I was or where I was headed. I was, of my own will, a stranger in a strange land. The one piece of a puzzle that didn't fit.

I was on the street and about to close the ambulance door when she spoke again. "Sam, I want you to know that I am grateful for everything you have done."

"I'm not sure what you mean," I said. I owed Mercedes an enormous debt, but I couldn't think of anything I had done that would warrant a shred of gratitude from her.

She shook her head. "It doesn't matter."

I supported as much of my weight as I could with my arms, at first on the side of the ambulance, then on the door frame of the house. Once I had the door ajar, I sat on the threshold to give my blistered feet a break. With a wave of my hand, I told Mercedes that I would be fine from there. As the ambulance rolled away toward wherever it was she went at night, I crawled my way into the house and closed the door behind me in the darkness. When I was halfway across the floor of the main room on my hands and knees, a small light appeared from the kitchen. Doña Rosario stood with her hands covering the sides of her face as if she we trying to steady her head.

I must have looked like a bad dog hoping for mercy.

"*Dios mío*," was all she said.

I slipped as quietly as I could into bed, thinking I would never be able to sleep with all that was racing through my mind. Then I fell almost immediately and deeply asleep. I woke up in the morning to the sound of Enrique rapping on my door. Doña Rosario wanted to see me, he said. There was urgency in his voice. The *señora* had never rousted me before. I was groggy still, and disoriented. Suddenly my head was flooded with images from yesterday – the funeral, the coca, the lightning strike, Mercedes.

"I'll be right out."

As soon as my feet hit the floor, they exploded with pain. I pulled on some clothes and shuffled into the main room. I wasn't going to force Doña Rosario to see me crawl again. No breakfast on the table yet. That was another first. Doña Rosario stood with her back to the front door and her fists on her hips, a perfect picture of Roman Catholic righteous indignation. Enrique stood to one side and fidgeted with anticipation. "What is it? What's the matter?" I asked.

Doña Rosario pulled open the door and backed away. There, in the rising light of dawn, centered on the concrete threshold was a circle, about eight inches across, formed of *chuño*. Inside the circle, on top of a small pile of ashes, lay a smooth stone with a jagged line like a lightning bolt scratched deep into its surface. Enrique moved to my side and together we stared at the strange composition as if spellbound. Finally I picked up the stone, breaking the spell, and turned to face the *señora.* She now stood with both hands clasped in front of her mouth. "Do you know what that is?" she asked.

I nodded. "I think so. It's for me. A gift, more or less." Her silence demanded more explanation. "It's not dangerous. Probably from someone in Huaynatambo." I considered carefully what to say next. "They seem to think I'm ... someone I'm not." I bent down and dragged my fingers through the ashes – burnt coca, I supposed – and the *chuño* in an attempt to make less of what might be seen as a portentous sign. "If you'll loan me a broom, I'll clean it up."

Doña Rosario made an 'Oh, never mind' gesture with her hands and her facial expression softened from revulsion and anger to mild disgust. She scooped the mess into a steel dustpan and swept the stoop clean.

Meanwhile, I was left to ponder a bigger mess. Here I was, trying to become an unobtrusive observer of the local culture, and where had I gotten? I'd been struck by lightning, for Christ sake, and now the local *campesinos* thought of me as some sort of a demigod. Well, that's unobtrusive, I told myself with self-inflicted sarcasm. On top of it all, I was being extorted for money by a local cop – oh, yeah, really unobtrusive – and followed, for God knows what reason, by an enormous man who apparently worked for a local bank president who just might also happen to be a drug lord. All in all, this did not bode well for my career as an anthropologist.

Comandante Rita had given Comrade Amador command of the operation. She wanted Comrade Sandra to take her orders from him on this particular occasion. Comrade Amador covered the bundle of dynamite as Comrade Sandra uncoiled the fuse wire. Their cadre had obtained the explosives in a raid on a mining camp near Cerro de Pasco only a few nights before. The headlines had called it a massacre.

The raid had been Amador's first operation to plan and lead. They surrounded the camp under cover of darkness and moved in pairs according to their assignments. Comrade Amador had assigned Comrades Sandra and Inocencio, a young *campesino* who spoke Quechua, to the workers' barracks. Amador and one other took the engineers' quarters. Four more took the guards and the equipment shed. The operation began with the sound of gunshots dropping the guards. Cassandra and Inocencio, wearing black balaclavas to cover their faces, and with guns held high, burst into the barracks. Cassandra shouted, "Stay where you are, brothers, and you will not be harmed. We are the liberators of the working people!" Inocencio repeated the order in Quechua.

There were several more gunshots. It sounded as if they came from the engineers' quarters. The workers, all *serranos*, peasants from the sierra, cowered in their cots. It seemed like just moments before Comrade Amador shouted, "It's done. *¡Vámonos!*" and the entire patrol moved at a jog down the road to their waiting cars. Comrade Sandra removed her balaclava and turned to Amador.

"There was resistance from the engineers' quarters?" she asked.

"They were lackeys of the puppet government," he responded with a flat voice. Comrade Sandra noticed the expensive watch Comrade Amador now wore on his left wrist.

It was the same wristwatch he consulted a week later when he said, "Everyone to your places." The patrol took cover on both sides of the railroad tracks as Amador twisted the wires into place on the detonator. He handed the plunger to Comrade Sandra. "On my command," he said. In a few minutes the tracks began to hum and the train that ran from Lima to Huancayo drew near. Another moment and the narrow-gauge diesel engine became visible. Cassandra gripped the plunger tightly and fixed her eyes on Comrade Amador. He shook his head as an order to wait. Closer and closer it came until Cassandra could see the engineer looking out the window. The engine had almost reached them when Amador shouted, "Now!" and Cassandra, startled, pushed the plunger.

The explosion ripped through the bottom of the engine, lifted its rear end slightly off the track, splayed the drive wheels and sent a riot of metal up through the engineer's cabin. The momentum of the train caused the smoking engine to jackknife across the tracks. The rest of the cars jolted, scraped and bumped into a more or less static zigzag. When the smoke and dust cleared, the engineer's body was folded double over the sill of the cabin window and Cassandra still clutched the detonator with both hands. She could see Amador's mouth moving, but no sound penetrated her consciousness.

Few of the passengers were hurt beyond mild concussions, cuts and bruises. Within minutes, the *Rojista* patrol, moving in through all the vestibules, had herded them out and onto the rocky ground. They made them sit. Anyone who spoke received a jab with a club or a rifle butt. Comrade Amador began to speak in a loud voice, "*Compadres*, you now have the privilege of supporting the people's war against the oppressive fascist regime. The comrades will be collecting your money and valuables. Place everything you are carrying on the ground in front of you." Some of the *guerrillas* began collecting personal items from the passengers while others searched through the luggage that was left aboard.

Cassandra watched it all in slow motion. With the push of a plunger, she had also flipped a switch inside herself. Until that moment, she had been along for the ride. An observer. An accomplice to violent revolution perhaps, but not a perpetrator. Now she had done it. She had killed.

Comrade Amador walked among the passengers, stopping only when he reached a foursome with stylish European clothing. Among them he counted four wallets and passports, four wristwatches and a thin gold ring. He picked up one of the passports. Italy. He pocketed all four of the passports and picked up the wallets. Each held one or two credit cards and a small amount of cash. He removed those and tossed the wallets back on the ground. He looked the larger of the two males right in the eyes. "This is all you have?" he asked.

The pallid Italian nodded his head.

"Comrade!" called Amador to Cassandra. She shook off the daze she had fallen into and joined him. "Remove this man's shirt."

Cassandra walked behind the man, took the knife from her belt and, with a firm hold on the man's collar, cut the shirt open clear through the tail. Showing just above the waistband of his pants was the strap of a money belt. Cassandra took hold of it, cut it, and pulled it free. She held it aloft for all to see and then she tossed it on the ground among the money and jewelry that had already been collected.

"This man would steal from the revolution!" cried Amador. "He would take the food from our brothers' mouths! Face down on the ground," he ordered, and the Italian hesitated.

Cassandra pushed the man over sideways with a boot to the shoulder and spoke softly, "Do as he says or he will kill you." The man flattened himself against the ground.

"This man must be punished. You," said Amador, leveling his pistol at the man's female companion, "stand up."

The young woman stood, trembling weakly. She was a pretty

woman with dark eyes, tanned skin and dark hair cut in a bob, streaked with golden highlights. “Comrade Sandra,” said Amador, “a knife.” Cassandra placed her knife in the hands of the trembling girl. She held it, confused by what it meant. “This man,” said Amador to the girl so all could hear, “will die. Kill him yourself and you will live.”

Her eyes slowly registered understanding, and then they grew wide with horror. She dropped the knife at her feet. Amador shot her in the knee and she crumpled. Inside, Cassandra winced. The man on the ground screamed and started to rise, and Amador put a bullet into his lower back, paralyzing but not killing him. He trained the pistol on the second Italian male. “Pick up the knife.” The man refused. Amador shot him in the forehead. The second girl lay prostrate, sobbing and pleading to God for mercy.

Amador took a step back and addressed the entire assortment of passengers and fellow *Rojistas.* His voice projected the tone of a theatrical performance. “¡*Peruanos*! These are the swine that suck the fat from your lands and your bodies! These are the capitalist pigs that pull the strings of the government that oppresses you! See how they fall before the revolution! Rise up! Rise up with *El Colibrí* and take back your country!”

Slowly at first, and then with greater ferocity, the Peruvian passengers yielded to the prodding of the guerillas, picking up stones and sticks with which to cast their votes against the foreigners and in favor of their own survival. Comrade Sandra removed herself to a distance from her circling countrymen where she squatted to observe the scene. She found the rising and falling of stones and clubs fascinating and primal. In the background, younger members of the patrol spray-painted revolutionary slogans along the length of the crippled train. Once again holding her knife, she rotated her wrist back and forth so the sun reflecting off the blade flashed in her eyes like a beacon. She wondered what tomorrow’s headline would read.

In the room she had taken for herself at the ranch at Puerta del Sol, *Comandante* Rita tossed her jacket onto the bed. She stacked two fine feather pillows against the dark, colonial era headboard and settled back into them on top of the bedspread. She considered the room. It wasn't luxurious in the way of the ostentatious styles she had seen in Lima or on television shows about the rich. There was no crystal in any of the light fixtures. There were no brocaded fabrics. No gilt picture frames. What the room had was substance. The fabrics of the bedspread and curtains were thick and tightly woven. The linens were soft but felt strong. The furniture, rather than ornate, was solid. She had admired the workmanship of the dovetail joints in the drawers and the hand-carved ornamentation of handles and pulls shaped like clusters of leaves. Someone had taken real pride in making them. Even the mattress beneath her felt substantial. More substantial perhaps than anything in her life had ever felt before. For a while, she allowed herself to daydream about what it would be like to have a room like this to come home to every night.

She reached for her jacket and withdrew a letter from the pocket. She read it with a wry smile on her face and then put it back. The letter represented possibilities that she would never have dreamed about a year ago. In fact, for the first time, it appeared that she might actually have choices in the manner of her future and her escape from the hell her life had been.

So far, the only real road out had been the Crimson Road. It had served her well. It provided her with security and community where there had been none. It taught her to expect more for herself than her station in society would have allowed. It had even allowed her to get an education. *El Colibrí* believed strongly in the power of education. Much of his power base existed in and through the university system, so much so that it had been possible to use the universities to provide deep cover for his most promising officers.

For her part, Rita had served the revolution well. Her work in Lima had been bold and inspired. The seduction of Cassandra Ganz, the foolish bitch, had been a major coup. Practically speaking, it had given the revolution a secure base of operations near Lima. Operations that Rita had strategized and executed. Symbolically, turning Cassandra demonstrated the real reach and power of the revolution. Most importantly for Rita, it had resulted in her promotion within the Camino Rojo. No one was now closer than she to *El Colibrí*. Sure, she had once been even closer, physically, as his lover. Those days were gone. When it had been necessary, she had even abetted Fortuna in his sexual liaisons with other women. The Ganz woman was a case in point. It had all helped to increase Rita's power. And power was what really mattered. Control. Conquest of the heart and mind. She had similarly, and calculatingly, used her own sexuality, whether through simple flirtation or outright seduction, to conquer the hearts and minds of weak-headed men.

No, her closeness to *El Colibrí* was no longer sexual. It was political and strategic. He trusted her completely. She was his right hand, his second in command. And if she could believe his rhetoric, one day she might actually convert that position to one of influence in a true revolutionary government. But Rita was no idiot. She knew that the revolution was at least as likely to carry her to death as to glory.

Lately, it had started to look as if there might actually be another road forward. Right now, it was just the shadow of a path that happened to run parallel with the road she was on. Right now, there was no need to choose a new direction. At some point, if that shadow path proved to be the real thing, she would have to make a choice, and it would be a life or death decision. But all that was in the future. Right now, all she wanted was to lie still and experience the gravity of the things around her.

I was walking alone through the *feria* this morning, my boots laced loosely to keep from putting to much pressure against my healing feet. I was more or less lost in my own thoughts. After a while, I realized something was different about the market. I couldn't tell what it was at first. I started paying closer attention to the sights and sounds. Then it hit me. It was as if I was walking around in a sound-deadening bubble. The *feria* was lively as usual, but as soon as I moved into an area, voices became muted.

In passing, I heard whispers. Most were unintelligible, but they didn't sound like the whispers of casual gossip. They carried more urgency. I turned a corner where an old couple tended a mound of mandarin oranges among a section of fruit vendors. The old woman nudged the old man, who appeared to be half asleep beneath a filthy, tattered fedora, and whispered to him. I heard the Quechua word *piqta*.

The old man, perhaps hard of hearing, grunted the Quechua equivalent of "Eh? What's that?"

The old woman leaned toward him, made a megaphone of her hands and croaked the words "*Kari Wakli-piqta*!" so loudly that she drew the attention of every eye in the immediate vicinity.

I stopped and faced the old couple. The man looked up at me with eyes clouded by cataracts. The woman dropped her gaze and pretended to study her wares. At the going price of ten oranges for one *sol*, I quickly estimated that they might go away with twenty *soles* at the end of the day if they sold everything they had.

"*Abuelita*," I said. Grandmama. "I would like one of your *mandarinas*, please."

Without ever raising her eyes, she took two of the glossy fruits in one gnarled hand and held them up to me. I took the oranges, thanked her, pressed a ten *soles* coin into her palm and asked her to please keep the change.

The sun had risen above the mountains and was now shining strongly among the vendors' kiosks. The warmth felt good. I walked to the *plaza de armas* and sat down on a bench facing the sun to eat the mandarins. The peels practically sloughed off in my hands. The segments were so juicy and tender that they disintegrated under the pressure of my tongue. Still contemplating the intense flavor, I stretched my arms out across the back of the bench, let my head roll back, closed my eyes and soaked up the radiant heat. I think I was just starting to doze off when I felt something touch my right forearm. I flinched and my eyes flew open. Cowering at the end of the bench, with his knees drawn up and his eyes nearly popping out of his head, was the twelve-year-old boy from the funeral of Benito Quispe.

"I'm sorry, *Wirakocha*," he said in a trembling voice.

Wirakocha? He was calling me Lord, the title for an Inca, a god.

"No, no!" I said. "Don't worry, *amiguito*! What's up?" Calling him 'little friend' seemed to reassure him that he wasn't in any mortal danger.

"Excuse me, *Wirakocha*, but my aunt wishes to know if you might be returning to Huaynatambo." He indicated his aunt standing across the street watching us intently with hands clasped in front of her chest. It was Gabriela Quispe.

"Does your aunt want me to stay away?" It would be par for the course.

"No, *Wirakocha*. She hopes you will come. It would be a great honor."

My heart leaped at the words. An invitation to visit the town. What a turnaround. This was potentially most excellent. "In that case, thank your aunt and tell her that I will be pleased to visit Huaynatambo."

Alex was glad to be back in el Valle del Cóndor for a few days. Even if the main reason for his return was inauspicious, at least this day had been pleasant. Thanks to the recent rains his flight from Lima was gorgeous. The valleys of Huancavelica wore their seasonal pools like diamonds. Waterfalls ribboned off every precipice. Not only were the fields and the mountainsides green, they *shouted* green. Even the normally drab rock faces sparkled as if with newfound self-worth.

Beautiful as it was, he would be making the flight between Lima and Ayacucho less frequently during the summer. For one thing, with the year-end approaching, he faced heavier workloads and more social obligations in Lima. Another reason was the weather. With the return of the summer rainy season, flight schedules had to be planned around the possibility of severe thunderstorms. Usually this meant flying in the early morning, if at all. Thunderstorms were practically a daily phenomenon but they tended to generate the most energy in the afternoons. Flying a small plane in the Andes at night was foolhardy at best, even with years of experience of flying with instruments. Although Alex employed a full-time pilot and mechanic, both he and Manolo were also adept pilots of the twin engine Aero Commander. Ganz had insisted on it.

Luz greeted him with good news when he arrived. Her coursework was done for the semester. She had passed it all and was separated from her teaching degree only by the required hours of practicum. Alex was happy for her. He said so. Still, he could tell she was disappointed that he didn't show more enthusiasm. She would have liked him to spend some time with her. Instead, he disappeared into his study with Manolito.

What had brought him back from Lima was the news of an

unsigned letter in his post office box in Santa Rosita. The letter contained nothing more than a date, time and place. It indicated the next day, mid-morning, at a farm high in the foothills of the *cordillera.* Manolo knew the route. It would take two hours, more or less, to get there in the Land Rover.

After dinner, Alex sat down and tried to read for a while. Other things kept intruding on his mind. Cassandra, for one. A novel. That had been a surprise. It was good that she had dedicated herself to something worthwhile and yet it seemed strange to think of her working reclusively, shunning social activity. Alex had often envied Cassandra her ease in social situations. He had always been the one inclined to hide away from others and lose himself in work.

And then there was Mercedes Marquez. Nearly every night she parked and camped so near his gate that he could easily walk down for a neighborly visit when he was at home in el Valle del Cóndor. Why didn't he? What was he afraid of? Lots of things. For one, he wasn't comfortable approaching women. Otherwise, he wouldn't have called on Madam Zenobia to solve the problem of his loneliness here in the sierra. He especially wasn't sure of himself with a woman so obviously independent-minded, although he was sure that any other kind would quickly bore him to distraction.

He had observed Mercedes a few fleeting times and only at a distance, but a drawer full of black and white photographs taken through Manolo's telephoto lens allowed him to consider her more closely and more frequently. There was the picture of her cooking dinner in her campsite by the waterfall: independence, he thought, self-sufficiency. Or reading a book: intelligence and sensitivity. Another showed her dressed like a college coed coming out of the church: a comforting level of sophistication and modernity. Yet another, dressed like a gypsy version of a peasant woman: a connection to the people underscored with a strong sense of the exotic. And then there were the close-ups of her face. Each one was a study in beauty and complexity. There was so much behind those images that he still couldn't fathom. Alex was a man who analyzed situations and then acted decisively. Mercedes Marquez was a problem that he must continue to approach with patience and care.

Finally, there was Luz. There was no denying he had a fondness for her. She was pretty. She was sweet. She was eager to please. Her companionship, which he valued far above its cost, basically amounted to quiet company in the evening hours and sort of a front-row-student approach to sex when he wanted it. She was anxious to learn more if it made the teacher happy. In exchange for her service, she was building a nest egg and sending a little money to her family in Ica each month. Zenobia had negotiated a good living for the girl and a hefty commission for herself. In addition, Alex had gone out of his way to see that Luz developed new skills that would carry her into a better life after she left el Valle del Cóndor. That departure might have to happen soon. Luz was beginning to show signs of melancholia, or attachment, or something. He needed to avoid the word love. When he took her to bed that night, he deliberately treated her a little roughly.

I had been in Santa Rosita for about three months. On November second, the Peruvian Day of the Dead, Pedro Buenaventura had conducted a special mass that packed the pews of the chapel of the *Santísima Virgen de Dolores* with somber townspeople. I stood in the back corner and observed without participating. Pedro's mass-giving voice was richer and more sonorous than his normal, quiet, conversational one. It rose and fell and wound itself in and out through the smells of incense, paraffin, bodies and wool. The candles surrounding the Virgin threw an undulating light that bathed the front of the church and hung tentative halos over the bowed heads of the parishioners.

The Virgin herself was a modest, approachable saint. Unlike many Madonnas with their golden crowns and fine, luxurious robes, this Lady of Sorrows wore a peasant's clothing, a simple, dark robe that only partially covered her head. In their one concession to ostentation, her makers had covered her hair in gold leaf. Much of the gold had long since rubbed away, but the statue remained undoubtedly and oddly blonde. Through this mother intercessor, on this day, the people of Santa Rosita hoped to bring some kind of blessing upon the souls of their dear deceased.

In my coat pocket my fingers warmed and softened the one-page letter I had received earlier that week from my mother. It was short, cordial. She had asked after my health, mentioned she would be organizing the tennis club's holiday charity fundraiser, said that Mitch had a studio and was doing some interesting work. Asked me to write when I found the time.

Day of the Dead, I thought. Day of the dad.

Father Pedro had begun to intone the names of the dead of Santa Rosita from a list compiled by his parishioners. One by one the names took wing in the heavy air. In my mind, I added the name Gregory Young to the list.

The rhythms of an Andean summer now fully governed the countryside and I was caught up in them. Every morning delivered a powerful sun and every afternoon a deluge. The *feria* came and went every week. Crops in the surrounding area were good and the animals were healthy. Precious coca leaf flowed unimpeded to the *campesinos.* Reports of *Rojistas* and of *sinchis* came from other parts of the province, but the news seemed irrelevant, almost foreign. The entire province had been placed under a state of emergency by the government and yet in Santa Rosita life went on as it had for generations. I supposed that even the monthly knock on the door by the cop, Sanchez, was part of the pattern of Andean life.

To my great delight, I finally found myself doing the work of anthropology. My feet had healed – although not without scars – which helped greatly. School ended for the summer break, which ran from December into March, and liberated Enrique to become my 'research assistant'. With him at my side, I formed a routine. Every Wednesday we visited the *feria*, where the highlight for me was spending a little time with Mercedes. She no longer snarled at me when I came around. In fact, she even asked me on occasion for a medical second opinion. If I noticed that the line at her clinic was particularly long, I would volunteer to help with the patient load, typically in a triage capacity. It actually appeared that Mercedes' patient load was increasing in terms of people with minor complaints. We speculated about the reason and decided that it might have something to do with the spectacle of the young witch and the Son of Lightning working together. Apparently demi-deification had absolved me from suspicion as a potentially murderous *pishtaco*.

On the other weekday mornings, Enrique and I tramped the seven kilometers to Huaynatambo where my local fame as the *Kari Wakli-piqta* turned out to be a special asset. While my feet had been healing, we took the Jeep, but I preferred to walk. All along the way, people waved or shouted greetings. Children ran alongside us and dared each other to touch me. I had begun building rapport by distributing gifts of coca leaf from the ample supply I had acquired at the funeral of Benito Quispe. Out of fear perhaps, at first, of the Son of Lightning, the *campesinos* allowed me to work alongside them in their fields. Because the fields prospered, they concluded that the *Kari Wakli-piqta*'s influence was benevolent. Their fear gave way to respect, which was no more deserved than the fear had been, but which served me better.

On the way to and from Huaynatambo, Enrique and I shared language lessons. We would take turns offering a phrase in Spanish, then I would teach Enrique the English equivalent and Enrique would teach me the Quechua word, if there was one. Enrique, it turned out, had the harder time of the teaching, not so much because he was less versed or less talented, but because Quechua had a limited vocabulary for discussing anything outside of agriculture, family, nature and the gods. The hour and a half each way flew by as only the most enjoyable times do. So accustomed was I to Enrique's company that I sometimes wondered how I would adjust to a life without him once my field work was completed and I returned to the States to write my dissertation.

Usually, we sat out the afternoon rains in Huaynatambo and still managed to get back to Santa Rosita in plenty of time for Enrique to take care of Doña Rosario's chores and errands. I would then complete my field notes for the day and drift over to *Los Tres Chanchitos* for dinner.

That summer, I filled several notebooks with field notes. I began to measure my success by their mass. My journal entries, which consisted of personal thoughts and feelings rather than observations and interviews, were more sporadic and rather pitiful. I only journaled when I felt particularly lonely or desperate or, on the other hand, elated. The writing read like the scribblings of a manic-depressive.

I also maintained my weekly reports to Fredo. Mostly, they were a running compendium of new observations and insights. For his part,

Fredo responded less frequently and without much indication of real interest. I did mention my brush with lightning, but I kept my local status as the Son of Lightning a secret from him. Although it was hard for me to resist the urge to tell the whole story, I didn't want to be forced yet to deal with the implications that accidental deification might have for the credibility of my research.

The next day, after a good breakfast, Ganz joined Manolo in the Land Rover and they set out for their designated meeting place. The countryside they traversed had all belonged at one time to the de la Vega *hacienda*. The ancestors of these *campesinos* had paid tribute to his ancestors, had in effect been owned by them. It wasn't slavery, but very nearly so. Were they better off now? Materially, he doubted it, but now they had the illusion of choice. Democracy, he mused, is the new opiate of the masses.

When they started up the road that climbed the last ten kilometers to their destination, Alex noticed a flash of light from high on the hillside.

"Did you see it?" he asked.

Manolo nodded. "Binoculars."

El Colibrí had not remained successfully a fugitive for all these years without being cautious.

The road climbed gradually for a while. A small stream tumbled along in the bottom of the canyon and Alex wondered if it still might harbor a few native trout in some of its deeper holes. Soon the road broke into switchbacks and, when it finally leveled out again, it was to render a view of a placid mountain lake with a tiny town at its farther shore. Midway around the lakeshore they came to a turnoff where an old *cholo* lounged on the grassy bank. He stood as the Rover approached, revealing beneath his frayed wool poncho a glimpse of an automatic weapon, and nodded in the direction of the side road.

From the outside, the little farm they found at the end of the road looked like any other they had passed along the way. Perhaps it had been more prosperous than most. The adobe house had been stuccoed and whitewashed, but the paint was wearing thin and the stucco was veined with cracks. There were no signs of long-term occupation by the *guerrillas*. Ganz figured they had recently commandeered the place for the purpose of this meeting and that it would be abandoned, bereft of any worthwhile food and supplies, soon afterward. He wondered if the previous occupants were still alive. If this meeting were reported to the authorities by some neighbor, the owner of the property would suffer gravely and needlessly. Probably, they would imprison and torture him for information he wouldn't have. *El Colibrí* and his retinue would be long gone and untraceable.

Manolo parked the Rover but left the engine running. Alex and he sat tight. The door of the house opened and a man and a woman came out, both with machine guns slung over their shoulders. They positioned themselves menacingly on either side of the door. A third person, whom Ganz had seen with *El Colibrí* before, a personal assistant perhaps, came out and walked to the passenger window of the Rover. He signaled for Ganz to get out of the vehicle.

"Wait here, Manolito. This won't take long." Manolo nodded very slightly and double-checked to make sure the safeties of the two weapons hidden within his reach were off.

As Alex stepped down from the Rover, he couldn't help notice how fresh and crisp the air was that came across the lake. *El Colibrí* came to the doorway and stood, Ganz fancied, like some sort of tribal chief about to hold court with his bodyguards standing before him.

"*Señor, qué gusto verle*," said Ganz. Some pleasure. "I trust you find yourself well." Dark bags had developed under *El Colibrí*'s eyes since their last meeting. Ganz wondered if the stress of life as a fugitive might be taking its toll on the man's health.

Miguel Fortuna chose not to answer. The chill in the air deepened as the two men studied each other.

"There has been some unwelcome activity in the *selva*," said Alex. "One of my workers was killed. I fear the people's army has let me down."

"A tragedy. That is a dangerous zone." *El Colibrí*'s tone communicated a transparently false sense of sympathy. "With the meddling of the murderous government and its imperialist North American puppeteers, it is difficult property to protect. Still, with adequate support, I am confident the revolutionary forces can secure the area. Comrade ..." His apparent assistant produced an envelope containing two sheets of plain paper with typed instructions and no other markings. *El Colibrí* handed it to Ganz. "These are the new terms for the defense of your agricultural holdings. Given their profitability and their vulnerability, I think you'll find this workable."

Ganz removed the papers and scanned the contents. There was a demand for money. As expected, the amount was substantially increased. But this time, the list also specified an array of weaponry, all of which was military issue. He refolded the papers, working his fingers slowly down the creases, and then put them in his jacket pocket. "This will take some time, but I believe I can get it. In the meantime, will you guarantee the safety of my interests?"

"For the time being," replied *El Colibrí.*

Alex turned and walked back to the Land Rover. Well, he thought, the cost of doing business continues to rise. It may be time to buy some insurance.

Christmas was the first time Alex had seen his sister since the morning after the bombings. It surprised him to see her drive up alone to the San Isidro home – she had always preferred to be driven – and to see the dusty condition of her car, which had always been immaculate.

"You cut your hair," he said as Cassandra stepped out of her car.

"It was becoming a bother," she said.

He expected her to pose and ask, "Do you like it?" But she didn't. She neither sought his approval nor courted his admiration. He was used to seeing Cassandra walk with slightly exaggerated femininity, almost like a runway model, but now she strode with a more athletic gait. He was also used to seeing artfully applied makeup. She now wore very little. She looked tanned and fit, with muscle definition in her arms and shoulders that had never been there before.

"Your new lifestyle seems to suit you," he observed.

She smiled only slightly and cocked her head as if she were examining his statement for deeper meaning. It echoed a statement made by *El Colibrí* months ago in the stable at Puerta del Sol.

"Obviously," Alex continued, "you've been doing something besides sitting at the typewriter."

"Well, of course the novel takes some time, but I'm also still running the ranch. You know, working the horses, making repairs. I've even taken up shooting." She wanted to say more, and she wanted to know more, especially about her brother's involvement with *El Colibrí* and the *Camino Rojo*. But on both counts, she was strictly forbidden. It was a vital security measure. Even the decision to allow Comrade Sandra to attend this family Christmas gathering had been motivated by security. No suspicion must be drawn toward the ranch at Puerta del Sol, which was now functioning as a base of operations for the cell under *Comandante* Rita's direct command. No, Comrade Sandra must go to San Isidro and keep up the charade of family tradition.

"You look awfully well, big brother." She gave him a kiss on the cheek and a hug with her free arm. A large jute bag full of gifts hung from the other. They locked arms and walked into the house. "What have you been up to lately?"

"Same old thing, I'm afraid. Keeping on top of the family businesses."

Cassandra was a little disappointed in the vagueness of his answer. She had been hoping for some cryptic clue about Alex and the *revolución*, but she attributed his response to discipline and security and felt slightly ashamed that she had wished otherwise.

In many ways, this Christmas was identical to the last several. There was the American-style tree, upon which Pilar de la Vega always insisted and which the serving staff always decorated with the same ornaments. There was the usual Christmas dinner, a stiff affair featuring a standing rib roast with all the trimmings, which only Alex approached with any enthusiasm. There was the usual procession of beverages, Pouilly-Fuissé to Burgundy to Armagnac. One difference did stand out. Pilar, who had worn nothing but mourning black since the death of her husband, had shed her somber affect. If not exactly festive, her pleated cream-colored skirt, ruffled silk blouse and red cropped jacket lent her a glow of resolute optimism. At fifty-seven she was still healthy and attractive, and for the first time in years, she really looked it.

"*Queridos*," she said, as dessert was cleared away. "My dears, I have an announcement. I have grown weary of my life here and I have decided to make some changes. After the first of the year I will be living in Florence."

"Florence!" Alex responded with surprise and delight. Cassandra's expression was more reserved.

"Florence," confirmed Pilar. "I have made the arrangements already. I will be leasing rooms not far from the Duomo."

"*Mamá*, that's wonderful," said Alex. "What will you do there?"

"Travel. Take in the art. I may even try my hand at painting."

"How long will you stay?" In contrast to Alex's, Cassandra's question had a tone of mild disinterest.

"Until I grow tired of it. Or until I receive a wedding invitation from one of my children."

Luz stood at the window and watched as columns of sunlight thrust their way through the tumble of clouds, lighting up first one and then another patch of rain-jeweled grass. The amount of sheer life energy on display almost overwhelmed her, a riot of photosynthesis, growth you could see and smell and almost hear in progress. The same sun on the coastal desert of Ica would have drained her strength, cowed her and driven her into the shade. She heard footsteps approach behind her, knew they were Juan Pablo's, and kept her eyes on the scene before her.

"*Niña*," said the old man, "will you join us now for Christmas Eve?"

It would be her first Christmas at el Valle del Cóndor. She spent the previous Christmas holiday with her family in Ica, spinning for them a story, mostly true, about her studies and the scholarship she received as an assistant to a well-to-do businessman. They were so happy for her, and so proud. But they also acted clumsy and withdrawn, as though they didn't know how to talk to her anymore. This year, she didn't feel comfortable facing them with the same story.

Luz turned toward Juan Pablo. The topography of his sexagenarian face showed a lifetime of wear and tear, but in his eyes shone a gentleness that was devoid of judgment. She felt undeserving of his open acceptance, for lately she had begun to judge herself more harshly. For two years, she had lived in this valley devoting her time to her studies, her occasional teaching and, of course, her *patrón*.

Patrón. She may as well get used to the word. How many times had she privately tried on other words? *Amante* had sounded good, but without love there was no lover. She might as well not kid herself. Her love for Alex was unrequited. Any more, she wasn't even sure that what she felt for him was love and not some illusion she had cultivated. God forgive her for having entertained, even in her most private moments, the word husband. The world was not kind to fools, she knew, and she had harbored foolish thoughts. Perhaps there were other words she should learn to accept as well. *Puta. Prostituta.* Whore.

Juan Pablo's frown lines deepened as if he had read her thoughts and they had saddened him. Then he looked past her out the window and said, "Look."

She turned. It was the rainbow.

Consuelo refused Luz's offer to help with the cooking or the table. "Another time," said the old woman. "What you *can* do is tell Indio and Manolito that dinner is nearly ready."

She could have used the telephone intercom, but on such a beautiful afternoon she preferred to walk. First to the caretaker's cottage for Indio. Although she stayed on the narrow footpath, the grass, still beaded with raindrops, brushed her bare ankles and dampened her canvas sneakers. Indio opened the door when she knocked. Luz couldn't tell whether he bowed to her or simply returned to his normally stooped posture.

"*Gracias, Señorita. Ahorita voy.*"

A narrower, lesser-used path led from Indio's cottage to the guardhouse where Manolo lived, usually, like tonight, alone. There were times when other men had been quartered there as well, for what reasons Luz couldn't guess and wouldn't ask.

When she knocked on the door, it opened so quickly that she jumped. To her further surprise she noted that Manolo was wearing a suit. Manolo, seeing her start, seemed embarrassed. "I'm sorry," he whispered. He hung his head as low as it would go, but it hung from such an altitude that she could still see his face plainly. His stance had gone slightly pigeon-toed. In that moment he looked like a gigantic schoolboy who had been caught at something naughty. Her mind completed the scenario by imagining her kneeling before him to provide a teacher's reassurance.

Luz couldn't help but smile.

Manolo lumbered just behind her on the path to the house. When they reached the door, he held forth an envelope. "I went to the post office today. This is for you."

She took it and turned it over, then over again. It was addressed to her in her mother's hand. Not now, she thought, and folded it into the pocket of her jeans.

Inside again, she took closer note of the special-occasion attire beneath Consuelo's apron. Luz excused herself and went to her rooms. She hurriedly shed her jeans and sweatshirt and slipped into a modest dove-gray dress and matching shoes, part of the extensive wardrobe Zenobia had put together for her.

Everyone was waiting in the dining room when she returned. Consuelo had removed her apron and stood behind the chair closest to the kitchen. Juan Pablo looked at ease in slacks and a cardigan. They both smiled their approval upon Luz's entrance. Across the room, Manolo couldn't seem to decide where to look. He sneaked a look at Luz, but when she tried to return eye contact, he looked at his feet. She looked away and his eyes tracked back to her. Noticing this, she looked his way, and he averted his gaze again. Old Indio stood at the far end of the table as stoic and solemn as a plaster statue of *San Martín.* His one concession to dressing up was the removal of the shapeless, once-gray felt hat that seemed never to leave his head. His hair, flecked with dandruff and quite thick for his age, was parted neatly in the middle.

"Well, let's not all just stand around while the food gets cold," exclaimed Consuelo. Then, indicating the chair next to hers, she said, "Luz, Sweetheart, you sit here."

With that one assignment made, the rest of the seating fell easily into place. Juan Pablo sat across from Consuelo. Next to him and directly across the table from Luz sat Manolo. Indio had moved to the foot of the table. The head of the table remained empty in *Don* Alejandro's absence.

Juan Pablo pronounced grace and all attention turned to the food. El Valle del Cóndor's traditional Christmas Eve meal was a thing of beauty. A suckling pig, roasted with a glossy orange glaze and surrounded by baby potatoes, took center stage on a silver platter. A pilaf of rice and raisins and a relish of fresh corn, onion and red pepper played supporting roles. Fresh bread and a medley of fruit rounded it out.

"Manolito," said Juan Pablo, "please pour the toast."

As Manolo moved from place to place pouring champagne into flutes, plates were passed and Juan Pablo carved the pig.

"My friends," said Juan Pablo, raising his glass. "To our God, to our *patrón* and to our country, let us drink. Peace."

A chorus of 'Peace' filled the air, twining through the many smells rising from the table. Then silence prevailed as everyone demonstrated proper devotion to the feast. They drained two more bottles of champagne in the course of their meal. Hearts began to warm and tongues began to loosen.

Consuelo and Juan Pablo reminisced about previous Christmases with the Ganz children in San Isidro. "What is she really like?" asked Luz about Cassandra. Juan Pablo entertained them with the story of a precocious child-actress recreating a scene, in English, from *My Fair Lady*. Luz didn't understand the movie reference. Her family couldn't afford movies when she was growing up. Books, however, she had enjoyed. She read everything she could borrow from her teachers, who were always willing to help a bright, inquisitive child. "I used to read to my brothers and sisters at night," she recalled. "*Oliver Twist* was their favorite. Of course, it was the Spanish translation. *Me encantaría poder leerlo en Inglés*," she said wistfully of her wish to read the original English.

Indio stood up, thanked everyone for the meal and excused himself. Luz noticed that Manolo had been quiet but attentive in a bashful kind of way. "Manolo," she asked to draw him into the conversation, "how did you come to be employed by *Don* Alejandro?"

Consuelo stood and motioned to Juan Pablo. "*Vámonos, viejo*, help me with the dishes. We know this story already. You two," she said to Luz and Manolo, "go on into the other room. We'll open gifts in a little while."

Luz and Manolo got up from the table with a show of reluctance and moved to the living room where several fresh-cut branches of eucalyptus arranged in an urn and decorated with glass ornaments served as a Christmas tree. Manolo waited for Luz to take a seat before settling himself into a comfortable armchair. He seemed to retreat into solitary contemplation. "So, are you going to tell me?" Luz asked.

"My father was a dock worker, a stevedore. I never knew my mother. One day, young Alejandro went with his father, *Don* Oswald, to tour a ship in the port at *El Callao.* Alex was only seven, but his father wanted to begin exposing him to some of the family business. Somehow Alex fell into the water. My father saw it and dove into the water after him. Alex could swim like a fish but, of course, my father couldn't know that. Someone threw life preservers into the water. Alex swam to one and was pulled to safety. My father drowned."

"My God."

"I was nine years old and suddenly an orphan. *Don* Oswald took me in and paid for my schooling. I've been with the family ever since."

Not knowing what else to say, Luz let the silence of the evening deepen. Manolo, seemingly unable to bear it for more than a minute or two, stood up and strode toward the dining room. "*¡Abuelos!*" He shouted in the general direction of the kitchen. He addressed Juan Pablo and Consuelo as grandparents. "Let's open the gifts. Are you going to make us wait all night?"

The old couple returned, Consuelo with a tray of cordial glasses and Juan Pablo with a bottle of brandy. Once everyone had something to sip, Consuelo asked Luz to do the honors and pass out the gifts. There was one for each of them and one for Indio.

"I will take it to him," said Manolo of Indio's gift and laid it aside. They all began the deliberate task of unwrapping. Juan Pablo's package was long and thin. Out came a fine American fishing rod. The old man hid his pleasure poorly. Consuelo's package yielded up a sterling silver frame around a matted picture of her and Juan Pablo standing with three children in front of a grand house. She passed it around for all to see and then clutched it to her breast. Luz correctly took the children for Cassandra, Alex and Manolo at the approximate ages of seven, ten and twelve. Manolo was already taller than either of his *abuelos*. Manolo's gift was a wooden humidor filled with Cuban cigars. He raised it to his nose, opened the lid a crack and inhaled deeply with his eyes closed.

Luz carefully unfolded wrapping paper, then tissue, to reveal a small box nested in a scarf of navy blue silk. The box contained a simple blue-sapphire pendant. It was beautiful, but what did it mean? She stood and held it to her neck. "Could you help me, Manolo?"

Manolo's big fingers were poorly suited for the delicate clasp and they trembled slightly, but soon the pendant was in place with the sapphire positioned just below her collarbone. She then knotted the scarf loosely around her waist. "What do you think?" she asked them as she gave a slow spin.

"Beautiful," said Consuelo. "Very nice," said Juan Pablo. Manolo bit his lower lip, took a deep breath and nodded his admiration.

"There's a card," said Juan Pablo. He slipped it from its envelope and read, "My dear friends, I am sorry I can't be with you on this holy night. In my absence, I hope you will love each other as I love you all. You are family. Alex."

Luz felt a lump in her throat as she choked back tears that she didn't fully understand. Consuelo got up and gave her a hug. "Good night, *Querida*," she said. And then to her husband, "Come on, *viejo*, it's time for bed." Manolo left with Indio's parcel, and Luz was alone. Back in her own rooms, she posed in front of the mirror to appreciate her gifts from *Don* Alejandro. You are family, he had said. She couldn't help compare the elegant reflection with the image in her mind of the poor urchin that had left Ica so long ago with three raggedy dresses and a prayer. As she dressed for bed, she found the letter from her mother and opened it.

> *Dearest Daughter,*
>
> *I hope this reaches you before Christmas. Thank you again for the money you send. It must be very hard for you. You should know that Jorge has joined the army. Can you believe it? He says the food is good and the clothes are warm. I joke with him and ask if they would take an old lady. Everyone is well. We miss you and are very proud. God bless and keep you.*
>
> *Love, Mamá*

She refolded the letter, placed it back in its envelope, lay down on top of the covers and wept.

Christmas in Santa Rosita passed quietly for me. Mercedes had gone to Huancayo to be with her Mother. Pedro Buenaventura put extra effort into his masses. I bought a music box for Doña Rosario, *Claire de Lune*, which earned me tears and my first-ever hug from the stout matron. For Enrique I got a portable transistor radio. To Pedro I presented a bottle of the best *pisco* I could find.

Throughout my own childhood, I had followed an annual holiday ritual of dropping not-so-subtle hints about the things I wanted for Christmas. I left catalogs or magazines lying around the house with pages dog-eared and certain items circled, sometimes with multiple circles or even exclamation points. Choosing which items to circle, and how boldly, was always a delicate task. If I circled more items than Mom and Dad were willing to buy (I'd caught onto the Santa thing earlier than I let on to my parents), I might not get what I most wanted. If my hints weren't plain enough, then I might also get items that I didn't want. If the gifts I wanted materialized, I would feign surprise, even if I had managed to figure them out already through late-night snooping under the tree.

In contrast, the pure, spontaneous joy in Enrique's face as he discovered his present was something to cherish forever.

I'd sent cards to my mother, to Mitch and to Marivela Santiana. For my own part, I received cards from Mitch and Mom. Mom's card carried well wishing and a short 'miss you' message along with a reference to a gift of See's chocolates. I would never see the chocolates. Such things never made it past the National Post Office without the extra push of a healthy bribe. Mitch's card spared more news. He was happily ensconced in a small house in Seattle's Queen Anne district with his new friend, Nan Chang, a Taiwanese stockbroker with a knack for investing profitably even in a recession. Thanks to Chang, Mitch was finally able to devote more time to his painting than to his survival. The card's illustration was a Mitchell Young original, a water-colored line drawing of an adolescent male angel with Asian features holding forth a salmon in his outstretched arms.

After a dinner of roast chicken and sweet potatoes that was Doña Rosario's contribution to the holiday, Enrique disappeared into his room with his new radio, and I decided I needed a long, leisurely walk. Wearing my wide-brimmed hat and poncho against the inevitable afternoon rain, I walked through the quiet town and beyond, in the direction of Uchurimac. The road, which skirted the foothills, was a maze of shallow puddles and deeper potholes. The afternoon rain fell lighter than usual, but there had been enough lately to fill all but the deepest holes.

As I walked along, staying to higher, dryer ground, I considered the legacy of my sporadically Episcopalian upbringing. Twice a year, at Christmas and at Easter, I made a half-hearted effort to define my religious beliefs. The exercise lacked urgency, because whatever my beliefs were or were not, they didn't seem to affect my daily life choices. What it comes down to is this: God is a freaking mystery. Nobody on the planet, not the Pope or anybody else, knows a damn thing more about God than I do. Those who say they do are liars and manipulators. I believe in the historical existence of Jesus, but not in his divinity. I reject completely the notion of virgin birth, chalk the miracles up to folklore and remain only slightly hopeful on the topic of resurrection or afterlife of any kind. What I do appreciate about Christianity is its value as a moral compass. I truly believe that if everyone who professed a religion, any religion, actually lived by its teachings, the world would be a veritable utopia. That I don't always live by Christian behavioral standards is a hypocrisy I've learned to accept, both as a fact and as a basis for reflection and improvement.

Such were my thoughts when, rounding a bend in the road, I found myself looking at a man lying crumpled in the track. I looked around to appraise the situation, wary of a ruse, such as a setup for robbery. Seeing nothing else suspicious, I approached with caution. Blackened bare feet stuck out from what looked like a oil-blackened harpy's nest. The man was curled with his head near his knees, one arm outstretched and the other clutched to his belly. He looked pretty big for a campesino, with a heavy brow and a strong jawline. There was no sign of blood. He was breathing and he was soaked. "*Señor,*" I said, "are you all right?" No response. Edging closer I got a whiff of stale liquor and urine.

I turned my nose away from the smell. I considered leaving the man to continue sleeping off his drunk, but then I thought better of it. A driver coming through the bend in the road might not see him in time to stop. "Hey, friend," I said, bending down this time to prod the man's outstretched arm. At my touch the man flew awake, his eyes wide with terror. The outstretched hand came up defensively in front of his face and the other hand emerged with a long, rusty, wicked-looking knife. I jumped back in alarm as the man scrambled in the other direction and then crouched at the side of the road with the knife held forward in a position more desperate than threatening. I recognized him now. It was the drunkard, Bonifacio Vargas, whom I had seen occasionally in the streets of Santa Rosita.

"Peace," I said. "No harm." Slowly I reached into my pocket and took out a thousand-*soles* note, not a fortune, but enough for a few meals and more than many peasants earned in a month. I unfolded it and laid it on the ground at the side of the road, and then I backed away.

"*Felíz Navidad*," I said.

Bonifacio and his older brother Camilo had shared reputations as good-for-nothings all their lives. Everyone in their village of Uchurimac knew that Camilo Vargas beat his wife. Most also believed the hard-drinking Bonifacio went to her bed and comforted her on nights when Camilo was out thieving.

Early one morning, a patrol of *Rojistas* had marched into Uchurimac – men, women and adolescents, some carrying carbines, others carrying machetes – with a list of names. All the residents were forced from their homes into the *plaza de armas* and ten men, including the mayor and the justice of the peace, were taken at gunpoint to the center of the square. A young man with a scruffy beard read off a list of charges against them. The mayor and the judge were each charged with 'fronting for the puppet government' and for 'conspiring with the *Guardia Civil* in the murder of workers and *campesinos'*. The other eight heard charges ranging from thievery to immorality. Next came a lengthy speech that included every imaginable pro-revolutionary slogan, none of which held any meaning at all for the terrified peasants. Finally, the leader of the militia asked the people in Quechua to speak freely and denounce any other villagers they had seen consorting with the *Guardia Civil.*

From within the crowd came a murmur and a fit of nervous laughter. "What is it? Speak up!" The leader demanded as he unholstered his revolver and took a step toward the muffled commotion. One old peasant, his face furrowed like a plowed field and his gums and lips a deep green from chewing coca, barely stifled another laugh. "State your business, you old fossil!"

"I was about to denounce Camilo Vargas," cackled the old man.

"What has he done?"

"He is consorting with the *policía.*"

"And where is this Camilo Vargas?"

"In jail. They hauled him away for stealing cattle."

The bearded youth glowered at the old man and the crowd stifled their laughter. The whole village heard the click as the *Rojista* pulled back the hammer of his revolver. Then he turned and pointed it at two of the larger male villagers. One of them was Bonifacio.

"You two hold this treacherous dog," he indicated the mayor, "on the ground. If he gets up, you will die."

The mayor was trembling as these two fellow townspeople gripped him by the arms and shoulders. He struggled and their grips tightened. They tried to force him down and he locked his knees. At this point, Bonifacio made a conscious decision. He placed his right leg behind of the mayor's left, pushed him backward, and sent him sprawling to the dirt. Then he dropped down and placed his knee hard on the mayor's shoulder. It took only a moment for the other man to overcome his shock and join Bonifacio in holding him down.

Still gesturing with the cocked pistol, the bearded *Rojista* selected two more of the villagers and indicated a large paving stone. "Lift it." One strong person could have lifted the stone with some straining. The pair did so easily. "Bring it here," said the leader, positioning them one on each side of the mayor's head. "Raise it higher." They lifted it to chest height. "Higher." They did. "This is the judgment of the people. Together we are liberated! Drop the stone."

Bonifacio resisted the mayor's sudden, violent struggle and felt the jolt of the stone through his own knee upon the man's shoulder. He saw blood trickling from the mayor's nose. He didn't know how badly the man was injured and he no longer cared. He resettled his weight harder as the leader motioned for two more people to raise the stone. When roughly half the townspeople had participated in the repeated bludgeoning of the mayor's ultimately pulverized skull, the leader turned the process on the justice of the peace, who was already on the ground praying to God for mercy on his soul. When the two executions were done, every resident of Uchurimac, no matter how old or young, had played a part. The other eight men, accused of lesser crimes, were beaten with sticks and sent home.

The militia placed red banners around the town, including on the bell tower of the crumbling, deserted church. They scrawled political slogans on the walls, looted the town for supplies and marched away from what looked like a ghost town. With them marched Bonifacio Vargas, his pant leg soaked with the blood of the mayor and the judge.

At first, Bonifacio took up the slogans and the violence of the *Camino Rojo* with something approaching vigor. However, given as he was to drunkenness, he could never maintain the level of discipline required by his leaders. One day, when an inspection found him secreted away with a flask of *trago*, the *comandante* of the patrol had Bonifacio beaten nearly to death and abandoned at the side of the road. He lay there through three days of hot sun and torrential rain, emerging only intermittently to consciousness. Each time he awoke, he was hounded by demons that drove him back into the black underworld. On the fourth day, with the sun turning the puddled countryside into a blanket of broken mirrors, Bonifacio had pulled himself up and started down the road with no sense of who he was or where he was going.

The Uchurimac-based patrol of the *Camino Rojo* came upon Bonifacio Vargas on Christmas day in the late afternoon. He cowered before them with a thousand-*soles* note clutched in his greasy hand. Most of the comrades remembered Bonifacio from his short time with the cadre that had taken his hometown. They took the money. When they tried to interrogate him about the source of it they found him pathetically incoherent. They remembered him as a drunkard and assumed that he was probably harmless. However, one wiry young man of about seventeen, called Pulga, suggested the money might indicate he was a paid spy or informer. They withdrew and observed him closely for an hour or so, long enough to be both bored and appalled by his depravity, and then the *comandante* of the patrol reduced the watch over him to one man, Pulga.

"Take this," said the *comandante*, handing Pulga an antiquated pistol with two bullets in the cylinder. "Follow him for a week. If you don't see anything suspicious, then come back."

"And if I see something suspicious?"

"Come back anyway and report it."

Pulga, whose nickname meant flea, dogged Vargas at a distance that was short enough for keeping an eye on him and long enough that Vargas didn't seem to notice or care. He followed him right into the town of Santa Rosita. In town, Bonifacio followed pretty much the same routine as he did in the countryside, periods of sleep or incoherent mumbling interspersed with bursts of raving and occasional movement. The difference was that, in town, there were more stimuli to pique Pulga's interest. Even though Santa Rosita had, for some reason, been declared off-limits to *guerrilla* activity, Pulga thought there was no harm in finding out who were its more prominent citizens and officials. So he began to compile a list of possible enemies of the revolution.

He was hanging around the *plaza de armas* when a *gringo* and a small boy came out of the church together. A *gringo*, thought Pulga, would be a sure addition to his list. Eventually he followed Vargas back to the countryside where he drifted from *chacra* to *chacra*, small peasant-owned farms where the vagrant was equally likely to receive a *pancito* or a thrown stone for his begging. When he was especially lucky, he could beg a drink of *chicha*. Pulga always fared better than Bonifacio as a result of the old revolver that he carried tucked in his belt and wasn't afraid to show.

Having heard nothing from Marivela at Christmas or in the ensuing days, I was feeling a little sorry for myself. Why do I have so much trouble maintaining a relationship with a woman who interests me? In this case, I admitted, distance had something to do with it. Being separated by a two-day drive filled with predatory cops and the possibility of terrorists was no help. Of course, close proximity hadn't always worked for me either.

Casual sex was even harder for me than relationships. All the girls I went with in high school had felt the need to preserve their virginity. And mine. I was the only guy I knew who had gotten out of high school as a virgin. Maybe because I was a pathetic romantic. I equated sex with love. I was in my freshman year at college when I first had that notion trampled.

Tammy was her name, a tawny Texas girl who seemed to live like a Cadillac heading ninety miles an hour down a dirt road. I met her at a frat party I crashed at the beginning of the school year. A kid from my roommate's hometown in Iowa was a Sigma Chi and had proffered an unofficial invitation. Tammy was deep into the keg of Sig hospitality when she latched onto me.

"So, you're pre-med," she had drawled. "Wanna play doctor?"

"I, uh, left my stethoscope in my other pants," was the best retort I could come up with.

"That's all right." She looked me up and down with the same expression I had seen on girls at department-store clothing racks then asked, "Got a car, Doc? I need some smokes."

"As your doctor, I'd have to advise you against it." She ignored the warning as she half-led and half-dragged me to the door.

After a quick stop at a convenience store, we were heading into the canyon west of the university in my old MG. Tammy's idea. In a matter of minutes, I had my car parked on the riverbank in a picnic area lit only by stars and a three-quarter moon. Almost before I had set the parking brake, Tammy was naked from the waist up and pulling at my belt. The moonlight on her breasts seemed redundant. My erection was into the game well before my mind was. I struggled with the toe of one shoe against the heel of the other one, afraid that, at the crucial moment, I would be unable to get my pants off from around my ankles. I groped at the button of her Levis.

"No need for that, Doc," she said, and her blonde head settled into the space between my lowest rib and the new seat of my entire consciousness.

The next day, I tried to follow up with Tammy for another date. I called the Dee Gee house three times, and three times was told that Tammy was unavailable. I called twice more in as many days with the same response. Finally, that Friday at around noon, I saw her walking across the grassy quad at the center of campus talking light-heartedly with two other girls. I loped over to intercept them.

"Hey, Tammy!" I called.

She looked at me then turned partially away to face the other girls, rolled her eyes dramatically, and exhaled audibly. "Get lost," she said.

I stammered, "Yeah, well … um, see you around." The day after that, I found her Delta Gamma sweatshirt and bra pushed halfway under the passenger seat of my car. The sweatshirt I stretched over the back of the driver's seat like a seat cover. The bra I threw in the dormitory dumpster.

I no longer equated sex exclusively with love, but making the conceptual distinction didn't help me satisfy my longing for either one as I spent my nights alone in Santa Rosita. I might be in love with Marivela, but it was too hard to tell. I certainly lusted for her. I probably would have fallen hopelessly in love with Mercedes or Luz at the merest sign of interest from either one. I thought briefly about finding a prostitute. Certainly, some of the young women in Santa Rosita or Huaynatambo must have plied the trade. Maybe I could find a pretty one, I fantasized, and arrange for some kind of exclusive deal as the Son of Lightning. I felt simultaneously charged up and dirtied by the idea. I also worried about the effects of the inevitable gossip on my research relationships. It was the worry that killed the idea for good.

Porfirio Sanchez had been hunting half-heartedly for Bonifacio Vargas ever since the interrogation of his brother Camilo, the cattle thief. Camilo had taken a good deal of guff from fellow prisoners over the issue of his younger brother's reputed opportunism with Camilo's wife. Therefore, when the detective held a pistol to Camilo's head and demanded the names of his *terrorista* associates, Bonifacio's name tripped off his tongue without so much as stubbing a toe.

Sanchez came upon Bonifacio on the road from Ayacucho to Santa Rosita. The morning was fresh and he traveled with his windows down, heartened by the prospect of collecting his monthly graft from Ganz and the *gringo* anthropologist. Driving with caution, as he always did, he saw Vargas from a distance and slowed his car. Wary of a trap, but seeing no one else around, he was delighted to recognize the down-and-out Bonifacio. It felt like a bonus, a freebie, an opportunity to appear heroic once again in the apprehension of a known terrorist.

Pulga had found a cozy spot for a nap behind a grassy hillock that hid him from the road. He woke at the sound of the approaching car. Slowly, he withdrew the old revolver and checked the position of the wobbly cylinder. He only had two bullets and if he had to shoot it was important that the hammer not fall on an empty chamber. He rolled to his belly, staying as flat as he could, and inched far enough around the hillock to watch what was happening at the opposite side of the road. In front of an empty, idling car, a top-heavy man walked with a slight limp toward Bonifacio, who sat in a crouch with his head down. Mr Top-Heavy took a fine looking pistol from a shoulder holster and held it close against his leg.

Top-Heavy was *policía.* He had to be. He began to goad Bonifacio, prodding him with a combination of insults. Without a clear and immediate intent to fire, but just in case, Pulga quietly cocked the pistol and took aim across the hillock. Bonifacio ignored Top-Heavy's insults, which irritated the cop. He stepped in front of Bonifacio and, with a swift backhand, pistol-whipped him across the side of the head. Bonifacio rolled with the blow and came to his knees with his knife in his hand. This brought a smile to the cop's face. He raised his fine *pistola* with a look of satisfaction that to Pulga resembled a hungry man assessing a tender bite of meat.

Pulga had to make a decision. Given the weight of the old revolver and the balkiness of its trigger, it was luck more than skill that guided the bullet from the wavering barrel into the overhanging flesh of Porfirio Sanchez's belly. Falling back on his training, Sanchez spun as he fell to the roadway and squeezed off several shots in the direction of his assailant. But Pulga had already flattened himself against the mound of earth and the bullets either whizzed by or churned up turf.

As Pulga lay pinned by fear, Sanchez began an arduous journey in his direction. With his right hand gripping the pistol and his left hand pressing hard against the hole in his gut, he used what leverage he could get from his elbows and knees to push himself forward a few excruciating inches at a time. Each time he forced his bulk forward, he left a fresh streak of blood, first on the hard-packed dirt, then on the damp grass. Each time he stopped to gather his strength, the streak of blood blossomed into a pool. By the time he had crossed half the distance from the road to the hillock, his strength was gone and his life was at an end. Bonifacio Vargas got to his feet, followed the trail of blood and hovered for a minute over the form that in his mind could as easily have belonged to the mayor of Uchurimac as to Porfirio Sanchez. Bonifacio needed a drink. Maybe he could find one back in the town.

When it occurred to Pulga that he wasn't going to die, he pushed himself to his knees, and then, once assured that the top-heavy cop wasn't going to move, he got to his feet. He watched Bonifacio Vargas shuffle along the road toward Santa Rosita and decided to let him go. The decision about what to do with a dead cop was harder. Pulga determined to take the decision to his superior. He collected the cop's excellent pistol and then pulled the still-running car alongside the body. There was no way Pulga could lift Sanchez into the trunk, so instead he opened the rear door and hoisted the heavy torso onto the floorboard. Then from the other side of the car he reached across the seat, got a grip on the dead man's sport coat and dragged him the rest of the way in.

My anthropological project proceeded as smoothly as I ever could have hoped. I was becoming well grounded in the daily rituals of the villagers of Huaynatambo. I understood their social structure, their values, their means of production and the myths with which they made sense of it all. I still couldn't answer my main research question about the results of intense external pressures on the culture, but I was close to establishing a baseline of cultural norms as a comparison.

It was a relief to no longer be embarrassed about my work. I continued my regular correspondence with Alfredo Ramirez and wrote, less frequently, to Jack Bentley. It turned out I was more than ready to have an outlet for my thoughts and observations. I still didn't reveal that I owed my successes to my masquerade as the Lightning God. It wasn't exactly standard anthropological procedure to impersonate deity. Also, I was more than a bit uncomfortable knowing that the first conquistadors owed their bloody successes to similar misunderstandings.

I wrote to Fredo every Sunday with a synopsis of the week's work. He would reply with gentle critique, usually in the form of questions about what I had observed. Fredo's questions helped me trace an interpretive thread through the mass of data I was accumulating. For some reason, Fredo also remained interested in less anthropological topics, especially Alejandro Ganz de la Vega. Had I met him? Had I been to his *hacienda*? What had I heard? I told him what I knew, which wasn't very much.

I received a postcard from Marivela not long after the New Year. It was short and sweet:

> *Querido,*
>
> *I was so happy to receive your card! Fredo says you are starting to feel more contented with the progress of your research. Congratulations. I hope you get everything you came for.*
>
> *Besitos, Marivela*

The card became the bookmark in my current set of field notes.

Of course, I still had a minor crush on Mercedes, despite the realization that it was unreciprocated. Now that all my illusions of romance with Mercedes were gone, we actually had become rather comfortably social. It was pretty obvious that she was nearly as lonely as I was. A couple of times a week, I persuaded her to let me buy her dinner at *Los Tres Chanchitos.* At first, we kept our conversations to medicine, townspeople and the like. I managed to learn a little about her history and to tell her a lot about mine.

One evening, she worked up the courage to ask me a question that caught me completely off-guard.

"Sam, if you wanted to help me financially with the clinic, why didn't you just come out and say so?"

"What?" I was genuinely bewildered. "I don't know what you mean."

"Don't lie about it now. What's the point?"

"I really don't know what you're talking about." I was confused, and I guess my face showed it.

"The money I get from the *padre* whenever I need it. That doesn't come from you?"

"I don't know anything about any money," I assured her.

For the first time ever, she looked as confused as I felt.

Cassandra peered in silence from the side rear window of the Mercedes-Benz and watched as the familiar sights of colonial downtown Lima rolled by. These stately buildings of government and church that had not so long ago been the highlights of her home landscape now appeared shabby and hostile. Where before they had represented nothing so much as opportunity – for stories, for fashionable intercourse, for the advancement of her media career – they now cast shadows of corruption and despotism. Behind the stone walls, the heavy wooden doors and the massive iron gates turned the machinery that ground the life out of her country and distilled it to a trickle of fantastic wealth, heady liquor for a few men drunken with ambition and self-importance. This, she now saw, was enemy territory.

The invitation she held was one of many that Cassandra still received routinely. *Comandante* Rita decreed that this one should be accepted.

"I think," said Rita, "it is time for the beloved Cassandra to once again enter society."

As an attractive single woman and a member of the media establishment, her presence at official parties was always welcomed. This particular party, being hosted at the presidential palace by none other than President Fernando López, was meant to help consolidate his administration's sagging public support. Elected three years earlier, the initially popular López, with his liberal rhetoric and his rugged good looks, had begun to lose credibility in economic and foreign affairs and as a peacemaker both at home and abroad.

López's policies had proven disastrous for the already sluggish Peruvian economy. All over the country, people had to line up early in the morning to buy such basic foods as sugar and cooking oil. He renounced the country's international debts and the World Bank had responded by cutting off all credit. He attempted to nationalize the banks within Peru and once again failed. Conditions for Peruvian workers deteriorated at the same time as the upper classes began building higher, stronger walls to protect their interests. National strikes had become commonplace and the general level of dissatisfaction and unrest created a tinderbox for the heated messages of the radical left. The strength of *El Colibrí*'s Crimson Road in particular had grown alarmingly.

The military responded to the rising unrest with increasing violence. *Sinchi* death squads sprang up and operated with impunity. Innocent civilians disappeared on the basis of the flimsiest suspicions of subversive activity. Young people, students in particular, were hauled from their houses or grabbed in the streets, forced into cars and carried to their deaths. Occasionally the government's draconian measures, like that of the mass execution in Lurigancho Prison, actually found their way into the international press. The heat of international opinion fell on López.

Outside the presidential palace, Cassandra stepped from the rear of the car wearing a black gown and carrying a small handbag to match. Her dress was slit in the back to just above the knee. Long sleeves hid the new muscularity in her arms while a deeply plunging back highlighted her sinuous figure. Her only jewelry was a double strand of pearls paralleling her scooped neckline, and earrings of matching pearls suspended from fine silver chains. At the door, she traded her engraved invitation for a flute of champagne and began to scan the room.

Before she could take another step, a small man with buzzed-short hair, deep-set gray eyes and acne scars across his cheekbones moved to block her path. An involuntary shudder rippled her spine. This was the publicly unobtrusive Adolfo Villarreal, current head of López's secret police. As a general in the army, Villarreal had been charged with anti-narcotics operations. In that role, he'd been invited to a drugs conference in Washington, DC, where it was rumored he had established contacts with the CIA. The suspicion, held by many and spoken aloud by few, was that he had successfully subverted the nation's anti-drug program into a powerful machine for personal profit. It was rumored that he replaced huge quantities of confiscated cocaine with flour or powdered plaster. The substituted product was burned and the real cocaine entered the vast international distribution network run by the cartel in Medellín, with profits reverting to Villarreal. Other whispers linked the shadowy figure to the death squads. One such rumor held that he had directly supervised the mass executions in Lurigancho Prison.

"*Señorita* Ganz, if you would permit me …" He reached out and took hold of her handbag. She tightened her grip defensively, and for a second they stood at an impasse. Then she released the bag with a cheaply manufactured smile. Such as this, she thought, are the pigs that spoil our country. With no attempt at discretion, Villarreal flicked through the small purse, which contained only her ID, a personal calling card with her private number in Puerta del Sol, a lipstick, a compact and a condom. He snapped it shut and handed it back. "Enjoy the party," was all he said.

Cassandra moved from small group to small group, greeting people and offering minimal answers to questions about her hiatus from television. No one could blame her for taking a break, especially in the wake of the bombings, and especially since it was common knowledge that she didn't need the money. The women she encountered unanimously focused on her new, boyish hairstyle with remarks ranging from "Oh, my God. What have you done?" to "I love it. It's so fresh. So bold!" The men said little with their mouths but spoke volumes with their eyes. Thinly disguised lust tracked every move she made. Although her path among the party guests appeared organic and natural, in reality it was a strategic course set to ensure that when *El Presidente* arrived at the head of the wide staircase descending from the interior of the palace she would be among the first things he noticed.

And she was. With her back to the staircase, she sensed his entry by the hush of the crowd. As all faces squared to his like sunflowers, she deliberately delayed long enough to be the last to turn. Long enough for his eyes to fix on her blonde head, to linger on her long neck and to trace down the curve of her naked back to the place where the vee in her dress pointed like an arrow to the fine territory below. When she turned, her eyes locked on his for a fleeting private moment, and then he resumed his public entrance, spreading his presidential gaze evenly across the ceremonial hall.

El Presidente López gave a short speech in which he made two promises designed to make peace with the nation's power brokers; one, that he would set the government on a stronger course of fiscal austerity to raise Peru from her economic doldrums, and two, that he would continue to strengthen the nation's defense against internal violence and subversion. Polite applause followed and Cassandra joined in. Then, as he descended to the floor of the hall, she moved to the center of the room to engage in superficial conversation and wait for López to make the next move.

It took nearly half an hour, but it happened just as she expected. President López moved in next to her with an extra flute of champagne to replace the nearly empty one she had been holding almost since her arrival. "Miss Ganz, how nice of you to come."

"Please, Mr President, call me Cassandra. I wouldn't have missed it for the world."

"I had hoped we might see your brother tonight."

Cassandra gave an empathetic nod. "I'm afraid Alejandro does not fully appreciate your policies regarding the banks."

"And you do?"

"I have always been one of your staunchest supporters, *Señor Presidente*."

"You may call me Fernando," he said, lowering his voice, and his eyes, to a more intimate level. "Perhaps we should meet again more privately to discuss your support."

Cassandra reached into her handbag and retrieved the card with her private telephone number and pressed it into his hand. "You may call me here with confidence any time."

Alejandro Ganz hung up the phone in the study. His conversation, encoded and decoded by a scrambling device, had confirmed what he already believed to be so. He could get the weaponry that *El Colibrí* demanded. But Christ, he thought, what an arsenal! The destructive power of the guns alone would be formidable, and *El Colibrí*'s list didn't end with guns. It included grenades and rocket launchers.

It was the Devil's bargain. He knew that if he didn't supply the weapons, someone else eventually would, and he would pay the price of reprisal. He also knew there was no guarantee he would be safe even if he *did* supply them. As an avowed capitalist, and US educated at that, he was the epitome of what the *Camino Rojo* despised. For how long could he buy his peace? How long could he protect the tranquility of Santa Rosita, el Valle del Cóndor and his coca plantations in the *selva*? *El Colibrí* was becoming bolder. Bolder and stronger.

Ganz declined to place an order. Better, he thought, to stall for time.

Outside of my deepening bond with Enrique, it was my relationship with Pedro Buenaventura that I found the most satisfying. We spent many weekend and evening hours in conversation. Our talks enriched my work as the priest provided reality checks for the information I gathered among the *campesinos*. Even more important, he offered me a type of friendship, adult friendship, which I had never before experienced. It seemed I could ask him anything, or tell him anything, without fear of judgment.

In one of our conversations, after a couple glasses of *pisco,* I asked him, "What's your story, *Padre*?"

"What do you mean?"

"I mean, what are you doing here? In the priesthood? Way out here in Santa Rosita? There must be a story."

We were sitting in his kitchen. Rain sheeted off the tile roof in a translucent, pleated curtain past the window. Pedro let his head roll back and gazed at the ceiling, which left me looking at his badly shaved throat with its pronounced Adam's apple.

Finally he spoke. "I grew up in the capital. I was born in the *barrio* la Victoria. What you would call a slum. My father was a corporal at the time, in the *policía.* In those early days, we were quite poor." He paused and I remained silent. "As I grew up, I developed an interest in law. My prospects looked bright. I was good at my studies and my father was moving up in the ranks of the *policía.* He had begun to develop influential contacts in the government. By the time I was in high school, he was a detective and we had become very well off. We moved out of La Victoria and into Miraflores, a respectable upper-middle class neighborhood. No one in the family ever questioned how that was possible on a policeman's salary. My mother had no income. Still, my father came home every night, we had a nice dinner, we talked about my studies, we talked about the news ..." The window lit up momentarily, followed by a muted clap of thunder.

"Then one day," continued Pedro, "he *was* the news. A woman in Miraflores saw three men stop a neighbor boy in the street. After a short struggle, they forced him into the back of their car and drove away. The woman had been on her way to a birthday party and was carrying a camera. She took a picture. The boy was never seen again."

The rain intensified.

"The woman took the picture to the boy's parents and they took it to an attorney. The license plate was legible and the men's faces, including my father's, were clear enough. Unfortunately, the boy wasn't recognizable in the photo. The attorney attempted to investigate, but he was obstructed at every step of the way. Stories were fed to the press. The woman with the camera became strangely mum. The boy was maligned as a subversive … which I knew was ridiculous.

"There was never a trial. The rest of the world – my mother, my friends, everyone – acted as if it had all been some lamentable, justifiable action, if indeed it had happened at all. But I knew better. I couldn't live with such deception anymore. It was unbearable, as if my own home had suddenly become a place of death, decay and indifference. My soul was in anguish.

"One afternoon, as I walked past the cathedral, I found my steps slowing. My feet seemed reluctant to move, as if they were obeying signals from some source other than my brain. I stopped and looked up at the massive façade, considered its detail and craftsmanship. I imagined the hours of human labor, the blistered hands and the aching muscles that lay behind each carved stone. I began to add it all up in my mind like some great tally sheet.

"Then something happened inside me. It was like a conduit opened between my soul and those of the ancient craftsmen. All their pain, all their joy poured into me like an avalanche. It was overwhelming, Sam. My heart was bursting. I felt I would be crushed by the weight of it. Then, when I thought I couldn't bear it anymore, the door to the cathedral opened and out walked an old woman with a little boy. The little boy turned and looked right at me. In that instant, the weight lifted from my soul.

"The next morning," he said, his voice turning from wistful to matter-of-fact, "I began my preparations to enter the priesthood."

"What was that like?" I asked.

"I was elated, at first anyway. I felt like I had done something very special, very courageous. I was engaged in righteous rebellion, breaking out of the mold, learning to live by a higher law. I felt I had God's approval, God's ear, God's guidance. In retrospect, I suppose I was probably insufferable and self-righteous. At least, I fear that's how my fellow seminarians must have viewed me."

"You think so?"

"*Sí. Creo que sí.* I refused to acknowledge the political realities of the priesthood. I didn't share the same ambitions as the others, so I didn't fit in. That's how I ended up in Santa Rosita. One day, the bishop said that if I wanted to keep my head in the clouds I would find it easier to do from the highlands." He gave a weak smile. "There aren't many priests left around Ayacucho. The *Camino Rojo* regards us as enemies of the revolution."

Something he had said earlier was nagging at my curiosity. "The boy who disappeared …" I ventured, "It almost sounded as if you knew him."

"I knew him."

"Was he a close friend?"

"More than that."

"More?"

"He was my lover."

A whole raft of realization came cascading down on me. The man who had become my best friend and confidant was a homosexual. How could I not have known? If I had known, would it have made a difference? It had made a difference between me and my brother, not to mention between my brother and my father. And then another thought: Pedro Buenaventura's father, the police detective, had known. The abduction and probable murder of a boy in Miraflores had been no mistake.

"Oh my god," was all I could say.

That night, I walked back to my *pensión* with my feelings careening like litter in a whirlwind. I slipped into my room quietly in order to avoid conversation. From my dresser drawer, I retrieved my Christmas card from Mitch. I studied the picture that Mitch had created for me: the young man, the angel's wings, the outstretched arms, the peace offering of a salmon. I had been such an ass. A fearful, arrogant, self-centered ass.

One morning late in January, Alex Ganz loaded his mother's new luggage into the trunk of the BMW he kept in San Isidro and drove her to the airport. There, he kissed her goodbye and waited until her Alitalia flight had disappeared into the gritty Lima sky. On his way to his office in Miraflores, he played out several potential courses of action with respect to *El Colibrí* and the *Camino Rojo*. None of them was desirable. Finally, he came to a decision.

Back at his desk Alex placed a call to his local contact in US intelligence. "How high up in the US Justice Department can you get a message? … That high? … Tell him that I would personally like to discuss my direct participation in the American war on drugs."

Ganz's conversation with Justice occurred a surprisingly quick half-hour later. The result of that conversation was quite satisfactory. He then picked up the phone again, activated the scrambler and entered a number he had memorized. The voice he expected came on the line. "I want to place an order," said Ganz, "with a few special provisions."

"Tell me, *Padre*, what's the secret of the peace here in Santa Rosita? I hear stories of *Rojistas* controlling villages as near as Uchurimac. What keeps them from overrunning this town as well?"

"I have often wondered. Have you heard the saying that foxes don't play in the lion's den?"

"No, but I get the drift. Ganz?"

Father Pedro answered with a shrug and upturned palms that seemed to communicate, "Who else?"

"Is he that powerful?"

"It's not the army that keeps the *guerrillas* away. Nor vice versa."

Three forces controlled the fate of this region: the government, *el Señor* Ganz and the *Camino Rojo*. On the side of the government, I had encountered only the corrupt cop, Porfirio Sanchez. The closest I had come to Ganz was as an apparent object of interest to Manolo Ruíz. And, to the best of my knowledge, I had never met a single *Rojista*.

"The lion's den," I echoed softly. I pictured the people of Santa Rosita as mice scurrying around unmolested by a powerful but languid beast while the foxes, the *Rojistas*, kept their wary distance. Then, thinking of Porfirio Sanchez and his monthly knocks at the door of the *casa* Flores, I envisioned a poisonous snake. I wondered if the snake was invited into the lion's den or merely tolerated. Dangerous to crush but impossible to ignore? And how does the lion see me? Fox, mouse or snake?

It didn't take long for me to get my answer. It was three days later. The *feria* had broken up and I had gone into a local *bodega* to buy a beer for me and an Inca Kola for Enrique. While I was paying for the drinks, the black Land Rover glided to the curb. As I left the store, the Rover's passenger-side window dropped smoothly into its door panel. It was Manolo Ruíz.

"*Señor* Young, *un momento, por favor*."

"*Señor* Ruíz, I believe?"

A nodded reply. "My employer requests your company for a drink at his home."

"Enrique," I said to the boy, "*nos vemos mas allá*."

I climbed into the black leather passenger seat with my unopened liter of cheap Peruvian beer and a heady combination of curiosity and misgivings. Manolo closed the window, muting the sound of the all-terrain tires on the cobblestone street.

Cobblestones yielded to dirt as the Rover pulled away from the center of town. Stuccoed adobe walls with tile roofs gave way to raw adobe walls with tin roofs, then to broken adobe walls studded with fieldstone, and finally across violet-flowering fields toward the partially terraced foothills of the *cordillera.* Manolo remained mute and expressionless. I wondered what went on inside that massive skull and whether or not I would really want to know. Walls, I thought, turning my attention back to the passing scenery and accepting the silence as a given. Walls, walls, walls.

The road angled upward, gently at first, then more steeply as it snaked up the narrowing canyon leading to el Valle del Cóndor. I felt my anxiety bubbling up in the form of stomach acid. I wondered who had seen me climb into the Rover. Enrique, I thought, and the woman from the bodega. I noticed that my right hand ached from its grip on the neck of the cold beer bottle. I may soon need this hand for a handshake, I thought, transferring the bottle to the plush-carpeted floor where I kept it from rolling with my feet.

The road surface transitioned again with a slight bump from dirt to a wide pad of asphalt before a plain wrought iron gate. The gate looked sturdy and, like all the gates and fences I had observed in Lima, this one carried spikes and serrations to deter would-be climbers. The iron fence that continued similarly on either side was anchored in concrete foundations set into steep hillsides. To the right of the gate, a vigorous stream bubbled through the fence and cascaded away in a confusion of mist and rocks. To the left and beyond the fence sat a blocky stone house and next to that a pair of matching Volvo farm trucks. Before I could figure out the mechanism for its triggering, the gate slid open and Manolo guided the Rover into the valley beyond.

The sight took my breath away. It was like a movie Shangri-La. The broad expanse of grass and wildflowers, still damp from their afternoon soaking, now shone like baskets of jewels in the shafts of sunlight piercing the clouds. Mist hung over the brook that divided the valley and llamas browsed along its banks. Looking at the sprawling colonial house, I could imagine its days at the center of a feudal empire. I envisioned the bent-backed peasants at the end of a hard journey, lugging their tributes of corn, potatoes, barley and quinoa to an overseer who would make marks in a large book. I could see the hope in the peasants' faces that the marks would be right and sufficient. The only signs I could detect of the current era were the wind sock atop the stone hangar, the nose of an airplane inside it and a subtle but complex array of antennae on the roof of each building.

A dapper man with short graying hair waited at the door of the house. "Juan Pablo will show you in," said Manolo. He seemed to have to force the words into the thick silence of the Land Rover as be brought it to a halt.

I nodded and climbed down. Before closing the door I placed the bottle of beer on the passenger seat. "For you," I said to Manolo. He nodded curtly.

Juan Pablo conducted me to a parlor with matching leather chairs and a light-colored wooden sideboard. I was about to decide whether to sit or stand when my host strode into the room and thrust out a hand for shaking. My first thought was, so young! He seemed not much older than I was. Not much older, but a lot more poised and sophisticated. Dressed in olive chinos, a pale yellow sweater and moccasin-style loafers, he looked like he had stepped right off the cover of GQ magazine. I regarded the dark shadow of a beard and the olive skin and suffered a fleeting pang of jealousy.

"Samson Young?" he inquired with an accent that hinted at the Northeastern US, maybe by way of Europe. "I'm Alex Ganz."

"Pleased to meet you."

"I'm glad you could come. What would you like to drink?"

"I was about to have a beer when your Mr Ruíz intercepted me." I heard a bit of irritation in my own voice that I only partially regretted.

"Yes. Well. I'm afraid Manolito uses his social skills somewhat sparingly. Still," he continued, pulling two brown bottles from a small refrigerator in the sideboard, "here we are."

I took a freshly opened bottle and observed the label. "Samuel Adams?"

"A holdover from my college days," said Ganz with a smile. "It sort of spoiled me for the local beers." The beer was good and the smile seemed genuine enough, but I remained wary. "We could sit here if you like," offered Ganz. "But it might be nicer to stroll about the property."

I made a lead-the-way gesture toward the door. Outside, the light had softened, heightening, if possible, the beauty of the surroundings.

"I've been wanting to meet you," said Ganz, "ever since you arrived in Santa Rosita, but the demands of my business made it difficult."

"So you chose to have me followed instead?"

"Ah. My apologies. In my position, the political climate being what it is, I tend to be a little overcautious. When an American comes unannounced to Ayacucho with the intention of staying, there is a chance that his presence will be, shall we say, a complication to my life here. Usually someone in your government extends me the courtesy of a call if there is going to be any official activity in the area. But still, I had to check you out."

Shit, I thought, courtesy calls from the US government? "And do you believe that I am such a complication?"

"Not where my business interests are concerned."

Where then? As we walked I sipped my beer, which became more flavorful as it warmed. We arrived in silence at a stream bank, and there we stood, a good ten feet apart, each peering into our own private understandings of flowing water.

"Are there fish?" I asked.

"A few native trout. The stream was nearly fished out twenty years ago. I considered planting it, but I decided against it. I'd like to give the indigenous fish a chance to come back."

"And hatchery fish …"

"Would be strong and robust, but they would probably drive the natives to extinction."

I turned my head just far enough to study the figure of Alex Ganz against the deepening green of el Valle del Cóndor. An intended metaphor? Is he talking only about fish? Or is he revealing feelings about the indigenous people? Late afternoon shadows crept into the contours of the valley walls. A breeze swept across the surface of the grass like an invisible sable-hair brush.

"What a beautiful place," I said.

"I love it here."

"I understand you are a bank president." He nodded. "You must spend most of your time in Lima."

"More than I like. But I have competent people working for me there and I can carry out a surprising amount of my work by phone and fax." At that moment, a frog that I hadn't seen before leaped from the grass of the far bank into the stream with a splash.

"Tell me, Sam – may I call you Sam? – why did you come to Peru?" Ganz turned to make eye contact. "And I don't mean the academic reasons. I understand anthropology. I mean as a man, why did you come to Ayacucho?"

"I don't know ..." I left the words hanging, and Ganz did nothing to rescue them. "I suppose I needed to get a sense of my own boundaries. At home I was white on white, too much a part of everything around me. There were no sharp edges. I had no clear sense of where Sam Young ended and the rest of the world began. Ayacucho has sharp edges. Of all the places in the world where I might have gone with my language skills, this seemed especially exotic, interesting, and I suppose dangerous."

"Hmm..." It came out as the first syllable of a chuckle. "I remember feeling that way once about Cambridge, Massachusetts." His face softened and I felt mine doing the same. "So, how is it going? Are you getting your fill of danger?"

"I guess I was pretty stupid about that part. I've seen my life dangling at the end of a gun barrel once already and, believe me, that was enough. Santa Rosita seems incredibly peaceful, though."

"We've been lucky. It's getting late. Do you have dinner plans?"

"The special at *Los Tres Chanchitos*."

"Then you'll stay. I've asked Consuelo to plan for an extra place at the table."

"Sure. Thank you. I'd like that."

As we walked back toward the house, Ganz broached another subject. "I know that Porfirio Sanchez has latched onto you. How deep is the bite?"

"Fifty bucks a month."

"What kind of burden does that create?"

"Painful. But not crippling. I haven't seen him yet this month."

Ganz nodded. "Sanchez learned a long time ago not to kill a cash cow."

We carried our empty beer bottles back into the house where Juan Pablo announced dinner. The dining table, a single expanse of dark, oiled wood on heavy legs, was large enough to seat eight people with elbowroom, but only six chairs were present. Three place settings of simple-patterned china, crystal stemware and a baroque silver service formed a triangle at one end. At the other, a silver candelabrum supported three partially burned tapers. Behind the chair opposite mine, wearing a loose-flowing skirt and a mohair sweater, stood Luz Castro.

"Sam Young," said Alex, switching to Spanish, "allow me to introduce Luz Castro."

"We've met before. *La Señorita* happens to be my young friend Enrique's favorite schoolteacher." Luz blushed. Ganz looked pleased.

After we had taken our seats, with Alex at the head of the table, Juan Pablo poured a Chilean sauvignon blanc and served the first course, a delicate seafood salad. I was in heaven. "Mmmm," I said. "This is delicious." Alex agreed. Luz kept silent.

For the second course, Juan Pablo ladled a wild mushroom bisque. "Oh, my," I exclaimed. "This is wonderful."

"It is quite good," agreed Alex. "Juan Pablo, my compliments to Consuelo."

"She would refuse the compliment, Don Alejandro. Miss Castro prepared the meal this evening."

Alex looked surprised. Luz struggled to keep her pride contained within the confines of a modest smile. The main course, sea bass baked with a sprinkling of breadcrumbs, parmesan cheese, capers and garlic in olive oil, with a side of asparagus, evoked equal reverence. Juan Pablo topped off the wineglasses again and our trio ate in silence. I was the first to speak.

"Alex, Luz, I don't think I've ever had a more delicious meal." They both smiled to acknowledge the thanks. "Forgive me for asking," I continued, "but are you …" I hesitated, looking from her to him and back to her again.

Luz looked at Alex. When Alex did not meet her eyes, she turned her flushed attention to the grain of the wooden tabletop. Alex answered, "Luz is a good friend. She's staying here until she completes her degree in education." Luz's look neither confirmed nor denied Ganz's description, but I couldn't help feeling that her mood had become heavy. "In fact," Ganz added with what sounded like a note of pride, "she's very nearly done."

Luz placed her napkin on the table and pushed back her chair. "Excuse me," was all she said. She left quickly through the serving door. I could taste the quiet she left behind.

"You'll be wanting to get back to town," said Ganz, ending the awkward silence. "Come on, I'll drive you down."

Darkness had engulfed el Valle del Cóndor. As the Land Rover rolled through the open gate, I noticed a faint glow coming from down below where the stream disappeared in a waterfall. It brightened, dimmed and then vanished, like headlights carving an arc against the stone, then clicking off. Ganz paid no particular attention and I assumed he was unsurprised by it.

Ganz seemed to be in no hurry to get back to Santa Rosita. Nor was he very talkative. In the relative quiet, there was one question I couldn't shake from my head. I decided to just ask it. "Alex, I'm curious. What can you tell me about the coca trade in this area?"

"Hmm," he vocalized with a slight upward nod of the head that said he had been expecting some such question. "Don't be coy, Sam. I own it. And I expect you knew that."

I grimaced at my own artlessness.

"Coca," he continued, "is a complicated topic in this country. Coca drives the Peruvian economy more than any other industry. I'm not just talking about its seamy underworld, either. You may not believe it, but coca money has been instrumental in building or improving hundreds of schools. Coca supports indigenous arts and artisan markets. It builds roads and airports. The only reason the business is even illegal here is because of pressure from the United States.

"But it is illegal, and so it has to operate without the official sanction of the government. Mind you, I said 'official' sanction. This government would collapse in a day without the support of coca dollars. At the same time, if it openly tolerated the industry, the repercussions from the G7, the World Bank and the IMF would be devastating. So the government has to play both sides. That inevitably leads to violence and conflict. And it leaves the coca industry vulnerable to extortion from terrorists. It also allows corrupt elements within the government to abuse their power to reap huge rewards.

"Imagine the efficiencies that would be created – the wealth, the good that could be done, the violence and waste that could be avoided – if the use of the drug were legalized and its distribution controlled and taxed."

Well, I thought, he certainly answered my question. A better, more straightforward answer than I'd expected. Everything I learned about this man only served to increase my esteem for him.

Ganz pulled into the lane alongside Doña Rosario's house and parked in front of my tarp-covered Jeep. He killed the lights but not the engine. I guessed it was his turn to ask a pointed question. His voice came at me the same way a bolt of lightning had several weeks before.

"Are you in love with Mercedes Marquez?"

I stiffened involuntarily in the seat and then I let my head roll back against the headrest. "I don't know," I said. "Probably not. No. Not really."

"Is she in love with you?"

"No." I took a deep breath and let it out slowly. "Why? Are you in love with her?"

For a long while he said nothing. Then he answered softly, "It was nice to meet you. Let me know if there is ever anything you need." I nodded. "I'm serious. You can always reach me through the bank."

My next letter to Fredo, in which I reported my visit to el Valle Del Cóndor, seemed to have roused him from a virtual coma. Suddenly he was interested in the minutiae of my observations. He wanted to know everything. How many people appeared to be living there? Whom had I met? What was the breakdown by age and gender? How many and what kinds of vehicles had I seen? Frankly, I found the energy level of his inquiries a little alarming. It was as though his interest in Alex and his home were not so much academic as … what? Tabloid? Maybe Fredo secretly worshiped power and celebrity in the way of so many Americans.

I answered his questions, despite a nagging feeling that something wasn't right, but a feeling that wasn't strong enough to make me examine or question my behavior. I wrote him that I had met fewer than a dozen people and that they all were members of the household, with the exception of one rather intimidating personal assistant. That the place was peaceful to an uncommon extreme. That the vehicles I had seen amounted to a Land Rover, a couple of farm trucks and a small airplane.

In the early hours of morning a diesel, stake-bed Volvo pulled away from an airstrip deep within Ganz's holdings in the *selva.* The cab of the truck was bright yellow, and brightly colored pom-poms hung from the visors. The stakes and railings that formed the sides and rear of the cargo area were painted red, blue and green. On the front of the wooden cargo box above the cab, in vivid blue script, were the words, *Vida de Perro*. A Dog's Life. The windows were open and a cassette tape of Peruvian folk music played in the stereo.

The driver of the truck wore the clothes of a laborer, as did the man on the passenger side. Each was lean and muscled and each one carried beneath his shirt a loaded automatic weapon. In the upper cargo box rode another man, similarly dressed and similarly armed, apparently relaxing on top of a long wooden crate covered with a canvas tarp and a split bale of straw. Three more rode in the bed and passed a liter of beer among them. Against the cab another wooden crate and another bale of straw formed a bench for two of them. The third lounged in a spare tire covered with a dozen blankets. The rest of the cargo area was filled with fruit and produce, sacks of beans and rice, and muslin-wrapped sides of beef and pork. The whole ensemble looked for all the world like a group of farmers taking a load to market.

The truck climbed for more than an hour through heavily

vegetated slopes. Eventually the vegetation thinned and terraced hillsides appeared. As the diesel clattered its way over a pass in the *cordillera*, the rider on top spotted a flash of reflected sunlight. He banged twice with the flat of his hand on the roof of the cab and the driver pulled the truck to a stop. Both the driver and the lookout climbed down and made a show of urinating at the side of the road. When they started up again they drove slowly, and all six men had thumbed off the safeties of their weapons.

A patrol of a dozen *Rojistas*, eight men and four women between the ages of about fourteen and twenty-five, met the truck around the next bend. They were fully prepared to intimidate a crew of farmers and to relieve them of their vehicle and their goods. The colorful *Vida de Perro* must have looked like a godsend to the revolution. Most of the guerrillas didn't even pick up their weapons as their leader swaggered toward the truck with his carbine across his chest, resting in the crook of his arm. The driver stopped the truck as if according to a script, and the lead *terruco* ordered him to step down. The door swung open and the driver turned toward the jaded-looking young man.

In a period of two to three seconds, several things happened. The guerrilla noticed the color of the driver's eyes. The discordant image of blue eyes on a campesino turned to doubt, then fear. There was a flash as two slugs ripped through the guerrilla's chest. The other five men rose from their positions in the truck and, with precision born of training, opened fire on the rest of the patrol. Not a single *Rojista* got off a shot.

The man up top lifted binoculars to his eyes and scanned the surrounding countryside to make sure no witnesses would tell the story. The others gathered the bodies of the slain *terrucos* and laid them shoulder to shoulder and face down at the side of the road. As a final touch, the driver retrieved the patrol's red flag from where it lay and planted it at the end of the row of bodies.

Within another hour, the truck was grinding through the wrought iron gate at the opening of el Valle del Cóndor. The six men unloaded the contents of the truck into the stone guardhouse, and then the fairer-skinned men washed dark makeup from their faces and hair. Thirty minutes later, another truck with a similar cargo, having followed the same road, arrived at el Valle del Cóndor unmolested.

One day, Enrique and I returned early from field work in Huaynatambo. I had banking to do in anticipation of my now overdue monthly visit from detective Sanchez, and Enrique was tagging along in order to avoid, for as long as possible, Doña Rosario and her list of chores. I noticed a farm truck, *Vida de Perro*, parked alongside the bank – one of two trucks I had seen at el Valle del Cóndor. Two men were lifting a sofa down from the bed of the truck.

"Do you know those men?" I asked Enrique.

"They're not from around here."

The two men carried the sofa to a doorway adjacent to the bank where they stopped and waited as if something prevented them from entering. A moment later, Luz Castro emerged wearing jeans and an oversized maroon Harvard sweatshirt. She squeezed by, and the men started in. From the angle the sofa took as it moved through the doorway, it appeared they were taking it to an upstairs apartment.

"*¡Hola, Señorita!*" Enrique shouted as he ran in Luz's direction.

"Oh!" said Luz, surprised, turning toward us, "Enrique! How are you?" I approached at a less exuberant pace and noticed that Luz' eyes looked a bit puffy. "Have you had a good summer?" she asked the boy.

"Yes. I'm learning to be an anthropologist."

"Really," she exclaimed. I thought she was putting extra effort into her enthusiasm.

"Enrique has been helping me with my field work in Huaynatambo," I explained with a hand on the boy's shoulder and a smile for the schoolteacher. "Are you moving in?"

"I guess I am." Her enthusiasm had ebbed but she retained a tired smile.

"Well, that's good news for us. What's the occasion?"

"School starts soon. I'll be teaching half-time, every morning, to finish my degree. It seemed more convenient to be here in town." She paused before she added, "Don Alejandro is letting me have the apartment above the bank."

"It will be nice to have you around. Won't it, Enrique? We live just up the street if there's ever anything you need."

Enrique and the American left, followed soon after by the two men in the now-empty truck. That left Luz alone to drop into the sofa, take in the bare walls of her new home and consider her situation. It had finally become clear to her on the night of her dinner for Alex and the American that her *patrón*, Don Alejandro, did not share her fantasies of a life together. Later that night, as if to salt her own wound, she confronted him and forced him to vocalize his feelings.

"You must know that I care for you, Luz. But you're right. I'm not in love with you."

She stiffened at the words. The walls accelerated away from her in every direction, leaving her cold, brittle and alone.

"Then why am I here?"

"Because I needed company and you needed a break. Was it not also your choice to be here?"

"Choice? I was bought and paid for!"

"I'm sorry you feel that way. You are not property, Luz. You may leave any time you wish … only, I hope you will not."

Luz swam in a maelstrom of feelings. She wasn't sure which she found more upsetting; that she had deceived herself about Alex's affections or that she might lose her only chance to complete her education.

"I could leave? Where? To Lima?"

"If you wish."

"To Madam Zenobia?"

"You owe no debt to me or to the madam."

"Why would you want me to stay?" She studied his face for an answer through the distortion of her tears.

"Because, Luz, you add beauty and goodness to your environment. Because here you can finish your education and, at the same time, teach the children of Santa Rosita. Because, here, you can make a difference."

God, she thought. Here was a man to love and to hate.

"I would like to finish my degree." She forced the words to come out. He remained quiet. "I love the kids at the school." Quiet. "But I don't see how I can continue to live here."

"I understand. Give me a day or two to work something out."

So here she was. Free use of an apartment in Santa Rosita. A *nice* apartment. Half-time teaching for a year, at the end of which she would have her diploma and teaching certificate. And no strings attached. Amazing. And amazing, too, that she still felt so hurt, angry and lost.

The pain had begun after dinner, a dull ache that sharpened to a searing blade in a matter of an hour. Now any movement at all increased Juan Pablo's agony. Alex considered flying him to Lima or Huancayo, but he didn't know whether such a flight was more likely to save him or to kill him. He needed a doctor fast, and he thought he knew where he could find one.

He jumped into the Land Rover and sped through the gate, barely giving it time to open. When he reached the turnoff to the waterfall, he began to honk the horn and flash the headlights. He felt relieved when he saw the van parked among the eucalyptus.

Mercedes had not yet fallen asleep and the racket brought her immediately to the sliding door. Alex gave her no time to ask questions and took no time for introductions. "I have a medical emergency," he shouted. "Please follow me. I need you – now."

Without a second thought, Mercedes jumped into the driver's seat and started the van as Alex turned the Rover around. The moment he saw her headlights, he pulled away. She followed the glow of the taillights to the road, up the steep hill and through the gate. A stone house to the left was illuminated, but they didn't stop there. Instead they sped toward a larger array of lights in the center of the small valley and pulled up to a rear door of a big Spanish-style house.

Alex and Mercedes jumped from their cars – Mercedes was still barefoot – and she followed him into the house. Manolo Ruíz opened the door for them and followed them to the quarters of Juan Pablo and Consuelo. Juan Pablo lay shivering in pajamas beneath a single sheet that was drenched in perspiration. Consuelo stood at the other side of the bed and another man stood in the far corner looking more ready than actually involved.

"This woman is a doctor, old friend," said Alex to Juan Pablo. Then he stepped aside for Mercedes.

Mercedes felt Juan Pablo's pulse. "What are the symptoms?" Then as Alex explained, she ran expert hands across his neck and torso.

"I have a plane ready to fly," said Alex.

"No time. In the back of the van there are two wooden boxes. I need them." Manolo went without a word. "We need to move him to a table." Ganz and the other man slid their arms beneath him and lifted as gently as possible. "Cover it with fresh linens." And Consuelo moved into action. Within less than three minutes, the large dining table was covered with a blanket and a fresh sheet, Juan Pablo was spread upon it and Mercedes' footlockers were open on the floor.

"*Señora*," Mercedes addressed Consuelo. "We'll need more linens. Also, is there a large syringe? Something for suction? If you can find one, boil it. Keep the water handy. The rest of you, wash your hands. Scrub them well. Hurry!" She pulled a bottle of chloroform and a gauze bandage from one of the footlockers. Then she leaned over and, with fingertips placed gently against Juan Pablo's temple, spoke to him in soft tones. "*Señor*, you have appendicitis. I need to remove the poisoned organ. I am going to place a bandage over your face and I need you to breathe in slowly and deeply. Can you do that?" He nodded, but panic or pain or both filled his eyes.

When Alex and Manolo returned to the room with sleeves rolled and hands drying, Juan Pablo lay calmly on the table. On a clean towel, Mercedes had laid out a scalpel and several needles threaded with sutures. Consuelo returned with a stack of towels, metal tongs and a pot of water just coming off boil.

With the tongs, Mercedes retrieved a turkey baster from the pot and set it aside with the surgical instruments. To Alex she said, "You stand here. You're going to be my clamps. Each time I cut through a layer of tissue, you need to get in there with your fingers and hold the wound open." He nodded his comprehension and willingness.

"*Dios mío*," moaned Consuelo with a quick genuflection.

"You," said Mercedes to Manolo, "stand there." She handed him the baster and continued, "There's going to be blood. Too much and I won't be able to see. You need to use this to keep it sucked away." He nodded and then reached behind him to a china cupboard for a delicate serving bowl to capture the blood he suctioned off.

Mercedes pulled her hooded sweater off over her head, revealing a white tank-style undershirt. She cleansed her hands to the elbow with a disinfectant solution and then passed it to Alex, indicating that he should do the same. With the same solution she swabbed the abdomen of the unconscious Juan Pablo. She took the scalpel gently between her thumb and index finger, looked to Alex, looked to Manolo and then drew a glistening crimson line across the smooth brown torso. "Separate," she said, and Alex spread the wound with his fingertips. "Suction," she said, and Manolo vacuumed away the blood. Beneath a thin layer of adipose she found the rectus abdominus and, using the scalpel again, she opened a division in the heavily striated muscle. "Separate. Wider. Suction. Again. Shit. More light!" The third man grabbed a floor lamp, ripped away the shade and held it aloft.

"*Gracias a Dios*, it hasn't ruptured. More suction please." With her hands she isolated the inflamed appendix, and then very carefully she trimmed it away and deposited it in the bloody china bowl. She picked up the nearest of the sutures and talked herself and Alex through each step of closing up layers of tissue and stitching them back together.

"There. It's finished … for now." Mercedes stepped away from the table and wiped her hands on one of the towels. The adrenaline and continued focus that had sustained them all as Mercedes closed the wounds no longer buoyed the rest of the participants. They stood around slump-shouldered and anxious. Sensing this emotional deflation, Alex excused Manolo and the other man with his thanks. Consuelo sat in a chair, counted rosary beads and prayed.

"As soon as he starts to come around," cautioned Mercedes, "we'll need to comfort him and keep him still."

"How long will it be?" asked Consuelo as she stood and began gathering soiled towels.

"Not long. Maybe an hour. He will be very sore. May I help you clean up, *Señora*?"

"No. No, *déjeme sola con ello*."

"Let me show you where to wash up," said Alex. Mercedes, still barefoot, padded along behind him, noticing gratefully when the wooden floors yielded to thick, Persian carpet. He led her to a large bathroom and started a stream of warm water into a marble basin. "Please," he offered, holding out a fresh bar of fragrant soap.

She looked at him closely for the first time. She knew who he was, generally – she had seen him come and go in Santa Rosita – although she knew little about his life or his business. Standing there in his blood-flecked tan slacks with his white shirtsleeves rolled to the tops of strong-looking forearms, she found him very handsome. "Thank you." She took the soap and plunged her hands and wrists into the running water. Feeling suddenly self-conscious, she watched the swirl of water, blood and Betadine solution spiral against the pale marble. When her hands were clean again, Alex slid his own cupped hands under hers to receive the soap.

"There's a towel behind you," he said. It was the softest towel Mercedes had ever felt. Alex washed and then dried with the same towel she had used. Mercedes backed up and settled her weight into the corner formed by the bathroom counter and the wall. She looked down at the few spots of browning blood on her ribbed cotton undershirt, exhaled roughly and began to cry.

Not knowing what else to do, Alex stood in front of her, placed his hand against her face so that his little finger cradled her chin, and with his thumb he caught a tear and smoothed it across her cheek. She looked up. He smiled and said, "I owe you a great debt, but right now I think you could use a place to sit." She nodded, sucked in a ragged breath and followed him to a living room and a big, soft sofa where she collapsed.

"What you did tonight was remarkable, Mercedes."

"It was my first major surgery." Alex raised his eyebrows, but otherwise didn't comment. "The patient is ...?"

"A servant. An old friend. He's been with my family since before I was born. Will he be all right?"

"I've given him some antibiotics to fight infection. If he gets through the next twenty-four hours, I think he'll be fine."

"I'd like you to stay until then."

"Of course. I do have one question. How did you know where I would be tonight?"

Enrique no longer comes along with me every day. Doña Rosario and I agreed that he needs to spend more time with children his age, and frankly Enrique didn't put up much of a fuss when we suggested he curtail his 'anthropology' to one or two days a week. Today, I came alone to Huaynatambo.

For most of the day, I helped Jainor, a cousin of Benito Quispe, with the construction of a new room on the rear of his house to welcome the coming of a new child. The new room will become the kitchen, freeing up some living space in the main part of the house. With nothing but string to use for measurements, he had laid out the dimensions of the room and leveled the soil. We were now constructing walls from adobe bricks cured over the winter. We worked together until it looked like rain was imminent, then we covered the cache of adobe bricks and the new construction with blue plastic tarps. The blue plastic tarp, according to a college girlfriend from Homer, Alaska, is the Alaska state flower. "It came down to a vote," she said. "It was either that or the fifty-gallon oil drum." I liked her. We dated for almost two weeks before she left me for a townie with a pick-up truck full of dogs.

Blue plastic tarps also happen to bloom like flowers all throughout the Andes. You see them pitched as solitary hillside shelters with sticks for tent poles and stones for stakes at the edges of potato fields almost anywhere you go. A blue splash on the mountainside during the harvest season indicates a crop being guarded from theft or harm. Often, a spiral of smoke from a small wood or straw fire will snake its way up from the peak of the tarp. Last year, according to the residents of Huaynatambo, a boy from a neighboring village went missing from just such a watch station. Some villagers believe a puma carried him off. Others say *Camino Rojo*. Recent puma sightings supported the first hypothesis. The quantity of missing potatoes supported the second.

With the blue tarps anchored down, we took a lunch break. Jainor's wife, Isabel, had prepared a dish from *charki* and potatoes. *Charki* is dried seasoned meat, and in a slightly varied form of the word, jerky, it is reportedly the only Quechua word ever to have crept into the English language. I'd started bringing gifts of *charki* and other meats from Santa Rosita after about the second week of lunching on nothing but baked potatoes.

Isabel comes from Huachatambo, a small village a half day's walk into the mountains from Huaynatambo. She served Jainor and me a plate of food and prepared to disappear back into the infinite domain of women's work. Before she could slip away, I asked her how life was different in Huachatambo.

"I don't know, *Wirakocha*."

She seemed reluctant to talk, but Jainor, who wanted to please me, wouldn't let her off the hook so easily.

"C'mon, woman. Tell him. Tell him about the rounds."

"The rounds?" I asked.

"Tell him. Tell him," insisted Jainor.

"*Sí, Wirakocha.* The rounds. Because they are afraid." She stared at her hands, which were engaged in a little dialogue of their own.

"I don't understand."

"*Sí, Wirakocha.* So no one sleeps in his own house. Everyone in the village sleeps together in the center while people do rounds."

Eventually, I learned that the village fears the *Camino Rojo* on account of stories they have heard from other nearby villages. As a defensive measure, the village's adult population, men and women over the age of fifteen, had been divided into thirds. Each third constitutes a watch. Every night, while the rest of the village gathers to sleep communally in a small cluster of houses in the center of town, a watch, charged with the entire town's meager weaponry, forms a circle and maintains a continuous perimeter. One watch does 'the rounds' from dusk until midnight. At midnight, the weapons are passed to another watch, which marches from midnight until dawn. Each watch gets a full night's sleep every third night. They had been doing this for a year.

I sat out a rain shower sipping Inca Kola and chatting with Doménico Quispe in the town's only *bodega.* Doménico is Gabriela's father-in-law and the old man from Benito's funeral. It looked like we wouldn't get the normal monsoon-like drenching today. The clouds began to break and the sun lasered through, raising steam from everything it touched, from pastures to metal roofs to the back of a dappled hog grazing at the side of the muddy street. It was gorgeous.

I bade good-bye to the folks in the *bodega* and strolled in the direction of the closest patch of sunlight, which happened to be falling in front of the door of the house across the street. In the first few steps I took, I felt the tightness in my hamstrings from working all morning and sitting around all afternoon. With my back to the doorway across the street, I bent over at the waist to stretch my legs. From behind me came a sound of hissing and great wing beats. Being bent over, I looked back between my legs and saw a gigantic grey goose flapping and running right at me from the doorway with its neck stretched forward and its little red tongue vibrating like a flame between two halves of a short, sharp beak.

Before I could get myself straightened up into a defensive posture, the goose bit me on the ass.

"Jesus Christ! Son of a bitch! Fucking goose!" All, of course, in English and incomprehensible, except in spirit, to the people of Huaynatambo.

I was running back toward the *bodega* as fast as I could with the goose lunging, flapping and snapping behind me. It was old man Doménico who saved me. He calmly, because at Doménico's age you don't hurry for anything, lowered himself from his stool and took two slow steps in my direction. As I ran past him into the *bodega*, he reached out with one hand, caught the goose around the throat, right below its nasty little head, and with his feet well planted gave just enough of a tug that the goose, by force of its own considerable momentum, snapped its neck and flopped to the street.

There was a moment of shocked silence before everyone in the village stood in the street laughing. Everyone except me (I was, literally, the butt of the joke) and the old lady standing in the doorway across the street, who was suddenly out one fine goose. I endured a few minutes of well-intentioned ribbing and then insisted that I must be on my way. Someone asked, and I promised that I and my poor bruised ass would certainly be back tomorrow.

The next day, after I'd spent several more hours building with Jainor, a small delegation of villagers came to escort us to lunch. Several other people, goose lady included, were already gathered in Doménico Quispe's garden. They were standing around a mound of sod that looked a lot like a smaller version of Benito's grave. Two men began to lift and move the chunks of sod. From beneath, they peeled back a large, dirty, steaming burlap sack. Out next came stones. The men plucked them out quickly, hot-potato style, and tossed them aside. Finally they scooped away a soggy, fragrant layer of well baked herbs and backed away so that all might behold. There in the pit, surrounded by potatoes and corn, nicely browned and dripping in its own juices, lay my nemesis, the goose.

The joke was lost on none of the people of Huaynatambo. A goose had bitten the Son of Lightning on the ass, but the last and best bite belonged to the Son of Lightning. The next day I came to the village carrying a gift for the goose lady: four live goslings I'd bought in the morning market.

The Friday night mass was one tradition that Pedro Buenaventura particularly enjoyed. A handful of devout worshipers always showed up, and always they occupied the same spots in the same pews. The young priest could close his eyes and visualize the pattern of their bowed heads as a familiar constellation of black stars against a wooden sky. Only tonight there was a new star on the horizon of the small chapel, one that remained behind after all the others had swirled together and blinked out the door into the broader night.

Father Pedro sensed the need to approach her gently. He slid into the pew just forward of hers so that the wooden seatback separated them. "*Buenas noches, Señorita.*"

Luz raised her head for the first time since the mass had begun. Her eyes showed the residue of tears. "*Buenas noches, Padre.*"

"I'm glad you came tonight," said the priest. "It's such a pleasure to see a fresh face." She sniffed and gave a shallow nod of acknowledgement to his words. "I noticed you have moved into town. Is there anything I can do to make you more comfortable?"

"Would you hear my confession?"

"Of course, *hija.* There is a booth, but we are alone here. So …"

"Forgive me father for I have sinned." She clasped her hands together so tightly that he could see the bloodless white of her otherwise caramel colored fingers. "It's been many years since my last confession. I have been guilty of pride, and that pride has led me to fornication." She spoke the words so quickly that the ensuing silence was caught naked and unaware.

"I see. Tell me. What was the nature of your pride?"

"I have desired to rise above my station. I left my family behind in their poverty with the vain hope of putting myself through college."

"Your 'station,' as you put it, was not decreed by God, daughter, but rather by society. In wishing to rise above it, you have not sinned against God, only against a social system that is cruel and unjust. Tell me about the fornication."

The girl took a deep breath, exhaled raggedly and explained how she had gone from her dire situation in Lima to live with Madam Zenobia, how she had lived among prostitutes and how she eventually was sent to el Valle del Cóndor as a companion for Don Alejandro Ganz de la Vega.

"How did you feel about that arrangement?"

"Afraid at first. But then I met Don Alejandro, and … I was in love with him, or so I thought. He has been so kind to me."

"Did he speak of marriage?"

"No. Never."

"Before *Señor* Ganz, was there …?"

"Nobody."

"And since?" She shook her head. "What is your situation now?"

"He has arranged for me to have an apartment, a teaching job, a chance to finish my education."

"With continued expectations for sexual favors?" Again she shook her head. Father Pedro closed his eyes and tipped his head back slightly, letting the chapel fill with a gauzy silence. When he reopened his eyes, it was to witness fresh tears forming in hers. "*Hijita*," he said, "you have traded your virginity for a better place in the world. That is a sin, but not one you have compounded with wantonness. When your heart has spoken with purity, you have listened. God asks no more than that of any of his children. I will, of course, impose some penance in prayer. Do you have a rosary?" She sniffed back tears and shook her head. The priest handed her his own. "Mostly I ask you to stay involved in the work you have chosen. Get to know the community while you are here. Teach the children about the world beyond Santa Rosita."

She heard her penance – a trifling, she thought – received absolution, thanked the priest for his time and understanding and slipped through the door like a ghost.

When Mercedes awoke the morning after Juan Pablo's operation, light was already stealing in at the edges of the curtains. She lay on her back, naked between the smooth sheets, with her thick black hair, still slightly damp in places, spread across the pillow. She stretched her limbs in all directions until her body felt like a tingling pentagram. Still she didn't reach the edges of the bed. The smooth, firm mattress was a piece of heaven. The linens not only were fresh and soft, but they matched. They matched each other and they even matched the draperies. Mercedes had never before spent the night in a room that was more than purely functional. In contrast, this room was like a perfect exercise in aesthetics. Every detail contributed to its harmony. Among them all, one detail revealed more than any other. Next to the bed on a wooden nightstand stood a lamp of ceramic and iron and a book of poetry: *Las Odas Elementales*, by Pablo Neruda.

This brought up all kinds of questions in her mind. Who was this Ganz, anyway? He had to be rich to live the way he did. But to be rich in Peru meant to be connected. And to be connected meant corruption, plain and simple. It was no secret, and there was no way around it. The economic system in Peru had always been a funnel for resources, whether monetary or human. The ruling elite distilled the blood and sweat and hunger of the poor and the working classes into a heady liquor of power and money. It had been so from the time of the Spanish conquistadors. This Ganz had to be part of the corrupt ruling elite. There could be no doubt. Were they not his coca fields that had employed Benito Quispe? And how could a drug trafficker possibly avoid the taints of violence and of payoffs to police and politicians?

Yet there were things that violated her preconceptions. The poetry, for one. Granted, maybe Ganz hadn't read, or even purchased, the volume by Neruda. But if he had, what did it mean? Neruda was both an avowed leftist and a shameless romantic, and his *Elemental Odes* were among the most sensitive, connected and loving poems of his long, prolific career. And what about the tenderness Ganz had shown toward old Juan Pablo? It didn't matter that the relationship between them was obviously close. True tenderness wasn't purely situational. Then there was the sweetness with which he had painted her cheek with one of her own tears in the aftermath of the surgery. There had been nothing feigned about the affection in that gesture. No, Mercedes felt sure she divined a deep current of kindness running through Alex Ganz. He was a paradox. A mystery. One thing was sure. Whoever he was, she wanted to like him, and she was pretty sure it wasn't just the sumptuousness of the bedroom making her feel that way.

But, my god, it was a wonderful bedroom. And better even than the bedroom was the bathroom only a few paces away. "The guest bathroom," Ganz had said. There are others? In addition to the sink where she had washed up from the operation, and made from the same marble, there was a shower with a glass door and an unbelievable supply of hot water. Her host had pointed out a copious selection of toiletries, many with labels in French, and handed her a heavy cotton robe to slip into between shower and bed.

Sometime between her sleep and waking, her clothes had disappeared, so she slipped back into last night's robe and wandered out into the quiet house. She found Ganz dressed and reading in the living room where they had sat a few hours before.

"*Buenos días*. How did you sleep?" he asked.

"Mmm. *Con los ángeles*." To Alex, she looked like an angel herself, standing there in her bare feet, without makeup, in a white terry cloth robe cut for a larger person. "How is our patient?" she asked with a yawn.

Even yawning she's beautiful, he thought. "Resting peacefully in his own bed. It hurts him to move, but Consuelo says his fever is down."

Mercedes felt a deep shiver of relief. It so easily could have turned out differently. She would check on him again before she left, but for now she accepted the broken fever as a sign that no infection had set in. She settled into the end of the sofa and curled her feet beneath her.

"My clothes?"

"Consuelo is washing them for you. They're in the dryer now, so it shouldn't be too long. Coffee?"

"Oh, yes, please." As Alex stood and walked toward the kitchen, she surprised herself by admiring the movement of his butt beneath the fabric of his slacks. "With cream and sugar," she tossed after him. She liked the way he moved, so unselfconscious. He returned carrying a tray with two steaming mugs, sliced papaya with lime juice and a sprinkle of cinnamon, and toast.

"I could get used to this," purred Mercedes.

His facial expression asked, could you? Then he changed the subject. "Tell me about yourself. How long have you been a doctor?"

So, as if he were not a near-perfect stranger, she told him about her childhood, about hanging around her father's garage, about his love of books and how his unschooled thirst for knowledge had infected her. She recounted her choice of college over domestic life and how her deeply Catholic mother had disapproved while her father had cheered her on. How her decision to study medicine had made him glow with pride. How the whole venture, so near completion, had slipped through her fingers with her father's death. And without actually saying it, she revealed how terribly she still missed her father.

"Let me make sure I understand. You finished all your courses?" She nodded. "And all that stands between you and your diploma is an internship?"

"Yes, but that's no small matter. After *Papá* died, I couldn't stand to move back home with *Mamá* – neither she nor my brothers were willing to help with the expenses – and I couldn't afford an apartment on an intern's wages. I had lost my only ally. So I used what I knew from helping *Papá* around the garage to fix up the van and I took my medical skills to people who don't care about a piece of paper hanging on a wall."

"It's an inspiring story."

"More so to hear it than to live it, I think."

A phone rang and Alex picked it up. "Go ahead." A frown formed and deepened as he listened. "I can be there before noon."

He held the hook down long enough to break the call and get a new dial tone. He pushed one button and spoke again, "Manolo, I need you to get the plane ready … Lima … right away." And then to Mercedes, "I'm sorry, but I'm afraid I have to leave you here."

"I understand. I'll get my clothes from Consuelo and I'll check on Juan Pablo again before I go."

"Thank you." He extended his right hand as if for a handshake. She offered hers in return. With his left hand, he covered them both. Mercedes added her own left hand and they stood for just a moment, the knot of their hands suspended between them, looking into each other's eyes and considering a multitude of unarticulated questions.

Then the moment was gone and Alex was striding toward the living-room door. A sudden realization caused him to stop short.

"Mercedes … I haven't paid you for your services."

"Another time," she smiled. "You seem to know where to find me."

"Inspector Castillo, what can I do for you?"

"Actually, it's the other way around, *Señor* Ganz. I'm here as a favor to you. May I talk frankly?"

Alex closed the door to the outer office.

"When was the last time you saw your sister, *Señor*?"

"At Christmas. Why?"

"I'm sorry to have to tell you this, but she's missing. Maybe dead. We should know more by this afternoon."

Alex said nothing. He merely waited for the Chief Inspector to continue.

"She has been staying at your ranch in Puerta del Sol, *¿verdad?*"

"As far as I know."

"The property has been abandoned recently. We don't know the extent of her complicity, but it is clear that she's been involved in the Villarreal affair."

"Please, Inspector. Tell me as much as you know."

Two days earlier, a call had come from the presidential palace. *Comandante* Rita set down the note card she had been writing on and picked up the phone.

"Yes, Miss Ganz is here. One moment, please." She signaled Cassandra to pick up the extension in the hall where they could maintain eye contact, muted her own extension and listened.

"This is Cassandra."

"May I speak freely?" It was a male voice she didn't recognize.

"You may."

"The person we both know would like to meet with you to continue a discussion you began at the reception."

"I remember."

"Can you be waiting outside the Hotel Crillón tomorrow at two o'clock?"

Comandante Rita nodded yes. "I can be there," confirmed

Cassandra.

As soon as the phones were resting back in their cradles, Rita closed her eyes, clenched her fists and tipped her head back as if smelling victory wafting through the coastal air. "Comrade Sandra," she barked, "call everyone together. We don't have much time."

The next afternoon, outside the Hotel Crillón, Cassandra waited in a pink cashmere dress with a tight bodice and a skirt that flared from the hips to just above the knee. Hanging loosely around her neck, she wore a white silk scarf. In her white purse, she carried a small tape recorder along with her basic cosmetics. This time she carried no identification card. The slim twenty-five-caliber pistol she preferred was taped high on the inside of her left thigh. She knew that Comrade Amador and the rest of the cell were watching from two nondescript sedans parked in the next block.

The plan was simple. When the president's car pulled to the curb she was to determine whether or not López was inside. If he was there, she had only to get in and play her rehearsed part. If he was not in the car, she was to fling her scarf over her shoulder as a signal to abort the ambush, keep her meeting with López and improvise.

The flaw in the plan turned out to be tinted windows.

When the car arrived right on schedule, Cassandra couldn't see the occupants. The chauffeur exited and moved briskly to open the door for her. She kept her right hand ready, touching the scarf, but instead of opening the door, the chauffeur gripped her elbow to guide her as the door opened from the inside. Not until her head was inside the limousine could Cassandra make out the other passenger, who had already slid back across the seat. It was Adolfo Villarreal, López's security chief.

"*Señorita,*" said Villarreal, dwelling too long on the first syllable, "your purse please." Cassandra made no effort to conceal her irritation as she handed it over. As he opened it up, she smoothed her skirt in her lap, conscious of the metallic shape pressed between her thighs. Villarreal pulled out the recorder, slipped it into the breast pocket of his suit coat and returned the purse. "You may have this back when our … meeting … is finished. Go," he commanded the driver.

Cassandra feigned indignation and turned to face out the window. What did he mean 'our' meeting? She wondered. Her mind raced. She hadn't given the signal. The plan would go forward. If it had been López, she had intended to occupy his attention seductively while she reached for the pistol. His ego would keep suspicion at bay. With Villarreal that ploy would never work.

The limo sped forward. Just before the intersection, a woman with a baby carriage stepped into the street, causing the driver to brake instinctively. Cassandra gave a shriek and allowed the jolt to throw her forward. At exactly the same moment, Villarreal cursed and drew a gun from a shoulder holster. The woman reached into the carriage, came up with an automatic weapon and sprayed the windshield with bullets, killing the driver. By this time, Cassandra was on the floor and Villarreal was on top of her. More bullets crashed through the side windows, and glass covered the back seat like gravel. Villarreal rolled back onto the seat, staying low, and trained the pistol on the blown-out window. With his left hand he reached across and grabbed Cassandra by the hair on the top of her head.

"Get up, you whore," he snarled, lifting her. "See who your friends are!"

Cassandra groped along her thigh, found the pistol and tore it free. As Villarreal dragged her upward, she managed to spin toward and on top of him, safely underneath his outstretched gun arm. The rest she had rehearsed until she could do it in her sleep. The small caliber pistol found the bottom of the rib cage and delivered two slugs to Villarreal's chest. She dropped the pistol, grappled with the door handle and flung herself headlong into the street.

Cassandra pulled herself to her feet and ran back in the direction of the hotel at the same time as the rest of the comrades scattered in other directions – all except for Comrade Luisa, the woman with the carriage. She walked to the side of the car with a bundle from the pram, pressed a button and prepared to lob it into the back seat. Villarreal had just enough life left in him to raise his pistol over his head and pull the trigger, but he lacked the strength to steady his hand. The slug hit Luisa in the belly, causing her to double over. Still clutching the bomb, but unable in her pain to throw it, she let herself fall with it on top of the expiring body of Adolfo Villarreal. The first explosion caused the car to bloat and spew unholy clouds from all its openings. The secondary blast, caused by the ignition of the gasoline in the tank, turned the whole affair into an incinerator.

The ranch was no longer a safe base. Somebody at the presidential palace knew of the planned meeting with Cassandra. The cell was now on the move.

The newspaper headline the next day read: *VILLARREAL ASSASSINATED*. The article reported the deaths of the President's chief of security, the driver of his government limo and an unidentified woman. Crimson Road terrorists were suspected of the crime, but speculation in some circles also pointed to a drug connection. Cassandra clipped the piece from the paper, folded it and placed it in a folder in her travel bag with several other articles, including two whose headlines read: *MINING CAMP MASSACRE* and *ITALIAN TOURISTS MURDERED IN ATTACK ON TRAIN*. In the folder also lay two German documents and the picture of her brother shaking hands with the notorious *El Colibrí*.

As Inspector Castillo had explained it to Alex, dental records proved that the woman in the car with Villarreal was not Cassandra Ganz de la Vega. However, at the time of the assassination, she had been in the car on her way to an appointment with the President. Her possible presence at the scene of the bombing was still unresolved. No physical evidence linked her to the bombing, but eyewitness accounts of a woman fleeing the scene could point to Miss Ganz. Evidence of a prolonged presence of troops at the ranch, including shell casings found in the dirt of the equestrian arena, made it clear that her connection to the assassination was not mere coincidence. It was at least possible that Cassandra was a victim of kidnapping. Worse, Castillo said he could not rule out the possibility of her complicity with the terrorists.

For the first time ever, Alex Ganz began to fear for his sister.

He was at his desk the next day when he received a call from the bank's chief of security.

"I see," said Alex. "You still have the security tapes? … No. I'll come down there."

Ismael Ordoñez, the graying, fifty-four-year-old former PIP detective, had served Ganz and the bank loyally for many years. As soon as word came of the robbery, he went personally to the scene to take charge of the investigation on behalf of the bank. Drawing on his friendships and credibility within the PIP, he arranged to have access to the security tapes for long enough to make copies before turning them over to the official investigators. When Alex arrived, the security chief indicated the relevant video monitors and rolled the tapes in sequence.

After a long stretch of usual pedestrian activity, including a few comings and goings of customers, the camera trained toward the street in front of the Chosica branch of *Banco Europa* picked up a sedan rolling to the curb. A man and a woman, attractive and well-dressed, emerged and entered the bank, passing the two uniformed men who stood guard outside the door with machine guns slung loosely over their shoulders. The woman wore a large hat and sunglasses and was largely unrecognizable. Only seconds later, another sedan pulled up outside. A burst of gunfire from the curbside windows dropped the two guards on the sidewalk before they could even unsling their weapons. Ganz winced as the two guards collapsed. These, he thought, were honest men working to support their families – working for me. From out of the second car, which remained double-parked with its engine running, came four people, three men and a woman, all carrying weapons and canvas bags and wearing balaclavas over their faces. One man stayed at the door as a lookout and the other three entered the bank. The relevant sequence ended less than three minutes later with all six people piling into the two cars and driving away.

The next tape, from a camera monitoring customers and the teller windows, showed the well-dressed couple approaching the counter. Just as they reached it, the faces and body language of the two interior guards registered a sudden surprise that would correspond with the shooting of the outside guards. At that moment, the man and the woman drew their own weapons, he from inside his jacket and she from a shopping bag. They shot the two interior guards, deepening Alex's anger and grief even more, and then turned their weapons on the two tellers and the branch manager.

The couple was joined almost immediately by three masked accomplices, who moved behind the counter and forced the tellers to empty the cash drawers. When they had finished, the masked woman bagged up the weapons of the slain guards. One of the masked men then killed the branch manager with a bullet to the forehead, which sent him slumping to his desk, where his hands had remained in plain sight throughout the robbery. The other man shot the two tellers, a young man and a middle-aged woman. They never even had time, thought Ganz, to plead for their lives.

The third camera, mounted above the door on the inside of the bank, presented an additional and mostly redundant view of the events captured by the second camera. Alex made himself watch it through to the end of the robbery, if only to reinforce his fierce anger over this outrage, committed on his turf and against his people. As the robbers scrambled out the door, one of them, the woman in the balaclava, hesitated and looked directly into the lens of the surveillance camera. In that instant, and only for that almost imperceptible instant, Alex Ganz's pupils dilated and he fought to keep his usual composure.

"What do we know, Ismael?"

"Not a lot. It appears to be *Camino Rojo.*"

"I thought as much. Listen, I want you to stay abreast of the police investigation and keep me informed of their progress. Your priority is to learn everything you can about the *Camino Rojo* and its operations in Lima. Do it as quietly as you can, but do it quickly. If there's anything you need and don't have, let me know. Use your contacts in the PIP, but only people you trust completely."

"*Bueno.* I'll start immediately."

"Good. And Ismael ..."

"*¿Señor?*"

"As I think you know, my sister may be involved involuntarily. I don't want her safety compromised. You'll want to check out the ranch in Puerta del Sol. The police have been over it already in relation to the Villarreal assassination, but ..."

"I understand."

"First," said Alex, as he wrote down a number he had used only to initiate contact with *El Colibrí*, "find the phone that belongs to this number. We need a record of all its activity, and absolutely no one but you and I must know."

"That will be no problem, *Señor*."

"Thank you, my friend. By the way," Ganz added, indicating the security tapes with a wave of his hand, "have you had these copied?"

"Not yet."

"Leave them with me. I'll get someone else to take care of it."

Ismael left and closed the door. Alex remained standing in front of the television screen. He rewound the last of the tapes and watched it from the beginning. As the three anonymous guerrillas swept through the door, and then again as they worked behind the counter stuffing currency into their canvas bags, he paid special attention to the woman. At the end of the recorded sequence, when her face turned briefly toward the camera, he paused the tape and studied the grainy image. He rewound a few frames and ran it again, then again, and again. The balaclava covered her face completely except for one oval cutout for the eyes and another for the mouth. The mouth looked familiar, but it was the eyes that gutted him like a fish. The eyes and a barely visible wisp of blonde hair. He rewound it to that point one more time, hit the record button, and let the tape run out.

It was near the end of a routine day of field work in Huaynatambo. Enrique was pitching in, helping Antonia Quispe, now visibly pregnant, with a load of washing. I could hear them laughing. I had spent the morning with Doménico Quispe, the village elder and de facto folklorist. At least twice a week, like this morning, I'd spent a couple hours with him, chewing coca and listening to stories ranging from the creation of man and the comportment of local gods or *apus* to common gossip about fellow villagers. I was beginning to hear the same stories over and over again.

This morning he retold the tale of his mother's disappearance. After the birth of her daughter, Doménico's now-deceased younger sister, his mother had refused to make an appropriate offering to the *apu* of the great peak to the east. The east wind whispered in her ear a curse of barrenness. Having already delivered two healthy children, she was haughty and ignored it. That year she suffered the first in a string of miscarriages. After five more years and five stillbirths, she wandered off to the east and was never seen again. Villagers believed the *apu* of the great peak opened the earth at its feet and took her into its womb. I listened attentively, bought Doménico a beer and then wandered over toward Enrique and Antonia. There I sat with my back against a low stone wall and watched an old ewe, a sow and a litter of white piglets browsing untethered in grass that was beginning to brown.

Watching that scene, at one level, filled me with a kind of joy. There is beauty in the simplicity of life in Huaynatambo, in the directness of the people's connection to the earth. They build their houses from the soil they live upon. They eat the food they plant and the animals they raise in these very pastures. The wool from their sheep becomes the clothing they wear. Their energy is reinvested into these fields, as is their waste. It is a small closed circle of life and death and rebirth.

The circle breaks open when they need or desire things their land cannot provide. A propane stove. A metal roof. Things that require cash. For that, they sell the surpluses from their fields or they go to work, as Benito did, in the coca fields or the mines. Once this circle breaks open, they begin to exist in the world I know best, the world where commerce is king. They enter a world that is vast and hostile. A world where it is easy to become lost, and from which to return is impossible.

Continuing to ponder this pastoral scene, I began to feel strangely hollow inside. It was as if I contained two worlds within me, theirs and mine, and the distance between them was like the vast emptiness of space. It was in that emptiness that I found myself suspended.

Perhaps what I felt was a lack of deep belonging. My work was going fine now. The people in Huaynatambo had opened their hearts and homes to me. I now knew as many of my neighbors in Santa Rosita and Huaynatambo as I once knew around campus. In short, I was as much a part of the community here as I probably ever would be anywhere, and still I felt utterly foreign. I'd learned to move comfortably on the surface of this landscape, but I had no depth here. No roots. No reality. In the end, in the lives of these people, I was a fiction. The young, pale man marked by *Wakli*.

It took me a while to identify my problem as homesickness. I'd experienced bouts of it before, but it was getting worse. Jack Bentley had warned me it would happen. My reaction? Not me! Homesickness presupposes a home, I'd said, and mine had already disappeared. But of course that was bullshit. Lately I'd caught myself longing for simple commodities from 'back there': A bowl of corn flakes with ice-cold pasteurized milk and granulated sugar. A Neil Young song whining from a car stereo. The freedom to surf channels on the television and to scoff at the quality of the programming. Christ, I even missed strip malls. I hate them, but I can't deny that they and I share the same linguistic DNA. I can go into any store in any strip mall in America and I know my role. I know my script. I know who I am. Or at least, I thought I did, once. Somehow I seemed to have lost my grip on my most basic cultural identity.

As I sat there soaking up the Andean sun, I realized that the coming weekend would mark my twenty-seventh birthday and four years since I had withdrawn from medical school. My choice had been either to withdraw or to flunk. The fall semester after Dad died had been hard, but at least I'd managed to keep my head in my studies long enough to finish out the term. By spring it had become impossible. I was utterly lost, and without my father's expectations looming over me, I had no motivation to go on. It became pretty clear that I wasn't in it for myself. Mom took it surprisingly well. "Whatever makes you happy, Dear," is all she would say. I'd like to know the answer to that riddle.

I remember the day I dropped out officially. I filed the papers then walked back to my apartment in the med-ghetto. I opened the door and stood there without going in. Who lives here? Everything I could see belonged to a Sam Young who was destined to be a physician, and who a half-hour earlier had ceased to exist.

I began with the bookshelves. They were filled with medical texts, notebooks and references. Five and six at a time, I carried them out into the hall and stacked them on the floor outside my door. When I was done, the bookshelves were empty with the exception of a dictionary. I understood a dictionary. It wasn't alien to me. I left it there. From the back of the chair I snatched a white lab coat, which I folded, carried out to the hallway and laid on top of the stack of books. To it I added another lab coat and some surgical scrubs I retrieved from the bedroom. Then from my desk, I gathered up the stethoscope, scalpels and other personal medical instruments I had been required to buy. I placed them on top of the clothing. Also on the desk, filled with pens, pencils and highlighters, was a coffee mug bearing the logo of the med school. I emptied it and carried it out to the stack.

I sat down at my desk and made a sign with a marking pen on a blank sheet of notebook paper. Then with Scotch tape, I stuck it to the hallway wall directly over the stack of alien possessions that signified the now-defunct Sam Young: *TAKE ANYTHING YOU WANT.*

To finish the job, I drove the Jetta to a dealership, traded it straight across for a well used Jeep CJ7 and relinquished the personalized license MD2B plate my father had so artfully chosen for me.

Back in the apartment, I looked around again. What was left? Was there an 'I' there? I began to take inventory. With any luck, if I were perceptive, I might actually be able to figure out some part of the identity of the person who inhabited this space and these things.

Well, to begin with, there was still the desk with a dictionary, pens, pencils and highlighters, a virgin notebook and a campus parking permit. The guy I was looking for appeared to be a student. What other clues could I find to his identity? I opened the kitchen cupboards. Mismatched glasses. A few plates and bowls from a once-larger set. Not much of a nester, I thought. And still there was nothing to disconfirm or add to the student hypothesis. In the other cupboard, I found breakfast cereals, packages of ramen noodles, pastas, a box of Krusteaz pancake mix, peanut butter, a jar of spaghetti sauce, a bottle of maple syrup … all foods that said 'college student'. But here there was a new clue. Among the standard condiments and seasonings stood a few oddities. There was a small bottle of fish sauce and another of toasted sesame oil. Asian? No, he's not Asian. Experimental? Maybe. I looked in the refrigerator and arrived at the same conclusion. The combination of cheap beer, cheddar cheese, catsup and mustard, and jug of milk all screamed 'student', as did the general emptiness of the appliance. Yet several varieties of hot sauce and chili paste suggested at least the possibility of a sense of adventure.

I moved to the bedroom where there was no sign of any feminine habitation or influence. If the guy had a love life, he didn't bring it here. That conclusion was reinforced by a look at the bathroom, which desperately needed cleaning. Maybe the closet could tell me something new. There I found the generic college-student wardrobe, but there was something else as well; a parka and a pair of technical hiking boots that were water-stained and scuffed by rocks. What could I infer? That this guy hikes or climbs, for sure. That something inside him says, "Get out of town. Get thee to a mountain."

At the back of the closet I saw something that made me pause. It was a wooden cigar box held closed by a brass latch. I took it out carefully, as if it might explode. This was my childhood treasure chest. I hadn't opened it for years. Did I dare to do so now? Under the circumstances, how could I not? I slowly thumbed open the latch and pushed back the lid. The box was not particularly full, but every item told a story. There were blue ribbons from two science fairs. There were three polished agates, my favorites from a long-gone rock collection. There was a hand-written piece of song lyric that signified the first and worst time I was ever dumped by a girlfriend. There was a bold blue feather from a Steller's jay, and there was a single, silver Mercury-head dime.

The dime evoked the essence of childhood adventure. I spent much of my childhood immersed in books – adventure novels, mysteries, science fiction and, especially, spy novels that brought all those other elements together. In grade school, I read all of the James Bond novels. I read *Thunderball* with a flashlight under the covers of my bed in one night, and then hid the book from my parents because it had a racy cover, Sean Connery and a mostly naked woman, that I knew would embarrass me. In my mind, Connery's Bond had looked just like my dad. I fantasized that I was an international spy, skulking around the college campus which, being only blocks away, was my playground, eavesdropping on conversations, peering into windows and arranging hideouts among shrubs, stairwells and other dark or neglected places. I crafted secret weapons from trash I pilfered from the university dumpsters. Blow guns, truth sera, lasers and spyscopes, all part of the arsenal I kept in somebody's cast-off attaché case.

Then there was my great cat-burglar caper. I was eight years old. Enrique's age. Late-afternoon light filtered through tall rhododendrons at the base of the old dormitory building. Parts of it were covered with ivy, but the wall above me was bare, the brick arranged in tiers with shallow recesses at even intervals like the inverted rungs of a ladder. Two stories up, the windows closed above heavy granite sills. Behind one of the windows a glass goblet shone with silver. Gripping the crevices with fingertips and toes, I scaled the wall, mindful all the time that I must not be seen. At the first-floor windowsill, and again at a ledge that separated the floors, I found enough support to rest and look around. The second-story window was cracked open. Bracing myself against the sill, I slid my hand, palm down, under the wooden window frame. Then, walking my fingertips toward my palm, I arched my knuckles upward, inching the window open. Careful to leave no fingerprints on the goblet, I reached in and lifted out a single silver dime, proof to myself that my adventure was real.

What is real and what is fantasy? Is Sam the anthropologist any more real than Sam the med student was? Or Sam the would-be international spy? Who is the real Sam Young? Based on the empirical evidence of one apartment at one moment in time, he was a student with a taste for mountains and adventure.

Adventure. Maybe that's what I was lacking now. Maybe I was just getting restless. I came to Ayacucho, in part, out of a desire to get as far away from my old ruts as possible. And here I was in a rut again. Maybe my symptoms of homesickness really grew out of boredom and frustration. I felt I had learned as much as I could from field work in Huaynatambo. I had come looking for cultural clash, and it seemed like Huaynatambo and Santa Rosita existed in some kind of bubble, some closed cultural loop that isolated them from the realities of the surrounding sierra. It had been good in a way. It helped me to understand some kind of status quo of life in the Central Andes, and I had heard some second-hand accounts of adaptation to external pressures. But sooner or later if I was going to answer my research question I was going to have to venture into areas where there had been more conflict.

Sensing this, I got up and went to look for Gabriela Quispe. I found her sitting on the ground with two other women, conversing and spinning wool from their fingertips onto wooden spindles.

"*Doña* Gabriela," I said when she looked in my direction. She would not hold eye contact with me for long. She never had. But her hands had grown still and I knew she was listening. "I wanted to let you know that I may not be coming back to Huaynatambo for a while."

She tightened her grip on the bundle of carded wool and her hands trembled. "We have offended you," she almost whispered.

"No! Oh, no, *Señora.* Your hospitality has been wonderful. I owe you and all of Huaynatambo a great debt. It's just that, well, there are other places I have to visit also."

She nodded and the three women stood up. Gabriela spoke softly to the other two and they picked up their skirts and ran off in opposite directions. Within minutes virtually the entire village, around three-dozen souls, stood surrounding me. Enrique worked his way to my side and, finally, moving very slowly, Doménico Quispe came to the center of the circle. Everyone became quiet.

"You leave us?" asked the old man.

"I must. At least for a while."

"We have chewed coca together."

"We have."

"And how do you leave us?"

I was puzzled by his question for a moment, and then I realized that he meant not "by what means do you leave us?" but rather, "in what state?"

"With my blessing," I answered. And then, although I felt silly and fraudulent saying it, I added, "May *Wakli* bless you and the earth beneath you all the days of your lives."

It took another half hour to finish up with hugs, pleasantries, reassurances of gratitude and friendship and declined offers of drink before Enrique and I managed to hit the road for Santa Rosita. By that time afternoon clouds had begun building in earnest. We were still within sight of Huaynatambo when the sky darkened, lightning flashed overhead, thunder pealed and a drenching downpour swept across the mountain.

Alex had waited out the weather and flown in late to el Valle del Cóndor. When he finally settled in, he slept badly. Images of his sister crowded his brain. From the tomboy to the schoolgirl actress to the Berkeley coed, what did he really know about her? He remembered a winter day, coming home from school when the family limo stopped at a busy intersection along *Avenida Javier Prado.* Standing barefoot on the median, with a tiny baby suspended in a woolen shawl over her shoulder, was a dark-skinned girl about Cassandra's size. Cass was ten or eleven. On the hip opposite the baby, the girl held a tray of Chiclets, which she attempted to sell for a few soles a box. Alex watched silently as Cassie slipped off her shoes then lowered the window and held them at arm's length. The expression on the girl's face went from hope as the window went down, to confusion when she saw the fine shoes, to disbelief when, just as the traffic cop signaled them forward, Cassie let the shoes drop. Alvaro, their driver, had pretended not to see, but Alex thought he noticed a repressed smile on his face as they accelerated through the intersection.

What about her college years? Did she have friends? Who were they? He tried to picture her in Levis and a teeshirt, hanging out and laughing with other students in a Berkeley coffee shop, but he couldn't solidify the image. She hadn't maintained any relationships from her college days. There were no names or faces that he could pull up. Had she felt alienated and alone? Abandoned? He despaired at the thought. He had been so busy with his own schooling and then with trying to fathom the complexities of Ganz Enterprises that he had lost his connection with her. But she had come home so determined, so focused, so self-possessed. He figured she must have done fine.

He thought he knew Cassandra, the career woman, the glamorous media professional, but what did he really know? There had been a few short episodes of excitement and personal triumph shared over the phone. There were the holiday dinners and the low-level battle of resistance between her and *Mamá*. But mostly there were the society-page clips and the highly produced images from television that he had occasionally tuned in out of … what? Brotherly pride? A desire to believe she was doing just fine because he didn't have the time or desire to deal with any other reality? And how did he reconcile those images with the woman he'd seen at Christmas, athletic, aloof, cryptic? And finally, the woman in the balaclava.

Had she been there at the bank of her own volition? Or was she being forced to cooperate? Was she there for the assassination of Villarreal? Under what circumstances? Where did the *TelePerú* bombings fit in? Did they push her over some sort of invisible edge? Or worse – unthinkable but possible – could she have been secretly involved with the Peruvian Communists all along? Since when? Berkeley? Could she have set the bombs herself? Could she have been the reason *El Colibrí* had come to him with such confidence, holding el Valle del Cóndor and Santa Rosita hostage for ever-increasing demands? Through most of the night, dark possibilities warred with things he thought he knew about his sister and now was forced to doubt.

Last night I had a dream that woke me in the middle of the night and kept me awake for what seemed like hours, tossing and turning and struggling with my conscience. After breakfast I sought out Pedro Buenaventura. I danced around the topic that was on my mind, remarking instead about the changing weather. About the continuing welfare of the people of Huaynatambo. Pedro just absorbed what I said, quietly, waiting me out. Finally, into the deep silence, I floated my true intentions.

"All this *Kari Wakli-piqta* stuff must be sort of distressing to you, *Padre*."

"How so?"

"Well, the religious aspects."

"Not really," he said. "Most of these people are Catholic in name only. Theirs is a Catholicism that embraces saints and *apus* – the old Incan nature gods – with equal alacrity. Your little miracle of resurrection is not likely to make the canon, but who am I to say that for them it is less valid than any other?"

"You're joking."

"I'm not. I can't control where people place their faith, Sam. And neither can they." I chewed on the priest's words for a while in silence. Which he broke. "Faith is like romantic love, Sam. You can be ready for it, but you never know when it will hit you or where it will attach."

That one also took some chewing.

"Still," I said. "It feels like a deception."

"Have you actually represented yourself as a god?"

"Not exactly, but ..."

"Have you threatened to bring down the lightning?

"No."

"Have you promised them salvation? From anything? No. Of course you haven't. Go easy on yourself over this, Sam. Think of yourself as a kind of ambulatory good luck charm."

Right. Sam Young, Son of Lightning, rabbit's foot.

The dream had been like this.

I was floating in a sea of colorfully dressed *campesinos*. The people were singing *Kari Wakli, Wakli-piqta! Kari, Kari Wakli-piqta!* Brown hands, cracked with labor, waved joyously in the air around me. Others held me up and carried me along. The sky was clear and blue, made bluer by contrast with a few billowing clouds scratching their bellies on the tops of the surrounding mountains. From somewhere in the distance ahead of us, across the green pastures, came a high keening sound that at first seemed to harmonize in counterpoint with the singing. Suddenly, a small cloud put our entire multitude in shade, making me shiver from the sudden drop in temperature.

The keening built to a wail that overshadowed the singing and finally silenced it. The multitude of people in front of me began to divide. I was on my feet now and suddenly I felt very heavy, as if the earth's gravity had been turned up. Through the breech in the crowd I could see a small party of women advancing toward us. They were the source of the wailing. All of them howled with grief except the one woman leading them. The woman was Mercedes Márquez. She carried a bundle wrapped in a colorful blanket. By the time the women reached the place where I was standing, the intensity of the wailing was such that it penetrated every cell of my body and set it to vibrating. I felt heavier and heavier, held fast to the ground by a weight that was too much for my muscles to overcome.

Mercedes set the bundle on the ground in front of me and the howling women fell silent. They formed a semicircle centered on me and the bundle. "Open it," said Mercedes. I couldn't. I was frozen in place. So she opened it, drawing back the corners of the blanket, first from the sides to the east and the west, then top and bottom to the north and the south. In the middle of the blanket lay the blackened remains of an incinerated infant. I knew at once it had been struck by lightning. I wanted to say something. That it wasn't my doing. That I was no god. But my voice was frozen too. The people in the multitude all turned their backs and disappeared. Then the women in the semicircle faded into mist. Only Mercedes remained. I had to say something, and nothing would come. She shook her head, turned her back on me and walked away.

The phone rang in Alex's office in el Valle del Cóndor. Three days had passed since the robbery at the Chosica branch.

"What do you have, Ismael?"

"The robbery was definitely *Camino Rojo*. We know the man to be one Amador Delgado. He's been imprisoned before. An actor and small-time thief. We suspect the woman in the hat to be a high-level *Rojista* known as *Comandante* Rita. The *policía* have been hunting her for years but they still don't know her true identity."

"And the rest of them?" Alex felt the reservation in his voice. He feared the answer.

"None of them is recognizable."

Relief.

"Any idea where they are now?"

"No, *Señor*. The cars they used were stolen and then abandoned on a busy street. They probably split up and left on foot or in different public microbuses. Impossible to trace."

"All right. Did you learn anything at the ranch?"

"Mostly what the police already know. They believe that up to a dozen people, more or less, have used it for many weeks, probably since right after the *TelePerú* bombings. From the trash, it appears they had recently prepared some fairly large and unimaginative meals. There were a lot of fingerprints, but only Amador Delgado's matched any records. They found a few stray shell casings buried in the arena dirt. Also, there was evidence of explosives having been stored in one of the outbuildings. "

"Any signs of violence, or …?"

"Nothing, sir." Ismael had correctly interpreted the question. After a respectful pause, he added, "Your sister did show up at a party at the presidential palace in January. Witnesses said she looked especially well."

As she had at Christmas. Oh, Cassandra, what are you doing? He thought about the plans he had set in motion back when he still believed Cass was taking a break from television and working safely on a novel. Damn it. He should have paid closer attention to her. Now it seemed she had somehow, inexplicably, joined forces with this Amador Delgado and *Comandante* Rita of the *Camino Rojo*. He wondered if he should call it all off. Cancel the weapons deal. Was there some way he could protect his sister, despite herself? If he did call it off, would Cassandra fare any better, or was she destined either way to end up as a sacrifice in this chess game with the devil? Christ, he didn't even know what side she was on … white pawn or black knight?

How could he have ended up in this position? The answer was simple: a worthy opponent. He leaned back in his office chair, let his gaze drift to his bookshelves – an assortment of poetry, literature and business books – and settle momentarily on a hardbound copy of *The Art of War* by Sun Tzu.

"And the phone number I gave you?" asked Alex.

"That turned out to be very interesting," replied Ismael. "The phone is located in a law office in Miraflores. It is a second, unlisted line. Are you near your fax machine?"

What had come humming out of the fax was a string of phone records. Alex set his copy on the desk in front of him and began to study it. Fewer than thirty calls in three months. No outgoing calls. None. Only incoming. In two places numbers had been blacked out. Alex looked at the dates and times and understood the reason. The calls had come from him. One other number, on a Lima exchange, was responsible for multiple calls. The rest of the numbers, mostly from outside Lima and all from public phones, showed up only once each.

"What is this Lima number that repeats?" asked Ganz.

"An office in the Department of Anthropology at National University."

"Now that *is* interesting. Follow up on all of them, but pay special attention to that one. Learn everything you can. Find me something I can use."

"*Muy bien, Señor.*"

"And Ismael …"

"*Sí, Señor?*"

"Your skills and discretion have never been more important to me than they are right now."

"I understand, *Señor*."

He does understand, thought Ganz. He had complete confidence in Ismael. He doubted there was a better investigator in all of Peru. He only wished he were as confident in his own plans and decisions.

Just before dawn, Porfirio Sanchez's car showed up outside the gate. It arrived, the headlights went out, the engine shut off and it sat there. Quiet. Waiting.

The security camera registered the car's presence but not the identity of its occupant. The night guard alerted Manolo who, in turn, alerted Ganz.

"Has anyone gotten out of the car?" Alex asked.

"No. *Nadie*."

"Then it's probably not a bomb. But it may not be Sanchez either. It's not his style to be out this early. How many in the car?"

"Can't tell yet. It's still too dark."

"Deploy a couple of extra men to guard the gate, but tell them to stay out of sight. I don't want anyone to suspect how much force we have up here. Then come get me in the Rover. Hide two extra men inside for backup."

Alex pulled on some clothes and a warm jacket. The morning would be chilly and the jacket would conceal a serviceable semi-automatic pistol. Manolo brought the Land Rover around. The rear seat was folded down and two of the men from the recently hired special security team lay flat in the back with automatic weapons ready across their chests. Alex took the passenger seat.

Manolo pulled the Rover to within ten meters of the gate and parked with the headlights still on. The gate remained closed. Only one person was visible inside Sanchez's car, a skinny youth leaning back in the seat with one hand raised against the glare of the Rover's headlights. Alex and Manolo opened their doors with their Kevlar armor and bulletproof glass and stood behind them, Manolo with gun in hand. The skinny youth pushed open the driver's door of the sedan, climbed out and approached the gate carrying two envelopes, one thin and one thick. Alex approached from his side.

"Who are you?" asked Alex.

"A messenger. I have something for *Señor* Ganz that requires a reply."

"I'm Ganz." Pulga passed the thin envelope through the bars of the gate and Alex read the contents. He folded the paper into his jacket pocket and said, "I'll be there."

Then Pulga handed him the thicker envelope. "I was told to give you this in case you developed any second thoughts." As Pulga slouched back to the car, Alex opened the second envelope. Inside he found PIP Detective Sanchez's badge and a long hank of familiar blonde hair.

The designated meeting gave Alex little time to prepare. He hurriedly breakfasted and showered. From the safe in his study he removed several stacks of American currency wrapped in plain paper and shoved them in a cloth bag. Then, with Manolo driving, he left el Valle del Cóndor.

They followed the map delivered by Pulga to a remote valley in the *cordillera* where the road ran straight and unobstructed for several hundred meters. At the south end of the valley Manolo pulled the Rover off the roadway and parked in a wide grassy area. Alex looked at his watch. It was time.

Manolo stepped out onto the short grass and lit a cigarette. By the time he had smoked it halfway down, they heard the growl of a small plane engine. The unmarked craft flew a circle over the valley, set down on the long stretch of road, taxied to the south end of the valley near the Rover, turned to a takeoff-ready position and stopped.

Alex walked toward the plane, forcing himself to hide the loathing he felt as first a bodyguard and then *El Colibrí* stepped from the fuselage. The bodyguard, armed with an automatic rifle, advanced, checked Alex for firearms and then nodded to *El Colibrí.*

"*Señor* Fortuna," said Alex by way of a greeting.

"*Señor* Ganz, I assume you have fulfilled your end of our agreement."

"I have the cash here." He proffered the cloth bag. "The rest of the order is waiting in a hangar in Panama City."

"You procured everything I asked for?"

"I had to burn a lot of favors, but I got it all."

"Very good," said *El Colibrí*, trading a folded sheet of paper for the bag of cash. "Here are the details of the drop. In two days – that's Tuesday – at eight in the morning, the cargo is to be delivered to the coordinates marked on the map. I think you will recognize the location."

Ganz unfolded the paper and scanned the map. It was his private airstrip, surrounded by coca fields in the middle of the *selva.* Alex had gambled on being able to predict *El Colibrí's* actions, and he had been right. The *terrorista* was becoming brasher and more arrogant. Having penetrated Ganz's world, *El Colibrí* was expanding inside it like a tapeworm. He had sullied Ganz's refuge at el Valle del Cóndor. He had dominated the ranch at Puerta del Sol. And now he was moving troops into Ganz's prime coca-growing properties. He had picked a good time. The main harvesting hadn't yet begun, and what few workers had remained after the death of Benito Quispe had been moved out. *El Colibrí* knew that Ganz had procured the protection of his coca fields from the government, making them a safe haven, through bribes to such people as Porfirio Sanchez, recently deceased.

Even if *El Colibrí*'s people were somehow betrayed, the coca fields and the surrounding jungle, with their heavy cover and dearth of roads, would make capture next to impossible. It made the fields a perfect place to hide out and stage further operations.

"The pilot will not land the plane," said Ganz. "The crates will be dropped by parachute." *El Colibrí* gestured the unimportance of the logistical detail. "There's one other thing. Your messenger delivered two envelopes."

"Ah, yes," replied *El Colibrí*. "Detective Sanchez will no longer be on your payroll. Shame. And …" he added, pausing to let the suspense build around Ganz's real concern, "you have my word that your sister will come to no harm from my people as long as we all keep our promises." With that, the chief *terruco* turned toward the plane.

In Ganz's stomach something cold and toxic began to churn.

I gathered up my maps of Ayacucho and carried them down to the chapel. Father Pedro was still in and appeared to be cleaning up after his breakfast.

"*Buenos días*, *Padre*. Have you got a few minutes? I need your advice on something."

"Spiritual matters? Matters of the heart?" I smiled and shook my head. "No? What a shame."

"Actually, this is work-related. And – who knows? – it may actually benefit my soul if it keeps me from departing too quickly into the next world."

"That would be a good cause. What's on your mind?"

"Uchurimac, I think." I spread the maps over the now-bare kitchen table. "I want to move my work to some area where the people have had encounters with the *Camino Rojo.* I have sort of a plan and I wanted to run it by you."

Pedro Buenaventura frowned. "Sounds like a bad plan already. Last I heard, the rebels were still in control of Uchurimac."

"I know. That's what I hear too. I figure that their strongest presence is probably right in the town. There must be outlying areas, though, farms and such, that have some contact, but without the constant threat."

"You are familiar with the game called Russian roulette?"

"Sure. In Russian roulette I have a pretty fair chance of encountering an empty chamber. I was hoping you might help me keep from walking into a fully loaded gun."

He stared at me for a long time. Then he said, "Mind you, this is the nearest church to Uchurimac that still has a priest, and I haven't seen anyone from there in months … with one exception."

He looked at my maps, leafed through them and selected the one with the highest level of detail that included Uchurimac. "This," he traced a line with his finger, "is the main road between here and there. Walk or drive in there and you would probably be ambushed either by *Rojistas* or by people from the community. Perhaps you heard of the massacre of journalists by the townspeople of Uchuraccay?" I shook my head. "Well, no matter. People who have been victimized either by the rebels or the government, or both, tend to become hostile to any outsiders."

"You mentioned an exception."

"Yes." Buenaventura tapped a section of the map corresponding to a high plateau on the near side of Uchurimac. "Here in the *alturas* above the village there are a few scattered farms. On occasion I've seen people from there, the Sonqo family, at the *feria* and in the Wednesday evensong mass. It's been two weeks since any of them came to mass. I'm not sure what it means."

"Is there a way to get there without traveling the main road?"

The priest nodded. "The same route they travel. From about here," he indicated a road that dead-ended in a canyon, "there is a footpath that follows the ridgeline. Where the ridge opens out you can see the first of the houses."

"Thanks, *Padre*," I said as I re-folded the maps. "I really appreciate this. I'm going to head up that direction, at least part-way, and see how things look."

"Be watchful, my friend."

I walked straight back to the *casa* Flores where Enrique was waiting for me. "Well, where are we going today?"

"I'm sorry, Enrique. I can't take you with me. It may be dangerous where I'm headed. Maybe later when I've had a chance to check things out." Enrique's face showed disappointment and some other combination of emotions that I couldn't read. He went into his room, closed the door and turned on his radio.

As I pulled the tarp from the Jeep, I thought about Enrique. He was a little bent out of shape about being left behind, but taking him was out of the question as long as there was any risk of hostility. I stowed the tarp loosely behind the seat and then returned to the house for my poncho and rain hat. The rains had become less frequent and less predictable, but they could still offer up a good drenching on occasion. As I passed Enrique's door, I could hear strains of music from the radio. "Hey, Sport," I said, "I'll see you tonight." He didn't answer. He's angry, I thought, but he'll get over it. I tossed the rain gear into the empty spot once occupied by a passenger seat, shifted to neutral and turned the key in the ignition.

The starter groaned a few times then gasped into silence. "Shit," I said under my breath. I slipped off the parking brake and hopped out. The grade was more or less level as far as the corner and then it was downhill all the way to the *plaza de armas*. Either the Jeep would start from engine compression or it would end up beached at the *plaza* until I could get another battery.

It started. Between the Jeep's natural rattles and the clatter of gears grinding, a spectator might have concluded the motor of the derelict Willys had been scared back to life.

With only a couple of looks at the map, I managed to find the right road up the right canyon. It turned out to be easy because, given the general lack of roads, there weren't many ways to be wrong. The road was rutted but drivable. Just a few meters before it petered out completely, I saw the footpath I was looking for. I pulled the Jeep to the side of the road and reached for the key. Then, remembering the condition of the battery, I turned the Jeep to face downhill before setting the brake, pocketing the key, grabbing my rain gear and heading up the trail.

Steep at first, the trail soon eased into a mild uphill that made hiking enjoyable. I took pleasure in the freshness of the air and the mild burn in my quadriceps. Before long the first small farm came into view. I saw no one outside. I considered approaching the house and attempting an introduction, but I decided against it. Whether uneasy about my mastery of Quechua or simply about the possibility of meeting suspicious or hostile strangers, I skirted the farm, staying on the far side of a fieldstone wall, and walked on. When I came near to another house, also without obvious human activity, I gave it a wide berth too. Two other small farms I managed to avoid with even greater distance and soon I stood at the crest of a hill overlooking a cemetery and, beyond that, the village of Uchurimac.

I sat down and considered the view. A crumbling hillside graveyard. A tiny enclave of adobe and tile nestled on both sides of a meandering stream. It was like a postcard or a calendar page. A perfect picture of pastoral bliss. Except that I now knew something about the conditions behind those adobe walls. I was acquainted with the statistics of infant mortality, of hunger and disease that fed the graveyard. And as if those hardships were not enough, I also knew something of the kinds of terrors inflicted on villages like this by men and women on both sides of the law, people with guns and agendas who valued the *campesinos* only as support for their own power bases or perverse personal pleasures.

From the mountains beyond the town a truck came into view, an old flat-bed Ford with stake sides. It looked as if a dozen or so people rode in the back. The truck rolled into the village and stopped in the small *plaza de armas*. From throughout the village another two dozen or so people materialized and formed around the truck. Some carried rifles, others had only machetes. Someone must have issued an order because, in unison, they moved to the rear of the truck and began climbing in. It was standing room only as the truck pulled out of the plaza.

Rojistas. On the move. It was my first look at any of the notorious rebels. They looked so young, so rag-tag. A little farther down the road they met with a car coming from the other direction. Wait a minute, I thought. That's Sanchez's car. This should be interesting. I imagined some kind of *policía-terrorista* showdown but I witnessed nothing of the sort. Both vehicles stopped for what looked like a very brief conversation between drivers and then they resumed in their original directions. The truck proceeded down the road toward the junction that would lead to Santa Rosita or, alternatively, toward the *cordillera* and the jungle beyond. Sanchez's car passed through Uchurimac without stopping and continued on the road that led, depending on turns taken, either toward the city of Cuzco or toward Lima via Ayacucho and Huancayo. What did it mean? Was Sanchez in bed with the *Camino Rojo*?

The sun warmed my back as I pondered the possibilities. With the vehicles out of sight down below, I began to slip into a contentedness induced by the peaceful landscape. Then, in less than the time it takes to formulate a coherent thought, a series of things happened. I sensed more than heard a footstep behind me. A shadow ascended in my peripheral vision. I rolled instinctively to the side away from the shadow just as the heavy iron blade of a hoe split the turf where I had been sitting.

I grabbed the near end of the hoe as it became dislodged from the earth. Wrestling with its other end, trying to raise it for a second blow, was a small *campesino* of about fifty. I could see panic in his eyes. The whites showed all the way around the black irises. I held tight to the hoe and struggled to my feet. The *campesino* released one hand and reached for his belt. Machete! I pushed back on the hoe, which sent my assailant to the ground. The *campesino* freed the machete and was scrambling to get to his feet again when another voice rang through the air.

"*Kari Wakli-piqta! Kari Wakli-piqta!*" Oh no! Enrique!

We both froze, I out of fear for Enrique's safety, and the machete-wielding *campesino* for some other reason I had yet to fathom. Then my attacker fell to his knees, his machete falling loose on the grass. The boy was still moving. His run had slowed to a walk. "Countryman," said Enrique in Quechua. "Do you not recognize the Son of Lightning when he visits your land?"

The man quivered and pressed his face to the ground. I was amazed. Beyond amazed. I was stupefied.

"*Señor*, stand up, please," I said in my deliberate Quechua. I reached into my pants pocket and felt the smooth stone with the lightning bolt etched in it. I had carried it with me ever since I retrieved it from the front step of the *casa* Flores.

"Forgive me, *Wirakocha*. I did not know."

"What do you know of the Son of Lightning?" I asked.

"I know that *Wirakocha* protects the people of Huaynatambo. I know that *Wirakocha* was struck dead by *Wakli* and rose from the grave. Please do not kill me, *Wirakocha*."

Shit, I thought, word gets around. "I will not hurt you." Enrique now stood solemnly at my side. "What is your name, countryman?"

His name was Ignacio Sonqo. He and all his extended family had heard of the *Kari Wakli-piqta* at the *feria* in Santa Rosita. By the time our conversation came to a close I had established several facts. First, every village and hamlet within walking distance – maybe farther – had heard of the Son of Lightning. Some of the farmers in those areas had even taken to raising poles at the windward edges of their farms with lightning bolts carved into them to ward off any evil influence that might visit them from this new god that apparently favored Huaynatambo.

Second, the arrival of a merciful *Kari Wakli-piqta* was a good omen for the Sonqo *ayllu*. Their crops were prospering. Their people were healthy. More importantly, in these highlands where lightning was a real threat, there had been no strikes on people or livestock all summer.

Third, for some inexplicable reason, the *terruco* devils had indeed packed up and gone from Uchurimac. Fortunately for me, it happened on this very day of the *Kari Wakli-piqta*'s appearance in the *alturas* above the town. Finally, it would be a great blessing for Uchurimac to have a visit from the *Kari Wakli-piqta*, and it would be especially valuable for the Sonqo *ayllu* to be able to make the introductions.

As Ignacio Sonqo picked up his machete and hoe, I couldn't help noticing the little bolt of lightning carved into the hoe handle. It had been smoothed and darkened by weeks' worth of sweat, dirt and labor. Ignacio led the way back through the farms, raising the hoe high overhead like a standard at each house, and at each house people came out to learn the story of how their patriarch had attempted to kill the *Kari Wakli-piqta* but was spared mercifully in his folly. Now this, I thought, is building rapport. At each house I received gifts of coca, and I promised to return very soon.

I compression-started the Jeep and Enrique stood in the empty passenger space gripping the top of the windshield frame. The wind tousled his hair like the hand of a friendly adult.

"Goddamn it, Enrique, that was dangerous," I chided him once we were underway.

"*¿Para quién?*" Enrique asked with the cockiness born of vindication.

"Dangerous for *you*, smart ass." I felt a peculiar brotherly pride. "Well, I'm glad you showed up when you did. How did you get there?"

Enrique smiled and pointed back at the tarp shifting in the breeze. I recalled the trip back into the house and the sound of the radio from Enrique's room and pieced the scene together. "I guess you'll be needing new batteries for your radio, hey, Sport?"

Comandante Rita, Amador Delgado, Cassandra and three other soldiers entered Ayacucho under cover of night, having traveled unmolested from Chosica in Cassandra's Mercedes-Benz. With Rita navigating, Cassandra guided the car to a stop on a back street where a high wall surrounded the outer courtyard of a private home. Rita got out and spoke into an intercom and the big wooden doors opened wide enough for Cassandra to drive through and park next to a tan-colored Plymouth.

The door to the house's interior opened and *El Colibrí* stood ready to greet them. Rita entered first and received a firm *abrazo* from their leader. Cassandra followed and *El Colibrí* also welcomed her with a warm embrace. *El Colibrí*'s arms then flung wide for Amador Delgado. While *El Colibrí* held Amador in the gesture of brotherhood, one of the *maestro*'s personal bodyguards stepped up quietly behind Delgado and slid a knife between his ribs and into his heart. The bodyguard caught Amador as he collapsed toward the floor and dragged him back out into the courtyard. So that all could see it, he laid the body face up on the paving stones, patted it down and removed a sheaf of currency and the expensive wristwatch. Then he peeled one bill from the stash of money and placed it like a flower in Amador's open mouth.

El Colibrí ushered Rita and Cassandra into a dining room where they were joined by Comrade Carlos, a ropy and intense young man recently and more familiarly called Pulga. "Please sit down," said *El Colibrí*. He remained standing at the head of the table, his hands gripping the chair back in front of him like a podium. He waited until he was sure he had everyone's complete attention, and then he waited a few seconds more for dramatic effect.

"We are a gathering storm," he pronounced. "We are very soon to become stronger than we have ever been before. In two days, we will receive a shipment of arms that will rival anything the treacherous puppet government can throw against us. As we speak, our armies amass around the drop site. *Comandante* Rita, you will accompany me to witness that great event." Rita swelled momentarily with pride and adoration, but she quickly recovered the disciplined deadpan that a soldier's decorum demanded. "Comrade Carlos, I have a special mission for you. The task and the promotion would have fallen to Comrade Amador, but he proved greedy and untrustworthy. Are you ready to assume the duties and title of a *comandante*?" Pulga nodded solemnly and *El Colibrí* continued. "Comrade Sandra, you will be *Comandante* Carlos' second-in-command. Congratulations, all of you. Now I need a private word with my new *comandante*."

The two women retired to sleeping quarters, each filled with her own combination of awe, suspense and guilty personal pride.

Pulga remained at the table bubbling in his own heady emotional brew.

"*Comandante* Carlos, a few additional troops are mustering along the road to Uchurimac. You and Comrade Sandra are to gather them tomorrow and proceed in that direction. Take the Plymouth. You will find a shortwave radio in the trunk."

El Colibrí turned to the bodyguard. "Make sure he knows how to use it."

"The great delivery of weapons of which I spoke takes place the day after tomorrow, in the morning. Once it is done, I will radio you. If all has gone well, as I assume it will, you will simply garrison in Uchurimac until further notice." Pulga nodded his understanding. "However, if something goes wrong or if you do not hear from me before noon, you are to take your patrol to Santa Rosita. There you will preside over the executions of every person on this list. This is for your eyes only."

El Colibrí slid a folded-over slip of paper across the table to Pulga. The names were basically the same ones Pulga had compiled after Christmas while dogging Bonifacio Vargas. There was one notable addition at the bottom of the list: Cassandra Ganz de la Vega, AKA, Comrade Sandra.

The pilot, copilot and two crewmen had received their final instructions early the day before. The cargo plane was already rigged with extra equipment originally designed for crop dusting but now adapted for a different purpose. At the moment of the plane's lift-off, only stars, a scrap of moon and a few ships' lights illuminated the surface of Panama Bay.

At five minutes before eight, the sun had rolled out a golden carpet across the misty canopy of the Amazon basin and up the eastern slopes of the Andes. Smoky ghosts lingered in the air above the recently abandoned sites of morning campfires surrounding the airstrip that constituted the bull's-eye of the drop zone. At two minutes before the hour, the copilot opened the rear cargo door and the crewmen rigged the first of four crates to its static line. At eight the copilot signaled, the crewman ejected the crate and its parachute blossomed. The pilot began to circle for the remaining drops.

The crates had been built to take extreme punishment without damage to their contents. Reinforced plywood and heavy steel bolts ensured that they not only would survive the impact of landing but also that they would require time and extraordinary effort to open. Thus it was that by the time the last crate touched down, the first was still intact. Guerrillas from all around the perimeter of the drop zone moved toward the crates like ants to honey. None of them paid much attention to the plane's final wide, low circle. Nor did they notice the heavy spray of flammable liquid it laid over the ring of foliage below it. The bolts of the first crate were barely loosened when the copilot pressed a remote detonator, turning each crate into a massive cloud of fire, shrapnel, blood, smoke and body parts. The plane's parting shot, an incendiary grenade lobbed into the fuel-sodden vegetation, created a circle of fire that would seal the fate of any *terrucos* unlucky enough to survive the initial blasts.

On a ridgeline high above the drop zone, a stunned Miguel Fortuna let the binoculars fall against his chest and took in the scene before him. An entire coca plantation blazed. Over two hundred of the *Camino Rojo*'s best men and women were dead or running to their deaths. What was to have been a great step forward in the revolution had become, instead, a giant step back. Well, *El Colibrí* could rebuild an army. There was no shortage of poor, hungry and angry citizens from which to recruit. And he could rebuild an armory. Ganz wasn't the only robber baron that would pay to grease the wheels of illicit commerce. It was a shame, though, *El Colibrí* thought, how he had miscalculated the value Alejandro Ganz de la Vega placed on his coca revenues. Had he also misjudged Ganz's fondness for the safety of Santa Rosita and for the life of his sister Cassandra? *El Colibrí* still had the means to make Ganz pay for this treachery. He picked up his portable shortwave radio and made the necessary call.

Standing next to him, *Comandante* Rita held her binoculars in place a little longer as the ring of fire expanded and closed on the dead and the dying. Then she lowered them slowly and without a word. This changes things, she thought.

Enrique and I rose early for our trip back to Uchurimac by way of the *alturas* and the farms of the Sonqo *ayllu*. I packed up my pouch of coca leaves and a bottle of *trago* that I kept in reserve for ceremonies requiring ingratiation or a return of hospitality. Anticipating Enrique's company as a passenger rather than a stowaway, I also had gathered up a box and cushion with which to craft an ersatz passenger seat. It turned out I needn't have bothered. Enrique much preferred the standing position he had adopted on our previous return to Santa Rosita.

"Hey, Sport," I said. The term of endearment had been a little puzzling to Enrique at first. Neither the noun nor the verb in literal translation made any sense as a name for a person, but he liked it because it was English and because I used it affectionately. It had led to a discussion of idioms.

"It's kind of like *pata*," I'd explained. "We understand it to mean *amigo* or *compadre*, even though it literally means a paw or an animal's foot."

Since that rather pedantic discussion, Enrique had taken to greeting me in English with the words, "What's up, animal foot?"

"*Las alturas de* Uchurimac are. Are you ready?"

"Ready," he said. So was I. It was a cool, clear April morning, a harbinger of fall, and the Jeep started without a push. I was beginning a new and vital stage of my field work. Finally I was going to be able to interview people who had lived under *Camino Rojo* occupation and who, if the stories were true, had witnessed tribunals and ritual assassinations. I would be able to compare life in Uchurimac to life as I had experienced it in Santa Rosita and Huaynatambo. I was more than ready. I was eager and optimistic.

We took the same route as we had two days ago. I even parked in the same indentations from my tires. The cool, dry air made for brisk walking, and in no time we were approaching the farm of Ignacio Sonqo.

"*Hallpakusunchis*." I greeted him with the formal Quechua phrase that meant 'let us chew coca together'. We traded *k'intus* and chewed ceremonially to underscore our good will and acceptance of each other. This ritual, which I had performed many times with the *campesinos* of Huaynatambo, was the cause of some initial consternation for Enrique and some rather heavy lectures on anthropology from me in return. He was forgiving of such long-winded explanations, and his presence as a sounding board helped me formulate my own ideas and understanding of the culture I was studying.

Ignacio waved out the rest of his family: his wife, Hortensia, a son, Emilio, a daughter-in-law, Marta, and a grandson named Marco. We traded greetings and proceeded to the rest of the farms in the *ayllu*, our procession growing in both length and animation. Each of us, with the exception of Enrique, had a wad of chewed coca leaves pressed into the cheek. It was a green-lipped and festive parade that wound down the mountain, through the graveyard and into Uchurimac.

The villagers were expecting us. From the moment our procession became visible from the town, people began congregating at the entrance of the cemetery. Plainly they wanted to get an early glimpse of the *Kari Wakli-piqta*. I was the excuse, if not the reason, for the festivity. The fifteen or twenty people from the cemetery swelled our ranks and our numbers continued to grow as we approached the *plaza de armas*. In the plaza stood most, I assumed, of the rest of the townspeople.

Since the night before, they had been preparing the feast called *pachamanca* or earth oven. In the *plaza de armas* they had dug a pit, lined it with stones and filled it with firewood. The fire had burned to coals and heated the rocks red. Into the pit had gone an entire hog, several fat guinea pigs and many kilos of corn and potatoes that had somehow been protected against the pillaging of the *Rojistas*. This earth oven, a larger version of the one that had cooked the demon goose, was covered over and left to bake. What came out the next day were the most succulent meats and vegetables I had ever experienced. In that moment Peru more than atoned for the countless mornings of bologna and instant coffee and the greasy fare of *Los Tres Chanchitos*.

Just before the feasting began, musical instruments appeared. There were flutes, fiddles and a string bass, all made of unvarnished woods. There were drums. There were sticks to beat together. There was even a horn section consisting of a tarnished silver saxophone and a battered, wobbly trombone. When the music started it delivered a major shock to my sensibilities. It evoked braying donkeys, lowing cattle and honking geese. Nails on chalkboards and rusty swing sets. Just tuning up, I thought. I was wrong. When the drums started up they didn't so much carry a rhythm as bludgeon a beat. It seemed like music fit for wild dancing and drunkenness. In that, I was wrong also. It actually settled into more of a dirge as the little band processed solemnly around the plaza.

In the festivities leading up to the feast I took it easy on the *trago* and beer, feigning swigs when bottles came my way in order to keep a clear head. I worked hard on the business of remembering the names of the people I met. Not facing the same constraints, the people of Uchurimac celebrated with zeal. Even without the excuse of a first visit from the Son of Lightning, the departure of the *terrucos* gave them reason enough to let off steam and take in alcohol. So it was that by the time the first of us noticed the overburdened tan Plymouth, it was too late to do anything about it. I recognized the car immediately, but it wasn't Porfirio Sanchez at the wheel. Whatever that meant, it almost certainly wasn't good for Sanchez, and it didn't seem to bode well for the rest of us, either.

There had to be at least seven or eight people riding inside and three others sitting in the trunk with the lid propped open. The first two people out of the car raised rifles and kept them trained on the crowd while the rest got out and formed a loose circle around the plaza. They looked agitated and humorless. Among the villagers all conversation had stopped. Heads hung. Eyes searched the dirt intensely for nothing in particular. No one moved at all.

Being whiter than the rest of the revelers set me apart. It only took the driver of Sanchez's car a moment to register his recognition of my face. I had seen him before too, in the plaza in Santa Rosita. He produced a pistol from a shoulder holster – I recognized it also as Sanchez's – and aimed it at me.

"You. Come here." I started to take a step and Enrique reached for my arm. The skinny *terruco* raised his eyebrows. "You too." He included Enrique in the arc of his pistol barrel. He made us kneel on the ground and ordered one of the soldiers to bring the other prisoner. From deep in the trunk they dragged a body. It was a woman. She was dressed like the other *terrucos*, except shoeless. A black balaclava was pulled over her head and turned backward so that she was unable to see. Through the holes meant for the face there showed only the improbable evidence of blonde hair.

The leader then addressed the crowd in a loud voice. "Which of you are also from Santa Rosita?" There was no response, but the townspeople huddled closer together. He held the pistol to my head. "Who else here is from Santa Rosita?" he asked me directly.

My insides cramped with fear. "*Nadie. Somos los únicos.* Everyone else is from Uchurimac."

"I will wait thirty seconds," announced the lead *guerilla.* "Anyone I see after that will be shot." There followed a few seconds of murmured confusion and the sound of footsteps retreating in every direction like the waves in a pond from a stone hitting the surface.

The *guerrillas* closed ranks and began to take note of the *pachamanca.* Their leader spoke to me again. "Take off your boots." He pulled off his own broken-down boots and tried mine on for size. Satisfied, he tossed his boots to another of the men whose own shoes were in the process of disintegrating around his feet. "Tie them up," he barked.

They bound our wrists behind our backs and then tied us together with a short rope that ran from my wrists to Enrique's and from Enrique's to those of the other prisoner. I didn't resist when the black muslin sack came down over my head. Instead I closed my eyes to replace the imposed darkness with one of my own choosing. Enrique did resist. I heard him strain against the arms that held him, and I heard the blow that silenced him. Someone forced me all the way to the ground.

“Enrique, are you okay?” I whispered in English, and for it I got a kick to my stomach so hard and unexpected that I had to fight to keep from vomiting into my hood. Enrique didn’t answer but he tugged twice on the rope to let me know he was there. Smart kid, I thought through the waves of pain and nausea. Then I heard the sounds of noisy eating. The rebels were devouring the remains of the *pachamanca*, a fact that I hoped would improve their dispositions.

I expected an immediate tribunal and execution, but those apparently were not the orders given to the patrol. I feared for us, and my fear was compounded with terrible guilt. I had brought us here against the advice of Pedro Buenaventura. I had allowed Enrique to come and had even felt glad for his company and grateful for his help in understanding the Quechua spoken by the *campesinos*. Now there was every reason to suspect that we would both be killed. And for what? For scholarship? For the possibility of another dubious contribution to the annals of anthropology? Because I had become bored with the work in Huaynatambo? I felt not only guilty and afraid; I felt vain, supremely stupid and angry with myself.

After a while I heard fresh milling about, muted conversations, an occasional belch. Out of the blackness came a prod to my ribs at the same time as a voice commanded me to get up. Enrique and our co-prisoner got the same treatment, and we were made to march. Almost immediately I stumbled and fell. With my hands behind me I twisted instinctively to land on my hip and shoulder. The rope yanked at my wrists and I felt and heard Enrique fall with me and then the woman prisoner too, like dominos. I must have lain there for a second too long, trying to figure out how to get up again without my hands, because my face suddenly exploded with the force of what I assume was the toe of a boot. I struggled hard to get to my feet and once again we were moving forward. With my tongue, I discovered a massively swollen, bloody lip and a rough fragment of tooth.

The trunk of the car slammed and then the doors – one, two, three, four. It sounded like a handful of rebels marched with us while the car, barely idling, followed behind us, probably carrying the rest. I thought I knew the direction of our travel from the lead rebel’s earlier question and also from the slight downhill grade. We were headed for Santa Rosita. It would be a long walk. I guessed that our captors would take turns riding in the car in order to avoid fatigue. I also guessed, correctly, that we prisoners would not be included in the rotation.

Curses and jabs dictated our pace, which was brisk. The rough road made walking difficult and the difficulty was exacerbated by the fact that the road was unfamiliar. I could form no mental picture of our position once we left the environs of the plaza. A few times I stumbled on a stone or a pothole in the road and caught myself before falling. Once Enrique fell down, yanking the rope between us, and I nearly fell back on top of him. He was hauled to his feet instantly by someone whose feet were striking the dirt just behind us. That same presence kept us from talking.

I tried to allow for the roughness of the road with my gait, lifting my feet high and setting them down with deliberate vertical movements. The simple fact of having to concentrate to keep my footing helped distract me, for a while at least, from thoughts of what most certainly lay ahead of us. As we marched, however, my body tended to slip into a cadence, which freed my mind to wander elsewhere. At those times, with no visual stimuli and without the sun's movement or even the rhythms of conversation to mark the time, I drifted into a black, timeless morass of imagination.

Unbidden scenes invaded my consciousness. I began to recall all the various horror stories I had heard or read about the treatment by *Rojista* rebels of their captured enemies. I imagined throats slit and arteries erupting, bombs exploded and bodies disintegrating, bullets fragmenting and soft tissue turning to mush. I recalled stories of the beheading of a priest, the public evisceration of a woman accused of succoring the enemy and the stoning of tourists whose only fault was being in a good place at a bad time. Then my morbid imagination began to supply faces to the victims: Pedro Buenaventura, Rosario Flores, Mercedes Marquez, Samson Young, Enrique Morales …

I tried to drive out the fear by imagining ways that rescue might come. The *policía* might arrive, led by Porfirio Sanchez, perhaps. But where *was* Sanchez? It seemed unlikely that he was still alive with his car being used by *terrucos*. Imagining Sanchez killed by rebels made me think of him in slightly fonder terms than I had before. Or maybe the army would save us. There would be a sound of trucks. Would the *terrucos* try to run? Would they leave us behind or would they drag us along? Surely the army would not shoot hooded prisoners, would they? At least not intentionally. Maybe we would be surrounded and the *terrucos* would be forced to surrender. They would let us live in order to save their own skins. No, the *terrucos* would surely resist. A gun battle would ensue. What would I do? Run? No. Fall to the ground. Protect Enrique. Play dead. Would we be valued as hostages? Would the *terrucos* try to use our bodies as shields?

How would the army find us? By sheer luck? No. The people of Uchurimac. Of course. They would contact the police and the police would call in the army. That's how it would happen. Why not? There were lots of reasons. Fear of *Rojista* reprisals, for one. The villagers had been terrorized before. They had seen two of their leaders murdered and had cooperated, at least on the surface, with the *guerrillas*. That would mark them as sympathizers and invite even more trouble from the authorities. Would they know that? Would they think of it?

What *would* they think? Who was I to the people of Uchurimac? Just some American? Some anthropologist? Hardly. I was the *Kari Wakli-piqta*, the Son of Lightning! What would that mean? Probably that I could take care of myself. I had lightning at my fingertips, right? And if I didn't, then what was I? A weakling god at the end of his season? A simple fraud? And how far from the truth was that?

At some point along the way, the little toe of my right foot connected hard with a stone embedded in the road. Pain blossomed and I fell hard to my right knee. The footsteps behind me stopped but no hands came forward to help me up. As I struggled to stand again without the use of my hands I favored the right foot and found that I could still support my weight. I hesitated to think what would become of me if I could no longer walk. When I was once again moving forward, I felt the slack disappear from the rope dangling at my wrist. Two distinct tugs seemed to communicate, '*Are you all right*?'

Enrique. My heart reached out to him. I gave him two quick return tugs to say, '*Yes, I'm still here*.' What I felt in that instant for Enrique Morales, I suddenly realized, was love. It was a purer love than I had ever felt before, purer not so much for what it was, but for what it was not. It was not at all like the groin-centered thing I felt for various women, feelings that shot through me like electroshock therapy and left me lying in bed in the middle of the night with my dick in my hand, my head muddled and my chest as empty as a pillaged grave. And unlike the love I felt for my parents, or even for Mitch, this love for Enrique was not about me.

I never doubted that I loved my family. But the feelings were conflicted and contaminated with resentments. I had resented all of them for the expectations that fell on me after Mitch broke away to follow his own path. I resented Mitch at the same time as I felt envy and awe at his courage in finding and following that path. I resented my father for his years of distance and silence. I resented his dying before I had a chance to bridge that distance and get to know him as a person and not just the imposing authority figure in my life. My god, I even resented my mother for her weakness while Dad was alive, for always living in his shadow, for not being her own person so much as an appendage of him. And after Dad died, I resented her even more for so quickly abandoning his memory. I realized, too, that all those resentments were less about my family than they were about me, about my shame for not being stronger, more honest with myself, more aware.

Enrique. Images of the boy filled my head. Running. Asking questions. Grinning after telling a joke. Earnestly translating a phrase I didn't understand. Every one of the images touched me in a way I had never fully experienced at the time. I wanted to celebrate Enrique. I wanted him to live, to prosper, to *be*. I wanted the world to belong to Enrique Morales. And now Enrique was about to become just one more tragic story, one more example of how Peru kills off her innocents. Enrique was going to die, and I would be an accomplice.

The pain in my toe had subsided to a nagging throb. Then that throb, like a tuning fork set to resonate with misery, began to elicit aches elsewhere in my body: my shoulders and elbows from being bound behind me; my lower back and inner thighs, probably from this cautious, high-stepping gait; my shoeless feet aching, probably bleeding. As a distraction I called up my memories of human physiology, mentally opening the conservative maroon cover of my old *Gray's Anatomy* and flipping to the illustrations of musculature. I envisioned each one, highlighting the places where I hurt. First the shoulder; strain on the rotator cuff, head of the biceps tendon, pectoralis major … down to the elbow; strain on triceps, lower biceps tendon, forearm flexor, impingement on ulnar nerve … and the lower back; Longissimus? Iliocostalis? What a mess of muscles we have to keep us upright. And that sharp pain emerging in my groin. Gracilis? And then of course back to the toe, the split lip, the broken tooth, the pounding in my head.

I wondered how Enrique was feeling. Better than me, I hoped.

And what about the other prisoner? Who could she be with that blonde hair? A hapless tourist? Then why the army fatigues? Then my wondering returned to Santa Rosita. How would we enter the town? Who would see us first? Would there be time to react? And with what weaponry? I began to conjure a picture of the rebels' hit list. For the crime of treason against the people's revolution; Mayor Domingo Gutierrez, Judge Pablo Cortez, Constable Carlos Sartori, Father Pedro Buenaventura, *la Señorita* Mercedes Marquez Acevedo, *la Señora* Rosario Flores … and on and on. In each case I fought against images of those people with guns to their heads. I saw images of beauty crushed, of faith betrayed, of innocence ended with a bullet or a blade. I saw the best parts of the world punished, vanquished by ugly brutality.

After interminable trudging and stumbling, I heard the sound of an airplane. A wild, irrational hope overtook me as the sound grew closer, and then it faded as the sound grew more distant. A second pass of the plane, although it sounded higher than the first, revived my hope, but my despondency quickly returned after its departure.

I tried to drive back my despair by forming pictures of my mother, of Mitch, of my father, but I couldn't hold onto them. They simply wouldn't solidify for me. I tried to reach out with my thoughts to God, except I had no real idea of who or what or *if* God was. I felt like that space probe – What was it? Explorer? Adventurer? – launched into the universe with its continuous radio transmissions of greetings in how many puny human languages? Prayer was just another desperate effort to communicate with somebody, anybody, with a better handle on the big picture than I had. And with predictable results. *Nada*. Nothing. Zip. Zero. Big surprise.

Above and underneath everything remained Enrique. No matter what my brain conjured in its attempt to thwart my fear, I still had the searing certainty that next to me and because of me, this bright, lively eight-year-old was marching to his death.

Eventually, it became clear that evening was on its way. The temperature was dropping. I had perspired heavily and a breeze carrying cool air down from the mountains had chilled me until I was shivering violently. Changes in the ambient sounds and smells indicated the approaching town. A door thudded and I imagined it blue in a reddish-brown frame. A pot clanged and a whiff of garlic caressed my nose. I imagined anonymous faces appearing in windowpanes then receding into blackness.

It wouldn't be long now. I knew the *Rojistas* preferred either dawn or twilight for their trials and executions. It was then that people's guards were down, then that the people named on their infamous lists were most likely to be at home, and then that the drama of revolution was most convincing.

The standard tactic of the *Camino Rojo* was to quietly surround a town and move in from the perimeter, sweeping their victims from their homes into the streets and then to the *plaza de armas*. My ears told me that they hadn't yet split up, even though we had reached the outskirts of town. I wondered why. Then it occurred to me. On this side of town only one bridge crossed the ravine dug by the river that collected local streams for their journey to the Apurimac and the Amazon basin. To cross anywhere else would be at best inconvenient and time consuming. They would take us across the wooden plank bridge and then they would split up and the operation would begin. I wanted to talk to Enrique, to tell him to be brave – although I already knew him to be braver than I was – to tell him to join the rebels if it would save his life, to tell him that I loved him like a little brother.

The first clear sign of our approach to the ravine was the smell. The river served the town as both culinary water and sewer. Naturally the drinking water was drawn from upstream of the town and the effluent entered below. This was only a small comfort. Everyone knew that every village and farm on every upstream branch used the same system. As a result the river almost always carried pungent overtones, but the smell today was worse. Layered over the normal odors was the stench of rotting flesh.

From the cadre ahead, I heard groans of disgust. What I smelled through the partial filter of a muslin hood, they were experiencing full-force. I wondered what had died and figured it was probably a dog. I had seen dog carcasses lying in the ravine before in varying stages of decomposition. Next to me, I heard Enrique cough. My own throat tightened. I wanted to swallow but my mouth was too dry. I hoped that neither Enrique nor I would vomit into our hoods. I heard the sound of boots on the wooden bridge then my own battered feet felt the rough planks.

The rhythm of footfalls was interrupted by a deafening blast as several sharp and near simultaneous explosions ripped through the air from below us on all sides. I froze. There were heavy thuds, clatters and more shots. Then a shot from behind me. Something slammed like a hot fist into my left shoulder, knocking me forward at the same time as the slack disappeared from the short rope between me and Enrique.

I dropped to my knees and fell to the ground. I rolled in the direction where Enrique had to be and tried to cover him with my own body. I expected to feel the stab of a bullet or a blade. I prayed I could protect Enrique.

The shooting stopped. Voices shouted. Objects were hitting the ground around me. Then more voices, urgent, then calmer.

"Enrique, are you okay?" No answer. "Enrique!" I said more loudly. He gave no response. "¡Enrique, *háblame*!"

I held my hooded cheek to his. Enrique lay lifeless.

My eyes burned with tears and dry, choking sobs wracked my ribs. I curled up next to Enrique with my head resting on his small body. It was all over.

Everything was over. My world had been reduced to a dark empty space surrounded by the shuffling and murmurs of ghosts.

After a time that seemed interminable a hand came down on my unwounded shoulder. "*Déjeme ayudarle, Señor*."

Two hands helped me get to my feet and removed the black hood. The third hostage, the blonde woman, was already gone. A soldier in a tan uniform carefully sliced the ropes from my wrists. Another was carrying Enrique's body gently like a bride's in the direction of town. What I could see of Enrique's face was plastered with blood-matted hair. One thin arm hung like the pendulum of a clock that had just stopped ticking.

Part Four: Finishing What I Came For

Yerba silvestre, aroma puro,
Te ruego acompañarme en mi camino.
Serás mi bálsamo y mi tragedia,
Serás mi aroma y mi gloria.
Serás mi amiga cuando crezcas sobre mi tumba.
Allí, que la montaña me cobije,
Que el cielo me responda.
Y en piedra lápida toda quedará grabado.

I pray the wildflowers, pure perfume,
To be my traveling companions.
You'll be my comfort and my tragedy,
My fragrance and my bliss,
The friend that lies down on my grave.
May the mountains give me shelter
And the heavens a reply,
And on headstones let everything be recorded.

Comandante Edith Lagos Sáez
Born: Ayacucho - November 27, 1962
Died: Andahuaylas - September 2, 1982

The earth danced through her orbit, holding her Southern reaches farther and farther from the sun. The nights became cool and the days dry. Sacks of potatoes and mounds of spent vegetation followed the harvest work of the *ayllus*. I spent many days pitching in, work that rewarded me with a sore back and the opportunity to interact constantly with the people of Uchurimac. On days when I didn't work in the fields, I spent time hanging around and chatting with the people who ran the shops, made the *chicha* and wove the wool in the village.

Some evenings, I observed the training of Santa Rosita's newly formed civil defense patrol, which extended to both Huaynatambo and Uchurimac. The patrol was, supposedly, armed and trained at the expense of Alex Ganz, although I privately speculated that the real source of money and weapons was the United States Government. I doubted that Ganz would sacrifice hundreds of acres of prime coca fields without extracting something in exchange from America's so-called war on drugs.

As for me, access to the many activities of the town and countryside became easier than ever. My notoriety as the *Kari Wakli-piqta* was only enhanced by my capture and my subsequent escape from the *terrucos*. As if I'd had anything to do with it. And while the actual work of anthropology went even more smoothly than before, I found I enjoyed it less.

Alex Ganz had predicted some kind of reaction to the double-cross in the coca fields. He had been mortally afraid for Cassandra, but he had resolved to carry out his plans anyway. He had done what he could for her, short of arming the entire *Camino Rojo* with state-of-the art weaponry. In the event she lived, he had made a deal with Inspector Castillo that might yet save her.

Manolo had been doing his third reconnaissance flyover for the day when he saw the small column of men followed by Sanchez's car.

He flew over once and then circled again to get a better view with his binoculars. As soon as he landed, he reported to Ganz, and Alex issued the order to mobilize.

The Volvo farm trucks were already loaded with weapons and medical supplies. The security team he had hired through a highly specialized company in the United States boarded the trucks and began to roll. Alex led the way in the Land Rover with Manolo and Mercedes.

He had chosen the jail as a headquarters for several reasons. It was reasonably spacious. For prisoners the cells would be useful. Finally, if it somehow became necessary to defend the town against greater numbers, the jail was its most defensible building.

The hired soldiers knew their jobs and did them with remarkable efficiency. They had planted the noisome canine corpses by the bridge as a distraction and prepared blinds for themselves up and down the ravine on both sides. As soon as the *Rojistas* were on the bridge, designated soldiers opened fire on the column, taking care not to hit the hooded prisoners. At the same time the remaining soldiers appeared from their hiding places in an impressive show of force. Only one *terruco* fired a shot as he went down. It was that shot that felled the child hostage and slammed into the shoulder of another. The *terrucos* that remained alive, including the ones in the car, dropped their weapons and surrendered. As the *comandante*, Pulga had been one of those riding in the car.

Immediately after the ambush, Manolo drove to the bridge in the Land Rover. He injected the third hostage with a strong sedative and scooped her up as easily as if she had been a kitten. He placed her in the back seat between two of the hired soldiers and left her hood in place until they were out of the view of witnesses.

When Cassandra finally woke up in a clean bed and pajamas in the house in el Valle del Cóndor, she had both Juan Pablo and Consuelo to see to her physical comfort. To tend to her other needs, Alex had retained Dr Miguel Valderrama, the psychiatrist to whose care she would be entrusted indefinitely.

Alex's agreement with Castillo would allow the Ganz family to create their own story of Cassandra's ordeal. In partial exchange, Cassandra would have to cooperate with Castillo's investigation, providing information about her experiences and her collaborators. Castillo was particularly interested in the female *comandante* that led the Crimson Road's Lima-based activities. Dr Valderrama assured both Alex and Castillo that, under his care, Cassandra's cooperation would be complete and her emotional recovery non-problematic. On those assurances he would stake his considerable reputation and earn a considerable fortune.

For the finer points of Cassandra's story, both the crafting and the telling, Alex had hired a very expensive, very discrete public relations firm in Washington, DC. It would begin with a tale of kidnapping and coercion by *El Colibrí*. It would include a diagnosis of Stockholm Syndrome, followed by a heroic rescue and a quiet, dignified and utterly successful period of professional de-programming. Finally, Cassandra would reenter society as the director of the soon-to-be-established Ganz Foundation, which would become Peru's premier philanthropic organization.

The soldier who had cut my ropes and removed my hood spoke to me in American English. "Let's have a look at that wound." Only then did I realize that blood was oozing down my back from a throbbing hole in my shoulder. Not that it mattered. I stood still while he cut away my shirtsleeve.

"Hmm. Looks like you're carrying a bullet. Got a name?"

"Sam."

"This isn't too serious, Sam." He wrapped my shoulder tightly with a length of gauze bandage. "We'll get you to the infirmary in just a few minutes." I nodded. It didn't really matter. Around me, soldiers gathered fallen weapons. Other soldiers dragged bodies to the end of the bridge. That didn't matter either. Nothing mattered. A wave of nausea washed through my stomach and I became light-headed. My mouth tasted metallic. My vision distorted and I started to black out. The soldier caught me and eased me to the ground. I only vaguely and disinterestedly tracked the transfer of my body from the ground to a stretcher and then to the back of a flatbed truck. The world that floated by made no impression on me. I had only one thought. Enrique Morales was dead.

By the time the truck stopped I was fully conscious again, cold and in pain. We were in front of the jail. An effort to sit up sent a saw blade through my shoulder.

"Easy," said the soldier riding with me in the back of the truck. He and one other man slid the stretcher from the truck bed and helped me to my feet.

The first thing I saw inside the jail was a blurred vision of Mercedes Marquez. She waved me to a chair next to a table spread with medical instruments. I sat. Mercedes swabbed the back of my hand and slid a needle into one of the veins there. Within a moment, she had attached an IV drip.

"I'm giving you something for the pain, Sam," she said as she injected the contents of a syringe into the IV tube. Morphine? Demerol?

Suddenly Pedro Buenaventura appeared in front of me. He handed me a cup of tea, which I recognized immediately as his special blend of coca leaves and chamomile. As I sipped the tea, Mercedes unwound my bandage. I began to feel dreamy and disconnected from the trauma in my shoulder. The room around me was an aquarium with people floating about in it. Alex Ganz drifted in through the door like a shark. Manolo Ruíz appeared at my side like a curious elephant seal.

Mercedes took the cup from me and set it on the table. Manolo knelt down next to me. He wrapped his huge arms around me and held me in a crushing bear hug. I was confused by that until I felt the stab of pain in my shoulder and the jolt of the bullet being pulled out. Mercedes washed and re-bandaged my wound and Manolo finally relaxed his hold. I slumped in the chair. "Enrique …" I said.

"Shhh," whispered Mercedes, and she pointed to the far side of the room. There, seated in a steel chair next to the Priest was Doña Rosario holding Enrique against her ample bosom. Enrique's head sported a clean white bandage.

"He'll be fine," said Mercedes. "A bullet grazed his scalp and gave him a concussion."

I felt like my heart was breaking from gratitude. Emotion was driving tears to my eyes and the breath from my lungs. I sobbed softly in my utter exhaustion.

Pedro Buenaventura knelt before me, took my hands in his and held them until I stopped shaking. Then he wrapped them once again around the mug of tea. The sweet concoction began to warm me and waken me to a better understanding of my surroundings. As my awareness broadened, I absorbed the rest of the scene inside the jail. Along one wall stood several weapons and boxes of ammunition. A few people stood and conversed in muted voices. I recognized some of Santa Rosita's community leaders. I noticed the abundance of supplies and the general state of medical readiness. I reflected upon the rescue at the bridge and on the overall attentiveness to humane details here in the jail.

"Pedro," I asked, "who's in charge?"

I followed the direction of his raised-eyebrows and saw Alex Ganz through the bars of a cell assisting Mercedes in the treatment of a wounded *Rojista.* Alex and Mercedes looked as if they belonged together.

Chief Inspector Castillo showed up a little after noon the next day in a Toyota Land Cruiser with two brawny *sinchis*, members of the National Guard, discernable by their red berets. Compared to the *Rojistas*, the *sinchis* looked like a different species. The *Rojistas* had the look of stringy, underfed coyotes. The *sinchis* looked like well-fed wolves that would kill for sport.

The rest of Castillo's bargain with Alex Ganz had included the gift of several *Camino Rojo* prisoners and the credit for their capture. The *militares* took the prisoners to a farm several kilometers away from Santa Rosita in the direction of Lima by way of Huancayo. The farmhouse had two rooms, one front and one rear. Castillo had the prisoners taken into the rear room and seated in a row with their backs to the raw adobe wall. There were six men, including Pulga, and one woman. Castillo paced the width of the room in each direction, looking the prisoners over while the two *sinchis* lounged by the door. The prisoners sat stoically. The oldest was probably thirty. The youngest maybe fifteen. The woman may have been seventeen. Castillo took his pistol from its holster and shot the youngest man through the forehead. The dead boy slumped forward and toppled across the lap of the bearded man next to him, turning his lap into a warm, sticky reservoir of blood. The bearded man never flinched.

"The rest of you," said Castillo, "will get a chance to talk to me."

With his pistol he indicated the bearded man.

"You," he said, "come with me, and bring him with you."

Castillo and one *sinchi* led the way into the forward room. The bearded man followed, dragging his fallen comrade by the arms. The dead boy's head painted a macabre trail on the smooth dirt floor. The second *sinchi* shut the curtain between the two rooms and stayed behind to guard the remaining prisoners. From his pocket he took a transistor radio, turned it on and fiddled with the dial until he found a station playing love songs. Through the lulls in the music, the prisoners could hear soft voices in the forward room, but they were unable to make out the words that were spoken.

In a few minutes, the voices stopped. In another minute Castillo pulled back the curtain and signaled to the oldest prisoner that he was next. The man stood up and looked fearfully at his comrades, but they made no eye contact. As he walked through the door, his fear congealed into a knot in his stomach. There had been no other shot fired. Maybe, he thought, if he talked he would walk. Castillo pointed him to a wooden chair in the middle of the room. The chair was unbloodied. He sat. He listened. He talked.

Twice more, Castillo appeared at the curtain and each time he called a male *Rojista* forward to the wooden chair. In each case, all that the prisoners in the back room could hear were muted voices and songs of romance. Only Pulga and the young woman were left. Finally, Castillo beckoned Pulga into the forward room. As before, there had been no gunshots and there was no blood. This time, in addition to the chair there was also a wooden table in the center of the room. Castillo stood in the open front door, smoking a cigarette. The volume of the radio rose to a level more appropriate to the ardent passions of the singers. Pulga sat. The *sinchi* cut the ropes binding Pulga's wrists. Then he looped a thin cord tightly around Pulga's right wrist and tied it off to the right forward table leg with enough slack that Pulga's hand rested in the middle of the tabletop. He repeated the procedure on the left side. Then, walking behind the chair, he looped a cord around Pulga's neck and tied it to the chair back. The noose wasn't tight, but it was there.

Castillo tossed the still smoldering cigarette butt to the dirt floor and walked to the front edge of the table. Pulga looked at him as impassively as he could, given the level of his fear.

"We have had quite fruitful little chats with your comrades," said Castillo. "For example, we know you are their *comandante*. We also know that you were promoted just recently by *El Colibrí* himself. You must be quite proud. We believe there is probably much more you can tell us. So here's what we are going to do: I will ask you questions and you will answer them. If I don't like an answer, my friend here will take one of your fingers. If you are very helpful, you could walk out of here still able to tie your own shoes. Now, shall we begin?"

Twice the sound of a love song was punctuated by a scream. Then there was only music. The expression on the face of the *sinchi* standing guard over the young woman never changed.

"That could have gone worse," said Castillo to Pulga.

The *sinchi* cut the cords and Castillo tossed Pulga a rag from the kitchen area of the room.

"Here. Take care of your bleeding."

Pulga stanched the flow from the former attachments of his right thumb and index finger.

"Go ahead. Stand up," said Castillo. "It's still a very pleasant day."

Castillo lit another cigarette and stepped out through the door into the sunlight. Pulga looked from Castillo to the *sinchi*. The *sinchi* gestured wordlessly in the direction of the door. Pulga took a tentative step in that direction. The *sinchi* just nodded and started in that direction himself. Pulga could hardly believe his luck. He walked to the door, stepped through and felt the sunshine on his face. Then looking down he saw his five comrades lying shoulder to shoulder, face up with their throats slit. At the very moment of recognition, he felt the first touch of the *sinchi*'s blade.

The *sinchi* cleaned his knife on Pulga's shirt then stood and looked back toward the curtained doorway where a new love song issued forth.

Castillo looked at his watch. "You can have twenty minutes with her," he said.

Enrique was more excited about school than he had been the previous spring and he credited his new teacher, *la Señorita* Castro. He said she made him want to go to school more than ever. For my part, firing up the Jeep every morning for the drive to Uchurimac began to feel almost like commuting to a job. Initially, the excitement of learning something new had carried me forward. I catalogued stories and observed behaviors that I knew would produce an acceptable dissertation. But the more deeply embedded I became in the local life, the more I realized my limitations in understanding it. I often felt more like a voyeur than an enlightened participant observer, and I never stopped feeling like an outsider. Life was happening around me but not to me.

The ways life happened were in some instances predictable and in other ways surprising. It was predictable, for instance, that Antonia Quispe would give birth at the end of her nine-month term. It was less predictable by half that the baby would be a son, and less predictable still that Antonia would insist on naming the healthy boy Marco, a name previously unknown in the village of Huaynatambo. The real surprise came a few days later when a young man named Marco Sonqo showed up at the door of the Quispe house claiming to be the infant's father. Marco and Antonia had courted briefly but passionately at the *feria* in Santa Rosita. Antonia, said the young man, would be welcome in the *alturas* above Uchurimac, but he was equally willing to stay and help work the land of the Quispe *chacra.* Marco probably would have been accepted warmly into the community of Huaynatambo in any case, but in the wake of Benito Quispe's death, his presence was all the more welcome.

It was predictable that Alex Ganz would take a continued interest in Mercedes Marquez and predictable, too, that his support would allow her to complete the internship that would lead to her final certification as an MD. On the strength of Alex's recommendation, and I would guess a sizable donation or two, the medical board agreed to count Mercedes' work from her mobile clinic, which she continued, as a major portion of her internship obligation. The rest she could fulfill with two days a week in a Lima hospital, made possible by the services of Alex's corporate plane. They usually managed to coordinate their schedules and fly together, necessitating only one round trip per week.

Somewhat surprising to me were Mercedes' continued refusals of

Alex's troth. She had moved into the house at el Valle del Cóndor where Consuelo and Juan Pablo spoiled her gleefully. I had a standing invitation for Sunday dinners and so I was able to see Alex and Mercedes interact weekly. She clearly was in love with him – I could see it in her every look and movement – and yet she resolutely refused to become his wife.

Even more surprising was the change in Manolo Ruíz. The man who had once been, for me, a menacing shadow became something of a benign fixture in Santa Rosita. I began seeing him two or three times a week, either hanging around the civil defense training sessions or coming out of the bank or even sipping a beer and making conversation with a shopkeeper. One Wednesday evening as I made my way to *Los Tres Chanchitos* for dinner, I spied Manolo sitting on a bench in the *plaza de armas*, facing in the direction of the bank. Dressed in a dark suit, a white shirt and heavy black oxfords, he sat slump-shouldered in a way that communicated some kind of burden. I thought about walking over to say hello, then I changed my mind. If Manolo Ruíz had a problem, there was little chance I could help him with it. Instead, I took a table with a view of the plaza and ordered the special, *picante de cuy*, guinea pig in a sauce of peanuts and hot yellow chilies. I sipped a *Cerveza Cristal* and watched the evening light soften.

After a little while, Pedro Buenaventura stepped out of the chapel of the *Santísima Virgen de Dolores* and propped open the door. A few of the faithful began to drift toward the church, and the priest stood out front to welcome them in. I saw the family of Ignacio Sonqo, without Ignacio. Doña Rosario showed up and others I recognized by sight but not by name. Certainly the widows' bench would be filled. Then, directly across the plaza from the doorway next to the bank, emerged Luz Castro. She wore a simple woolen suit, purple with a cream-colored blouse that would have looked more natural in Lima or Portland than it did here in Santa Rosita.

As it turned out, Manolo was battling a case of nerves. The moment Luz appeared on the sidewalk, Manolo popped to his feet. He stood there in the middle of the plaza, looking like a humble colossus, as she approached. She greeted him with a smile, they spoke a few words and, side by side, they continued toward the chapel and the evensong mass. About that time, my dinner came out and I had to smile. Spread-eagled on top of a mound of rice, feet and head still attached, was my *cuy*. Its expression reminded me of Wile E. Coyote splattered at the bottom of a cliff. I think that was when it really hit me that it was time to go home.

A team of *sinchis* under the command of Chief Inspector Castillo raided a safe house in Ayacucho. *El Colibrí* was not there, but he had been. Either he had left in a hurry or he had fully expected to be coming back, because he left physical evidence behind. It was a first for the investigation. There were vestiges of tire tracks and traces of blood in the courtyard. There was food in the larder and medicine in the bathroom. There were butts from Marlboro cigarettes in the trash. No single clue was enough to track him by, but together they contributed to a pattern. Castillo was getting closer.

Marivela's letters and postcards had been coming less frequently of late and they had been less upbeat. It had been weeks since had I heard from her. Then, one day in June, I received the following:

My Dear Sam,

I hardly know how to start. There are so many things I long to tell you. Some I can only tell you in person. I miss you, Sam. I wish you were here.

I don't know how much longer I can continue my work in the shantytowns. It's draining me dry. Fredo wants me to go on, but to be truthful, I think there is little more I can learn there, and even less that I can accomplish for the residents. It seems I have worked my way into a narrow, suffocating space, when the world should be opening up to me. What is worse, I have begun to fear for my safety. I don't know what to do.

I care deeply for you, Sam, and I suspect you care for me as well. When do you think you will be finished with your work in Santa Rosita? I may be fooling myself, but I feel as if being with you will make everything all right again.

Yours always, Marivela

Wow, I thought, as I read it again. She missed me. Wished I were there. I began to reconsider my own feelings for Marivela, which, for long months, had hung suspended in some kind of weightless state between my loneliness and my desire, bouncing around each time I received a new letter from her. Those letters had been sporadic and mostly nonchalant, flirtatious and without gravity. Now, suddenly, it seemed as though she needed me. Wanted me. What was going on, I wondered, to make her afraid for her safety?

I replied the same day:

Dear Marivela,

Of course I care for you. No matter what you do, please don't put yourself in any danger. I should be finishing my field work in Uchurimac very soon now – probably within the next two weeks. Then there will be nothing to keep me from returning to Lima.

Have you considered continuing your doctoral studies in the US? It's something to think about, anyway. I can hardly wait to see you again.

Love, Sam

Marivela picked up the letter from her campus mailbox and carried it unopened to her room in the graduate-student dorm. With a kitchen knife she slit the envelope and removed its single page of contents. She smiled as she read it; then she folded it back into its envelope. Soon, she would make an appointment at a beauty salon and then she would get passport pictures taken.

In the meantime, she thought, she would need to treat Fredo very gingerly. In fact, she thought, it might be best to stay away from him as much as possible. Ever since the news of the recent major blow against the *Camino Rojo*, Fredo had been acting nervous. Jittery, even. The action, for which the Army claimed responsibility, had made all the headlines: *CRIMSON ROAD DEVASTATED BY MILITARY ATTACK!*

SCORES OF TERRORISTS DEAD IN COCA FIELD INFERNO! EL COLIBRÍ, DEAD AT LAST?

Alfredo Ramirez was, in fact, very nervous. He had talked with *Comandante* Rita shortly after the coca fields debacle, so he knew it hadn't been an act of the Peruvian Army. It had been a double-cross by Alejandro Ganz de la Vega. And the Ganz siblings had been, in large part, Alfredo's responsibility.

Not so long ago, he had been recruited by *El Colibrí* himself to play an important part in the rebellion – not the part of a soldier, but rather of a scholar, a researcher. Like many members of the Peruvian intelligentsia, especially those who had witnessed first hand the exploitive excesses of capitalism, Alfredo had sympathized with the Communist ideals espoused by Miguel Fortuna. Fredo, too, had nurtured dreams of a Peru that was free of corruption and grinding poverty.

Slowly and cautiously, he had drawn closer to Fortuna's revolution. At first, he had merely stood, as an observer, at the fringes of rallies and protests. Then, tentatively, he had approached someone, an organizer he had observed at several of the rallies, and expressed his interest and support. After that had come invitations to more secretive meetings. Then, finally, came the visit from *Comandante* Rita and a trip, blindfolded, to meet the legendary Miguel Fortuna. What a day that had been. Fredo had felt so proud, and so humbled. He had felt chosen.

Fredo's job was to gather intelligence, something for which he felt particularly well suited. The targeted enemy in this case had consisted of the over-privileged Alejandro and Cassandra Ganz, symbols of everything that was wrong with Peru. Alfredo had studied them meticulously, reading everything that had ever been written about either of them. He'd spent countless days in newspaper archives. He'd read business news, entertainment news and editorial columns from sources on the left, on the right and in the mainstream. He'd even prevailed upon his old mentor, Jack Bentley, to help dig up the truth about the identity of the patriarch, Oswald Ganz. What a coup that had been. And when the chance came out of nowhere to assist Bentley's newest doctoral student with a research site, it had been Fredo's idea to place him in Santa Rosita, as close as possible to Ganz. At a minimum, that ploy had earned him an additional perspective of el Valle del Condór and its personnel situation.

Now, it seemed to Alfredo, things had gone terribly wrong. Rita had characterized the Ganz double-cross as 'merely a setback' and as something 'overblown by the press', but Fredo had his doubts. What he had wanted more than anything in the days following the disaster was some reassurance from *El Colibrí*, himself. To that end, after much internal debate, he had picked up his phone and dialed the number he had been given to initiate urgent contact.

"Hello," a voice had answered. Alfredo replied with his password message.

"Who is this, please?" asked the voice. It was the wrong voice. Alfredo quickly hung up the phone and stared at it as if it were transforming into a poisonous snake.

And so, somewhat hurriedly, I completed my field work in the Department of Ayacucho. For my research needs the site had turned out to be excellent, almost like a field experiment. I had Santa Rosita with its bank, its church, its *bodegas*, its *feria* and its *Tres Chanchitos* restaurant with which to compare life in the outlying villages. In close proximity, I had two villages of similar size and distance, Huaynatambo and Uchurimac, one which had stayed mostly clear of the pressures of the Crimson Road and the other which had suffered a brutal occupation. By the time winter began its yearly browning and brittling of the landscape, I knew I had sufficient data to write a dissertation.

I was anxious about Marivela. I wrote to her again and told her when to expect me back.

My thoughts also turned more and more to Oregon. I grew up there, and its geography remained imprinted on my soul. The Willamette River was my aorta. The coastline with its rocky fists pummeling the surf, and Mount Hood, rising above the Cascades like a white-haired god, were the guardians of my childhood. I could, at any moment, close my eyes, conjure up a map of Western Oregon, pinpoint a spot on it and find myself transported there on the wings of familiarity. It could be to a specific chair at a specific wooden table in Powell's City of Books, with a book and a steaming cup of coffee partially covering initials carved in a tabletop heart. Or it could be to a strawberry field north of Hillsboro where I'd kneel in the loamy, volcanic soil between mounded rows, feel the earth's moisture bleeding through the knees of my jeans and pluck a burnished berry the size of child's fist. It would show the first furry signs of mold where it had touched the ground, and when I squeezed it gently, it would collapse into mush, releasing its wild scent through my fingers.

Hard as I tried, the one spot I couldn't pinpoint on my mental map of Oregon was home.

I sent a letter to my mother letting her know my work in Peru would be coming to a close within a month or so. She wrote back a long letter, by far the longest she had ever written to me. In it, she said that she was proud of me. That she had missed me. That she had been visiting regularly with Mitchell and Nan Chang and how well-suited they were for each other. That she had started writing poetry (!), some of which had been published (!!). Finally, she said that Mitch was on the verge of the first showing of his work at a new Seattle art gallery. She mentioned the date of the opening and I made a mental note of it. For the first time since I came to Peru, I got the sense that maybe there was something to go back to.

One morning, as they sipped their coffees and witnessed the first fingers of sunlight reaching across the rocky peaks to the east, Mercedes gave Alex an answer to the question that had been hanging between them almost since Juan Pablo's emergency appendectomy. She gripped the warm cup with both hands and studied the tableau they made. She avoided looking at Alex's face because she wasn't ready to see it marred by disappointment.

"I was married once before," she said very softly.

The words sat there between them like confused children who

didn't know what to do or where to go next. Alex said nothing, but he studied her face and posture looking for the meanings the timid words did not convey. Finally, Mercedes resumed the burden of disclosure.

"I may still be." Silence. She braved a look at Alex. His face told her she was the center of his universe. In that moment nothing else existed. She saw love there, and support. She let out a breath she didn't realize she had been holding. "It's impossible to know for sure. It was in college. His name was David Escobedo. We wanted to sleep together and I insisted on marriage first. We did the wedding quietly with a justice of the peace. I didn't even tell my parents. It was mid-semester and I was waiting for a better time to break the news. We had only been married a week when David decided to go with some friends to a political demonstration. Police came to break it up. There was resistance, confusion. David disappeared that night and I never saw or heard from him again. It was later that week that my father died."

Alex reached across the corner of the table and placed a hand on her wrist.

"What do you want most of all?" he asked gently.

"Just to know."

It was done. I said my good-byes on Saturday in Uchurimac and on Sunday in Huaynatambo. In each village I left a gift of a pair of breeding hogs. Manolo Ruíz had helped me procure them from a farm near Huancavelica. We left early on Friday morning in the *Vida de Perro*. Manolo picked me up at the *casa* Flores. When I climbed up into the cab, I felt my eyes widen at the sight of two semi-automatic pistols arrayed on a chamois in the center position of the bench seat.

Manolo grinned. "Just in case."

The most dangerous part of the trip was Manolo's driving. He drove the big diesel-powered truck over the primitive dirt highway as if it were an Alfa Romeo on the autopiste. For over three hours, not counting down time for lunch and for actually buying the pigs, he barreled along, jamming gears, passing on blind curves or at the edges of precipices, overtaking lumbering trucks with loads of bricks, and microbuses jammed with passengers, and laying on the horn almost constantly. All with the cavalier calm of a suburban Sunday driver. I kept telling myself, no worries. He knows the road. This is how they all drive down here.

With Doña Rosario's blessing, Enrique helped me deliver the hogs. The hardest part of the task was getting the sizable pigs into the old Willys. We ended up leashing them with ropes and drafting a couple of available townsmen to help coax and heave them in. We placed a board across the back where the tailgate should have been. Finally, by tying the hogs with short tethers to the sides of the Jeep, we managed to keep them out of the driver's seat. However, they completely filled the rest of the vehicle. Enrique solved the problem of passenger space by simply sitting on top of the big sow. Having worked out the logistics on Saturday, we made a relative snap out of the Sunday delivery.

The notion of communally owned swine was easy for the *campesinos* to grasp. It fit right in with their system of cooperative *ayllus*. Just as they all chipped in to plant or harvest each family's crops in turn, they would also take turns as piglet beneficiaries. As the sow and the boar continued to produce litters, the piglets would be distributed in breeding pairs until each household in the *ayllu* had received a pair of its own. Then the distribution process would begin again in the reverse direction.

The pigs of the Lightning God became instant celebrities. In Huaynatambo, the villagers threw a party for the swine. They adorned their necks, tails and hocks with colorful ribbons and gave each beast a large bowl of boiled potatoes and beer. In Uchurimac, they painted the hogs with bright blue lightning bolts and led them in a procession around the little town square to the accompaniment of the same musical *conjunto* that had played for my first visit.

In each case, it took all day long to say good-bye. Gabriela Quispe hugged me so tightly and for so long that I began to think maybe she would try to keep me from going at all. When she finally let go and backed away with tears in her eyes, she took a big raw chunk of my heart with her. Ignacio Sonqo squared off with me and placed an ancient hand on my shoulder. "You will not be back," he said knowingly. "But we will be fine here."

He was right about the first thing. I hoped he would be right about the latter.

"Two pages were ripped out of the arrest records for the night of the demonstration," said Ismael, the head of security of Banco Europa. "I figured if I could find those two pages, then we might have something. But the man who was in charge of the police action that night in Ayacucho is dead. You may know him."

"Porfirio Sanchez," said Alex. Mercedes looked from the former PIP detective to Alex and back to Ismael again.

Ismael nodded.

"But that wasn't the end of the line. I learned that Sanchez's only heir is a niece, Elena de Roncesvalles, in Chiclayo. I tracked down her address to a run-down tenement at the foot of a hill that looks like a war zone. The Roncesvalles had moved out a few days before, leaving most of their possessions behind. The apartment had already been inhabited by squatters. I asked the neighbors if anyone knew where they had gone. One old lady volunteered that they had moved *alla donde los ricos*.

"It took me a couple of hours to track down the Roncesvalles' new house. The house was mostly empty. Hardly a stick of furniture there yet. We sat at a table and chairs that still had price tags on them. Elena didn't want to talk until I convinced her that she was in no trouble and that I was a friend of her uncle from the old days in the PIP. I think she was afraid I had come to make trouble about her inheritance.

"She claimed she barely knew her uncle and that she hadn't spoken to him for years. It was his lawyer who contacted her right after his death. The lawyer came to their apartment – they had no phone – to deliver an envelope with Elena's name on it. Inside she found a letter with her uncle's blessing and the key to a bank box in Lima.

"I acknowledged that Porfirio had been a frugal man and that he would be glad to know he had left her well cared for. What I needed to know, I told her, was if there had been anything inside the bank box other than the money he left for her. Something that would be of no value to her.

"She just fidgeted on the edge of her chair. So I played a hunch. I assured her that I meant no harm to her or the good name of her uncle. What I was looking for was just a list of names, and perhaps dates, that had been lost and that could make some good people very happy. She left me for a minute and came back carrying this." Ismael produced a small paper sack. "I think you will find this interesting."

Ismael emptied the sack onto the table in front of Alex and Mercedes. There were dozens of official identification cards. He then reached into his shirt pocket and produced a card he had kept separate from the rest. "Miss Marquez, this one belongs to you."

The name on the card was David Escobedo.

On my last day in Santa Rosita, I said goodbye to the people who had been my family for the last several months. To the man I owed the most, Father Pedro Buenaventura, my sponsor in the community, my champion with Mercedes Marquez, my father confessor, my maker of herb teas, my sharer of secrets, my provider of perspective when I felt completely lost, and the older brother I never had, I gave the Jeep. I didn't want to risk the danger of a drive back to Lima, even though popular wisdom held that the strength of the *guerrillas* was greatly reduced. I had learned too much. I had learned to be afraid. Alex had offered to fly me down in his plane, and I'd accepted.

"What will I do with a Jeep, Sam?"

"I don't know. Drive it. Sell it. Use it to extend your ministry."

"I could use it," he said with a grin, "if I knew how to drive."

So we spent the next hour and a half in a driving lesson that became the biggest spectacle in Santa Rosita since the arrest of the *terrucos*. Pedro wanted a demonstration before he dared take the driver's seat and we made several circles of the *plaza de armas* with me driving and Pedro stiffly on his feet in the seatless passenger space. With Pedro standing there like a human mast, black raiments billowing, the little yellow Willys must have looked something like an eerie schooner. I shouted out my lecture about accelerator, clutch, brakes and gearshift mechanism and he shouted back his questions. Between the rattling and gear-grinding noises of the Jeep and our shouting to make ourselves heard above the din, we made more than enough noise to attract every person within running distance. People flowed to the sidewalks around the plaza as if it were a parade day.

After we switched places for Pedro's 'practicum', the scene became even more comical. The Jeep lurched, bounced, rocketed and wove like an angry, spastic bull or a robot with several short circuits. Twice, I was nearly hurled out onto the cobblestone street. At one point, Pedro was concentrating so hard on making the shift from first to second that he forgot about steering. We jumped the curb into the plaza and laid waste to a garbage can and several rose bushes before he finally stalled the motor and ended the destruction amid the *ooh*s, *aahh*s and *ha-ha-ha*s of the crowd.

After two successful circumnavigations of the plaza, we took the driving lesson to the unpaved side streets of Santa Rosita. Once Pedro felt himself to be the master of the machine, we returned to the plaza and to the chapel, laughing and feeling a warmth of friendship that exceeded any we had experienced before, even during our many hours of conversation over the last several months.

"That was fun," I said as we entered the chapel together.

"It was, wasn't it?" Pedro didn't say it as a matter of simple agreement. He said it as if it were a surprise. An epiphany. "You know, I haven't done anything I would call fun since I was a child."

"You're not serious."

"No. You are wrong, Sam. That is exactly what I am. Chronically serious. I need to change that about myself."

His words trailed off into the silence of the chapel of the Virgin of Sorrows.

"You know, Sam, there is something I need to tell you."

"Well?"

"You must know that I love you like a brother. Having you here to talk to as a peer, not as a parishioner, has been a great blessing for me. Maybe it's your professional orientation – you know, as an anthropologist – but you listen without judging. Do you realize how rare that is?"

"You've done the same for me."

"Yes. Perhaps we have that in common. But there is more. Something else that we share. I can tell that, like me, you have a great empty space inside of you. Maybe because people have hurt you. Maybe because you have felt abandoned at some critical point in your life."

I was listening.

"Anyway, what I wanted to say is … that empty space isn't necessarily a bad thing, even though at times it aches like a broken tooth exposed to the air."

I was feeling the exposure at that very moment, as if his words had begun to lacerate my emptiness.

"What is empty can be filled. And you have the ability to fill it with anything you want."

Penetrating the emptiness and forcing it open.

"But nothing can be done to fill that hole as long as it is closed up and protected by all the flesh that surrounds it. You have been working on opening yourself up ever since you got here. Maybe before. And you have helped me find access to my own great emptiness. For that I will always be grateful."

Forcing it open and exposing the raw nerves of my psyche.

Carried by Pedro's words, the pain that had been working around the edges of my emptiness suddenly blossomed within me like some kind of exquisite bouquet of roses. Glass roses with razor-sharp thorns.

"There is one thing I know that can ease the pain," he continued. I couldn't respond. Any words I might have uttered were too big for the constricted throat that blocked their way.

"Forgiveness. You need to forgive those who have hurt you. And you need to forgive yourself."

"How do I do that?" The words came out as something between a whisper and a croak.

"With love, Sam. Maybe I can help you."

I only nodded.

"Good. Sit down and close your eyes." I did. "I want you to think of someone you love deeply and without reservation. It may be your mother or your father …"

Each of their faces passed through my mind, and with each passage I felt a swelling of love mixed with sharp impulses of pain.

"… or your brother …"

I tried to get a fix on Mitchell's face, but it wouldn't materialize.

"… or a good friend."

And there he was. Pedro Buenaventura. And next to him in my mind stood Enrique Morales. Two people I could honestly say I had come to love deeply and without reservation or hesitation.

"Focus your thoughts on that person."

I did. On both of them.

"Now, while you have that person in mind, change the focus of your attention. Instead of focusing on the person, focus on the feeling of love the person evokes in you. Have you got it?" I nodded. "Good. Now hold that love in your mind and heart. Let it fill you up, because love is infinite. See it as a globe of warm, golden light."

I did. It was beautiful. Pedro Buenaventura and Enrique Morales, side by side, bathed in sunshine.

"Now, Samson Young, shine that love on yourself."

I did. And, oh my god, how it hurt. It was a searing, blinding, purifying pain that entered through my chest and guts and burned its way into my cranium. It turned my organs to soup and my bones to rubber and set every cell in my body into some kind of sympathetic vibration. I slumped in the pew and buried my face in my hands. I tried to hold back tears and my nose started to run. The sobs that had been building up within me came flying out like escaping birds, each one with a frantic flutter of wing beats. What the hell was happening to me? How could I make it stop? How could I be sure I could make it happen again?

After a few minutes, I started to gather my composure. Pedro laid a hand on my shoulder, and the whole outpouring started again.

None of the bodies of the people whose ID cards showed up in Porfirio Sanchez's bank box has ever been recovered. However, the cards alone, along with Ismael's affidavit, proved sufficient for the issuance of death certificates. Officially a widow, Mercedes was free to accept Alex's proposal of marriage. Which she did. With a show of reluctance. "I like being your mistress," she said.

Alex had a single wedding announcement engraved and sent by courier to a villa in Tuscany.

What can I say about Doña Rosario? She's like the matron aunt who takes you in as a family obligation even though she senses you are going to be trouble from the very first day. Doña Rosario, into whose home I had brought danger and intrigue; who had watched me crawl across her floor with feet that had been boiled by a pair of electrified boots; who had forgiven me for nearly causing the death of her precious adopted grandson, Enrique. Doña Rosario actually became teary-eyed when it was time to say good-bye. The hug I got from her was big, warm, soft and unforgettable.

Saying goodbye to Enrique was more difficult. We stood on the street in front of the house. On the step sat my flight bag and a nylon duffel stuffed with my notebooks. I dropped to one knee to be at eye level with him. I grasped his shoulders and said the only words that I could make surface from my cauldron of emotions.

"I'm going to miss you, Sport."

He looked at me as if he were trying to figure out what was the big deal.

"When are you coming back?" he asked.

I hadn't been prepared for that. The fact was, I had no plans to return. I had accomplished what I had come to accomplish.

"I don't know, Enrique. I don't know if I will be back."

Enrique's face clouded over and developed deep lines I had never seen there before. He trembled visibly. It was as if I had slapped him.

"You're not coming back." He turned and ran into the house, leaving me standing there as if alone on a high Andean plain. How selfish could I be? I had become like a brother to Enrique and now I was about to abandon him as if it all meant nothing.

At that moment, the black Land Rover rounded the corner from the *plaza de armas* and pulled to a stop in front of the house. Manolo Ruíz stepped out and asked if I was ready to go.

"Not quite," I answered, and I ran back into the house. I found Enrique in the room that had been mine since I first arrived in Santa Rosita. He was sitting on the edge of the bed, closed up like a book.

"Enrique," I said. "Enrique. Listen, little brother." He continued staring into the empty space of my ex-room. "The United States is a long way away. I hope I can come back some day, but I don't want to make a promise that I may not be able to keep."

No response.

"Enrique, I want you to know that I have never had a friend that I valued as much as you. Without you, I would have been lost here. We're language brothers. My Quechua and your English are proof of that."

Finally he looked at me and sniffed back a tear.

"That's true, isn't it?" he said.

"Of course it is. We can write to each other as often as you like. In English or Spanish. Your choice."

"English."

"English, then. And Enrique? I have a little present for you. It is my most precious possession and I want you to have it to remember me by."

His face brightened with suspense. I reached deep into my pocket, pulled out the stone etched with a bolt of lightning and pressed it into his hand.

"You, little brother, will have to be the sole representative of *Kari Wakli-piqta*."

He smiled. Then he said something that made me love him even more: "Sam, you're not really *Kari Wakli-piqta*, are you?"

I couldn't suppress a grin. "No. But let that be our secret. Now can I have a hug before I go?"

He flew into my arms. I held him tightly as I turned a circle there in the middle of the floor and walked us back out to the street.

Once we got to Lima, Alex dropped me off at the University. Lunchtime was past, and I found Alfredo Ramirez in his office.

"Fredo," I greeted him, and asked him literally about his work and figuratively about life in general. "*¿Cómo va la chamba?*"

"Well enough." He said it with a note of distraction, as if he were a little on edge. "How about you?"

"All right. It's good to be back in Lima." I only partially lied. In many ways, Lima was a shock to the senses for someone accustomed to the earthbound life and rarefied air of the Andes. So much of Lima was ugly, filthy and tragically poor. Still, with its regular strikes, blackouts and protests, it was a city that defied boredom. And Marivela was there. That, I hoped, would make up for a lot.

"Sit down." He leaned forward and considered me in silence, as though deliberating what to say next. Just as the silence began to feel thick and uncomfortable, he broke it with a question that should have had the tone of small talk but, instead, seemed freighted with meaning. "How did you get back to Lima?"

"I flew back with Alex Ganz."

There was a visible, reflexive tightening in Fredo's facial features, almost like a wince of pain.

"You must be pretty close to Mr Ganz." It was like an accusation. Suddenly and unexpectedly, I got the feeling of being a witness on the stand. A hostile witness.

"Oh, I don't know. We became acquainted." I recalled games of college poker, struggling to break even in games with only beer at stake, shielding my hand and trying to conceal my emotions.

His eyes never blinking, never leaving my face, he said, "And what about the sister?"

"Sister?" By this question I was bewildered and my face must have shown it.

"Cassandra Ganz?"

I shook my head and offered a gesture of unfeigned ignorance.

Then he relaxed back in his chair and asked, "So, what is this *Kari Wakli-piqta* business I've heard about?"

"Oh, nothing much." That question caught me off guard even more than the one about Alex's sister. I wondered how he had heard about the Son of Lightning. I hadn't told him about it. Marivela? No, I hadn't told her either. Father Pedro? The *padre* had never mentioned any conversations with Alfredo. It put me back on my guard. I had hidden, and now continued to minimize, the whole Lightning God business because I was afraid it might cast aspersions on my research. "It's just a nickname I picked up after the lightning strike I told you about. I guess it kinda stuck. The *campesinos* got a kick out of calling me that."

He studied me as if he sensed I wasn't telling him everything. More than ever, I sensed that I shouldn't.

"Tell me more about your relationship with Mr Ganz," he probed. Back to Alex. Red flags jumped out all over the place.

"Well, he pretty well keeps to himself. I mean, you know, guys like that live in a whole other world. And," I added as an afterthought that seemed like a coup of deflection, "he didn't seem particularly sorry to see me leave Santa Rosita."

"I guess you got yourself a glimpse of the revolution." Again, a change of topic and tone. Friendlier. Designed, I thought, to put me more at ease.

"I'd say I came too close for comfort to being on the evening news." Of course, he knew the story of the *Rojistas*' fatal march on Santa Rosita. It *had* made the news and I had described it in a letter to him soon after it happened.

"Would you say the community is better prepared now for the possibility of attack?"

"Well, fortunately for me, they were *already* pretty well-prepared."

"Yes?" He was trying to draw me into elaboration. I just nodded. Here I was, back on my guard again. He asked, "Who was leading their defenses?"

I shrugged and feigned cluelessness.

"What kinds of weapons did they have?"

"Wow," I shrugged, as though shrinking under his barrage of questions. "It beats me. I don't know anything about guns. Do you?" His face revealed no answer, but I sensed disdain for my cloud of unknowing. I decided to change the subject. "You know, I was really kind of hoping to talk with you about cultural preservation and coca-chewing rituals. Do you think we might do that after I get settled down here?"

"Maybe," he said without enthusiasm. He started straightening papers on his desk. "I've got a lot to do in the next few days."

"I'll keep my options open. By the way, have you seen Marivela?" He shook his head and continued to pour on the expression of a prosecuting attorney. "If you do, would you mind telling her I'm back at El Moro?" On the topic of my relationship with Marivela, whatever it was destined to be, I also felt guarded around Fredo. So I lied again. "I would like to see if I can get her to help me with some library research."

It was an easy lie and it felt believable. Or at least as believable as anything else I had told him. Ramirez nodded dismissively. I backed out of his office and, as I walked toward the hotel, I pondered my newfound uneasiness. I felt as if I were caught up in a game I didn't understand. Yet what kind of game was it? I didn't know. I didn't know who all the players were, or for what sides they played. I didn't even know what the *sides* were. I didn't know what constituted a win, and I didn't know what the consequences of losing might be.

At El Moro the lobby was deserted but I could hear the sounds of the television from the back office. "*¡Buenas tardes!*" I said loudly. The same woman who had checked me in last spring came forward and checked me into the same room as before. I unpacked and took a long soak in the tub. I was just lying down on the hammocky bed when there came a soft knock on the door.

"Come in," I said. I'd left the door ajar. It made me feel less lonely, as if somehow it increased the likelihood of receiving a visit.

The door opened a little way into the room and Marivela peeked around it almost timidly.

"*Hola*," she said in a voice that seemed uncharacteristically soft.

"Hey! Come in!" I jumped up from the bed. "It's great to see you!"

And it was. She looked good. She was wearing a flouncy floral print skirt with a snug, sleeveless sweater and sandals. She looked thinner than before. Her long hair had been cut in a stylish bob and had more highlights in it.

"I like your hair."

"Really? I was afraid you'd hate it."

I shook my head. "How have you been?"

"So-so," she said. I thought I detected a note of sadness. "You?"

"Well. I've been well."

With her hands behind her, she backed up against the door and clicked it shut. For a few seconds, she just leaned there against the door, looking at me and letting me look at her. Then she pushed away from the door, took a couple of coy steps and stopped in front of the room's antique dresser. I couldn't quite judge her mood. It came off as somewhere in the realms of playful and tentative. She leaned into the dresser and with the tip of her index finger pushed the room key in a gentle circle. She looked at me sideways with her head slightly cocked and a strand of hair hanging down onto her face, partly obscuring one of her dark, probing eyes.

"Did you miss me?" she whispered.

I had missed her. But seeing her now, biting her lower lip, seeing the brightness in her eyes, the fierce angularity of her face, the pressure of her breasts against the soft knit of her sweater, the curve of her calf above the delicate Achilles … I could hardly believe I hadn't missed her more. "I sure did."

"Are you going to kiss me?"

I nodded and crossed the rest of the short distance between us. I extended my hands. She took them in hers and moved in until our bodies touched lightly where her breasts met my lower ribs. She looked up into my eyes and stretched just enough to invite a kiss. I bent down and let our lips merge. She let go of my hands and laced her fingers behind my neck. I drew her closer with one hand in the curve of her lower back and the other between her shoulder blades. Her tongue came forward and we tightened our embrace. Nothing else in the whole world mattered but that kiss and the warmth of her body against mine. Eventually she broke the kiss, let her hands drift to my shoulders and laid her cheek against my chest.

"That was nice," she said.

"Mm-hmm."

"You can't imagine how many times I've dreamed of this."

"Yeah? Actually, I can."

Then she walked past me, catching my hand, turning me and leading me toward the bed.

"Sit down," she said with a soft smile. "I have a present for you."

I sat on the edge of the bed and her smile broadened.

"Lie back," she said with a little shove to my chest. "It's a very good present."

The phone in Alfredo Ramirez's office rang once and fell silent. He had been pacing back and forth with a section of the morning newspaper in his hands, trying to squeeze more information out of it than it actually contained.

The phone rang again, two rings this time, and again fell silent. The next time it rang he picked it up.

"I'm here."

"You left a message for me to call." It was *Comandante* Rita.

"Have you seen the papers?" asked Fredo. It was not a casual question.

"I've seen them."

The daily papers had reported their new list of Peru's most wanted fugitives. The name Miguel Fortuna, AKA *El Colibrí*, naturally headed the list. Several known criminals also made the list as usual. What had changed was the name in second place. It was a new name, Margarita Novara, AKA *Comandante* Rita, of the *Camino Rojo*.

"What should we do?" Despite his efforts to mask it, there was a streak of anxiety in his voice.

"Nothing," said Rita. "Don't panic. All they have is a name. There's nothing else to lead them to me. Or to you. Oh, and Fredo …"

"Yes?"

"Don't use the urgent-contact phone number. It has been compromised."

Comandante Rita hung up the phone, leaving Alfredo alone with a silent handset and a head swirling with questions. Shit! He had called that number. But it had been days. And he had hung up right away. That meant there wasn't time to trace the call, right? And how had the press learned about Rita? And the police! How close were they to tracking her down? What were the chances their search would lead to him? And if it did? No. Don't even think about it. He was too unimportant. Not even a real player. Not a real revolutionary. Not like Rita. But still …

Fredo flashed back to his first meeting with Rita. He had been investigating, *very* cautiously, participation in the Peruvian Communist Party. He had made a few furtive inquiries, and once had a quiet but impassioned conversation with an organizer he believed he could trust. Then, one day, Rita had simply shown up at his office door.

With her youthful demeanor, he had mistaken her for a student and wondered how he could possibly not have noticed her before. She was strikingly pretty in an intense and almost feral kind of way.

She had stepped inside the door and asked, "Professor Ramirez, may I have a moment of your time?"

Yes, she could. Of course she could. She could have all the time she wanted.

She had closed the door and settled into the chair opposite his desk, crossed her legs and rested her hands atop a handbag in her lap.

"I understand," she began, with a forward-leaning tilt of the head and a slightly lowered voice that affected a conspiratorial atmosphere, "that you may be interested in supporting the Communist Party."

This had been a surprise. How to answer? "I didn't get your name," he ventured. She merely shook her head with a gentle, close-lipped smile. He looked for some sign in her face that he could trust her. "I've been considering it," he answered at length.

"Can you tell me why, please?"

It was one of those moments in life that offered a crossroad that would never appear again. He could feel it. So he picked a path and answered her. He answered and she listened. Listened until he had convinced not only her, but himself as well, that communism held the only real hope for a free and just Peru.

That had been the beginning, a desire to make a difference and a seductively powerful woman offering to make it possible. Until now he'd never looked back.

Now, however, he wondered; where had Rita been lately? Certainly not around campus. What, besides the tragedies reported in the news, was going on in the revolution from which he had been kept, presumably for his safety and that of the movement, so completely insulated? God, he thought, he wished he knew more.

He hung up the phone, which had been dangling dead in his hand since Rita had disconnected, and spent the rest of the morning meticulously combing through his office for any evidence that might implicate him in subversive – that is, patriotic – activities. One couldn't be too careful. Alfredo had always been very selective about where and with whom he had shared his communist ideologies. He believed in activism against corruption and abuse, which were personified in the current administration, but he also believed in survival. He believed in covering his tracks. Among other things he pulled for destruction were all his files of research on Alejandro and Cassandra Ganz.

It was almost noon. I had checked out of El Moro and was waiting in the lobby for Marivela to return with her own luggage. As I waited, I replayed in my mind the sequence of the previous night. Marivela had made love to me in unimaginable ways. After I came the first time, she convinced me I wasn't through. Several times after that she transported me to a place where all my muscles were on the verge of cramps, where my bones felt like they might melt spontaneously. Each time, she would ease off enough to let me catch my breath again, and then she would start something new. Every time, I wanted to split her in two and wrap myself in the halves.

Later, as we lay naked and exhausted on the bed, she spoke. "Sam?"

"Hm?"

"*¿Me quieres?*" There was that question. 'Do you love me' also translates to 'do you want me?'

"Desperately." She snuggled up against me. I felt her lips brush my shoulder. Her fingertips caressed my temple. I wanted to purr. To melt. After a moment she spoke again.

"Sam."

"Hmm?"

"I'm afraid."

I felt my entire body shift involuntarily into a state of readiness. "Afraid of what?"

"Can you keep a secret?"

"Of course."

"It's about Doctor Ramirez."

"Fredo?" The mention of his name put my warning systems on alert.

She sat on the bed with her knees pulled up in front of her. "I think he is *Camino Rojo*." There was no lightness in her voice now. I raised myself up on one elbow to get a good look at her while this message sank in. She looked away. "It's true."

I sat up and pulled a section of sheet into my lap. I had no idea what to do with this information, so I waited in silence. Marivela drew her knees tight to her breasts. "Sam."

"Yes?"

"It terrifies me. If anyone else found out, as his assistant they would probably accuse me of collaboration. I could go to jail. Or worse ..." She seemed genuinely lost and afraid.

"Jesus. That's heavy. How did you find out? What makes you think it?"

"I have suspected for a long time, partly because of his politics. Not that I mind his politics very much. I mean, you know, I lean to the left myself. But there were other signs too. Cryptic hints, strange phone calls."

"Okay, but that could mean anything." As I said the words, my mind was racing through my own recent interactions with Fredo, resurrecting my misgivings.

"No," she said, with a note of authority. "It became clear to me yesterday. He told me you were here and that you might want help with some research. He asked me to steal some of your notebooks."

"What?! Why?"

She winced at the strength of my reaction. "It has something to do with Santa Rosita. And a *Señor* Ganz. He's obsessed with this Ganz."

I stared at her. She rocked slightly back and forth with her arms locked around her knees, closed her eyes and squeezed out a tear.

"I'm afraid, Sam, and I don't know what to do."

"Maybe you should turn him in."

She shook her head forlornly. "I can't. Even if I could, the *Rojistas* would probably kill me for it."

My own mood followed Marivela's into an abyss. *Goddammit*. This explained so much. I thought I understood why Ramirez might have wanted my field notes. In them I had kept predictably detailed records of all I observed in Santa Rosita and the smaller villages, including details of their leadership and their new civil defense program. Naturally, I had also recorded everything I knew about Alex Ganz. My correspondence with Ramirez had been vague on the topics but my notes were explicit. They could be a severe liability to the safety of my friends. The extent to which Fredo had been using me started to dawn on me. That son of a bitch.

It also dawned on me, as Marivela sat huddled and naked on my bed, that she was risking her life for me. I was sure now that I loved her. That she needed me and I needed her. That all of my previous ambivalence about her could be explained away by this terrible revelation.

"Come on, let's try to get some sleep." I pulled her back down into the bedding. "We'll figure something out." Already I was hatching a bold and crazy idea.

In the morning, I woke up before Marivela did. She lay facing the wall. I raised the covers far enough to admire the relief of her well-defined shoulder blades and the contour of her spine all the way down to the two dimples that punctuated her lower back like a colon that precedes a long list of wonders. I wanted to rescue her, and I knew how I wanted to do it. I kissed her awake, we cleaned up, and I explained my plan over breakfast.

First, we moved to the Grand Hotel Bolívar where we would be harder to find. Next, instead of the library to do research, which was where Ramirez would expect us to go, we went to the municipality where we were married by a justice of the peace. I'm sure no young groom could have looked more anxious, more animated or more starry-eyed than I did. Marivela looked like the happiest woman on earth.

From there, we went to the American Embassy for Marivela's visa and immigration papers. When the clerk asked for Marivela's passport, she reached over and held my hand. As she placed her passport on the counter she squeezed my hand hard and kept the pressure on.

"Italian?" asked the clerk with a double-take at Marivela's Incan features.

"On my father's side," she said. "My mother was Peruvian."

I looked at the picture on the passport. It was definitely Marivela's, and it was definitely an Italian passport. How about that?

On the way out of the embassy with her visa intact and the immigration papers in process, I said, "Dual citizenship? I didn't know your father was Italian."

She smiled. "*Mi Corazón*, I'm sure there are many things we don't know about each other yet. But we should have plenty of time to learn."

Fredo's nightmare had begun early in the morning when two PIP investigators banged on the door of his house. They ordered him to sit still while they overturned every item in every drawer and cabinet searching for something that might incriminate him. The entire time they worked, Fredo stood by looking appropriately worried and, he hoped, naively innocent.

"Maybe," he said, "if you tell me what you're looking for …"

They ignored him.

"Have I been accused of something?"

They gave no response. He fought down panic. Something had brought them here. Some clue. What had it been? Was it something he could explain away if he had to?

The cops confiscated nothing obvious, but they did take several pages of seemingly innocuous notes and several photographs. From there, they went to his office at the university and went through the same thorough routine. They had asked many pointed questions about books in English that turned out to be anthropological monographs. He was glad he had so recently given his office a complete sanitation treatment. Some of the papers he had disposed of would surely have landed him in jail.

The PIP investigators also asked him about his relationships with numerous people, mentioning among them friends and acquaintances, fellow faculty members and students Fredo knew to be ardent leftists. They asked him about Marivela Santiana, whom he defended as a promising and completely apolitical graduate student, and Margarita Novara, whose name he said he had seen for the first time in yesterday's news. He hoped his carefully phrased answers to their questions had satisfied them without endangering him or any of his friends.

When they left, Fredo breathed a sigh of only partial relief. He was far from relaxed. They had given him a business card and forbidden him to leave the city without first checking in with PIP headquarters. He rang Rita's number. There was no answer. Where was she? Then he tried to reach Sam Young at the Hotel El Moro only to learn that he had already checked out. Yes, the desk clerk had said, in the company of a young woman. He hung up and stared at the phone. What the hell was going on?

Fredo was overtaken by an epidemic of dread. Like fully incubated viruses, fears and realizations that previously had lingered below the surface of his consciousness now began to blossom and spread. The PIP suspected him of something. What did they know? What *could* they know? And from what or whom? They had asked him about *Comandante* Rita. If they thought he knew her, how far would they go to get that information out of him? How far *wouldn't* they go? Could he give her up? Hide behind a story of innocence and fear for his life? Would that spare him?

Maybe he could run. But where? He had no place to hide. And wouldn't flight confirm his guilt?

And what about Rita? Could he warn her? Give her a chance to go to ground? To disappear? Where the hell was she? He could leave a message at their regular drop, but what if he was followed and a note intercepted? Wouldn't that prove his complicity? And what if she had already gone to ground? That would save her, right? But what about him? What about Alfredo Ramirez?

Fredo sat and buried his face in his hands. Through his fingers he saw the black gloss of the telephone. Suddenly he knew. It was the phone. Somehow his call to the secret contact number had been discovered. Rita had told him it was compromised. But not soon enough. At least, now he knew what he had to do. He had to wait. He had to play it cool. The call could have been a wrong number. The PIP could just be fishing. If not, if somehow they knew more or believed *he* knew more, well ... he would talk. He would talk to save his life, and he would hope that was enough.

I used up most of my remaining Peruvian money on two plane tickets for the following day. The flight was scheduled to leave around midnight, so Marivela and I had almost two days to kill. We spent much of the time in our hotel room, either making love or making plans. We discussed the kinds of topics she might study as a doctoral student under Jack Bentley. We speculated about what we might do to support ourselves while I finished my dissertation and looked for a teaching job in a saturated market.

I mentioned that, within a few days of our arrival, my brother Mitchell had an opening at an art gallery in Seattle and that I would like to attend. It would be an ideal opportunity for me to reconnect with my family and to introduce them to Marivela. Marivela asked how I thought my family would take the news of our marriage. I explained that since Mitch had eloped at the age of eighteen with a male lover, I suspected they would take the news pretty calmly.

"Your brother is a *maricón*?" she asked, her eyes widening.

"He prefers the term 'gay', but yes, he is."

"Well, what do you know?" she said with a tone of wonderment.

We took our meals in the hotel. The only time we went out was to buy a new carry-on bag for Marivela and an outfit that she found suitable for a gallery opening, just in case there wasn't time to shop once we got to Portland.

With about five hours to flight time we began packing our very minimal luggage. We would have my leather flight bag, my duffel full of notebooks, Marivela's carry-on bag and her oversized handbag. We wouldn't have to check anything. Marivela insisted on organizing the luggage, and she started by laying everything out on the bed.

"What's this, Sam?"

"That? Oh, that's a lead-lined bag for carrying film. It protects it from exposure to X-rays in airports. I don't really need it because I've already developed all the photos from my field work."

"Interesting." She peeked inside and turned it over and over in her hands.

Once inside the airport, we began to negotiate a bureaucratic gauntlet of long lines and armed men. We stood in one long line at immigration. At both ends stood soldiers with machine guns. Marivela seemed tense. Her eyes were restless.

"Are you okay?" I asked.

"What? Oh, sure. It's just I've never been here before. It's a little overwhelming."

It felt good for a change to be the experienced one in a situation, to be in charge and confident.

We stood in another queue to pay airport departure taxes and paraded past more soldiers. Then came the line for security to enter the international terminal. We put the three carry-on bags through the X-ray machine and I walked through the metal detector without a beep. Then Marivela placed her handbag on the belt and walked into the metal detector. It went off with a red light and a strident squeal.

"Oh, my," said Marivela. All eyes were on her, including those of the official manning the X-ray machine. And why not? She looked beautiful. “It must be this.” She reached up and removed a large metal barrette from her hair. She dropped the barrette into a small tray, walked through cleanly, retrieved her handbag from the belt and took hold of my arm for the walk to the concourse.

The day after ravaging both his home and his office, the two PIP investigators showed up again at Fredo’s door on campus.

“Doctor Ramirez,” said the older of the two. “You are under arrest. We have reason to believe you have abetted enemies of the nation in acts of treason.”

The younger man produced a pair of handcuffs from his jacket pocket. Fear blanched the professor’s face.

Alfredo Ramirez had walked these halls virtually every day for the last decade and a half. He knew them like his own home. There wasn’t a paint chip or a crack in the walls that he didn’t know. They were among the most reliably tangible aspects of his daily reality. And yet, in walking down them now, flanked by these two policemen, they seemed surreal. It had to be a dream, he thought. His feet shouldn’t feel this heavy. The air shouldn’t feel so thick. The light through the windows shouldn’t be bending and distorting this way. I’ll just go along, he thought, and wait to wake up.

Of course, he didn’t wake up. The nightmare intensified. Once outside the building, the detectives loaded Alfredo into the rear seat of an unmarked sedan. The whole rear passenger area, including the seat and the floor, was covered loosely with a sheet of heavy clear plastic.

Oh, God, thought Alfredo, and he began to search his soul for courage.

The younger detective drove them to an industrial area between downtown and the airport and into an alley between two dilapidated warehouses.

“Doctor Ramirez,” said the detective in the passenger seat, “we have been given a great deal of latitude in how we deal with terrorists. The problem is, after all, of the gravest national concern. Wouldn’t you agree?”

Alfredo nodded once, very slightly.

"I thought you would. We are strong advocates of due legal process. The other problem is that too often the individuals who support terrorists are simply released to the streets to resume their activities. It is such a waste of time and effort. In these days of national crisis we are often encouraged to create simpler, more permanent solutions."

At this point the detective rested his arm on the seat back and leaned forward as though taking Alfredo into his confidence.

"Do you comprehend my meaning, Doctor?"

Alfredo nodded.

"Good. Then here's the thing. You are an intellectual. I won't play games with you. My partner and I believe very strongly that you are not a major player in the affairs of the *Camino Rojo*. However, we also believe very strongly that you know someone who is. We are looking for the big fish, not just the little ones. If you are willing to give us a big fish, then we are likely to let you keep on swimming. If not, then we will play you on the end of our line until we get what we are looking for. Do I tire you with the fishing metaphor, Doctor Ramirez?"

Marivela sat with Sam in the waiting area near the boarding gate. She was less than an hour away from take-off and the beginning of a new, better life. Alfredo had been good to her. The revolution had been good to her. *El Colibrí* certainly had been good to her. But given what she had seen in the last few weeks, she was afraid it might all come down around her. Sam was all right, she thought. Naïve and earnest. So easy to control.

She first sensed that something was wrong when she spotted the two men without luggage talking together in the concourse between her and the main terminal. Noticing her, but pretending not to notice. She kept her eye on them as she reached into her handbag and felt for the small semi-automatic pistol inside the lead-lined film protection bag.

Her vigilance was now on its highest setting. She began

methodically examining every person in the vicinity. Did anyone else appear to be deliberately inconspicuous in his awareness of her? Was anyone else traveling without at least a briefcase or carry-on? Did any of them wear a sport coat loose enough to hide a shoulder holster?

Yes. There they were. Two more men farther down the concourse. Probably PIP. Blocking her escape in that direction. *Mierda.* They left her only one clear way out, through the gate door. With the speed of a born strategist, she spun out escape alternatives. Once through the gate door and down the Jetway, she might try to commandeer the airplane. But what if the door were closed? Or if there were no pilot on board yet? And how would the plane be pushed back from the gate? No. The plane was a dead end. A deathtrap. Her best bet was to get down to the tarmac. There, she could hijack a baggage cart or a shuttle. Or a fuel truck. That was it. Her first choice was to grab a fuel truck. If it was still attached to the plane, so much the better. Spraying jet fuel would create panic, and confusion would be her best ally. Once away from the terminal, her options would increase.

The gate door was locked. She could wait until it was opened at flight time and make her move then, but the police might not wait that long to close in. Alternatively, she could grab one of the airline employees at the gate counter and force her to open it, but that would cause a panic. A panicky employee might freeze up and leave her trapped. Maybe there was another way.

"Sam, *Cariño*, wouldn't it be wonderful if they were to put us in the first-class cabin? Do you think they might if we tell them we're honeymooners?"

"It's possible."

"Come on. Let's check it out."

We walked to the gate counter. Wary of theft, I lugged all three carry-ons with me. As I pulled our tickets and boarding passes from their paper jacket, Marivela held my upper arm and drew herself close. I appreciated the apparent warmth of the gesture.

"*Buenas tardes*," said Marivela, pleasantly and with a small smile, to the gate attendant. "If you scream or make a scene, I will have to kill you."

I stiffened. Had I misheard her? She held a pistol in front of her so that only the frozen gate attendant and I could see it. I started to back away.

"Stay where you are, *Cariño*, or I will shoot you. Now you," she said to the attendant, "go directly and not too slowly to the gate door and open it up for me. Don't do anything silly and get somebody hurt." She pressed the gun into my ribs.

"Jesus," I whispered. "What are you doing?"

"Surviving. Now, pick up the bags and stay right by my side."

I did. The gate attendant punched a combination into the lock and opened the door a crack. Marivela steered us toward it. She was still smiling. I moved carefully and obediently, no longer even trying to disentangle this incomprehensible situation. My mind was occupied by a vivid picture of a bullet bouncing around inside my rib cage.

I sensed movement in the gate area behind us. From there came a commanding voice and words that added no clarity to my understanding.

"Margarita Novara, if you wish to leave the airport alive, put the gun down."

Who? Novara? The name half-clicked for me. I'd read it recently. Of course. The news. This was a mistake. A misunderstanding. Thank God.

Marivela turned us slowly to place me between her and four suited men with guns drawn. Police. They had to be. Sideways now, to her and to them, I saw everything, or parts of everything, as my eyes darted manically from side to side and my brain raced to put it all together.

"You'll let me leave here," she called, "or you'll have a dead American on your hands." What are you saying? Tell them it's a mistake.

The gate area was crowded with people, mostly international travelers, all backing away. Marivela and the armed men seemed locked in a stalemate.

"No one has to die," she said. "Now, one at a time, from left to right, lay your guns on the ground and kick them over here."

The four policemen stood, shoulder to shoulder, with their weapons out of reach. Marivela let go of my upper arm and felt behind her for the handle of the Jetway door, but she kept her eyes on the cops the whole time.

That was her mistake.

Just as she tugged on the heavy door there came, from low in the shadows, behind it a deafening crack. Marivela's face burst into a bouquet of red roses. I felt a warm spray. The gate door flew open and I was slammed to the floor. There were screams. Shouting. I was dragged, handcuffed and hauled away. Minutes later, as I was being force-marched back through the airport, I heard crackling loudspeakers announcing a change of gate for the Los Angeles flight.

I moved through a fog, dragged, pushed and steered by men I couldn't distinguish, until I ended up at a jail somewhere in Lima. I was placed in a cell without my possessions. The cell was a tiny room with four walls, an attached bench, an iron door, a filthy, bare toilet and a sink. With the exception of the toilet and sink, everything was covered with peeling paint in the same hospital green color. I sat on the bench and felt my mind go completely out of my control. Thoughts and images flashed through at random, crashing into each other or chasing each other out, and I was incapable of latching onto any of them. Time was impossible for me to perceive, let alone to measure. I had nothing to go by but a constant shade of green, an unchanging glow of artificial light, and a nightmarish mental landscape where I had no volition.

At one point, it may have been many hours later, a guard came to the cell. He looked at me and said, "Oh, Shit. Wash your fucking face." I did, and the wash water turned red. I blotted my face dry with my shirtsleeves and the guard took me to an interrogation room. I was seated in a steel folding chair in the center of the room. There was no other furniture. After some time, one cop came in wearing a white shirt and tie. He closed the door behind him, leaned back against it, and stood there looking at me.

I looked back.

"What is your role in the *Camino Rojo*?" asked the cop with no particular intensity, almost as if he were bored.

"I have nothing to do with them."

He looked at me as if I had strained his credulity. "Nothing?"

"Nothing."

"How did you know Margarita Novara?"

There was that name again. "Who?"

"Margarita Novara," he said as if he had all the patience in the world. "The woman you were with at the airport."

"Marivela Santiana," I said. He looked at me as if I had irritated him with an amateurish and obvious lie. "I was with Marivela. We were just married. Where is she?"

"Why did you marry?"

"Where is Marivela?" I said.

He pushed away from the door where he had been leaning, stood in a wide stance with arms folded. "She's dead."

Oh, God, I thought. Or I may have said it out loud. Like a flashback, I relived the confusion of Marivela's strange behavior, the echoing boom, the ensuing pandemonium and, somewhere in the middle of it all, Marivela's face with a halo of rubies and rose petals. It was a flashback I was destined to repeat again and again over the next few days.

"Why did you marry?" His voice barely penetrated my gauzy unreality.

"What?" Dead. I had to believe it. Hadn't I known it all along?

"I said, why did you marry?"

I struggled to clear my head. "We were in love. She was in danger. She was afraid."

"Afraid of what?"

I need help, I thought. "Can I make a phone call?"

"Tell me what she was afraid of."

"Alfredo Ramírez. *Rojistas*."

"She was afraid of the *Camino Rojo*?" He said it with disdain, as if I had insulted him with the stupidest of lies.

"Yes. Can I make a phone call?"

"She told you that?"

"Yes." I found myself gripping the front of the chair seat with both hands.

"What were your plans?"

"Study … work … teaching."

"How long have you known Novara?"

"*Marivela*. Marivela Santiana."

"How long?" He leaned into his words for emphasis.

"About a year. Since I first came here. Can I make a phone call?"

"Which of her associates have you met?"

"Alfredo Ramirez. Only Fredo."

"In a year," he said, pacing toward my left, hands behind his back, "with the woman you married," circling now behind me, "you only met one associate?"

I turned to look over my right shoulder, where he was now standing, and a backhand slap sent my head snapping back to the front.

"It's the truth."

"One associate."

"Yes. Alfredo Ramirez."

"How is that possible, Mr Young?"

"She was in Lima. I was in the sierra."

"Where in the sierra?"

"Santa Rosita. Ayacucho."

"Ayacucho?"

"Yes."

"And you have nothing to do with the *Camino Rojo*."

"That's right. Look, I'd really like to make a phone call."

Again, my interrogator released a spring-loaded backhand, sending a jolt of pain through my head and neck.

"Let's begin again," he said, calmly as before. "What is your role in the *Camino Rojo*?"

I closed my eyes and thought a quiet, abortive little prayer to no god in particular. When I opened them, the cop was, once again, a picture of patience with his arms folded across his chest. "Alex Ganz will vouch for me," I said.

"Who?"

"Ganz. Alejandro Ganz de la Vega. He's a friend."

The interrogator studied me for a minute in silence then barked in the direction of the door, "Guard! Get him out of here."

And then I was back in my cell. It could have been night. It could have been morning. It could have been a day later. I had no way of knowing. I slept on and off and woke from bizarre dreams that I only remembered for seconds after waking. After a while, it seemed like I had been in the cell forever and that I would be there forever more. It became my only reality. Everything else was dream.

I sat down on the floor, my back to the wall, and let my eyes unfocus. I was engulfed in a sea of green. I concentrated on my breathing. Jail sounds receded until my breathing was the only thing I heard. With each complete breath I rose in the water of that green sea and sank back down. I breathed in and the air in my lungs lifted me to the surface. I breathed out and the water dragged me back down. In and up. Out and down. Hovering between air and water. Hovering between life and death. In and out. In and out. In and out.

In its green, aquatic state my mind floats freely. Into it comes a creature that I recognize. It is the young man with angel's wings from Mitch's card. From the surface of my green sea existence, he picks me up with his outstretched arms, arms that once before held a gift of salmon. He wraps his arms around me so that we are spooned together, and with a few strong wing beats he lifts us high over the ocean. In the distance I see land, strips of beach trimmed in green.

Soon I can see the jewels of Lima; Miraflores, San Isidro and Monterrico, neighborhoods that still bask in colonial wealth. Here there are rooftop gardens, walled courtyards and watered lawns. Here are the guard dogs and the supermarkets, the palaces, the parks and the private police.

Flying east, we reach the hill towns, whole hills blanketed in concrete homes with no electricity, no glass in the windows. Defensible bunkers for armies of the night. The pungent smells of survival hang in the air; garlic and oil and fish, sewage and rotting flesh, sweat, fear and disease, the exhaust of a million cars and trucks, and over it all a hint of cinnamon.

Farther east we pass the *pueblos jóvenes*, the shantytowns, whole cities erected on shifting sand from scavenged wood, tin and cardboard. These are people from the sierra, squatting their way into new lives. This is the architecture of desperation. But also of hope.

We circle around and upward. All Lima lies beneath us. It is Dante's inferno with hints of paradise, Peru's pride and her shame, her hope and her despair. Around and upward we circle again, into the clouds that dominate the Lima sky. It's blinding, insubstantial. Only by the force of the air from the young man's wings can I even tell down from up. And up and up and up, until once again we surface, only this time upward from a sea of clouds. It's the heaven I envisioned as a child.

And there before us, rising from the frothy sea, lies a new continent. Lima is a distant memory, a conflicted Atlantis at the bottom of an ocean of clouds. There is a path upward and we follow it, the central highway, a twisted ribbon of dirt and broken pavement. Next to it, and braided around and through it, run the railroad tracks and the *Río Rimac*. Dirt, stone, steel and water. We pass mines and farms, terraced gardens and precipitous canyon breaches. Oxen, pigs, lambs and goats dot the landscape cared for by the colorful people of these ancient places. And up and up we fly. Herds of llama browse in high meadows. Higher still, delicate vicuñas grace the lower flanks of snowcapped peaks, wary of the puma that stalks them silently. Higher still, we share the sky with a condor, the monarch of the Peruvian sky.

Cresting the Western range, we bank and dive down across mountain valleys decked out in green velvet and adorned with the polished silver of streams and lakes. Stone wall petroglyphs tell the story of human habitation. Strains of music drift past us on the cold mountain air. *Huaynas*, the blues of the Andes, cry with the sounds of wooden flutes, pan pipes, *charangos* and plaintive voices forged in stone and sorrow and hope.

Soon we are gliding over the *alturas* of Uchurimac. Ignacio Sonqo lifts his hoe in salute. The wind carries us over Huaynatambo where the *apu* of the great southern peak, fed by the offerings of Doménico Quispe, stands sentinel over the infant Marco Sonqo Quispe and his young parents. We make a low circle over Santa Rosita. Pedro Buenaventura stands in the door of the chapel talking with Doña Rosario. Luz Castro strolls in the *plaza de armas* with Manolo Ruíz. On the flat roof of the bank building, where they have their apartment, the wires of a clothesline stretch like a musical staff. On it, brightly colored garments, from tiny infant clothing and slender dresses to a huge man's shirts and trousers, undulate in the crisp Andean breeze intoning a perfect visual harmony.

In all this flight, I have not yet spoken to the young man whose wings have borne us to these great heights. I look over my shoulder to express my thanks, and the face smiling back at me is that of Enrique Morales.

Eventually, the shock of the cumulative events of the last few days subsided into a dull, aching grief and I began trying to arrange my thoughts into some semblance of order. It was like trying to capture smoke rings and pin them to a moving board. Marivela was dead. We had been less than a day away from a life in the US, and now she was gone forever. I was in jail, accused of aiding the *Camino Rojo.* Alfredo Ramirez had also been named as a *Rojista.* Was it true? What was real? I wondered if Alfredo also sat in a cell in this same jail. Or if he was even alive. I wondered how much longer *I* would be alive. And who was Margarita Novara?

I was wrong about the passage of time. It was possible to judge it, even here in this unchanging cell. For one thing, my face that began clean-shaven transformed, first to a sandpapery roughness and from that to a palpable stubble. My smell grew more pungent as well, but in here it was masked by so many other foul smells that it wasn't noticeable to me unless I deliberately focused on it. My body had other clocks as well. There were the pendulums of breath and heartbeat that served to mark short periods of time. For longer stretches there were the clocks of bowels and bladder. I had shat once and pissed seven times since entering this cell. Then there was the food clock. Such as they were, I had taken six meals; three of bread and soup and three of bread and watery coffee.

Three days, then. Probably two days since my brief interrogation. Why had there been no more questioning?

Not long after my third meager breakfast, I heard the grind and clunk of the lock, and the cell door opened. Standing there with the guard was a man I hadn't seen before. From his silvering hair, I guessed him to be in his late fifties. He wore a navy blue suit with a pale yellow shirt and striped tie. His shoes were plain black oxfords. Although he had an executive look about him, he looked as though he either worked out regularly or had a high level of residual physical fitness from an earlier time in his life. He looked me over like someone who knew what he was seeing and exactly what it meant.

"Sam," he said, "my name is Ismael Ordoñez. I work for Mr Ganz. Come on. Let's get you out of here. I'm sorry you had to stay so long. We learned of your incarceration the day before yesterday, but this wasn't an easy one to fix."

Ismael had already liberated my belongings, but he insisted that I look them over to make sure nothing was missing. The only things I cared about at that moment were my passport, my notebooks and photos, and the money I would need to get home. The passport was there, but the wallet was empty.

"Don't worry about the cash," said Ismael. "You will have enough to get you home. I assume that is still what you want to do?"

"Yes. Yes, it is."

"I took the liberty of confirming you on tonight's flight to Los Angeles with a connection to Portland. The ticket you purchased for … the young woman … will be refunded, but no time soon. If you are willing to sign it over to Ganz Enterprises, I can pay you for it today."

I could hardly believe the extremes of viciousness and generosity inherent in everyday Peruvian life. I puzzled over the complexities of Alex Ganz, struggling to reconcile the many facets I had seen of him. In him I had witnessed generosity, openness and tenderness living alongside shrewdness, toughness and a deep potential for ruthlessness and violence. In fact, I had seen the same characteristics in Marivela Santiana. Did they also live inside me? Perhaps, I thought, those potentialities exist in all of us, but it takes a crucible like Peru to refine them to the degree I had seen in Alex and Marivela.

Then, I found myself wondering what that crucible would do to the beautiful child Enrique Morales. Certainly it would toughen him. What paths would he choose through the mountains and valleys of life in Peru? What paths would even be open to him? What chapters of the history of this place would thrust themselves into his consciousness? I believed in the profound goodness of Enrique Morales. I believed that in Enrique and others like him lay the seed of a better future for this country. I vowed that I would keep in close contact with Enrique and that if he ever needed me, I would come running as fast as I could.

My notebooks were all intact. I looked deeply enough into my flight bag to verify a clean change of clothes and a razor. Then, from something in my bag, I caught a whiff of Marivela. Until that moment I hadn't noticed that I associated a particular scent with her. Yet there it was, a floral aroma with notes of cinnamon and clove, rising from a mess of clothing, both hers and mine, that had been folded and separate when we'd left for the airport.

Ismael showed me to a tan Land Rover that I figured must be a company car.

"Sorry about the smell," I said.

"I tell you what. We'll just keep the windows down for now." His voice was kind.

I didn't even ask where we were going. We drove through an industrial area for a while, alongside a sprawling slum for a while longer, and finally we came to the front of a three-star hotel.

"Here's a room key. I've asked them to supply you with any toiletries you need and to take you to the airport this evening."

"I don't know how I can possibly thank you enough. And Alex, of course. Would you please thank him for me"

"He is happy to be able to help. Now, is there anything else at all that I can do for you before I go?"

I thought a moment and then I asked, "What day is it?"

"Wednesday, the twenty-third."

"Do you think you could help me change my ticket from Portland to Seattle?"

I got to SeaTac airport in Seattle at about four in the afternoon after a long layover at LAX. I took a shuttle into town, picked up a newspaper and walked down to the waterfront. I sat at a booth in a Pike Street café and ordered clam chowder and a beer. It was hard to believe I had been a prisoner in a Peruvian jail only twenty-four hours earlier. Already the experience, all of it, seemed distant and unreal. I finished my chowder, ordered a second beer and opened the paper. In the metro-entertainment section I found the listing I was looking for:

Mitchell Young. 'Saving Myself,' Works in watercolor and acrylic. Birdsong Gallery. 7:00 – 9:00PM.

I had just enough time to walk there and to pick out a good bottle of champagne on the way.

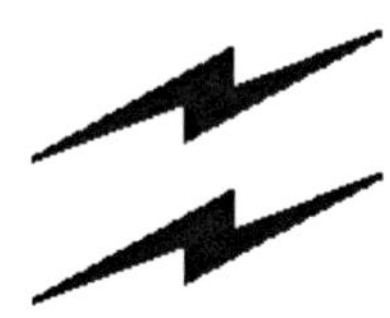

Acknowledgements

They say the first one is the hardest. I hope they're right. This novel owes its existence to many people beyond its author. Most important has been Diane Martin, my confidante, collaborator and lifelong traveling companion, who identified the monster within me and urged me to write it out. Along the way and through numerous revisions I've had the help of insightful, sensitive readers. Diane, thank you a thousand times more. For the other reviews I saved and labored with, thank you Sara Brant Guest, Margot Singer and Kirk Colvin. To my agent, Monique Raphel High, special thanks for investing your support in such an unproven and risky proposition. Finally, to Neil Marr, who may be the most skillful editor on the planet, I tip my sweat-stained baseball cap in gratitude.

Also Available from BeWrite Books

A Thousand Beauties by Mark Adam Kaplan

Overweight and jaded, rich and lonely, Rupert Ruskin clings to an obsessive belief that if he can witness a thousand beautiful sights in a single day, his shattered and sordid existence will turn to bliss.

But his dreamquest for A Thousand Beauties is stalled when beloved and eccentric ex wife, Elaine, bursts back into his life with disturbing news.

Ruskin now has to make room for a more immediate and secret plan … but should it be for a wedding or a funeral?

Mark Adam Kaplan navigates the peaks and troughs of co-dependency and mutual punishment in a magnificently spun story of love and loathing. His urgent, yet poetic prose trap the reader like a spider traps a fly in an intricate web both beautiful and deadly.

ISBN 978-1-905202-94-2

The Black Garden by Joe Bright

A young university student from Boston takes on the summer job, in a small rural town, of clearing the accumulated rubbish from the house and garden of an elderly man, George O'Brien, and his granddaughter, Candice. The task is not as straightforward as he at first thought and Mitchell finds himself drawn into the mystery surrounding the Black Garden and the lives of his employers.

Can he solve the secret behind the animosity of the townspeople? Can he do so without endangering George's freedom and leaving Candice even more isolated?

ISBN 978-1-905202-98-0

Also Available from BeWrite Books

Sleep Before Evening by Magdalena Ball

Marianne is teetering at the edge of reason.

A death in the family sends her brilliant academic career and promising future spiraling out of control until resentment towards those who shaped her past leads her on a wild and desperate search for the truth about herself.

On the seedy side of New York, she meets Miles, a hip musician busking the streets and playing low-rent venues in a muddled bid to make his own dreams come true.

In her new life, she finds anarchic squalor, home grown music and poetry, booze, drugs, sex, violence, love, loss … and, above all, exhilarating freedom on her troubled journey from sleep to awakening.

This gritty, relentless story unfolds with the same cool detachment that motivates the central character to peel back the layers of her life and expose the painful scalding within.

ISBN 978-1-904492-96-2

The Bad Seed by Maurilia Meehan

Her young daughter has disappeared, sparking a massive murder hunt, and now her husband has gone walkabout in the bush with no plans to return.

Nothing is coming up roses for small-time gardening correspondent Agatha.

So she plants the seeds of a new life in an isolated village … in the dilapidated former home of a renowned witch.

A strange new lover and mysterious visitors from half a world away will not allow Agatha's own ghosts to rest … and her garden produces dark honey and poison as Maurilia Meehan's tale builds to a chilling climax.

Sinister flora and phantoms flourish in this rich and unforgettable work from the pen of the award-winning author of the acclaimed "Performances", "Adultery", "The Sea People" and "Fury".

ISBN 978-1-905202-12-6

Breinigsville, PA USA
12 October 2009

225594BV00001B/1/P